THE WO[illegible]
THE DOUBLE EAGLE

"Meet Tom Kirk, hero of the nimble global romp
The Double Eagle and heir to the throne
of the twisty international thriller,
a seat that has belonged to Tom Clancy's Jack Ryan
for more than two decades."

Cleveland Plain Dealer

"Twining's obvious research pays off
as we are treated to a compelling fusion
of real historical events and modern thrills. . . .
Kirk [is] an action hero as adroit and charismatic
as Clive Cussler's Dar Pitt."

Library Journal

"Twining lunges into the thriller genre
with this globe-trotting adventure . . .
[and] writes with enthusiasm,
giving us meaty characters and
a story that fairly stampedes along."

Booklist

THE BLACK SUN

"There's something for thriller fans of all types
in James Twining's second novel . . .
The Black Sun never loses speed—
all the way to the story's culmination
in an abandoned mine in Austria . . .
The chapters are short and to the point,
and always end with some satisfying drama . . .
The Black Sun is pure, unadulterated fun."

USA Today

"The author follows *The Double Eagle* (2005)
with this equally entertaining sequel. . . .
Fast paced and exciting,
with a bigger-than-life villain,
a conflicted hero, and a solid payoff:
What more does a thriller need?"

Booklist

"If you want a damned good, traditional,
commercial thriller . . . then Twining is just the ticket."

Telegraph (London)

"Once again, Twining offers
a tremendously well-researched and
exciting adventure that delves into the secret orders
of the Nazi hierarchy and traces the history and lore
of Nazi plunder. This work takes readers
on a journey full of twists and surprises as Kirk races
to find Russia's legendary Amber Room."
Library Journal

"If you enjoyed James Twining's action-packed
art-theft thriller *The Double Eagle*,
you're sure to get a similar charge
from its sequel, *The Black Sun*."
Chicago Tribune

"A story that harks back to the Nazis,
Hitler, and a legendary treasure.
What more could you want?
If there's a better thriller this year,
I would like to see it."
Jack Higgins,
bestselling author of *The Eagle Has Landed*

By James Twining

THE GILDED SEAL
THE BLACK SUN
THE DOUBLE EAGLE

JAMES
TWINING

THE GILDED SEAL

HARPER

An Imprint of HarperCollins*Publishers*

This is a work of fiction. Names, characters, places, and incidents are products of the author's imagination or are used fictitiously and are not to be construed as real. Any resemblance to actual events, locales, organizations, or persons, living or dead, is entirely coincidental.

HARPER

An Imprint of HarperCollins*Publishers*
10 East 53rd Street
New York, New York 10022-5299

ISBN 978-0-06-167186-9

First Harper paperback printing: June 2009

HarperCollins® and Harper® are registered trademarks of HarperCollins Publishers.

Printed in the United States of America

Visit Harper paperbacks on the World Wide Web at
www.harpercollins.com

10 9 8 7 6 5 4 3 2 1

To Amelia and Jemima

"When the first baby laughed for the first time,
its laugh broke into a thousand pieces,
and they all went skipping about,
and that was the beginning of fairies."
J.M. Barrie, Peter Pan

ACKNOWLEDGMENTS

My thanks to my indefatigable agent, Jonathan Lloyd, and the whole team at Curtis Brown in London, who have done such a fantastic job in looking out for me over the past few years.

Thank you also to my editor Wayne Brookes, who I value not only for his editorial skill and unshakeable faith in me, but also for his boundless enthusiasm, which is a constant source of energy and hope. My thanks of course also go to Amanda Ridout and the rest of the team at Harper Collins in the sales, editorial, marketing and creative departments that Wayne pesters so effectively on my behalf, and who have continued to work wonders for me.

For their help in researching this novel I would like to acknowledge the Queensbury Estate (Drumlanrig Castle) in Scotland, Apsley House (Wellington Museum) in London, the Musée du Louvre in Paris, El Museo Napoleónico de La Habana in Cuba and the staff of the Claremont Riding Academy in New York City.

As ever, many people helped in the original conception and writing of this novel, but special thanks go to my family, Ann, Bob and Joanna Twining and Roy, Claire and Sarah Toft for their guidance and support. Many others have also helped in the (painful!) editing process, most particularly Anne O'Brien, Jeremy Green, and Jeremy Walton.

Victoria, Amelia and now Jemima—I know that the writing is tough on all of us at times, but you especially. Thank you.

LONDON, JUNE 2007

Historical Background

This novel was inspired by the theft of the *Mona Lisa* in 1911 and its eventual recovery in 1913, an event which triggered one of the largest criminal investigations in history and to which the *Mona Lisa* owes much of her present-day fame.

All descriptions and background information provided on works of art, artists, thefts, forgery detection techniques and architecture are similarly accurate. Unfortunately, the Claremont Riding Academy, which is briefly featured in this novel, announced its closure shortly before publication, but the description was left unchanged as a tribute to the sad passing of a much loved New York landmark.

For more information on the author and on the fascinating history, people, places and artifacts that feature in *The Gilded Seal* and the other Tom Kirk novels, please visit www.jamestwining.com.

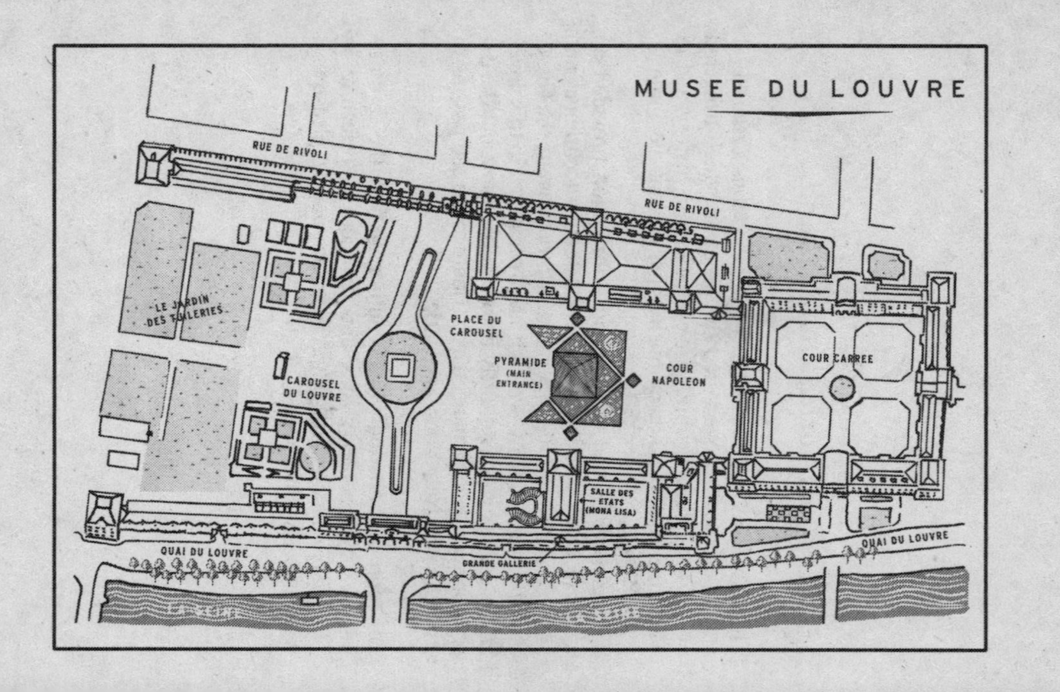
MUSEE DU LOUVRE
RUE DE RIVOLI
RUE DE RIVOLI
LE JARDIN DES TUILERIES
PLACE DU CAROUSEL
PYRAMIDE (MAIN ENTRANCE)
COUR NAPOLEON
COUR CARREE
CAROUSEL DU LOUVRE
SALLE DES ETATS (MONA LISA)
QUAI DU LOUVRE
GRANDE GALLERIE
QUAI DU LOUVRE

Extract from *Lives of the Most Eminent Painters, Sculptors, and Architects* by Giorgio Vasari (1568), translated by Gaston du C. de Vere (1912)

Leonardo undertook to execute, for Francesco del Giocondo, the portrait of Mona Lisa, his wife.

In this head, whoever wished to see how closely art could imitate nature, was able to comprehend it with ease; for in it were counterfeited all the minutenesses that with subtlety are able to be painted . . .

. . . The nose, with its beautiful nostrils, rosy and tender, appeared to be alive. The mouth, with its opening, and with its ends united by the red of the lips to the flesh-tints of the face, seemed, in truth, to be not colors but flesh. In the pit of the throat, if one gazed upon it intently, could be seen the beating of the pulse. And, indeed, it may be said that it was painted in such a manner as to make every valiant craftsman, be he who he may, tremble and lose heart.

And in this work of Leonardo's there was a smile so pleasing, that it was a thing more divine than human to behold; and it was held to be something marvelous, since the reality was not more alive.

***The Washington Post*, 13th December 1913**

Mona Lisa, *Leonardo da Vinci's great painting, which was stolen from the Louvre, in Paris, more than two years ago, has been found [and a man arrested]. It is now in the hands of the Italian authorities and will be returned to France.*

Mona Lisa *or* La Joconde *as it is more properly known, the most celebrated portrait of a woman ever painted, has been the object of an exhaustive search in all quarters of the globe. The mystery of its abstraction from the Louvre, its great intrinsic value, and the fascination of the smile of the woman it portrayed . . . have combined to keep alive interest in its recovery.*

On being interrogated, the prisoner said his real name is Vincenzo Peruggia . . . "I was ashamed," he said "that for more than a century no Italian had thought of avenging the spoliation committed by Frenchmen under Napoléon when they carried off from the Italian museums and galleries, pictures, statues and treasures of all kinds by wagonloads, ancient manuscripts by thousands, and gold by sacks."

PROLOGUE

There is only one step
from the sublime to the ridiculous.

Napoléon I

MACARENA, SEVILLE, SPAIN

14th April (Holy Thursday)—2:37 A.M.

It started with a whisper; a barely voiced tremor of suppressed anticipation that rippled gently through the expectant crowd.

"*Pronto. Pronto estará aquí.*" Soon. She'll be here soon.

But the whisper evaporated almost as quickly as it had appeared. Snatched from their lips by a capricious wind, it was carried far above their heads into the warm night, only to be casually tossed between the swirling currents like autumn leaves being chased across a park.

It was replaced, instead, by the distant sound of a lone trumpet, its plaintive, almost feminine cry echoing down the winding, cobbled street. This time, people made no attempt to conceal their excitement, and their faces flushed with a strange inner glow.

"*Ahora viene. Viene La Macarena.*" She's coming. La Macarena is coming.

The crowd, almost ten deep on both sides of the street, surged forward against the steel barriers that lined the route, straining to see. In between them, the dark cobblestones flowed like a black river, their rippled surface glinting occasionally in the flickering light.

The man allowed himself to be carried forward by the breathless host, sheltering in the warm comfort of the anonymity they provided. In the crowd, but not of it, his eyes skipped nervously over the faces of those around him rather than the approaching procession. Had he lost them? Surely they couldn't find him now.

He caught his own reflection in the polished rim of a lantern being carried by a woman in front of him. His leathered skin, dark eyes glowing like hot coals, the steep cliff of his jaw, the ruby-colored razor slash of his lips, his wild mane of white hair. The unmistakable mask of despair. He had a sudden vision of an aging lion, standing on some high promontory, taking one last look at his territory stretching toward the horizon and at his pride, lazing beneath him in the setting sun's orange-fingered embrace, before heading quietly into the bush to die.

A cheer drew his gaze. The first *nazarenos* had swung into view. Sinister in their matching purple cloaks and long pointed hats, they trooped silently past, their faces masked with only narrow slits for eyes, a black candle grasped solemnly in one hand. Behind them, a marching band dictated a steady pace.

"*¡Está aquí! ¡Está aquí!*" She's here! She's here! A small boy with long golden hair had fought his way through to where he was standing and was jumping to try and get a better look. The man smiled at his eagerness, at his uncomplicated and breathless excitement and, for a moment, forgot his fear.

"*Todavía no. ¿Ves?*" Not yet. See? He swept the boy off the ground and lifted him above his shoulders to show him how far the procession still had to run before the solid silver float containing the statue of the Virgen de la Esperanza Macarena would appear.

"*Gracias, Señor.*" The boy gave him a faint kiss on the cheek before diving through the legs of the people in front with a snatched wave.

The first flower-strewn float shuffled past—the sentencing of Christ by Pontius Pilate. The faint aroma of incense and orange blossom drifted to him on a mournful sigh of wind and he breathed in deeply, the smells blending harmoniously at the back of his throat like cognac fumes. How had it come to this? It had all happened so long ago now. Forgotten.

He looked back to the procession and saw that the *nazarenos* had given way, temporarily at least, to two rows of *penitentes*—those who sought to repent of their sins by walking the processional route barefoot and with heavy wooden crosses slung over their shoulders. He smiled ruefully at the sight of their bruised and bloodied feet, part of him wanting to take his place alongside them, the other knowing it was too late.

A sudden break in their somber ranks afforded him a clear view right through to the other side of the street. There several *monaguillos*, children dressed as priests, were handing out sweets to the people standing in the front row. They were all smiling, the peal of their laughter filling the air. All apart from one man who, his phone pressed to his ear, was staring straight at him.

"They're here," he breathed. "They've found me."

He turned away, instinctively heading against the flow of the procession to make it harder for anyone to follow him. Elbowing his way through the crush, he came to a narrow street and darted up it, past a drunk pissing in one doorway and some kids making out in another, the boy's hand shoved awkwardly up the girl's top. Halfway along, he veered right down a side alley where bright banners and wilting flowers hung lazily from low, sagging balconies.

He skidded to a halt outside a large wooden gate. The sign nailed to it indicated that the building was currently being renovated by Construción Pedro Alvarez. That meant it was empty.

It only took him a couple of seconds to spring the padlock open. He stepped inside and carefully closed the gate behind him, finding himself in a small courtyard littered with paint-spattered tools and broken terracotta tiles. A dog had fouled the large pile of sand immediately to his left.

In the middle stood a well. He made his way to it. It was disused, a black grille over the opening rendering the bucket suspended above it purely ornamental. This was as good a place as any.

A match flared in the darkness and he held it to his small

notebook. The dry paper clutched at the flame, drawing it in like water, the fire gnawing hungrily at the pages' pale skin until only the charred spine remained. He glanced toward the gate. He still had time. Time to leave some clue as to what he had discovered before it was too late.

The knife bit into his palm, the blood welling up through the deep gash and then oozing through his fingers, sticky and warm. He had barely finished when the gate burst open.

"*Está allí. Te dijé que le iba a encontrar. ¡Venga! ¡Venga! Antes de que se vaya.*" He's in here. I told you I'd find him. Quick! Quick! Before he gets away.

He looked up and recognized the little boy he had lifted above the crowd earlier pointing triumphantly toward him, a cruel look in his eyes, blond hair shimmering like flames in the darkness.

Five men shot through the doorway, two of them overpowering him instantly by bending his right arm up behind his back and forcing him to his knees.

"Did you really think you could hide from us, Rafael?" came a voice from behind him.

He didn't answer, knowing it was pointless.

"Get him up."

The grip on his arm relaxed slightly and he was dragged to his feet. A cold, blinding light snapped on. Rafael held his other hand up to his face, shielding his eyes. A video camera. The sick *putas* were filming this. They were filming the whole thing.

A shape materialized in front of him, a solid black outline silhouetted against the white light's searing canvas, the world suddenly drained of all color. The figure had a hammer in one hand and two six-inch masonry nails in the other that he had scooped up off the floor. A kaleidoscopic undershirt of tattoos disappeared up each sleeve and formed a rounded collar where they reappeared just below the neckline of his unbuttoned shirt.

Rafael felt himself being lifted so that his wrists were pressed flat against the wall on either side of an open doorway. The video operator took up a position so he could get both men in the shot.

"Ready?"

Outside, Rafael heard muffled cheering and the faint sound of women wailing and crying. He knew then that La Macarena had finally appeared on the adjacent street, glass tears of grief at the loss of her only son frozen on to the delicate ecstasy of her carved face.

She was here. She was here for him.

PART I

Forsake not an old friend;
for the new is not comparable to him;
a new friend is as new wine;
when it is old,
thou shalt drink it with pleasure.

Ecclesiasticus 9:10

CHAPTER ONE

DRUMLANRIG CASTLE, SCOTLAND

18th April—11:58 A.M.

As the car drew up, a shaft of light appeared through a break in the brooding sky. The castle's sandstone walls glowed under its gentle touch, an unexpected shock of pink against the ancient greens of the surrounding hills and woodlands.

Tom Kirk stepped out and drew his dark overcoat around him with a shiver, turning the black velvet collar up so it hugged the circle of his neck. Ahead of him, blue-and-white police tape snapped in the icy wind where it had been strung across the opposing steps that curved up to the main entrance. Six feet tall, slim and square shouldered, Tom had an athletic although not obviously muscular build, his careful gestures and the precise way he moved hinting at a deliberate, controlled strength that was strangely compelling to watch.

It was his eyes that were most striking, though, an intense pale blue that suggested both a calm intelligence and an unflinching resolve. These were set into a handsome, angular face, his thick arching eyebrows matching the color of his short brown hair, the firm line of his jaw echoing the sharp edge of his cheekbones and lending an air of measured self-confidence. The only jarring note came from the series of small fighting scars that flecked his knuckles, tiny white lines that joined and bisected each other like animal tracks across the savanna.

Looking up, he was suddenly struck by the almost deliberate extravagance of the castle's elaborate Renaissance splendor compared to the artisinal, gray functionality of the neighboring village he had just passed through. No doubt when it had been built that had been precisely the point, the building a crushing reminder to the local population of their lowly status. Now, however, the castle looked slightly out of place, as if it had emerged blinking into the new century, uncertain of its role and perhaps even slightly embarrassed by its outmoded finery.

In the distance, a police helicopter made a low pass over the neighboring forest, the chop of its rotors muffled by the steady buzz of the radios carried by the twenty or so officers swarming purposefully around him. Tom shivered again, although this time it wasn't the cold. This many cops always made him nervous.

"Can I help you, sir?" A policeman on the other side of the tape shouted over the noise. At the sound of his voice the thick curtain of cloud drew shut once again, and the castle faded back into its gray slumber.

"It's okay, Constable. He's with me."

Mark Dorling had appeared at the top of the left-hand staircase, a tall man wearing a dark blue double-breasted suit and a striped regimental tie. He waved him forward impatiently, Tom recognizing in Dorling's ever so slightly proprietary manner evidence, perhaps, of weekends spent visiting friends with houses of a similar size and stature.

The policeman nodded and Tom stooped under the tape and made his way up the shallow and worn steps to where Dorling was waiting for him, shoulders back, chin raised, fists balanced on each hip like a big game hunter posing over his kill. Oxford had been full of people like Dorling, Tom reflected. It was the eyes that gave them away, the look of scornful indifference tinged with contempt with which they surveyed the world, as if partly removed from it. At first Tom had been offended by this, resenting what appeared to be an instinctive disdain for anyone who didn't share their privileged background or gilded future. But he had soon come to understand that behind those dead eyes lurked a cold fury at a world where the odds had so clearly been stacked in their favor, that their lives had been robbed of any sense of mystery or adventure. Far from contempt, therefore, what their expression actually revealed was a deep self-loathing, maybe even jealousy.

"I wasn't expecting you until later." Dorling welcomed him with a tight smile. Tom wasn't offended by his accusing tone. People like Dorling didn't like surprises. It disturbed the illusion of order and control they worked so hard to conjure up around themselves.

"I thought you said you were in Milan?" he continued, sweeping a quiff of thinning blond hair back off his forehead, a large gold signet ring gleaming on the little finger of his left hand.

"I was," said Tom. "I got the early flight. It sounded important."

"It is," Dorling confirmed, his pale green eyes narrowing momentarily, his jaw stiffening. "It's the Leonardo." A pause. "I'm glad you're here Tom."

Dorling gripped his hand unnecessarily hard, as if trying to compensate for his earlier brusqueness, his skin soft and firm. Tom said nothing, allowing this new piece of information to sink in for a few seconds before answering. The *Madonna of the Yarnwinder.* One of only fifteen paintings in the world thought to have been substantially painted by da Vinci. Conservatively worth $150 million. Probably more. In his business, it didn't get much more important than that.

"When?"

"This morning."

"Anyone hurt?"

"They overpowered a tour guide. She's bruised but fine. More shocked than anything."

"Security?"

"Rudimentary," Dorling gave an exasperated shrug. "It takes the police thirty minutes to get out here on a good day. These chaps were in and out in ten."

"Sounds like they knew what they were doing."

"Professionals," Dorling agreed.

"Just as well it's insured, then, isn't it?" Tom grinned. "Or aren't Lloyd's planning to pay up on this one?"

"Why do you think you're here?" Dorling replied with a faint smile, the lines around his eyes and tanned cheeks deepening as his face creased, his eyes darkening momentarily.

"The old poacher-turned-gamekeeper routine?"

"Something like that."

"What does that make you, I wonder?"

Dorling paused to reflect before answering, the pulse in his temple fractionally increasing its tempo.

"A businessman. Same as always."

There were other words dancing on the edge of Tom's tongue, but he took a deep breath and let the moment pass. He had his reasons. Dorling's firm of chartered loss adjusters was the first port of call for Lloyd's underwriters whenever they had a big-ticket insurance claim to investigate. And during the ten years that Tom had operated as an art thief—the best in the business, many said—Dorling's company had cooperated with the police on countless jobs which they suspected him of being behind.

All that had changed, however, when word had got out a year or so back that Tom and his old fence, Archie Connelly, had set themselves up on the other side of the law, advising on museum security and helping recover lost or stolen art. Now the very people who had spent years trying to put them both away were queuing up for their help. The irony still bit deep.

Tom didn't blame Dorling. If anything he found his shameless opportunism rather endearing. The truth was that the art world was full of people like him—crocodile-skinned and conveniently forgetful as soon as they understood there was a profit to be made. It was just that the memories didn't fade quite so fast when you'd been the one staring down the wrong end of a twenty-year stretch.

"Who's inside?" Tom asked, nodding toward the castle entrance.

"Who isn't?" Dorling replied mournfully. "The owner,

forensic team, local filth." The slang seemed forced and sat uneasily with Dorling's clipped sentences and sharp vowels. Tom wondered if he too felt awkward about their past history and whether this was therefore a deliberate attempt to bridge or otherwise heal the gap between them. If so, it was a rather ham-fisted attempt, although Tom appreciated him making the effort at least. "Oh, and that annoying little shit from the Yard's Art Crime Squad just showed up."

"Annoying little shit? You mean Clarke?" Tom gave a rueful laugh. In this instance the description was an apt one, although Tom suspected that it was a term Dorling routinely deployed to describe anyone who hadn't gone to the same school as him, or who didn't feature on his regular Chelsea dinner-party circuit.

"Play nicely," Dorling warned him. "We need him onside. We're cooperating, remember, not competing."

"I will if he will." Tom shrugged, unable and perhaps unwilling to suppress the hint of petulance in his voice. Clarke and he had what Archie would have called "previous." It didn't matter how much you wanted to draw a line and move on, sometimes others wouldn't let you. Tom felt suddenly hot and loosened his coat, revealing a single-breasted charcoal-gray Huntsman suit that he was wearing with an open-necked blue Hilditch & Key shirt.

"There's one more thing you should know," said Dorling, pausing on the threshold, one foot outside the house, the other on the marble floor, his square chin raised as if anticipating a blow. "I had a call from our Beijing office. They only just heard, but Milo's out. The Chinese released him six months ago. No one knows why."

"Milo?" Tom froze, not sure he'd heard correctly. Not wanting to believe he had. "Milo's out? What's that got to do . . . you think this is him?"

Dorling shrugged awkwardly, his bluff confidence momentarily deserting him.

"That's why I called you in on this one, Tom. He's left you something."

CHAPTER TWO

NEW YORK CITY

18th April—7:00 A.M.

They hit traffic almost immediately when they turned on to Broadway, brake lights shimmering ahead of them like beads on a long necklace, umbrellas bobbing impatiently along the sidewalk. The rain, thick with the evaporated sweat of eight million people, crawled in greasy rivulets down the glass, flecking Special Agent Jennifer Browne's faint reflection in the passenger-side window as she sipped coffee from a polystyrene cup.

Most agreed that she was a beautiful woman, perhaps even more so since she'd broken thirty, as if she'd somehow grown into the slender, elegantly curving five foot nine frame that had made her appear a little gawky when younger. She had light brown skin and curling black hair, her father's African American coloring having been softened by her mother's Southern pallor. But her large, honeyed hazel eyes were pure Grandma May, a fierce woman who claimed to have met the devil on two separate occasions; once on the ship over from Haiti, the other on her wedding night. To her regret, Jennifer had been too young to verify either of these stories with her grandfather before he'd died.

And yet despite what others said, Jennifer had never really

considered herself to be attractive, citing her younger sister as an example of a far more natural and intuitive beauty. Besides, she'd never been that concerned with what people thought about how she looked. It was, after all, a poor proxy for character, which is what she preferred to be judged on.

She stifled a yawn, the mesmeric fizz of the wipers across the windshield exposing the effects of too many late nights. She certainly could have done without today's early start. Then again, she'd not had much choice. Not when FBI Director Green himself was calling the shots.

"This is taking forever," she said restlessly as they shuffled forward another few feet and the caffeine began to bite. "Cut across to Eighth when you hit West Fourteenth." She glanced up and caught the driver eyeing the firm outline of her breasts in the mirror.

"Sure thing." He nodded awkwardly, his eyes flicking back to the road.

She sat back, her annoyance with the driver offset by her amusement at herself. Only nine months in and she was already well on her way to being a real New Yorker—not only irrationally impatient but also utterly convinced of her ability to navigate to any point in the city faster than anyone else. Not particularly attractive traits, perhaps, but ones that nonetheless gave her a sudden sense of belonging that she hadn't felt for a long time. Too long.

Twenty-five minutes later they turned on to West 89th Street and drew up outside the elegant façade of the Claremont Riding Academy, the oldest continuously working stable in the state, according to the sign fixed to the wall outside.

Jennifer scanned the street—Green's usual security detachment was already there, a lucky few sat in one of the three unmarked Suburbans, the rest sheltering in the doorways opposite, water dripping on to their shoulders and the toecaps of their polished shoes. He was early. That was a first. Whatever he wanted, he clearly didn't plan to hang around.

She stepped out of the car, a long coat worn over her usual urban camouflage of black trouser suit and white silk blouse. Not the most exciting outfit, she knew, but then she'd learned the hard way that people would grasp at anything to categorize you into their rigid mental taxonomies. Certainly, given how hard it was to make it as a woman in the Bureau, let alone an African American woman, she'd rather be classified as frigid than as a potential fuck, which, convention had it, were the only two points on the scale that female agents could operate at. Besides, in a way it suited her—it was one less decision to make in the morning.

A ramp covered with a deep carpet of dirt and wood shavings led up to the riding school itself. She made her way inside, suddenly aware of the smell, an incongruous mixture of horse and leather and manure amidst Manhattan's unforgiving forest of steel and concrete and glass. There was a time, she mused, when the whole city would have smelled this way, when the clatter of hooves and the foghorns of ships arriving in the harbor had signaled the forging of a new city built on hope and ambition. She decided she liked this smell. It seemed somehow real. Permanent. Relevant.

Ahead of her a single horse was trotting robotically in a wide circle defined by the space between the walls and the bright blue pillars supporting the whitewashed brick ceiling above. A young girl was perched unsteadily in the saddle, golden braids peeking out from under a pristine black velvet helmet. An instructor was standing in the center of the school, swiveling on the heels of his scuffed brown riding boots as he followed the horse around and around, occasionally bellowing instructions.

"Excuse me," Jennifer called, as the horse rode past and the man turned to face her. "I'm looking for Falstaff."

"Falstaff?" He eyed her curiously as he walked over, his muscled thighs sheathed in pale cream Lycra jodhpurs. "You're here for Falstaff?"

She nodded firmly, hoping that he had not noticed the slight uncertainty in her own voice. Green's call had been hurried and muffled by the sound of a passing siren. *Seven thirty a.m. Claremont Riding Academy. Ask for Falstaff. Don't be late.*

"How many times? Keep your heels down," the instructor suddenly barked, his eyes fixed beyond her shoulder. Jennifer glanced behind her and saw the young girl blush crimson as she wheeled away, heels firmly pressed down against her stirrups, braids bouncing frantically off her shoulders. The instructor's searching gaze followed her as she circled past, his face set into a disapproving frown.

"Yes, Falstaff. You know where I can find him?"

The man glanced at her skeptically, before giving a vague nod to his right.

"They're waiting for you upstairs. First floor. Back and right. That's it. Good girl. Hands out in front. Now remember your posture. It all comes from the posture."

With a faint word of thanks, Jennifer headed over to the spot he had indicated. A wide, curving ramp led up to the stabling floor above, the stone worn and gouged by generations of hooves and overindulged Upper West Side kids.

Two more of Green's men were positioned at the top of the ramp, transparent earpieces snaking inside their collars. They waved her down a central aisle that led to the far end of the stables, narrower passageways containing loose-boxes leading off to the left and the right. The boxes themselves were painted white and in various stages of decay and disrepair, with wooden slats missing or broken and the wrought-iron railings thick with rust and overpainting. Saddles, reins and various other pieces of tack and frayed rope were hanging haphazardly from the peeling walls or slung over skewed gates. A stereo dangled from an overhead beam, the music clearly more to the taste of the Mexican workers mucking out than the horses whose mournful heads she could see peering over the stable doors.

Another of Green's men was waiting for her at the end of the main aisle. He silently steered her to the right. The sound of voices drew her to the final stall where a tin plate was attached to the door with twine. A name had been punched into it with a blunt nail—Falstaff.

Jennifer frowned, momentarily disconcerted. She'd assumed Falstaff was someone whose parents had either had an irrational love of Shakespeare, or a questionable sense of humor. Not a horse.

With a shrug, she stepped into thc box. Jack Green had his

back to her and was locked in conversation with two smartly dressed men, one noticeably older than the other. The younger man looked up sharply when he saw her. Picking up on his cue, Green spun around to greet her.

"Browne." He gave her a fleeting smile. "Good."

Green was one of those cookie-cutter DC insiders who seemed to roll off a secret production line in some rich white neighborhood on the outskirts of Boston. Crisp creases in his suit trousers, ironed parting in his brown hair, plump cheeks, perfect teeth and irises like faded ink spots on crisp linen sheets, his gaze constantly flitting over your shoulder, in case someone more interesting should come into the room behind you.

He'd lost weight since the last time she'd seen him, adding substance to the Bureau gossips who contended that he'd recently remarried and that his new, much younger and richer, bride had him on a treadmill three times a week. True or not, he still had a way to go; the material around the top button of his trousers was buckling under the stress of holding his stomach in. And if there was a new wife, she'd certainly done nothing to improve his taste in ties, this morning's offering a garish blend of different shades of orange.

"Morning, sir." She shook his hand.

"Thank you for coming. I know it's early."

"It's not a problem," she said generously. "I normally go for a run at this time anyway."

He gave her a look that was caught somewhere between sympathy and admiration, before gesturing first toward the older man, then his younger companion.

"I'd like you to meet Lord Anthony Hudson, Chairman of Sotheby's, and Benjamin Cole, his opposite number at Christie's. Gentlemen, this is Special Agent Jennifer Browne from our Art Crime Team."

"Call me Ben."

Cole gave a wide, teethy grin, his dark brown eyes searching hers out earnestly and then darting away when she tried to hold his gaze. She wondered if the others knew he was gay. Probably. He was immaculately dressed in a black suit and open-necked white shirt, the glint of a thin gold chain just visible in the cleft of his collarbone. She guessed he was in his early forties, although he looked maybe ten years younger, the healthy glow of his long pointed face betraying a daily routine of wheat grass, exfoliation, free weights, soya milk, pilates and expensive moisturiser.

"But whatever you do, don't call him Tony," he continued.

Hudson looked as jaded and shopworn as Cole was bright and fit, the dated cut and frayed corners of his pin-striped suit suggesting that it was some sort of family heirloom or hand-me-down. His eyes had almost disappeared under his eyebrows' craggy overhang, while his cheeks were lined and drooping like a balloon that has had the air let out of it, and his lips were cracked and frozen into a permanent scowl. She placed him at about fifty-five; not quite retirement age, but definitely counting the days. She had the sudden impression that he was weighing her up, as if he was gazing at her through the crosshairs of a rifle on some distant Scottish moor and estimating the distance and wind speed before pulling the trigger.

"I recognize you both, of course." She nodded, reaching out to shake their hands.

Hudson was a Brit, a blue-blood distantly related to the Queen who'd been shipped in to schmooze Sotheby's mainly North American clientele with canapés and a touch of old-fashioned class. Cole on the other hand was a Brooklyn-born hustler who, despite barely being able to spell his name when he first joined the Christie's mail room, had risen to the top on the back of a silken tongue and an unfailing eye for a good deal. The two of them neatly represented the social spectrum of both the auction world and the clients they served.

"Then you'll also know why I asked you to meet us here." Green waved semi-apologetically at their surroundings. Hudson shifted uncomfortably in mute agreement, his eyes fixed reproachfully on the thin coat of dust, straw and feed that had already settled on his gleaming handmade shoes.

"I can guess," Jennifer confirmed with a nod.

A few years ago both Christie's and Sotheby's had faced antitrust cases over allegations that they were fixing commission levels through a series of illicit meetings in the back of limousines and in airport departure lounges. Huge corporate fines and even jail sentences had resulted, although Sir Norman Watkins, Hudson's predecessor, had managed to avoid incarceration so far by refusing to return to the United States. The stables, therefore, offered a suitably discreet venue for Hudson and Cole to get together, given that in the current climate they daren't risk being seen in the same room, let alone meeting in private as they were now.

"Anthony," Green turned to Hudson, "why don't you explain what this is all about."

"Very well." Hudson loosened the inside button on his double-breasted suit jacket, the lining flashing emerald green. He bent down stiffly and picked up a gilt-framed painting that Jennifer had not noticed leaning against the stall.

"*Vase de Fleurs, Lilas,* by Paul Gauguin, 1885," he pronounced grandly, as he held it up for her to see. It was quite a small painting, featuring a delicately rendered vase of bright flowers against a dark, almost stormy background. "Not one of his most famous works perhaps, since he had not yet adopted the more primitive, expressive style that characterized his work after moving to Tahiti. Nevertheless it already betrays his more conceptual method of representation, as well as reflecting clear influences by Pissarro and Cézanne."

"Don't worry, I don't know what he's talking about either," Cole laughed.

Hudson twitched but said nothing and Jennifer suspected he quite liked Cole and his irreverent manner; probably even slightly envied it.

"You're auctioning it?" she guessed.

"Next week. It belongs to Reuben Razi, an Iranian dealer. A good client of ours. So far, we've had a very positive response from the market."

"Is it genuine?"

"Why do you ask that?" Hudson snapped, pulling the canvas away from her protectively, his eyes narrowing as if he was again lining her up in his rifle's crosshairs.

"Because, Lord Hudson, I'm guessing you didn't ask me up here just to show me a painting."

"You see?" Green smiled. "I told you she was good."

"Don't worry about Anthony." Cole clapped Hudson on the back. "You just hit a nerve, that's all."

"Show Agent Browne the catalog," Green suggested. "That'll explain why."

Cole flicked open the catches on his monogrammed Louis Vuitton briefcase and extracted a loosely bound color document that he handed to Jennifer.

"This is the proof of the catalog for our auction of nineteenth and twentieth-century art in Paris in a few months' time. A Japanese conglomerate, a longstanding client of ours, has asked us to include a number of paintings in the sale. One in particular, stands out." He nodded at the document. "Lot 185."

Jennifer thumbed through the pages until she came to the lot mentioned by Cole. There was a short description of the item and an estimate of three hundred thousand dollars, but it was the picture that immediately grabbed her attention. She looked up in surprise.

"It's the same painting," she exclaimed.

"Exactly," Hudson growled. "Someone's trying to rip us off. And this time, we've bloody well caught them with their hand in the till."

"This time?"

"Both Lord Hudson and Mr. Cole believe that this isn't an isolated incident," Green explained solemnly.

"And that, Agent Browne," Cole added, suddenly serious, "is why we asked you up here."

CHAPTER THREE

DRUMLANRIG CASTLE, SCOTLAND

18th April—12:07 P.M.

It seemed less a castle than a mausoleum to Tom; a place of thin shadows, cloaked with a funereal stillness, where muffled footsteps and snatched fragments of hushed conversations echoed faintly along the cold and empty corridors.

It was an impression that the furnishings did little to dispel, for although the cavernous rooms were adorned with a rich and varied assortment of tapestries, gilt-framed oil paintings, marble-topped chests, rococo consoles and miscellaneous *objets d'art*, closer inspection revealed many of them to be worn, dusty and neglected.

"This place reminds me of an Egyptian tomb," Tom whispered. "You know, stuffed full of treasure and servants and then sealed to the outside world."

"It's a family home," Dorling reminded him. "The Dukes of Buccleuch have lived here for centuries."

"I wonder if they've ever really lived here or just tended it, like a grave?"

"Why don't you ask them? That's the Duke and his son, the Earl of Dalkieth," Dorling hissed as they walked past an old man being supported by a younger one. Both men nodded at them solemnly as they passed by, their faces etched with a mournful, almost reproachful look that made Tom feel as though he had invaded the privacy of an intimate family occasion. "Poor bastards look like somebody died."

"That's probably how it feels," said Tom sympathetically. "Like somebody who has been a member of their family for two hundred and fifty years has suddenly dropped down dead."

"It's much worse than that," Dorling corrected him, eyebrows raised playfully. "It's like they've died and left eighty million quid to the local cat's home."

The hall had been sealed off; a square-shouldered constable was standing guard. From behind him came the occasional white flash and mechanical whir of a police photographer's camera. Tom felt his chest tighten as they stepped closer, Dorling's words echoing in his head: "He's left you something."

The disturbing thing was that Milo and he had always had a very simple agreement to just keep out of each other's way. So something serious must have happened for Milo to break that arrangement now, something that involved Tom and this place and whatever was waiting for him on the other side of that doorway. The easy option, Tom knew, would have been to refuse to take the bait, to walk away and simply ignore whatever lay in the next room. But the easy option was rarely the right one. Besides, Tom preferred to know what he was up against.

Seeing Dorling, the constable lifted the tape for them both to stoop under. To Tom's right, some forensic officers in white evidence suits were huddled next to the wall where Tom assumed the painting had been hanging.

"There's nothing here." Tom almost sounded relieved as he glanced around. Knowing Milo as he did, he'd feared the worst.

Dorling shrugged and then motioned toward two men who were standing at the foot of the staircase. One of them was speaking to the other in a gratingly nasal whine, a shapeless gray raincoat covering his curved shoulders. The corners of Tom's mouth twitched as he recognized his voice.

"It was opportunistic," the man pronounced. "They walked in, saw their chance and took it."

"What about the little souvenir they left behind?" the other man queried in a soft Edinburgh burr. "They must have planned that."

"Probably smuggled it in with them under a coat," Dorling agreed. "Look. I'm not saying they didn't plan to come here and steal something, just that they weren't that bothered what they took. Probably wouldn't know who da Vinci was if he jumped up and gave them a haircut."

"Would you?" Tom interrupted, unable to stop himself, despite Dorling's earlier warning.

The man swiveled around to face him.

"Kirk!" He spat the name through clenched teeth, yellowing eyes bulging above the dark shadows that nestled in his long, sunken cheeks. His skin was like marble, cold and white and flecked with a delicate spider's web of tiny veins that pulsed red just below the surface.

"Sergeant Clarke!" Tom exclaimed, his eyes twinkling mischievously. "What a nice surprise."

Tom could no longer remember quite why Clarke had made it his personal mission to see him behind bars. It was a pursuit that had at times verged on the obsessive, Clarke's anger mounting as Tom had managed again and again to slip from his grasp. Even now, he refused to believe that Tom had gone straight, convinced that his newly acquired respectability was all part of some elaborate con. Still, Tom didn't mind. If anything he found Clarke mildly amusing, which seemed to make him even angrier.

"It's *Detective* Sergeant Clarke, as well you know," Clarke seethed, the sharp outline of his Adam's apple bobbing uncontrollably. "What the hell are you doing here?"

"I invited him," Dorling volunteered.

"This is a criminal investigation." Clarke rounded on him. "Not a bloody cocktail party."

"If Tom's here, it's because I think he can help," Dorling replied tersely.

"For all you know, he nicked it himself," Clarke sneered. "Ever think of that?"

The man standing next to Clarke turned to Tom with interest.

"I don't believe we've met." He was about fifty years old, tall, with wind-tanned cheeks, moss green eyes and a wild thatch of muddy brown hair that was thinning from the crown outward.

"Bruce Ritchie," Dorling introduced him to Tom. "The estate manager. Bruce, this is Tom Kirk."

Tom shook Ritchie's outstretched hand, noting the nicotine stains around the tips of his fingers and the empty shotgun cartridges in his waxed jacket that rattled as he moved his arm.

"I take it you have some direct . . . experience of this type of crime?" He hesitated fractionally over the right choice of words.

"Too bloody right he does," Clarke muttered darkly.

"Can I ask where from?"

"He's a thief," Clarke snapped before Tom could answer. "That's all you need to know. The Yanks trained him. Industrial espionage. That is until he decided to go into business for himself." Clarke turned to Tom, a confident smirk curling across his face. "How am I doing so far?"

"Agency?" Ritchie guessed, his tone suggesting that, far from scaring him off, Clarke had only succeeded in further arousing his interest.

"That's right," Tom nodded, realizing now that Ritchie's stiff-shouldered demeanor and calculating gaze probably betrayed a military background. Possibly special forces. "You?"

"Army intelligence," he said with a grin. "Back when we didn't just do what the Yanks told us."

Clarke looked on unsmilingly as the other three men laughed.

"So you don't agree that this was opportunistic?" asked Ritchie.

Tom shook his head. "The people who did this knew exactly what they were here for."

"You don't know that," Clarke objected.

"Opportunistic is settling for the Rembrandt or the Holbein

nearer the entrance, not deliberately targeting the da Vinci," Tom retorted, sensing Clarke flinch every time he moved too suddenly.

"Do you think they'll try and sell it?" Ritchie pressed.

"Not on the open market. It's too hot. But then that was never the plan. Best case they'll lie low for a few months before making contact and asking for a ransom. That way your insurers avoid paying out full value and you get your painting back. It's what some people say the National Gallery in London had to do to get their two Turners returned, although they called it a finder's fee."

"And worst case?" Ritchie asked with a glum frown.

"If you don't hear from them in the next twelve months, then chances are it's been taken as collateral for a drugs or arms deal. It'll take seven years for it to work its way through the system to a point where someone will be willing to make contact again. The timings run like clockwork. But I don't think that's what's happened here."

"You're just making this up," Clarke snorted with a dismissive wave of his hand. "You don't know anything about this job or who pulled it."

Tom shrugged.

"Four-man team, right?"

"Maybe." Clarke gave an uncertain nod.

"I'd guess two on the inside and two on the outside—a lookout and a driver. The getaway car was probably stolen last night. Something small and fast. Most likely white or red so it wouldn't stand out."

"A white VW," Ritchie confirmed, his obvious surprise giving way to an irritated frown as he turned to Clarke. "I thought we'd agreed not to release any details yet?"

"We haven't," Clarke spluttered.

"I know because it's his usual MO," Tom reassured him.

"Whose?"

"His name is Ludovic Royal," Tom explained. "He's known in the business as Milo. French, although he would argue he's Corsican. Turned to art theft after five years in the Foreign Legion and another ten fighting in West Africa for whoever could afford him. He's ruthless and he's one of the best."

"Why's he called Milo?"

"Back when he first got started a client, some Syrian dealer, stiffed him on a deal. Milo hacked both the guy's arms off, one at the elbow, the other at the shoulder, and left him to bleed to death. When the photos leaked to the local press in Damascus they dubbed it the *Venus de Milo* killing. The name stuck."

"And that's who you think did this?" Ritchie sounded skeptical.

"It's too early to say," Clarke intervened.

"Have you found the gambling chip yet?" Tom asked. "It's a small mother-of-pearl disc about this big, with the letter M inlaid in ebony."

Clarke glared furiously at Dorling. "What else have you told him?"

"Nothing," Dorling insisted.

"I don't care who's told who what," Ritchie said firmly. "I just want to know what it means."

"Milo likes to autograph his scores," Tom explained. "It lets the rest of us know how good he is."

"The gambling chip is his symbol," Dorling confirmed. "They're pretty common in the art underworld." He paused, deliberately avoiding Tom's gaze. "Tom's was a black cat, you know, like the cartoon character. That's why they used to call him Felix."

Ritchie nodded slowly, as if this last piece of information had somehow confirmed a decision that had been forming in his mind.

"What do you know about the painting?" he asked.

"I know it's small, about nineteen inches long and fifteen wide, so it won't be hard to smuggle out of the country," Tom began. "I know it was painted between 1500 and 1510 and that a total of eleven copies were produced by da Vinci's workshop. Yours was the original."

"What about its subject matter?" Ritchie pressed.

"Who cares?" Clarke huffed impatiently.

"It shows the Madonna pulling the infant Jesus away from a yarnwinder, a wooden tool used for winding wool," Tom replied, ignoring him. "It's meant to symbolize the cross and the fact that even her love cannot save him from the Passion."

"Some of the copies even have a small cross bar on the yarnwinder to make the reference to the crucifixion more explicit," Ritchie confirmed with a nod. Then he paused, as if he couldn't quite bring himself to continue.

"Is there something else?" Tom ventured.

"You tell me," Ritchie said with a shrug, pointing to his right.

The forensic team had shifted to one side and Tom could now see the paneled wall where the painting had hung between two other works. But instead of an empty space, something seemed to have been fixed there. Something small and black.

"They found the gambling chip you described in its mouth," Ritchie explained, earning himself a reproachful glare from Clarke.

"In what's mouth?" Tom breathed.

He stepped closer, his heart beating apprehensively as the shape slowly came into focus.

He could see a head, legs and a long black tail. He could see a small pink tongue lolling out of the side of its mouth. He could see trails of dried blood where it had been nailed to the wall and a pool of sticky dark liquid on the top of the display case beneath it rendered a translucent pink by the light shining through the glass.

It was a cat. A crucified cat.

He glanced sharply at Dorling who gave him a telling nod.

"I told you he'd left you something, Felix."

CHAPTER FOUR

CLAREMONT RIDING ACADEMY, NEW YORK

18th April—7:55 A.M.

As a precaution against being seen in Hudson's company, Cole had allowed five minutes to elapse before following the older man down the ramp and out of the stables, leaving Jennifer and Green standing in an awkward silence.

"Any questions?" Green asked as Cole's footsteps faded away, only to be replaced by the muffled thump of hooves from the floor below.

"What about the case I'm on now? We've got a warehouse under surveillance over in New Jersey. I'm due on the next shift."

"It's all taken care of," Green said firmly. "I explained the situation to Dawkins. He understands this takes priority."

Although Jennifer felt bad about walking away from her team halfway through, she couldn't deny that part of her was relieved. After the month she'd just had, the prospect of another two weeks of sleepless nights and weak coffee was not one she had been particularly looking forward to.

"Anything else?" Green asked.

"Just one thing . . ." Jennifer hesitated, not entirely sure how she should phrase this. "If you don't mind my asking, sir, what's this got to do with you?"

Green nodded, having clearly been expecting this. After all, it usually took a bit more than a suspect painting to get the Director of the FBI personally involved in a case, let alone wading through horse shit at 7 a.m. to a briefing.

"Let's head back down," he suggested. "I need to get out to LaGuardia for nine."

She followed him out of the stall and back down the main aisle. A hosepipe had been left running, the end twitching nervously as water spilled across the floor, a ridge of straw and dirt forming at the edges of its wash. She stepped over it carefully, not wanting to ruin her shoes any more than they already had been.

"Hudson and I read law together at Yale," Green explained as they picked their way down the ramp to the ground floor, his men jogging ahead to ensure the route was secure. "Or rather I read law and he played polo. We've stayed in touch ever since."

"I see." She fought off the dismayed look that had momentarily threatened to engulf her face. Great. Screw up and she'd carry the can. Get a result and Green would step in to look good in front of his old college buddy. Either way, she couldn't win. In fact the best she could hope for was to get this over with as quickly as possible. "Did he call you?"

"As soon as he found out about the second Gauguin," Green confirmed, pausing under the building's arched entrance. "He's convinced that his client's version is genuine, of course. But then Cole's client is the one with the certificate of authenticity."

"Can't they just cancel the sale and sort it out between them?"

"You want the short answer or the long one?"

"Either will do."

"If they pull the lots, people will start to ask questions. Questions they can't answer until they can identify the fake."

"They could control the story if they wanted to."

"Perhaps. But they've got enough on their hands fighting off all these Holocaust claims without adding to their problems. And after the antitrust case, neither of them can risk another big scandal. That was the long answer by the way."

Jennifer nodded. Both firms stood accused by descendants of Holocaust victims of auctioning off art works stolen from their families by the Nazis. Nothing had been proved, but news of them both selling the same painting would hardly help restore their already battered reputations.

"So I'm guessing you want this kept low key."

"Until we know what we're dealing with." Green wagged his finger in agreement. "Ask around. See what you can find out without making too many waves. Both Cole and Hudson agree that this isn't an isolated incident. If there's an art forgery ring here in New York, we'd all like to know about it. I don't want to scare anyone off until we've got something solid."

"One more question, sir," Jennifer said as Green made to step out on to the street where one of his flunkies was hovering with an umbrella, ready to escort him to the limousine's open door. "Why me?"

The question had been gnawing away at her all morning. After all, it had been nearly a year since she had last spoken to Green, and even then it had been the briefest of conversations. She knew she should feel flattered that he had selected her for this, but she had been in the Bureau long enough to suspect an ulterior motive.

"Because you're good. Because you deserve it."

"The Bureau's full of good agents."

Green turned to face her, his eyes meeting hers and steadily holding her gaze. She had the sudden feeling that he was doing this deliberately, as if to try and convince her of his sincerity.

"The press office got called up by some bullshit journalist a few days ago," Green began. "Leigh Lewis. Writes for one of the check-out rags—*American Voice*. You know it?"

"No," said Jennifer, unsure where this was leading.

"That figures," he sniffed. "Sometimes I wonder if anyone actually reads that shit. Anyway, he must have some good sources, because he was asking about the Double Eagle case."

Jennifer's eyes widened in surprise. As far as she knew, that case was still classified. Highly classified. And for good reason. At its heart was the cover-up of an old CIA industrial espionage operation and a theft from Fort Knox that led all the way to the White House. No wonder Green was being cagey.

"What did he know?"

"Not much. But he had a name."

"Mine?" she guessed.

Green nodded.

"Obviously we didn't comment, but, given the extreme sensitivity of that investigation and your previous history . . ."

He didn't have to complete the sentence for her to know what he was referring to. A few years back, while on a DEA-led raid, she'd accidentally shot and killed a fellow officer, her one-time instructor from Quantico. During the inquiry it came out that they'd been seeing each other. It was a real mess. Though she'd been cleared of any wrongdoing, that hadn't stopped the press speculation and the Bureau gossips. It certainly hadn't stopped her being shipped out to the Atlanta field office until, in their words, things had "blown over," when in reality they had just wanted her out of the way.

"You don't think Lewis is going to drop the story?"

"We're doing what we can behind the scenes. But these things take time. That's why, when Hudson called, I thought of you. Given the circumstances it seemed like a good fit."

"I don't follow," she said with a frown. "What circumstances?"

"This case needs to be run in stealth mode. That means you'll be flying way beneath Lewis's radar for a few months. It's perfect," he exclaimed, clearly pleased with himself for devising such a creative solution.

Jennifer's heart sank. Far from singling her out as she'd somewhat vainly assumed, all Green wanted was to banish her to the nursery slopes where she couldn't do any damage. Suddenly two weeks of surveillance didn't look quite the bum deal she'd thought.

"Am I being suspended?"

"Of course not," he spluttered, a little too forcefully for Jennifer's liking. "I wouldn't have put you on this case if I didn't think it was important and that you could do a good job. This is an opportunity, not a punishment. But until we find out what Lewis knows and where he's getting it from, I don't want you to take any risks. You know the potential embarrassment to the Bureau and to the Administration if the Double Eagle story gets out. We'll all be in the firing line. This is for your own protection."

Somehow, Jennifer seriously doubted that. There was a rumor that Green, armed with his new wife's money, was thinking of running for office. A tilt at the Senate, some even said. The only protection he was worried about was his own.

CHAPTER FIVE

APSLEY HOUSE, LONDON

18th April—5:13 P.M.

The hall was dark and still. Several marble busts, once milky white and now curdled a creamy yellow by age, flanked its square perimeter and glared unblinkingly into nothingness. On the walls, a series of somber paintings. Archie glanced at each piece as he waited, fidgeting longingly with the cigarette packet and solid silver Dunhill lighter in his pocket, the sharp click of his heels amplified by the cloying silence.

"Mr. Connolly?" A female voice suddenly rang out.

Archie swiveled round to see a short woman striding toward him purposefully, her lips shining in the gloom.

"Yeah?"

"Hannah Key." She thrust out her arm and grasped his hand firmly. "I'm the curator here."

"Nice to put a face to the voice," said Archie.

She was much younger and prettier than he had guessed from their phone conversation a few days ago, with a pale oval face and large, inky eyes that reminded him of a Vermeer painting. Her long black hair was pulled back into a ponytail that was fixed in place with an elastic band, suggesting she was more concerned with the immediate practicalities of keeping her hair out of her eyes than she was with looking good. This impression was further confirmed by her simple blue dress, complete lack of jewelry and makeup, and the unsightly chips in the pearl varnish along the edges of her nails. What struck Archie most though were her shoes, which were new, clearly expensive and a startling shade of emerald green. Perhaps, he speculated, these revealed a rather more impulsive and indulgent character than the severe and forbidding persona she projected at work.

Then again, Archie knew he wasn't without his contradictions either. His accent, for example, straddled a broad social divide, occasionally hinting at a wholesome middle-class education but more often suggesting a rough apprenticeship amidst the traders who operated at the sharp end of the Bermondsey and Portobello antiques markets. And while he wore an elegant handmade suit and bright Hermès tie that wouldn't have looked out of place in a Pall Mall club, his gold identity bracelet, square-shouldered physiquc and closely cropped blond hair suggested a journeyman boxer of some sort.

In a country that invested so much meaning in external markers of social class, he knew that people often struggled to reconcile these seemingly conflicting signs. Some even questioned whether this was, in fact, deliberate. Archie chose not to elaborate. He'd always found it paid to keep people guessing.

"Not everyone who works in a museum is an antique," she remarked wryly, seemingly reading his thoughts. "Some of us even have a social life."

"Not many." Archie grinned. "At least not that I've seen over the years."

"Maybe things have changed since you got started?"

"I'm forty-five. That's thirty five years in the art game and counting," he said with a smile. "Everything's changed since I got started."

"By art game you mean museum security?"

He paused before answering. Sometimes he had to remind himself that Tom and he were running a legitimate business. Museum security was certainly not how he would havc described his years as a fence, although it was probably the best training he could ever have received for what he was doing now.

"One way or another." He nodded. "Never been here before, though."

"So you said on the phone." She adopted a slightly disapproving tone.

"Nice gaff. Perhaps you could show me round?" he ventured. She wasn't really his type, but there was no harm in chancing his hand.

"Perhaps we should finish up here first," she replied curtly.

"What's worth seeing?" She hadn't said no. That was pretty much a green light as far as Archie was concerned.

"Everything. But most people come for the paintings in the formal rooms on the first floor."

"Most people including your thieves?"

"Thief, not thieves," she corrected him. "And no, he didn't come for them. In fact that's what's most strange about this whole thing."

She steered Archie over to a large rectangular room on the left side of the house that looked out on to a small walled garden.

"This room contains some of the gifts bestowed on Wellington after Waterloo," she announced proudly. "The Waterloo Shield. His twelve Field Marshal batons. The Portuguese dinner service."

She indicated the mahogany display cases that lined the walls, each brimming with porcelain, gold and silver and decorated, wherever space allowed, with swooping copperplate inscriptions extolling Wellington's brilliance and the eternal gratitude of the piece's donor.

Archie's attention, however, was immediately drawn to the two-tier glass-sided cabinet positioned at the center of the room. Dominating the space like a small boat, the lower level was filled with decorated plates while the upper level appeared to contain a twenty-foot-long scale model of an Egyptian temple complex, complete with gateways, seated figures, obelisks, three separate temple buildings and sixteen sets of matching sacred rams.

"What's that?" It didn't happen that often anymore, but he was impressed.

"The Sèvres Egyptian dinner service," she explained. Archie noted how the cadence of her voice quickened whenever she spoke about any of the exhibits. "One of two sets made to commemorate Napoleon's successful invasion of Egypt in 1798. Each plate shows a different archaeological site, while the centerpiece is made from biscuit porcelain and modeled on the temples of Luxor, Karnak, Dendera and Edfu. This particular example was a gift from the Emperor to the Empress Josephine after their divorce, although she rejected it. It was eventually gifted to Wellington by the newly restored King of France."

"And this is what your villain wanted? The centerpiece. Or part of it at least."

"Yes," she confirmed, her voice betraying her surprise. "How did you know . . . ?"

"This glass is new," Archie explained, pointing at the cracked varnish where an old pane had been removed and a new one inserted. "And someone has tried to pick the lock." He ran his finger across the small scratches at the edges of one of the cabinet's brass locks.

"Tried and failed. That's why he smashed the glass."

"When was this?"

"March thirtieth, so a couple of weeks ago now. One of the guards disturbed him before he could take anything. They chased him outside, but he had a car waiting."

"It don't make no sense," Archie said with a frown, reasoning with himself as much as anyone. "The most he could have got away with would have been a couple of pieces. And what would they have been worth? A couple of grand, tops."

"Exactly. Any one of the swords or batons would have been worth a lot more."

"And been easier to flog," Archie added. "He certainly doesn't sound like a pro."

"To be honest, I don't care who he is," she retorted. "All I want to know is how we make sure nothing like this happens again."

"The bad news is you can't," Archie said with a sigh. "Not

for certain. But there are some things you can do to even the odds. Upgrade the locks, install security glass in all the cases, reconfigure the patrol cycles, that sort of thing. Anything more will cost you. If you're interested, I'll pull something together laying the options out. Maybe we could run through them over dinner?"

"Do you think there's any chance he'll try again?" she persisted, ignoring his suggestion.

"Normally I'd say no," Archie said with a shrug. "But this guy seems to be making it up as he goes along. It might be worth watching out for him, just in case."

"The problem is we don't know what he looks like," she said. "The guard only saw the back of his head."

"What about the cameras outside?"

"He had his head lowered in every picture. The police said he must have known where they were."

Archie frowned. If this intruder had taken the trouble to scope out the cameras, then maybe he wasn't quite the amateur he had assumed. Was he missing something?

"This is the best shot we could come up with," she said, taking a manilla folder from a side table and removing a photograph of a man, his head dipped so that only a narrow crescent of the bottom half of his face could be seen. Archie studied it for a few seconds and then looked up, straining to keep his voice level and face impassive.

"Mind if I hang on to this?"

"Why?" she asked, a curious edge to her voice. "You don't recognize him, do you?"

"No," Archie lied. "But you never know. Someone else might."

CHAPTER SIX

CLERKENWELL, LONDON

18th April—8:59 P.M.

Tom was finishing a call when Archie let himself in, the chatter of the refrigeration unit on a passing lorry gushing through the open door before draining away the instant it was shut behind him. Removing his coat, Archie tossed it over the back of one of the Georgian dining chairs arranged in the shop's two large arched windows.

Tom had bought this building just over a year ago now, transferring the stock from his father's antique business in Geneva after he'd died. As well as the dimly lit showroom area they were in now, the ground floor consisted of a large warehouse to the rear and an office that Tom and Archie shared as a base for their art recovery work. Tom himself lived on the top floor.

He killed the call and threw the phone down on the green baize card table he was sitting at, his right hand deftly manipulating a small mother-of-pearl casino chip through his slender fingers. Behind him, a grandfather clock lazily boomed the hour, triggering a sympathetic chorus of subtle chiming and gently pinging bells from the other clocks positioned around the room.

"All right?" Archie asked, leaning against the back of one of a pair of matching Chesterfield armchairs.

Tom caught a flash of cerise pink lining as Archie's jacket fell open and smiled. Subtlety had never been Archie's strongest point and even in a suit, a uniform Tom had rarely seen him out of, his forceful character seemed to find a way to flaunt itself. He had at least recently shed one of the two phones that he used to juggle from ear to ear like a commodities trader, although from the occasional involuntary twitch of his fingers, like a gunfighter stripped of his .45, Tom knew that he still missed the buzz of his old life.

"Good. You?"

"Not bad, not bad," Archie sniffed.

Tom nodded, struck by how, the better you knew someone, the less you often needed to say.

"Dominique in?" Archie glanced hopefully toward the rear.

"Not seen her." Tom shrugged. "Why, are you going to ask her out?"

"What are you talking about?" Archie laughed the question away.

"You know exactly what I'm talking about. What are you waiting for?"

"Leave it out, will you?" Archie snorted.

"If you don't make your move, someone else will."

"If I wanted to make a move, I would have done," Archie insisted.

"Well, it's probably just as well," Tom sniffed, his eyes twinkling at Archie's discomfort. "She'd only have said no. Better to avoid the rejection."

"Very funny." Archie smiled tightly. Tom decided to change the subject before he completely lost his sense of humor.

"That was Dorling, by the way." Tom nodded toward the phone.

"What the hell did he want?" Archie bristled. While Tom had understood the need to forgive his one-time pursuers if he was to move on, Archie was less sanguine. His scars ran deep, and he was suspicious of Dorling's Machiavellian pragmatism, sensing the seeds of a further about-turn should the circumstances require it.

"He just got the initial results of the forensic tests back."

"And?"

"And basically they've got nothing. No prints at the scene. The getaway car torched. Zip." In truth, he'd have been more surprised if they had found something. From what he'd seen, this crew weren't the sort to make mistakes.

"Any idea who pulled it?"

Tom flicked the chip down on to the card table, enjoying the expression registering on Archie's face as he stepped forward for a closer look.

"Milo?" he exclaimed. "Pull the other one! He was down for a ten-year stretch, minimum."

"According to Dorling, he got out six months ago. They found one of these at the scene." He nodded toward the chip. "This is one he gave me after a job we pulled together in Macau. Back when we were still talking."

"Well then, all we have to do is wait. He'll just follow his usual MO and ransom it back."

"I think he's picked up some new moves while he's been away. This time he left a message."

"What sort of a message?"

"A black cat. Dead. Nailed to the wall. The chip was in its mouth." He shook his head, as if to shake the grotesque image from his mind, but found that every time he blinked, its ghostly outline reappeared in front of him, as if it had somehow been seared on to the back of his eyelids.

Archie sat down slowly on the opposite other side of the card table. He picked the chip up and considered it for a few seconds, then locked eyes with Tom.

"And you think it was meant for you, don't you?"

"I think it was meant for Felix, yes." Tom was surprised at the instinctive anger in his voice. That name sat uncomfortably with him now, reminding him of a past life and a past self that he was trying to forget, to leave behind. Only Milo was trying to drag him back.

"It's a bit bloody crude, isn't it, even for him?"

"He's a showman. He likes to shock people."

"What do you think he wants?"

"To let me know he's back?" Tom speculated irritably. "To show me that he's not lost his touch? That he's still number one? Take your pick."

"You don't think it's a threat?"

"No." Tom gave a confident shake of his head. "We have an understanding. More of a debt, really. Milo operates by this old-fashioned code of honor, a hangover from his days in the Legion. According to his code he owes me a life, because I helped save his once. Until he repays it, he won't touch me."

"But now you've swapped sides," Archie reminded him. "Whatever debt you two had don't count for nothing no more."

"You mean *we've* swapped sides," Tom corrected him, with a nudge.

Archie mumbled something under his breath and fumbled for his cigarettes.

"Do you have to?" Tom frowned as he lit up.

"I've been gagging for one all afternoon." He took a deep drag and sighed contentedly.

"Why, where have you been?"

"Over at Apsley House, remember?"

"Oh, yeah."

"You should have seen the bird that runs the place." He rolled his eyes. "Fit as a butcher's dog."

"So you're glad you went?" Tom laughed.

"I was till she gave me this," Archie sighed, handing over the CCTV still. "Now I'm not so sure."

Tom studied the picture for a few seconds, attempting to extrapolate the man's face from the narrow sliver of his features that hadn't been obscured. He suddenly fixed Archie with an incredulous look.

"Is that Rafael?"

"That's what I thought too. It's the only shot they got of him. He dodged the other cameras."

"It can't be him." Tom shook his head in disbelief. "He'd have let me know if he was over here."

"You were away when this happened."

"What was he after?"

"Part of a dinner service. They rumbled him before he could get to it. He's a better art forger than he is a thief."

"A dinner service?" Tom looked up with a frown. "The Egyptian dinner service?"

"You know it?"

"It's one of a pair. I saw the other one once at the Kuskovo Estate near Moscow."

"Well, next time maybe he should try his luck there instead," Archie laughed. "He certainly ballsed this one up."

Tom silently considered the grainy image, his brain furiously calculating all the possible reasons Rafael might have had to try and pull off a job like this. The problem was, none of them made sense. Just like this picture didn't make sense. If Rafael had managed to avoid all the other cameras, why allow himself to be seen in this one, even if he was only barely recognizable? He would have known it was there, same as the others.

Unless that was the whole point. Unless he wanted to be seen. The question was, by who?

CHAPTER SEVEN

GINZA DISTRICT, TOKYO

19th April—6:02 A.M.

This was a sanctuary. A refuge. A place to escape the sensory assault of the outside world. The choking fumes from the long ribbons of traffic, cut into neat strips where the streets crossed. The deafening floods of people, the roar of their heavy footsteps as they funneled obediently along the sidewalks in different directions, depending on the time of day. The blinding strum of the persuasive neon, the advertising signs preaching their different religions high above the heads of those passing below, heads bowed as if in prayer.

Here there were no windows, and no way in, apart from a solitary, soundproofed door that could only be opened from the inside. The air was filtered and chilled, the walls covered in the same black Poltrona Frau leather used by Ferrari, the recessed lights waxing to nothing more than a lunar glow before waning back into darkness at the press of a switch.

There was a single chair positioned in front of a blank screen that took up almost an entire wall. A man was sitting in it, naked. To his left was a glass of iced water. His head, face, chest, arms, legs and groin were totally bald, giving him the appearance of a grotesque oversized baby. From the way he was sitting, it was also impossible to see his penis, giving him a strange, androgynous quality that his distended stomach, swollen breasts and delicate bone structure did nothing to dispel.

He pressed the small remote balancing on his lap. The screen flickered on, a searing rectangle of white light that made the colorful brocade of tattoos that snaked over his entire upper body ripple as if alive. From all around him came the low hum and hiss of the concealed surround speakers.

Now an image appeared. A man. Terrified. His arms pressed flat against a doorframe. Then someone else stepped into the picture, a hammer in one hand and two nails in the other. The first man's eyes widened in sudden understanding. The nail went through his wrist, the metal stretching his median nerve across its blunt tip like the strings over the bridge of a violin, his thumbnail drawing blood where the reflex had caused it to embed itself into his palm. He screamed, the saliva dribbling down his chin, then fainted. Reaching for the remote, the viewer turned the volume up.

They waited until he regained consciousness and then hammered in the second nail. He shrieked again, his body momentarily rigid with pain, hands clenched into white talons, before sagging forward as the men released him and let his wrists take the strain. The camera never left his face, silent tears running down his cheek, a sudden nosebleed drawing a vivid line across his upper lip and chin before dripping on to his chest.

His tortured breathing echoed through the room, a steady metronome that marked every few passing seconds with unfeeling regularity until slowly, inevitably, the gap between each rasping breath grew. For a few minutes it seemed as if time itself was slowing, his lungs clawing for air, his lips thin and blue, each breath shallower than the last until little more than a whisper remained.

Then he was still.

Taking a sip of water and freeing his penis so it lay across his stomach where he could touch it, the man settled down to watch the film again.

CHAPTER EIGHT

CLERKENWELL, LONDON

19th April—1:16 A.M.

With a sigh, Tom threw the bedclothes off and swung his feet down to the floor. He'd never been a good sleeper, and experience had taught him there was no point trying to wrestle his mind into submission when it had decided it had better things to do.

He pulled on the jeans and shirt he'd thrown over the back of a chair and negotiated his way across the open expanse of the living room, the orange glow of the slumbering city seeping in through the partially glazed roof overhead. Unbolting his front door, he made his way down the staircase to his office, the rubber soles of his trainers squeaking noisily on the concrete steps.

The desk light snapped on, a brilliant wash of bleached halogen sweeping across the worn leather surface. He prodded the mouse and his computer blinked reluctantly into life, the screen staining his face blue.

He scanned through his emails—junk mail mostly, offering to improve his sex life or his bank balance. For a moment his cursor hovered over the three unopened messages from Jennifer Browne that lurked at the foot of his inbox. Two from the year before, one sent this January. Then nothing.

Not that that was surprising. Jennifer had better things to do than waste time writing to him if he couldn't be bothered to reply. But then it wasn't that he hadn't wanted to read them. It was just simpler that way. His was a life that could only be lived alone and there was no point in pretending otherwise. And although he would never admit it, he drew a perverse satisfaction in his asceticism; in proving that civilian life had not blunted his self-discipline. Even so, he hadn't quite been able to bring himself to delete her emails yet. That would have been a little too final. Perhaps, deep down, he liked to believe that there might be another way.

A noise made Tom look up. The roller-shutter over the entrance had been activated and was retracting itself with a loud clanking. He crossed over to the window that looked on to the warehouse below, just in time to see a powerful motorbike pull in, the dazzling beam of its headlamp picking out a series of packing crates and cardboard boxes before both it and the engine were extinguished. Almost immediately, the shutter unfurled behind it.

Dominique jumped to the ground and removed her helmet, blonde hair spilling out on to her shoulders. Looking up, she waved at Tom with a smile, before turning and making her way up the spiral staircase toward him.

"Welcome home." She kissed him on both cheeks, her blue eyes sparkling under a silvery eye shadow.

"Thanks. You're late back."

"You checking up on me too?" She grinned, unzipping her leather jacket to reveal a strapless black cocktail dress. "I've already had two missed calls from Archie tonight."

"I just didn't know where you were," said Tom.

Although it was against his natural instincts to worry about anyone other than himself, Tom felt strangely responsible for Dominique. Responsible because, as she had revealed to him a few months before, it was his father who had offered her a way out of Geneva's callous streets and a spiraling cycle of soft drugs, casual scams and brutal young-offender institutions. Responsible because, after his father's death, she was the one who had picked up the reins of his business, first transferring it to London and then agreeing to stay and help run it. Protecting her was, therefore, a way of preserving the delicate thread of shared memories that led back to his father. Not that she wanted or needed much protection.

"I can look after myself," she said, arching her eyebrows knowingly. "What are you doing up?"

"Can't sleep."

"Anything you want to talk about?" She laid a concerned hand on his arm. "You were only meant to be gone a few days. It's been three weeks."

"I got a lead on the Ghent altarpiece," he said defensively. "I followed it up."

"You look tired."

"I've got a lot going on."

"You need to slow down," she cautioned.

"I like to keep busy."

"Keeping busy won't bring any of them back, you know. Your father, Harry—"

"I don't want to talk about him." Tom felt his teeth clenching at the mention of Harry Renwick. A family friend and surrogate father to Tom, Renwick had revealed himself to be the murderer and criminal mastermind known as Cassius. The shock of his betrayal the previous summer still hadn't left Tom; nor had the guilt he now felt at his role in Harry's death, or his anger that Renwick had taken the truth about Tom's father's true involvement in his murderous schemes to his grave. There were still so many questions about the sort of man his father had been, about the people he'd known and the things he'd done. Questions, always questions, but never any way of answering them.

"You never want to . . ." She broke off suddenly, reached behind him and snatched the CCTV still off the desk where Tom had left it. "Where did you get this?"

"Archie. It's from that break-in at Apsley House."

"I know that man." She pointed at the blurred image.

"Rafael?" Tom gave a disbelieving frown. "I doubt it."

"He was here," she insisted. "The morning you flew off to Italy. He left you something."

"What?"

She pointed at the bookcase under the window. A long, narrow object had been placed there, wrapped in what appeared to be a white linen napkin.

Tom picked it up and carried it over to the desk. As he stood it up and undid the knot, the material fell away, revealing a porcelain obelisk, just over two feet long, inscribed with hieroglyphs.

"What is it?" asked Dominique, frowning.

"It's part of the Egyptian dinner service from Apsley House," Tom answered, grim-faced.

"But they told us nothing was taken."

"That's exactly what he wanted them to think."

"You mean he swapped this for a replica?"

"I should have known better than to think he'd have run away empty-handed. He's too good."

"Who is he?"

"A crook and a friend." Tom gave a wry smile.

"In that order?"

"He never saw the difference. Was there anything else?"

"A letter." She handed him an envelope. It was made from thick, good-quality ivory paper and a single word had been written across the front in a swirling copperplate script. *Felix.*

Tom snatched a knife out of the desk drawer and sliced it open.

"It's empty," said Dominique, looking up at him questioningly. "What does that mean?"

"Only one way to find out," Tom said as he reached into the desk for his address book.

"Have you seen the time?" she warned him.

"He's up to something," he muttered, nodding at the stolen obelisk and the empty envelope. "What if he's in some sort of trouble? What if he needs my help?"

He found Rafael's number and dialed it. A few seconds later a voice answered.

"Digame."

"Rafael?" he asked in a tentative tone, not recognizing the man's voice and wondering if he'd misdialed.

There was a pause.

"Who is this?" There was a suspicious edge to the man's voice.

"Oliver Cook," Tom improvised a name and a reason for calling. "I work for the London *Times*. We were hoping to get a quote from Mr. Quintavalle for a piece we're running tomorrow. Who am I speaking to?"

"Officer Juan Alonso of the Seville Police," came the heavily accented reply.

"The police? Is Mr. Quintavalle in some sort of trouble?"

Another pause, then the man replied in a hesitant, almost apologetic tone.

"Señor Quintavalle is dead."

"Dead?" Tom gasped. "How? When?"

"Last week. Murdered. If you like, I transfer you to my superior," Alonso suggested eagerly.

"That's kind, but I'm on a deadline and I'm a quote down," Tom insisted, trying to keep his voice level. "Thanks for your help. *Buenas noches.*"

He punched the off button. There was a long silence. Dominique placed a sympathetic hand on his shoulder.

"I'm sorry."

"I was too late," he said slowly, shaking her off. "He came here because he needed my help. He needed my help and I wasn't here for him."

"It wasn't your fault," she said gently.

"It's somebody's fault," Tom shot back.

"He's dead, Tom. There's nothing you can do for him now."

"I can find out who did this," Tom said coldly, his eyes rising to meet hers. "I can find out who did this and make them pay."

CHAPTER NINE

SOHO, NEW YORK

19th April—8:50 A.M.

Reuben Razi's gallery occupied the ground floor of one of Soho's characteristic cast-iron warehouses, the rusty scar of its fire-escape zig-zagging up the recently painted white façade.

Jennifer had yet to see anyone enter the building, but it was still early. She'd been sitting in her car, parked outside the model agency on the opposite side of the street, since seven-thirty, watching the neighborhood slowly stretch, yawning, into life. The early start had been deliberate. Razi's receptionist had told her he would not be in until after nine, but she wanted to get a feel for the world Razi lived in before she met him.

According to the file spread across her lap, Razi had fled to the U.S. from Iran after the fall of the Shah. Penniless and not speaking a word of English, he had begun importing Middle Eastern antiquities, and from those modest beginnings had evolved the small but prosperous fine art business he ran today. He specialized in the mid-market, selling second-tier artists and minor works by some of the bigger Impressionist and Post-Impressionist painters—the sort of piece that was worth hundreds of thousands rather than millions. It was a formula that seemed to have worked, given that Razi was able to afford a sprawling compound out in Long Island from where he commuted every day.

The only slight question mark on his resumé had been over the sale of a number of paintings reported to belong to the Fanjul and de la Torre families. As refugees from Fidel Castro's regime in Cuba, their art collections had been seized by the Communists, but some of the more valuable works had reappeared several years later in U.S. and European auction rooms. Razi had been named by an informant as the link man between the Cuban government and an Italian art dealer who had arranged for the works to be smuggled abroad. Nothing had ever been proven, of course, and Razi's name had been just one of several in the frame. It certainly wasn't enough to undermine his credibility or the trust that Lord Hudson so clearly had in him.

A Range Rover swept past her, its tires drumming noisily over the cobbled street, the sunlight winking in its heavily tinted windows. She checked the plates, confirming that it was the same car that had already driven past twice this morning. According to the list she had in front of her, it was registered in Razi's name.

This time, rather than drive on, the Range Rover drew up outside the gallery. As the driver's door opened, a girl ran out of the building. A man stepped from the vehicle and scurried inside, Jennifer just catching a glimpse of the back of his head before he vanished. The girl meanwhile clambered in, adjusted the driver's seat and pulled sedately away, Jennifer guessing that she had gone to park it somewhere. She gave it a few minutes and then followed the man inside, the file clutched under one arm.

The gallery was a large, open-plan space, every inch of which had been painted an unforgivably clinical white. Despite its size, there couldn't have been more than fifteen paintings on display, small islands of color marooned amidst the walls' featureless expanse, each illuminated by a single brushed-steel spotlight that protruded from the ceiling like a medical implant.

"I'd like to speak to Mr. Razi, please," Jennifer instructed the receptionist, holding out her ID.

"He's in a meeting right now," the receptionist trilled through a saccharine smile. "Can I take a message?"

"You must be Agent Browne."

Jennifer looked up to where the accented voice had come from. A man was beaming down at her over the mezzanine level's railings like a ringmaster welcoming her to the circus.

"Mr. Razi?"

She stepped back to get a better view. He had a swarthy face and a pencil-thin mustache dyed an unlikely shade of black to match his carefully styled hair. According to the file he was in his early fifties, but he looked older, and the diamond stud in his left ear suggested someone clinging by his fingertips to the rock-face of youth. Amidst the sterile surroundings, his vibrant purple velvet suit seemed almost unreal, and made him look as if he had been superimposed against the gallery walls.

Without answering, he stepped away from the balustrade and made his way down to her, each heavy footstep making the spiral staircase vibrate with a dull clang. He held out his hand and, as she shook it, he bowed theatrically. A thatch of long dark hairs poked out from under the cuff of his starched white shirt and now that she was closer she could see that his face was pitted with acne scars.

"Hudson said you'd come." He pressed a hand over his mouth, affecting surprise, his English strangely stilted. "Was that very wrong of him?"

"Not wrong. Just not ideal."

"You must forgive him," Razi pleaded, bringing his hands together as if in prayer, the large gold rings that adorned every finger glinting like brass knuckles. "He thought I should know. It is my painting, after all."

"It doesn't matter," she said with a shrug, not wanting to put Razi on the defensive. Not yet at least. "We're all after the same thing."

"And what is that?"

"To figure out what's going on, as fast as we can."

"Exactly!" He smiled in agreement, the faint glint of several gold teeth coming from the back of his mouth. "I hope you didn't waste too much time this morning?"

"What do you mean?"

"I drove past at eight o'clock and saw you outside. And again at quarter past. Were you hoping to see anything in particular?"

Jennifer paused. She was less worried at having been spotted than intrigued as to why Razi had felt it necessary to drive past his gallery twice before finally going inside.

"Why don't we sit down?" she suggested.

"By all means." He nodded toward a secluded area at the rear of the gallery where a white leather divan had been provocatively placed at a forty-five-degree angle across the floorspace. Jennifer instinctively wanted to straighten it. They sat down and he turned to face her with his palms resting on his knees.

"We should start with a few questions, if that's okay?"

"You are very beautiful, Agent Browne." Razi smiled, his nostrils flaring slightly as he spoke. "But I expect many men tell you that."

Jennifer gazed at Razi unblinkingly. She knew that in his business, the ability to read people was the key to convincing someone to pay a hundred thousand for something worth fifty. She therefore took the compliment as a sighting shot to calibrate how he should play her, rather than a line. Having said that, from what she'd seen so far, Razi was also a performer. One who clearly liked to keep his audience slightly off-balance. Either way, her best policy was not to react.

"When did you buy the Gauguin?"

Razi sat back resignedly and began to slowly crack his knuckles in turn. "About ten years ago. At the time, people said I overpaid, but a Gauguin is a Gauguin, whatever the period."

"And you never doubted its authenticity?"

"Never." Razi was adamant, his hand movements becoming more animated. "Its provenance was beyond suspicion. The documentation proved it. I can supply you with copies of everything."

"So the existence of a second work has taken you by surprise?"

"Absolutely." Razi gave a vehement nod.

"The seller is a major Japanese corporation."

"It's always the Japanese these days." He shrugged. "The economy's not what it used to be. Russia, on the other hand—now that's a market."

"Have you ever come across a forgery yourself?"

"Not that I can recall." He gave another shrug.

"And yet you buy and sell a lot of paintings, don't you?"

"It depends on what you mean by 'a lot.' "

"Lord Hudson said that you were a good client of his." She opened her file and consulted one of the typewritten pages inside. "I counted fifteen purchases and twenty sales in the past three years from Sotheby's alone."

"Is that file on me?" Razi's tone hardened.

"Parts of it, yes." Jennifer flipped the cover shut. Although it wasn't exactly standard procedure, she'd brought the file in with her precisely to see how Razi would react when he saw it. So far, he seemed more offended than concerned.

"Am I a suspect, Agent Browne?" He drew back and glared at her.

"No more than I am, Mr. Razi," Jennifer said in a conciliatory tone. "But if we're going to get a result, we need to have a fuller picture of you and your business. After all, this could have been done by a client or a supplier. Someone who bore a personal grudge and wanted to damage your reputation."

"I have no enemies." Razi shook his head firmly. "I left them all behind in Iran. Here, in America, I am with friends. Many, many friends."

"What about Herbie Hammon?"

Again she saw a flash of impatience in his eyes.

"Herbie and I are . . . are very close."

"Close enough for you to break his arm?" she pressed, thinking back to the paramedic's deposition she'd read in the file while she'd been waiting. "Close enough for him to sue you for assault?"

"The case never went to trial." His humorless tone belied his easy smile. "It was a simple misunderstanding. I never meant to hurt him . . ." A pause. "Are you married, Agent Browne?"

"No."

"No," he repeated. Jennifer found herself bristling at his tone, which implied she'd provided the answer he had been expecting. Was she that easy to read? "Well, Herbie and I are like a married couple, and married couples argue. Things are said and done in the heat of the moment. But they don't mean anything. The important thing is that we always kiss and make up in the end."

There was a long silence as Jennifer waited to see if he would continue. If nothing else, the mention of Hammon's name seemed to have thrown him. It was an angle worth following up on, even if Razi wasn't prepared to volunteer anything more himself.

"Mr. Razi, is there something you're not telling me?" she asked eventually. "Something that might have provoked someone out there to try to get at you?"

"I've already said no," he said with a simple shake of his head. "Why, do you . . . ?" He glanced accusingly at the file on Jennifer's lap and then snatched his eyes back to hers.

Jennifer remained silent. The truth was that she had more questions now than when she had walked in. Like why had Razi driven past his gallery twice before finally sprinting inside? Or, more to the point, what had prompted him to carry the revolver that she had glimpsed strapped to his right ankle as he'd made his way downstairs?

These were hardly the actions of a man who supposedly had no enemies. But then again, as the existence of two identical Gauguins had shown, in this world, appearances could sometimes be deceptive.

CHAPTER TEN

ALAMEDA, SEVILLE

19th April—5:15 P.M.

The wooden gate creaked open, ripping the police notice forbidding entry in half and revealing a small courtyard. Tom stepped in warily, the walls of the two-story building rising on all sides to frame a small slab of sky overhead, gray and sullen.

The ground was littered with broken tiles and shattered terracotta bricks. The dog turd on the large pile of sand to his left had been stepped in, the crumbling imprint of a ridged sole still visible. A pile of wind-blown rubbish had drifted into the far corner where Tom thought he could make out the fluorescent glow of a discarded condom. He shook his head angrily. Rafael had deserved better than this. Much better.

"This way."

Marco Gillez shouldered past him and strode into the middle of the courtyard. Tom paused to secure the gate behind them before following, fluttering his T-shirt against his body to cool himself. It was warm for this time of year, even for Spain.

Gillez was wearing an outfit that looked as if it had been lifted from a bad fifties musical—blue flannel trousers worn with a pastel green jacket and cream shoes that were in need of a polish. He had a long, pale face and small muddy brown eyes that were separated by a large nose that narrowed to an almost impossibly sharp edge along its ridge, casting a shadow across one half of his face like the arm of a sundial. His ginger hair and goatee had been dyed black, the resulting color a dark mahogany that changed hue depending on the light.

"There—"

He pointed with a dramatic flourish at an open doorway; his fingernails were gnawed right back, the cuticles sore and bleeding. Tom looked up and saw two holes on either side of the door frame, dark rivulets of dried blood running from beneath them to the ground. White chalk marks had been drawn around the outline of the bloodstains, forming a large, looping line like an untightened noose.

"Cause of death: *asfixia*," Gillez continued as he consulted a file produced from a small brown leather satchel, his voice colored by a heavy Spanish accent. "The weight of the body suspended on the two nails made it impossible to breathe. It only took a few minutes." He ran his hand over his goatee as he spoke, smoothing it against his skin as if he was stroking a cat.

"That's why the Romans used to nail people's feet too," Tom added in a dispassionate tone. "So they could push themselves up and catch their breath. It prolonged the ordeal."

"So it could have been worse?" A flicker of interest in Gillez's voice. "He was lucky?"

"He was crucified, Marco," Tom snapped. "Nailed to a doorway in a yard full of dog shit and used rubbers. You call that lucky?"

He turned away and stared angrily at the open doorway. The small part of him that had voiced a faint voice of hope that Rafael could not be dead, that this must all be some terrible mistake, was suddenly tellingly muted. This was where Rafael's life had ebbed away, retreating a little further out of reach with every agonized breath. He almost wished he'd taken Dominique's advice and stayed away.

There was a long silence. Gillez, his jaw clicking as he exercised it slowly from side to side, appeared to be waiting for Tom to say something.

"Would you like to see the photos?" he asked eventually, thrusting the file hopefully toward Tom.

"No." Tom turned away in distaste, a brief mental image forming of Gillez as a child, pulling the legs off a crab and watching it struggle at the bottom of his bucket. "Just tell me what it says."

Gillez gave a disappointed shrug and turned the page.

"Rafael Quintavalle. White male. Age fifty-six. Found dead on the *Domingo de Resurrección*—Easter Sunday. *Homicidio.* The coroner estimated he'd been here two to three days. He was identified by his stepdaughter."

"Eva?" Tom asked in surprise. "She's here?"

"You know her?"

"Used to." Tom nodded with a sigh.

"She's a wild one," Gillez said with a whistle. "It says here the FBI arrested her for diamond smuggling."

"That was a long time ago. What else does it say about Rafael?"

"He was last seen at the Macarena procession on *Jueves Santo*—Holy Thursday. At least two people claim they saw him going for *confesión* in the Basilica de la Macarena just before the procession set out."

"Confession?" Tom gave an incredulous frown. "Are you sure?"

"That's what it says." Again Gillez thrust the file toward him.

"What does it say about his apartment? Did the police find anything there?"

"It had already been searched by the time they arrived. They were too late."

"I was too late," Tom murmured to himself.

"You knew him well?" Gillez, fanning himself with one of the photographs, sounded intrigued.

"Rafael and I did a couple of jobs once," Tom confirmed. "In the early days. I don't know why, but we clicked. We've been friends ever since."

He paused, thinking back to when he'd left the CIA, or rather when they'd decided that he'd become a dangerous liability that needed silencing. Rafael had been there for him when he'd gone on the run, had helped set him up in the business, introduced him to the right people, Archie among them. He thought back to their friendship and the good times they'd shared. All that was gone now.

"Rafael was old school, a real character. He taught me a lot about the way the game was played. He taught me a lot about myself. I trusted him. He trusted me. In our business, that doesn't happen very often."

"They say he was a good forger."

"One of the best," Tom agreed. "He's got two in the Getty and three more in the Prado. And they're just the ones he told me about."

"But he'd retired?" Gillez sounded uncertain.

"That's what he told me." Tom shrugged. "But retired people don't get crucified."

Gillez nodded at this, as if he'd come to the same conclusion. Tom locked eyes with him.

"What is it?"

"*Aquí.*"

Gillez stepped toward the small well and pointed at the stone step leading up to it. More white chalk marks had been drawn on the floor and the stone.

"We think he set fire to something before they killed him. A small notebook or something like that. Then he cut himself." His eyes shone excitedly, his razor-edged nose quivering as if he'd picked up a scent. "The index finger of his right hand was covered in blood."

"He wrote something, didn't he?" Tom guessed breathlessly. "Show me."

CHAPTER ELEVEN

LEXINGTON AVENUE, UPPER EAST SIDE, NEW YORK

19th April—11:25 P.M.

"The thing is, Special Agent Browne . . . I'm awful busy."
If Jennifer had heard those words once since leaving Razi that morning, she'd heard them ten times.

Each visit she'd made had played out the same way: an expectant smile from the gallery owner that had wilted the moment they realized she was not a potential client. Then a slow, deliberate nodding of the head to feign interest in her questions, their eyes glazing over all the while. Shortly thereafter came hesitation, and a sudden distracted interest in a painting that needed straightening or a chest requiring a polish—anything to play for time. Finally, an excuse along the lines of the one that had just been given.

"Mr. Wilson, this won't take long."

With a weary sigh, Wilson took his spectacles off, folded them carefully and placed them on the desk in front of him. His pinched features and fussy, slightly arch movements suggested to Jennifer the type of person who insisted on cataloguing their CDs not only by year of recording, but also by conductor.

"Very well."

"Do you know Reuben Razi?"

"Is that who this is about?"

"You do know him then?"

"I know *of* him. He's a buyer. In this business that gets you known." He gestured at the paintings carefully arranged around the walls of his gallery, as if to indicate that he too was well known in the art world. "But I've never met him. He isn't really involved in the art scene here in Manhattan."

"He's a competitor of yours."

"Competitor is such a vulgar word," Wilson said, his top lip lifting off his square teeth as he wrinkled his nose. "We're partners, really; partners in a shared cultural enterprise. We're not like those sharks on Wall Street. We don't take lumps out of each other anytime someone swims too close. Our business is a bit more civilized than that."

Jennifer bit her tongue, wanting to pick Wilson up on almost every point he'd just made, but knowing she'd only make things more difficult than they already were. Besides, she wasn't sure whether she was annoyed because she disagreed with him, or because of his pompous, self-satisfied manner.

"But it *is* a business. At the end of the day, surely you're all in it to make money?"

"We're in it for the art," he corrected her tartly. "The money is just a happy coincidence."

Judging from his immaculate handmade suit and glittering Cartier wristwatch, it was a coincidence that Jennifer sensed Wilson was taking full advantage of.

"Would you say Mr. Razi is a well-respected member of the Manhattan art community?" she probed.

"Of course." Wilson nodded, perhaps just a little too emphatically, she thought.

"You've never heard of him falling out with anyone?"

"Not as far as I know," he said, with a firm shake of his head. "In fact, I heard he can be . . . quite charming." Wilson bared his teeth with what she assumed was an attempt to look charming himself. She stifled a smile.

"Did you hear about a fight that he was involved in a few months ago?"

"I don't listen to gossip," Wilson sniffed disdainfully.

"It was picked up by the press. A man had his arm broken. An attorney here in Manhattan, by the name of Herbie Hammon. Have you any idea what they were fighting about?"

"I don't follow the news either," said Wilson with a perfunctory shake of the head. "All doom and gloom and celebrity tittle-tattle. I suggest you go and ask Mr. Hammon yourself."

"I have an appointment to see him later today," she said with a thin smile, noting a rolled-up copy of that day's *New York Times* peeking out from his trash can. "It's strange—not a single dealer I have spoken to today seems to have heard of that fight, or have an opinion as to what it was about."

"It must have been a private matter." Wilson perched his spectacles back on his nose and peered at her impatiently. "Personally, I find people's lack of willingness to speculate on the causes commendable rather than strange."

This was going nowhere. Jennifer decided on a change of approach.

"Have you ever been a victim of fraud here, Mr. Wilson?"

"Fraud?" The question seemed to take him by surprise and his watery gray eyes blinked repeatedly.

"Artistic fraud. Has anyone ever tried to sell you a forgery? Have you perhaps bought one without realizing what it was at the time?"

"What sort of a question is that?" Wilson asked haughtily, stepping out from behind his desk and drawing himself up to his full five feet six—still a few inches shorter than Jennifer. "What do you mean?"

"I take it you haven't been working in the art world long?"

"Less than a year," she admitted icily. His condescending tone was beginning to rile her, although she comforted herself with the thought that he was probably like this with everyone. Part of her couldn't help wondering, however, if he would speak to a man in the same way. Probably not.

"It shows." He took up a position close to the door as he spoke, Jennifer taking this as a rather unsubtle attempt to bring their conversation to an end. "A bit more experience would have taught you to tread more carefully when using f-words."

"F-words?"

"Fake, forgery, fraud. Bring them up in the wrong context and you'll find yourself on very dangerous ground." His tone was growing increasingly strident, almost angry.

"I wasn't suggesting . . ."

"People's reputations are on the line. Reputations that have taken years to establish. An accusation is made and pfff—" he snapped his fingers "—it's all gone. But what if you get it wrong? By the time you realize your mistake, lifelong relationships have been destroyed, trust shattered. Forgery is the pedophilia of the art world. Once the suspicion is raised, you're presumed guilty even when proven innocent. It's a shadow that never leaves you, poisoning everything you touch. So you need to be either very brave, or very sure that you're right, before you cry forgery in this city."

"Even so," she said with a frown, "given the sums involved, I would have thought that forged works appear on a fairly regular—"

"I've already told you," he snapped, his hand hovering over the door handle, his cheeks flushed, "none of us do this for the money. It's . . ."

"For the art, I know." She completed the sentence for him unsmilingly. It wasn't the first time today she'd heard that familiar and infuriating refrain.

CHAPTER TWELVE

ALAMEDA, SEVILLE

19th April—5:25 P.M.

Gillez led Tom round to the other side of the well. There, hastily daubed against its weather-stained stone base, were three letters, or at least what appeared to be letters, arranged in a triangle. At the top an F, to the left a Q, to the right an almost indistinct N.

"Any ideas?" Gillez asked hopefully, wiping the sweat off his forehead with his sleeve.

Tom shrugged.

"Not really," he lied.

The triangle was Rafael's symbol, an oblique reference to the mountainous region of Northern Italy his family came from and from which his name derived—Quintavalle literally meant the fifth valley. The top letter was who the message was addressed to. F for Felix. The Q was who it was from. Quintavalle. As for the N, Tom was certain that it wasn't an N at all but an M that Rafael had been unable to complete before his attackers pounced. An M for Milo, to tell Tom that that was who was about to kill him.

"Did you find a small gambling chip anywhere? Mother-of-pearl, inlaid with an ebony letter?"

"What?" The confused expression on Gillez's face told

Tom they hadn't. Not that surprising, on reflection. Murder was probably not something Milo would want to advertise.

"Show me the photos." Tom demanded icily.

"I thought you didn't want to . . ."

"Well now I do," Tom insisted, his earlier reluctance forgotten.

With a shrug, Gillez pulled a handful of black-and-white photos out of the file and handed them over. Tom leafed through them slowly, his face impassive, trying to divorce the pictures of the carcass that had been strung across the open doorway from the living, feeling person he had once known. It was an impossible task and Tom knew that from now on both images were condemned to an unhappy marriage in his mind, each intimately bound up with the other.

He looked back to the inscription written in his friend's blood. He had not given much thought to the events up at Drumlanrig Castle since he had learned about Rafael's fate. In fact, he had called Dorling on his way to the airport to excuse himself, temporarily at least, from the investigation.

Now, however, the image of the black cat nailed to the wall and its parallels with Rafael's agonizing death came sharply back into focus. Milo was clearly involved in both cases and wanted him to know it. The question was why.

He looked up sharply, the noise of approaching sirens interrupting his thoughts and prompting an instant, almost instinctive reaction.

"Are they for me?"

"Of course not," Gillez laughed. "I wouldn't do that. Especially not to you."

Tom stared at Gillez for moment and then cuffed him across the face. The man's head snapped back as if it was on a spring. A small cut opened up on his right cheekbone.

"Yes, you would," Tom said stonily. If there was one thing he had learned to rely on, it was Gillez's pathological dishonesty.

Gillez glared at him angrily, his hand clutching his face.

"Don't you trust anyone anymore?"

"Cut the bullshit, Marco. How long have I got?"

Marco's shoulders slumped into a sullen sulk.

"It's not my fault. They still want you for that Prado job. I had to give them *something* in exchange for the file."

"Don't try and pretend you did me some sort of a favor," Tom snarled. "This was all about you. It always is. What did they catch you at this time? Bribing a judge, sleeping with the mayor's wife? Something that made it worth selling me out for, in any case. How long have I got?"

"One, maybe two minutes," Gillez admitted, still massaging his cheek. "They're locking down the whole area. They don't want you slipping away again."

"Then I'd better make this look convincing."

Tom stepped forward and punched him in the face, breaking the sharp ridge of his nose with a satisfyingly loud crack. Gillez screamed and clutched his face, the file dropping from his hand, blood seeping between his fingers and dripping on to his pastel jacket and cream shoes.

"You don't want them thinking you let me get away, do you?" Tom shouted as he scooped the file off the floor. The anger and frustration of the last twenty-four hours had found a strange release in the sharp stab of pain across his knuckles and Gillez's animal yelp. He went to hit him again, but then drew back as the sound of approaching feet and muffled shouts of "*Policía!*" reached him. Spinning around, he darted through one of the open doorways and up the stairs just as someone began pounding on the heavy gate. He was glad he'd taken the time to lock it behind them.

He continued up the crumbling staircase until he arrived at a flimsy metal door. Kicking it open, he emerged on to the flat roof. The city stretched out around him, slumbering in the dusty heat, the surrounding rooftops of burned terracotta forming stepping stones across which, if he was quick, he could make his way to safety.

From the courtyard below came the sound of the gate splintering. Gillez's plaintive cry echoed up the stairwell. Tom's Spanish wasn't fluent, but he knew enough to understand what he was blubbing.

"Don't shoot, don't shoot! It's me, Sergeant Gillez. He's

upstairs. Someone get me a doctor. The bastard's broken my nose. I tried to stop him, but he had a gun. Shoot him. Oh, my nose. Somebody shoot him, for God's sake!"

Despite everything, Tom smiled. Cops like Gillez gave most criminals a good name.

CHAPTER THIRTEEN

SOUTH STREET, NEW YORK

19th April—3:17 P.M.

The sound of sirens echoing down Broadway's steel canyon reached Jennifer several blocks before she turned on to South Street and saw the reflection of the blue strobe lights in the glass walls looming around her. New York was one of the few cities where sound traveled faster than light.

As she drew closer, she could see that a small crowd had gathered at the foot of one of the buildings, straining to see what was going on from behind a hastily erected set of weathered blue police barriers. As she watched, the crowd parted reluctantly to let two paramedic teams through, before snapping shut hungrily behind them.

"Stop here," she instructed her driver, who tacked obediently right and eased to a halt about fifty yards from the building's entrance.

Jennifer stepped out. A local news channel was already broadcasting from across the street, presumably tipped off by one of the cops that they kept on the payroll for just this sort of eventuality. And given the manpower that the NYPD was already lavishing on the scene, the networks wouldn't be far behind.

"What's going on?" she demanded, grabbing the arm of a

passing officer and flashing her badge. He glanced at it suspiciously, checking her face against the photo.

"Homicide. Some hot-shot attorney." He shrugged disinterestedly, giving Jennifer the impression that either this was a fairly routine occurrence in this part of Manhattan, or that a small part of him felt that one less attorney in the world was probably no bad thing.

"He got a name?"

"Yeah, Hammon. At least that's what it sounded like. Half the time you can't hear a goddamned thing on this piece of shit—" He smacked his radio resentfully. "Now, if you don't mind . . . ?"

Jennifer waved him on and took a deep breath. Hammon dead. Coincidence? Possibly. Probably. Until she knew more, it was pointless to speculate.

"Special Agent Browne?"

A questioning, almost incredulous voice broke into her thoughts. As she turned, a man in his mid-fifties broke away from the crowd at the base of the building and walked toward her, his rolling gait suggesting some sort of longstanding hip injury. Every part of him appeared to be sagging, his clothes hanging listlessly from his sharp, bony frame, the excess skin under his eyes and chin draped like folds of loose material. Brushing his straw-colored hair across his balding scalp, he smiled warmly as he approached, the color of his teeth betraying that he was a smoker, and a heavy one at that.

Jennifer frowned, unable to place the man's chalky face and pallid green eyes, her mind feverishly trawling back through distant high school memories and her freshman year at Columbia. Now that she was closer, she noticed that he had a mustard stain on the right leg of his faded chinos and a button missing from the front of his blue linen jacket.

"Leigh Lewis—*American Voice*." He held out a moist palm, which Jennifer shook warily, still uncertain who he was. "Here, Tony, get a shot."

Before Jennifer knew what was happening, a flashgun exploded in her face. The fog lifted. Lewis. The journalist Green had warned her about.

"So, what's the deal here? You know the vic?" Lewis jerked

his head at the building behind him, a tape recorder materializing under her nose.

"No comment," Jennifer insisted as she pushed past him, her annoyance with herself at not having immediately recognized his name only slightly tempered by her curiosity at what he was doing here.

"Was Hammon under federal investigation?" Lewis skipped backward to keep up with her.

"No comment," Jennifer repeated, shielding her face from the camera's cyclopic gaze as she marched purposefully toward the building's entrance.

"Or had you two hooked up? The word is you like to party."

"Get out of my way," Jennifer said through gritted teeth. She was only a few feet from the security cordon now and she gripped her ID anxiously in anticipation of escaping Lewis before she lost her temper.

"The only catch, of course, is that everyone who screws you winds up dead." Lewis was standing directly in front of her now, blocking her way and moving his head in line with hers every time she tried to look past him. "In fact, maybe I should call you the black widow, Agent Browne."

"Fuck you." Jennifer pushed Lewis roughly in the chest. He stumbled backward, tripping over his photographer and sending him sprawling.

She caught the shocked yet triumphant expression on Lewis's face as she stalked past them, the camera still chattering noisily as the photographer continued to shoot. She flashed her badge at the bemused officer controlling access into the building and stalked inside, her eyes brimming with tears of silent anger. From behind her she could hear Lewis's voice ringing out in an annoyingly singsong tone.

"Can I quote you on that?"

CHAPTER FOURTEEN

LAS CANDELARIAS, SEVILLE

19th April—9:23 P.M.

Tom had waited for the protective cloak of darkness to fall before venturing over to this side of town. Although Gillez and his colleagues were reassuringly incompetent, there was certainly no point in tempting fate by walking around in broad daylight. The trail left by Rafael's killer was cold enough already, without Tom being arrested and delayed by yet another round of pointless questioning.

He had therefore spent the intervening hours holed up in the tenebrous anonymity of a small basement bar in the Barrio Santa Cruz, trying to forget what he had felt upon seeing the place where Rafael had died, and focus instead on what he had learned there.

On reflection, of all the things that Gillez had told him, two stood out. The first was that Rafael had been seen going to confession at the Basilica de la Macarena which, given Rafael's attitude toward religion in general and the Catholic faith in particular, seemed about as likely as the Pope being spotted in a strip bar.

The second was that although Gillez had mentioned Rafael's apartment being searched, he'd said nothing about his studio. It was just possible, therefore, that the police didn't know about it. This was hardly surprising given that, as far as Tom could remember, the property was registered in the name of Ignacio Sánchez Mejías, a once-famous Sevillian bullfighter and longstanding resident of the Cementerio de San Fernando.

The crumbling street of tattered warehouses and tumble-down workshops was deserted, but Tom stuck to the shadows all the same. When he was satisfied that he was alone, he crossed over, sidestepping a decomposing car raised on bricks. The wreck had been set alight at some point and the seats were melted back to their frames, scraps of fabric and foam clinging stubbornly to their blackened skeletons like skin.

There were no lights on inside Rafael's two-story building, and as he drew closer Tom could see that the padlock securing its heavily graffitied roller-shutter to the ground was still intact. Above him, a small fern that had somehow taken root under the flaking plaster swayed lazily in the sticky heat.

Checking around him one last time, he sprang the lock, raised the shutter high enough to slip under it and then rolled it back behind him. The noise reverberated along the length of the windowless room that stretched in front of him like a deep coffin. Grabbing a chair, he leaned it against the shutter and then balanced the padlock he'd removed from the door on its seat. It was an old trick, but an effective one.

Locating the flashlight in its usual hiding place, Tom crept along the narrow corridor formed by the assortment of unwanted furniture, old tires and children's toys that had been piled up on either side of the room, dolls' eyes glinting accusingly every so often out of the darkness. A few of the nicer pieces had been covered in protective sheets; as Tom walked past, they lifted slowly as if reaching out to touch him, before settling back with an inaudible sigh.

Compared to the ground floor, the upstairs room was light and airy, with large windows front and back and a high, glazed roof. There was a full moon, its anemic glow chased away every few seconds by the red-blooded pulse of a large neon advertising sign high on the wall of a neighboring building.

Despite the shifting light, Tom could see that the room was every bit as chaotic as he remembered. The concrete floor, for example, was almost lost under a layer of dried paint, thin veins of random colors that crackled underfoot like dry twigs on a forest floor. Discarded sketches and half-finished canvases were gathered in the corners as if blown there by the wind, empty paint tubes and worn brushes emerging from the gaps between them like the masts of a ship half-buried in sand.

And yet not everything was the same. A chair had been flipped over on to its front, its legs extended helplessly into the air, its innards spilling through the deep gash that had been cut in its seat. Two easels were lying prostate on the ground. All the cupboards and drawers had been yanked open and their contents scooped out on to the floor beneath. Tom's face set into a grim frown. Whoever had turned over Rafael's apartment had clearly been here too.

Kneeling down, he plucked a small photo frame from where it was sheltering under a crumpled newspaper. Although the glass had been shattered, he recognized Rafael's grinning face through the sparkling web of tiny fractures. He had his arm around Tom on one side and Eva on the other, and the three of them were sitting on the edge of a fountain in the Alcázar. The mixture of anger and disbelief that he had felt on seeing the crime-scene photographs welled up in him again. *Why?*

There was a thud downstairs. Steel on concrete. The padlock falling off the chair he'd left leaning against the shutter. Someone had come in behind him.

He placed the frame back on the ground and crept over to the top of the stairs, positioning himself out of sight to the left of the doorway. From below he heard the sound of careful footsteps and then the tell-tale creak of the staircase. The third step, he remembered from when he had made his own way up.

He readied himself, ready to send whoever was coming up sprawling across the room, when the faint scent of perfume reached him. A perfume he recognized.

"Tom?" An uncertain voice filtered through the open doorway.

"Eva?" Tom edged forward, his shadow further obscuring the already dark stairwell. A figure advanced toward him.

"Still using that old chair routine?" A flash of white teeth amid the gloom.

"Still wearing Chanel?" Tom smiled as he stepped back and let Eva into the room.

"If that's a line, it's a bad one," she sniffed, brushing past and then wheeling to face him. In the intermittent neon glow she looked even more striking than he remembered: dark oval eyes glinting impetuously, an almost indecently suggestive mouth, shimmering black hair held off her face by an elasticated white band and tumbling down on to olive-skinned shoulders that might have been modeled on a Canova nude.

"I heard you'd gone straight." She sounded skeptical.

"I'd heard the same about you," he said softly, trying to keep his eyes on her face rather than tracing a line from her slender ankles to her skirt's embroidered hem and the suggestive curve of her legs. Now, as when he'd first met her, she radiated sex. It wasn't deliberate, it was just the way she was. The animal dart of her pink tongue against her lips, the generous heave of her breasts under her black silk blouse, the erect nipples brushing the material, the open thrust of her hips. Sex seasoned with a hint of unpredictability and a dash of temper for good measure.

A pause.

"It's good to see you again, Eva."

He meant it.

"What are you doing here?" she demanded.

Her tone didn't surprise him. Their break-up had been messy. She'd been hurt. No reason she should be anything other than cold with him now. In fact, it made things simpler.

"Same as you. Looking for answers."

"He's dead." Her voice was hollow. "What more of an answer do you want?" She paused, her eyes boring into his.

"Go home, Tom. You're not needed here. You're not wanted here."

"He left a message before he died."

"I know." She gave a sad nod. "They showed me the photos."

"Then you saw who it was addressed to?"

"You two and your little codes and secrets." Her bottom lip, pink and full, jutted out indignantly, nostrils quivering.

"It was never like that," he insisted.

"Yes it was. Rafael only ever invited me in when it suited him. And even now that he's dead, nothing's changed." Tom remembered now that she'd always insisted on calling her stepfather by his first name.

"What was he mixed up in?" Tom pressed.

"I don't know. Things were never simple between us." She fixed him with an accusing stare. "You walking out on me didn't help. It forced him to pick sides."

"Is this about Rafael, or us?"

Eva flew forward and slapped Tom across the cheek, the sharp crack of the blow echoing around the room.

A pause.

"Feel better?" Tom asked slowly, rubbing his face.

"Go home, Tom," she said wearily.

"He came to see me in London."

"What?" This, finally, seemed to have registered.

"Three or four weeks ago. I don't know what he'd got himself involved in, Eva, but I think he was in trouble and that he wanted my help. He stole part of a Napoleonic dinner service. An obelisk. What was he up to?"

She looked down, the toe of her black patent leather shoe poking absentmindedly through the debris strewn across the floor.

"He lied to us, Tom." She glanced up, looking unsure of herself for the first time. "He lied to us all. I could tell from his voice. He'd signed up for another job."

"For Milo." Tom nodded, thinking back to the unfinished letter *M* scrawled in blood across the base of the well. "Have you checked the drawers yet?"

"What do you mean?"

He pulled one of the drawers out, emptied what remained inside it on to the floor, and then released a small catch underneath. The bottom of the drawer folded back, revealing a hidden compartment about an inch deep. It was empty.

"He used to hide things he was working on in these," Tom began, before realizing from the expression on Eva's face that this was yet another secret Rafael had not chosen to share with her. Maybe she had a point after all.

"Open them," she muttered hoarsely.

There were six drawers, but like the first, they were empty. All except the final one. This opened to reveal a painting. A painting that a small part of Tom had almost been expecting to find. There could be no doubt now that the two cases were connected.

"Is that a da Vinci?" Eva exclaimed.

"It's the *Madonna of the Yarnwinder*," Tom confirmed grimly as he carefully lifted it from the drawer. "But it's not the original. That was stolen a few days ago by Milo. This must be one of your father's forgeries. I expect that's what his killers were looking for when they turned this place and his apartment upside down."

"You mean all this was for a stupid painting?" Her voice broke as she gestured, the sweep of her arm taking in the ransacked room but also, Tom knew, the invisible trail of blood that led to the courtyard on the other side of the city. She pinched the bridge of her nose, trying to keep her emotions in check. He said nothing, giving her time to regain her composure. As she lowered her arm, Tom caught a glimpse of the silver bracelet he'd given her many summers ago, before she hurriedly tugged her sleeve back down to cover it. Perhaps she hadn't totally banished those times from her mind after all.

"They didn't take everything," he said gently. "They left you this—"

He handed her the photo he had found on the floor. This time there was no holding back her tears.

CHAPTER FIFTEEN

SOUTH STREET, NEW YORK

19th April—3:26 P.M.

As soon as she was certain that the doors had closed behind her, Jennifer let out an angry cry and struck her fist against the side of the elevator. The noise echoed up the shaft above her like thunder presaging a heavy storm. How could she have been so stupid? Lewis had just been fishing and she'd grabbed the bait at the first time of asking. She'd even knocked the guy over. On camera. What would Green say? Assaulting civilians was not exactly how the Bureau liked to handle its PR. If it wasn't so bad, it would almost have been funny.

Less funny was how Lewis had known she would be there. Had someone leaked her schedule? Unlikely, given she had only arranged to see Hammon after leaving Razi earlier that morning.

Maybe it was just an unfortunate coincidence. After all, years swimming through the lurid waters of popular scandal had given Lewis and his kind a nose for a story somewhat akin to a shark's for a wounded seal. He would have smelled the blood in the water from the other side of the city.

The doors whirred open. A camera flash exploded, momentarily burning an image on to the back of her retina. A corpse sprawled on the floor in front of the reception desk. Two bullet wounds in her back suggesting she'd been gunned down as she tried to run away. A dark shadow of blood beneath her, matting her long blonde hair with dark streaks.

"Who the fuck let you up here?" A man stepped into her field of vision. He had a mottled complexion, a deep scar across the bridge of his nose and a lazy right eye.

"Special Agent Jennifer Browne, FBI."

The man glanced at her ID and then looked up again, his chin jutting out defiantly. Judging from his graying brown hair, she guessed he was maybe forty, forty-five years old. Behind him, she saw two people from the coroner's office flip the girl over before lifting her into a body bag and zipping it shut.

"You're kidding, right? The bodies are still warm and already you're trying to crowd us out?"

"I had an appointment with Mr. Hammon." She nodded at the large nameplate on the wall behind the reception desk. "I only just found out about the shooting."

"Hey, Sutton," the man called out without looking around. "You got anything in the book today with a Julia Browne?"

The body bag was lifted on to a stretcher and wheeled into the open lift behind her.

"Jennifer," she corrected him sharply.

"Whatever." He shrugged.

A woman standing on the other side of the desk leaned over the terminal, her finger leaving a greasy mark as she slid it across the surface of the on-screen diary.

"Sure," she called out. "Three-thirty. Special Agent Jennifer Browne." She looked up and gave Jennifer a fleeting nod that she took as sisterly encouragement not to let herself be pushed around. There was no danger of that.

Grudgingly, the man reached out to shake her hand.

"Jim Mitchell, Homicide. I'm afraid Hammon's going to miss your three-thirty."

"No kidding?"

"You a client?"

"I was hoping to talk to him about a case I'm investigating."

"Yeah, well, talking's the one thing he won't be doing again," Mitchell said with a smirk.

"What do you mean?"

"See for yourself."

He threw open the large mahogany double doors behind him and waved her through. Hammon's office was located in the corner of the building, its two glass walls framing the graceful sweep of the Brooklyn Bridge as it unfurled against the East River. At that moment a chopper took off from the nearby heliport, its red-tipped rotors carving a steep circle in the thin air.

Beyond the view and the extravagance of a large fish tank set into the facing wall, however, the room was a triumph of minimalist design. The only furniture consisted of two Barcelona chairs neatly arranged around a square glass table and a massive cherrywood desk that was empty apart from a folded copy of the *Wall Street Journal* and an open laptop. A fax machine and a printer sat on a low table that hugged the desk's right leg.

"We've got three fatalities. Hammon, the receptionist and a security guard in the lobby."

"When?"

"An hour ago, maybe two. Eyewitnesses put two men at the scene, with two more waiting in a car outside. Initial reports suggest they were Oriental—Japanese or Korean, maybe. You know . . ." he shrugged helplessly and for a moment Jennifer thought he was actually going to tell her that they all looked the same to him. This guy was a real sweetheart.

"Were all the victims shot?"

"Point-blank range. Probably a .45. Only Hammon didn't get off quite so easy as the other two." Mitchell nodded grimly toward the desk and the large black chair with its back turned toward them.

Jennifer stepped around the edge of the desk and realized, as she caught sight of a wrist secured to the chair's metal arm with a plastic tag, that Hammon was still there.

"He's next, as soon as they've loaded the other two up," Mitchell explained as she shot him a questioning glance.

Moving closer, she could see that the lawyer's balding head was slumped forward and to one side; his chin and monogrammed shirt were soaked in blood. One of his expensive leather shoes seemed to have half come off as he had struggled, although the black handle of the Tanto knife that was protruding from his chest, his Ferragamo tie draped around it like a scarf, suggested it had been a short and uneven contest.

Most shocking though were his eyes, or rather the gaping, livid sockets where his eyes had been until someone had prized them out, leaving red tears frozen on to his face like wax.

"There's no sign of them here," Mitchell volunteered. "We figure they took them with them."

Jennifer looked up, her face impassive. The longer she did this job, the less instances of random sadism such as this seemed to shock her.

"Some sort of trophy?"

"Maybe."

She leaned forward with a frown, having caught sight of something soft and pink that seemed to have been skewered on to the tip of the knife before it was plunged into Hammon's chest.

"What's that?"

"His tongue," said Mitchell, watching her closely.

"His tongue . . ." It was more of a statement than a question and Mitchell seemed disappointed by her muted reaction. "So it's got to be some sort of a revenge killing, right? A punishment for something he'd said or seen. Or both."

"You tell me." Mitchell shrugged. "I'm normally pulling hookers out of dumpsters and junkies out of the East River. What was your angle?"

"Hammon got into a fight with someone who's involved in my case. I wanted to find out why."

"The guy's an attorney. What more of a reason do you need?" Mitchell laughed.

Jennifer smiled as she moved around to the other side of the desk, slowly warming to Mitchell's black humor.

"You got any paper?" she asked suddenly.

"What?" Mitchell frowned.

"Paper?"

Mitchell continued to stare at her blankly.

"For the fax," she explained, pointing at the light blinking on the fax machine. "Looks like something's caught in the memory."

With a nod of understanding, Mitchell opened the printer tray, removed a few sheets of paper, and placed them into the fax. Moments later, the machine began to whir and hum, sucking a fresh sheet inside and then spitting it out on to the floor.

Mitchell picked the sheet up, studied it for a few seconds, then handed it to Jennifer. "Go figure."

Three items were listed on the page: First an alphanumeric code—VIS1095. Then a sum of money—$100,000,000. And beneath them, a letter in a circle.

The letter M.

CHAPTER SIXTEEN

LAS CANDELARIAS, SEVILLE

19th April—9:33 P.M.

Eva seemed reluctant to leave the workshop. Tom understood why.

Unable to sleep the night of his own father's funeral a few years before, he had wandered through Geneva's wintry streets, vainly looking for answers to questions that he couldn't yet quite bring himself to ask. As dawn broke, he had found himself standing outside the front door to his father's old apartment, drawn there as if by some ancient magic. Sitting on the foot of his father's bed, seeing his cufflinks glittering on the marble-topped chest and his ties peeking out from behind the wardrobe door like snowdrops nosing their way aboveground in early spring, it was almost as if he had still been alive.

Now he sensed that Eva was doing the same, absorbing the memories of her father that swirled stubbornly around this room like paint fumes. The half-empty wine glass with a ghostly lip-print on its rim. The pocket knife, its bone handle smoothed by use. The discarded sunglasses, one arm bent back on itself where he had sat on them. Part of Tom wanted to hold her, to tell her that it would all be all right. But he knew it wouldn't, not for a long time, and that this was something she was going to have to come to terms with on her own.

"We should go," Tom muttered eventually as he carefully wrapped the painting in a cloth and placed it inside his bag.

"Where to?" she said mournfully. "The police are in and out of his apartment. I can't bear it there anymore."

For a moment Tom thought of suggesting that they go to his hotel, but quickly changed his mind. Chances were she would take it the wrong way, and in any case the cops were probably there by now. The best thing would be to get out of Seville as quickly as possible, but there was one more place he needed to go first. According to Gillez, Rafael had been seen going to confession at the Basilica de la Macarena the night he was killed. Assuming that he hadn't been gripped by a sudden bout of evangelical fervor, Tom wanted to see for himself what had drawn him there. But she interrupted him before he could suggest it, her voice breathless and hurried.

"There's something you should know. Something Rafael told me about your father. About how he died. I should have told you before only I was so angry with you that I never—"

The words stuck in Eva's throat as the glass roof above them suddenly imploded. Tom pulled her to the floor and threw his coat over their heads, the shards embedding themselves into the thick material and crashing around their feet. The next instant he was up, dragging her toward the exit, but heavy footsteps announced someone pounding up the staircase toward them. He turned back, hoping to get to the window, but two other men rappelled into the room, guns drawn, blocking their path. They were trapped.

"On your knees." The man to their left stepped forward, his accent and appearance suggesting that he was of North African origin—Moroccan, Tom guessed, his heart pounding. His two companions were white; one of them had a long pink bullet scar down the side of his head.

"Where's Milo?" Tom asked, knowing immediately who these men were and who had sent them. Eva pressed herself to him, her eyes flashing defiantly.

"Shut up."

"Let her go," Tom insisted. "This is about me, not her."

"It's about both of you now." The Moroccan's eyes narrowed. "Take her outside."

The man standing behind Eva shoved her roughly toward the staircase. She turned and cuffed him hard across the cheek, the sharp crack of the blow echoing off the walls. Clutching his face, he raised his gun to her chest, his thumb pulling back on the hammer, his eyes blazing.

"No!" The Moroccan's voice rang out. "He wants them both alive." He turned to the other man and ordered, "Help him."

Eva flashed Tom a desperate glance but it was no use. One man grabbed her arms and pinned them to her sides while the second grabbed her legs, lifting her off the ground. She began to scream, the sound cutting into Tom, her body jack-knifing as she raised her legs to her chest and then kicked out again and again. But they had her in a firm grip and her cries were soon muffled by a paint-soiled rag that one of the men scooped off the floor and jammed into her mouth.

Tom stepped forward, his fists clenched, but was immediately warned off by the Moroccan waggling his gun at him. Exhausted and gagging on the filthy rag, her struggling slowly subsided.

"Put her in the trunk," the Moroccan ordered.

"I'll find you," Tom called out as they half-dragged, half-lifted her out of the room and down the staircase. She gazed at him blankly as she sank out of sight, leaving the room still and empty and Tom's head ringing with the echo of her labored breathing and the deafening plea for help that he had seen framed within her dark eyes.

"Get over there," the Moroccan instructed Tom as soon as they were alone.

"If you're going to shoot me, do it here," Tom retorted.

"I said move!" He stepped forward and jabbed Tom in the chest with his gun. Sensing his moment, Tom reached down and grasped one of the shards of glass that had lodged in his coat. Pulling it free, he plunged it into the man's wrist. The gun dropped from the Moroccan's grasp as he clutched his arm to his chest, screaming in pain.

Tom grabbed one of the rappelling ropes that were dangling

like vines from the roof, looped it around the Moroccan's neck and tugged hard. The man's hands flew to his throat as he clawed at the thick nylon cord, his legs dancing wildly underneath him as he tried to wriggle free, his lips turning blue. Tom held firm, managing to throw another loop over the man's head and then pulling down with all his weight. In a few minutes, the Moroccan had gone limp, the rope holding him upright like an oversize puppet. In the intermittent red neon light, it appeared that he had been drenched in blood.

"Youssef?" A voice from downstairs. "You okay?"

Tom heard the tell-tale creak of someone making their way up the stairs.

Scrabbling around on the floor, Tom found the Moroccan's gun and raced to the stairwell. Edging his head around the doorway, he fired a shot at the approaching figure, catching him in the shoulder. The man cried out in pain, firing three shots wildly in Tom's direction as he staggered back downstairs.

Tom bounded down after him and burst on to the street, only to be met by a violent shriek of rubber as the waiting car accelerated away. He lowered his gun, not wanting to risk hitting Eva, and quickly made his way back upstairs to retrieve his bag.

Milo wanted them alive. That's what the Moroccan had said. That meant there was still time to find her, still time to bargain for her life, perhaps even with the forged *Yarnwinder* painting he had just recovered. What was certain was that this time, he wouldn't abandon her. He owed it to her. He owed it to Rafael.

And given what she'd said about his father and how he'd died, maybe he even owed it to himself.

CHAPTER SEVENTEEN

SOUTH STREET, NEW YORK

19th April—3:40 P.M.

"You got any idea what it means?" Mitchell asked Jennifer as she returned the piece of paper to him.

"Nope," she said. "But a hundred million would buy you a hell of a lot of legal advice. Even if the guy giving it has to pay for this sort of a view."

She gestured toward the window and Mitchell stepped forward, nodding appreciatively. A lone yacht was slicing through the whitecaps out into the Long Island Sound, its red sail flexing in the crisp breeze. In the distance towered the Statue of Liberty, her face tanned by the afternoon sun, the corrugated folds of her robe alternating between ridges of burnished green and plunging shadow.

"It sure is special," he agreed, with an admiring sigh. "Weird how much more peaceful the city looks from up here. Like all the dirt and ugliness got washed away."

"So why not look at it?" Jennifer asked with a frown, nodding at the way Hammon's desk had been arranged to face into the room. "If you were paying these prices, wouldn't you want to see what your money was getting you?"

"Maybe he preferred fish," he suggested, only half seriously.

Jennifer nodded. He may have been joking, but Mitchell had a point. The desk was positioned squarely in front of the fish tank.

"I guess so." She approached the tank and peered through the thick glass, a light positioned somewhere above it refracting through the water.

"That's odd," she mused. "I wonder if . . ." She strode back to the desk.

"What?"

"Turning your back to that view I could just about understand," she replied, running her hands along the underside of the polished cherrywood surface. "Maybe he had vertigo or something. But staring at a tank that doesn't have any fish in it? That I don't buy."

Mitchell's bulging eyes snapped to the tank, clearly only now seeing what Jennifer had only just observed herself—apart from the steady stream of bubbles fizzing their way to the surface and a few slivers of weed swaying in an unseen current, it was empty.

"There!" she exclaimed as her fingers detected the button she had guessed she would find. She pressed it and looked up. There was a low hum from the fish tank as it slid back a few inches and was then lowered out of sight. The space it had vacated was immediately filled by a white panel that descended from above and then edged forward until it was flush with the rest of the wall. And in the center of the panel, housed within an elaborate gilded frame, was a painting.

"You've got to be kidding!" Mitchell had a dazed grin on his face.

The painting showed a table covered in a bright purple napkin. Resting on the napkin was a bowl of vividly colored fruit and a vase exploding with red flowers.

"Chagall," Jennifer said slowly, recognizing the style and confirming her instinct against the signature in the bottom right corner.

"Valuable?"

"Valuable enough to hide it."

"What's wrong with a bank?"

"Maybe this way he could see it whenever he wanted without the risk of hanging it out in the open."

"I thought half the reason these rich fucks bought their expensive toys was to show them off."

She frowned. Again, she couldn't fault Mitchell's logic.

"Maybe he didn't want anyone to know he had it. Maybe he wasn't meant to have it? Maybe . . ."

She paused, struck by a sudden thought, then reached into her bag for the catalog Cole had given her the previous day. Hurriedly she leafed through it, pausing about twenty pages in.

"*La Nappe Mauve* by Marc Chagall," she read. "Estimate one million dollars."

"What's that?" Mitchell inquired with a curious nod.

"The proof of a catalog for an auction in Paris," she explained, measuring her words. "Hammon was hiding the painting because, according to this, someone else owns it."

CHAPTER EIGHTEEN

BASILICA DE LA MACARENA, SEVILLE

19th April—10:31 P.M.

The rhythmic tolling of the Basilica's bell ushered Tom inside. It was a muffled, almost sleepy strike that seemed to be bemoaning the lateness of the hour, despite the fact that some of the neighboring bars were only now rousing themselves for the night ahead, taking advantage of the warm weather to conjure up chairs and tables on the wide pavements.

The interior was dimly lit, the swaying flames from the many votive candles arranged down each aisle painting the walls with a warm glow that disguised the functional simplicity, some might even say ugliness, of its relatively modern construction.

The altar, by contrast, sparkled as if a thousand Chinese lanterns had just been released into the night sky, a small oasis of light amidst the rest of the building's restrained gloom. A few shadowy figures were spaced along the pews in front of it, peering up hopefully at the crucified figure suspended high overhead or threading a rosary between their fingers, their eyes closed.

Tom sat down. He wasn't quite sure what he was expecting

to find here. He only knew that, less than an hour after supposedly coming for confession, Rafael had been dead.

There must be something here that Rafael had wanted to see or do. Something that he might be able to use to get Eva back before it was too late. Eva. He shook his head, banishing his final image of her from his thoughts, knowing that the memory, still raw, would only cloud his judgments.

Tom flipped open the file he had snatched off Gillez and found the relevant pages. The witness reports pinpointed the confessional Rafael had been seen going into. Second on the left. Right-hand booth. Tom got up and made his way over to it. It seemed as good a place to start as any.

The booth was empty, a sign over the middle door where the priest normally sat indicating the times confession could be heard. He smiled, amused by the thought that even God had opening hours.

He slipped inside and pulled the door shut behind him. Settling on the hard bench, his eyes adjusting to the dusty gloom, he quickly scanned the small space around him to see if there was an obvious place where Rafael might have secreted something away.

It only took a few minutes of feeling his way around, however, to see that there was nothing here. Nothing, apart from bare wooden walls and a faded red velvet curtain across the blackened grille through which sins were spoken and penances heard. Nothing, apart from the musty smell of guilt, tears and stale alcohol, although it was difficult to judge whether these came from his side or the priest's.

Nothing, unless . . . he leaned forward, his hands reaching between his legs and feeling under his seat. There. The tips of his fingers had brushed against something. A piece of paper? A package?

It was an envelope. A large brown envelope, its flap gummed shut. What he noticed immediately, however, was the small symbol in the top left-hand corner—a triangle. Underneath it was a small note written in English in Rafael's distinctively spidery script.

Look after her.

His heart beating, Tom gingerly unsealed the flap and reached inside, carefully removing a further padded envelope and a computer memory stick.

Placing the memory stick down on the seat next to him, Tom opened the second envelope and gingerly pulled out what at first seemed to be a piece of board but which he could see now was wood. Painted poplar wood.

He heard himself breathe in sharply as he realized what he was holding, the sound seeming strangely disembodied, as if for a moment he had floated outside of himself. A pair of velvety brown eyes and a teasing smile returned his awestruck gaze and slowly drew him back down to earth.

It was a forgery, of course, a product of da Vinci's genius and Rafael's talent for imitation. But it was glorious all the same. And it provided him, finally, with the explanation he had been searching for.

This was what Milo was really interested in, not the *Yarnwinder*. This was what Rafael had been working on for him. This was why Milo had had him killed. This was how Tom could get Eva back.

He grabbed his phone and dialed a number. It was answered on the third ring.

"Archie, it's Tom. I need you to meet me in Paris. It's Milo—I know what he's up to."

He paused and let his fingers brush against the silent figure's soft cheeks and the gentle curve of her slender neck before continuing.

"He's making a play for the *Mona Lisa*."

PART II

You might as well pretend that one could steal the towers of the cathedral of Notre Dame.

THÉOPHILE HOMOLLE,
DIRECTOR OF THE LOUVRE 1910

CHAPTER NINETEEN

115TH AND CENTRAL PARK WEST, NEW YORK

20th April—6:15 A.M.

I thought we'd agreed that you were going to keep your head down?" FBI Director Green elbowed past her, his heels tip-tapping officiously across the parquet.

"I can explain," Jennifer stammered as she fastened her dressing gown around her waist, any hint of tiredness instantly evaporating under the harsh light of Green's tone. As she closed the door, one of the secret service agents who had accompanied Green upstairs winked at her sympathetically through the shrinking crack.

"You'd better make it good."

His fleshy face had gone a deep pink, a shiny slick of sweat forming on his top lip and forehead. Jennifer wasn't sure if this reflected his mood or the fact that he'd had to walk up six flights of stairs. The elevator was out of action. Again.

"Have you any idea how bad this looks?"

She unfolded the newspaper that he had thrust angrily toward her, her heart sinking as she saw that the front page was almost entirely taken up with a picture of her shoving a shocked-looking Lewis to the ground. By some cruel coincidence, the photographer seemed to have caught her at her most angry, eyes ablaze and teeth bared like a rabid animal.

"*Black Widow Strikes Again*," Green, grim-faced, quoted the headline. "*Now FBI femme fatale attacks our man*."

There was an inset picture of a mournful-looking Lewis holding up his shirt to show where it had been ripped open at the elbow. The picture was so clearly staged that at any other time she would have laughed. Green, however, clearly wasn't getting the joke.

"What the hell were you thinking, Browne? We've got civil liberties groups crawling up our ass and you go and give them a new pin-up boy. I mean, there are four pages of this shit. Four fucking pages." He began to quote from the paper again, nailing her with an indignant look every few words. "*Agent Browne has been involved in a number of high-profile incidents since joining the Bureau. These include the fatal shooting of fellow agent and lover Greg Durand on an ill-fated DEA-led raid, and the imprisonment of a corrupt agent during a top-secret investigation into a daring theft from Fort Knox.*"

"Sir, I . . ." She allowed her voice to tail off. There was no sense in trying to reason with him. Not yet, at least. Not until he'd cooled off.

"Oh look, there's a picture of me," he observed in mock excitement. "That's nice. Something to cut out and stick on the refrigerator."

He pointed at a photo of himself on page three. It had to be at least fifteen years out of date, but Jennifer suspected it was still the one he insisted be included on the Bureau's website and in all their publicity material.

He slumped on to the sofa with a sigh, throwing the paper down on the coffee table in frustration. Jennifer allowed a few seconds to pass before attempting the explanation that she sensed he was now ready to hear.

"It was an accident," she began. "Dumb luck, really. I was on my way to interview someone. An attorney who'd been in a fight with Razi a few weeks ago. But when I showed up he was dead."

"Yeah, I saw the bulletin. Triple homicide. No suspects."

"Lewis was outside, sniffing around for a story. He saw me and started asking questions. About Greg and the shooting.

About my private life. I pushed past him to get inside. He tripped and fell. That's all there is to it."

"That's all there ever is to it," Green growled. "That's why guys like Lewis are radioactive. They poison everything they touch."

"I never meant . . ."

"I know, I know." He waved his hand at her with a sigh. "But out there, they just see the headlines and a picture of Lewis flat on his ass. They just see what they want to see." A pause. "Go and get dressed. Then we'll try and figure something out."

Five minutes later, Jennifer reappeared. From the slightly puzzled expression on Green's face, she guessed that he had had a quick look around the sitting room and found himself struggling to reconcile the orderly person he knew from work with the unstructured chaos of her apartment—pairs of shoes kicked off in the far corner, books spilling off the end of the bookcase, clothes peeking out from behind the sofa cushions. The truth was that, while at home, she found a certain comfort in letting things slide a little. It was her own crude way of delineating the two parts of her life which so often threatened to merge into one.

"Can I get you a coffee?" she volunteered.

"You got whole milk?" he asked hopefully. "I only get skim at home now."

"Two percent any good?" she offered, the mournful expression on Green's face giving her a sudden insight into the guerrilla war he was seemingly engaged in with his new wife over low-fat food and regular exercise.

"Three sugars," he added eagerly as he perched himself on a stool on the other side of the breakfast bar, his mood seemingly lifted by this impending act of defiance. "So what's the story with the attorney?"

Jennifer quickly recounted the circumstances surrounding Hammon's murder as she boiled the water and measured three spoons of coffee into the cafetière.

"You think Razi's involved?"

"I don't know," she sighed. "He knew Hammon. Broke his arm in a fight a few months ago. And his name was vaguely linked to a Cuban smuggling scam. But so far his story checks out; he has an alibi for this afternoon and everyone I spoke to said he was a stand-up guy. Then again, he carries a gun, so maybe they were too scared to say anything different."

"Licensed?"

"Yeah. He travels a lot, mainly buying in the States and Europe and selling in the Far East."

"And how did he know Hammon?"

"Apparently Hammon represented a number of international buyers. The sort of buyers who like to keep their name out of the gossip columns and their business well beyond the reach of the IRS. Razi was one of the dealers he bought from on their behalf."

"There must have been more to it than that. It can't be a coincidence that they both own paintings with identical twins, and that both twins are being auctioned."

"Or that the same Japanese company is selling them." She pressed the plunger down and poured the coffee out. "Takano Holdings."

"Takano? Why do I know that name?" He frowned as he concentrated on levering three heaped teaspoons of sugar into his cup and topping it up with milk.

"It's a privately owned Japanese trading house with operations in mining, energy, banking, electronics and construction. But there's been some talk that it's a front for the Takeshi Yakuza family."

"Takeshi? Wasn't he the guy the Triads poisoned?" he asked, stirring furiously.

"They contaminated his food with some sort of radioactive spray," she confirmed. "He nearly died. Since then, no one's seen him. He refuses to leave his apartment."

"And he's definitely behind Takano Holdings?"

"There's no proof. Just rumors."

"Well, either way, it would be good to run some forensic tests on the paintings, so we can work out exactly who's being ripped off here."

"We can ask. But so far Takano refuse even to say where or when they bought them. Maybe they don't want to have to explain where the money came from."

"Where are the paintings now?"

"Christie's is holding them in Paris until the sale."

"Okay." Green took a long, grateful swig of coffee. "Good job, Browne. This will give whoever takes this case on a real head start."

"Sorry?" Jennifer wasn't sure she'd heard him right.

"Well, I can't exactly have you out in the field," said Green. "Not anymore."

"Why the hell not?"

"Because you assaulted a civilian. Because the longer you're in the public eye, the greater the chance that the whole Double Eagle story will leak. I'm only talking about a couple of weeks' vacation until everything blows over. You know the way the game's played."

"It's not a game to me," she countered. "This is my career we're talking about."

"Well, what do you expect me to do?"

"I expect to be allowed to do my job, not pulled off a case at the first bump in the road."

"I know you're upset, but this isn't easy for any of us."

"You're damn right I'm upset," she snapped, her dark eyes flashing dangerously. "I didn't ask for any of this. You were the one who pulled me on to this case, remember? Now you're kicking me off. For what? Because some moron tripped over his own feet. What about listening to my side of the story? What about a little loyalty?"

"Don't try and pin that shit on me," he retorted, his voice hardening. "And don't forget who you're talking to either. The guy may be an asshole, but you hit him, Browne. Whatever the reason, you hit him. The Bureau can't just carry on like nothing's happened. You've got to think how this looks. You've got to consider the optics."

"I'm not interested in your DC politics."

"Careful, Browne," he warned her again. "I'm on your side . . ."

"No you're not." The rumors of Green running for the Senate suddenly seemed to make a hell of a lot more sense. "You're on the side of making sure none of this sticks, either to you or to the administration."

"I'm on the side of facing the facts. And until this sorts itself out, I won't have you and Lewis playing hide and seek all over the city."

There was a long pause, Jennifer fixing Green with a challenging stare, Green seemingly seeking inspiration from the bottom of his coffee cup. Jennifer had a sudden thought.

"What about if I left the country?" she suggested, thinking back to something Green had said earlier.

"What?" He gave a confused frown, as if he was only half listening.

"You could send me to Paris," she prompted, her voice gaining in confidence. "Even Lewis will struggle to trip over me there."

"That's a crazy idea."

"It's your idea."

"It is?"

"You asked whether the Japanese would agree to forensic testing. Well, let's ask them. If we can get all the paintings together, then maybe we can figure out which ones are the forgeries and focus the investigation on them. And this way I stay on the case, but out of Lewis's way."

He tapped his lip slowly, considering her suggestion.

"What would it take to set up?"

"A couple of phone calls from you to smooth things over with the NYPD and push the paperwork through. Hudson to call Razi and get his permission. Cole to convince the Japanese. It's not easy, but it's doable."

"It's not really standard procedure," he demurred.

"I'm sure Lord Hudson would appreciate you going out of your way, like this," she prompted gently. "Not to mention the rest of the art community."

"There's a lot of money, a lot of jobs, tied up in the art trade here in New York," Green conceded solemnly, sounding ever more as if he were rehearsing for the campaign trail. "We need to do what we can to protect it." He drained his coffee and stood up. "Let me make a few calls. I'll be in touch. Until then, stay here."

"If it's okay with you, sir," she said with a smile, "I might just go back to bed."

CHAPTER TWENTY

CAFÉ VOLTAIRE, 15TH ARRONDISSEMENT, PARIS

20th April—12:30 P.M.

The air was heavy with a swirling mist of cigarette smoke into which the chipped blades of the juddering ceiling fan periodically vanished like propellers cutting through clouds. Two men were at the bar, each holding a drink in one hand and a betting slip in the other, their gaze fixed on the TV screen overhead. The sound was turned down, but Tom could still just about make out the frantic crescendo of the commentary as the race reached its climax.

Behind them, the barman was hunched over that day's form guide, a white tea towel over one shoulder and a half-finished beer to his left. An overflowing yellow Ricard ash-tray was strategically positioned between the three men. Tom paused for a second, struck by the timelessness of this scene. He was certain that he could have walked into this place at almost any time on almost any day, and the picture of controlled boredom that was being presented to him would have been exactly the same.

"Where is he?" Tom asked in French, rapping his knuckles sharply against the bar.

The barman looked up grudgingly, nodded toward the rear and then sank back into his newspaper.

"Two espressos," Tom ordered, squinting briefly into the darkness that he had just indicated. "And lots of sugar."

The barman rolled his eyes and then made a great show of closing his paper and folding it carefully away. Tom walked toward the back of the café, his eyes adjusting. A lone figure was hunched over a table near the entrance to the toilet, the only light coming from the intermittent flashing of the neighboring pinball machine.

"Jean-Pierre?" Tom called as he approached the figure. The man's head lifted slightly at the mention of his name. A cigarette was clenched in his left hand, a line of ash beneath it where it had burned down to the butt and then extinguished itself.

"*Je suis occupé, Felix*," he muttered from behind a curtain of lank hair.

"Yeah, I can see you're busy," Tom said with a smile, slipping on to the chair opposite him. There was a pause.

"You heard she left me?" he mumbled eventually, in English this time.

"I heard you started drinking again."

The man looked up, lifting his hair off his face and brushing it back behind his ears. Tom smiled a welcome, but had difficulty in masking his surprise. He'd been friends with Jean-Pierre Dumas for well over ten years now. It was Dumas, one of the DST's best agents, who had arranged his disappearance and then fed bogus DNA evidence back to the Agency to convince them that he was dead. In return, Tom had helped out on a couple of dubious operations on behalf of the French government, before striking out on his own. But he sat there now, a pale ghost of the man Tom had once known.

In fact, Dumas had the look of someone clinging to life by his very fingertips, his cheery face and ready smile having faded into a hollow-cheeked, haunted gaze that reeked of defeat and self-pity. Knowing Dumas, probably the only reason he hadn't let himself plummet into the abyss yet was his sheer bloody-mindedness. He was alive to deny others the satisfaction of seeing him dead, rather than because he wanted it for himself. He was alive in order to be difficult.

"Are you here to buy me a drink?" His tone was suddenly hopeful, although the rest of his face remained anchored in an unsmiling scowl, his bushy mustache twitching occasionally like a flag in a limp breeze.

"Your coffee." The barman had appeared at their table.

"They're both for him," Tom gestured.

The man deposited the cups on the table with a clatter, spilling half of one into the saucer.

"Sugar's on the table," he grunted as he shuffled away.

Dumas wiped the back of his hand across his large, blunt nose, his eyes bloodshot and puffy from lack of sleep. The knot on his nondescript tie was pinched and greasy, suggesting that he simply loosened it every night to take it off so he wouldn't have to re-tie it the following morning. Tom realized then that he had probably been wearing the same clothes for days. Maybe even weeks.

The silence was broken by the pinball machine behind them suddenly flaring into life to the accompaniment of the theme tune from *Star Trek: The Next Generation*. Dumas turned and glared balefully at the man who had just started a game.

"Milo's out," Tom said over the machine's loud pinging and the occasional slap of the player's hands on the controls. "He cut a deal with the Chinese."

Dumas's eyes snapped back to Tom's, then he looked down with a shrug.

"Pas mon problème."

"He's planning a job."

"He's always planning a job."

"Not one like this."

There was a pause.

"Like what?"

The corners of Tom's mouth twitched. He'd known Dumas wouldn't be able to help himself. Whatever might have happened, twenty-five years in the French secret service were not as easily shaken off as his personal hygiene.

"The Louvre. The *Mona Lisa*."

"Pfff." A disbelieving smile crossed Dumas's face. "That's impossible."

"It's been done before."

"In 1911," he said with a dismissive wave of his hand. "Things were a bit different back then. Now . . . He'd never dare."

"Welcome to the Enterprise," the disembodied voice of Captain Jean-Luc Picard trumpeted from the machine behind them.

"Really?" Tom said, placing the memory stick that Rafael had left him on the table between them.

"What's this?"

"A download of the Louvre's entire security set-up. Blueprints. Codes. Guard rotas. Wiring grids. Surveillance systems."

"Sensors are picking up a distortion in the space-time continuum," the pinball machine announced as the steel ball struck one of the targets.

"Where did you . . . ?"

"Rafael hid it for me the night he died."

"Rafael's dead?" Dumas seemed to be shaken sober by this news. "How?"

"Milo."

"You're sure?"

"He's had Rafael working on a forged *Mona Lisa*. I think he's planning to swap it for the original. And he's got Eva, too."

"Eva. Your Eva?"

Tom nodded, feeling his jaw tense with silent anger as he explained what had happened in Rafael's workshop, although he left out what she had said about his father and how he'd died. That was for no one else but him. That was for when he found her.

"You went back to Spain? Aren't they looking for you?"

"They are now." Tom grimaced, Gillez's betrayal still rankling. "Getting in was no problem, but I had to look up some people I know down in Gibraltar to organize an exit. They're more used to moving cigarettes and whiskey, but they made some calls. I landed two hours ago."

"And came to see me? Why?"

"Milo used to work for you. You know what he's capable

of. I need to stop him. I need to get Eva back before he kills her."

Dumas emptied one of the coffee cups and lit a fresh cigarette, a hint of life creeping back into his ashen cheeks.

"What's the plan?"

"We warn the Louvre. Tell them what Milo is planning. Set a trap. He doesn't know that I'm on to him. He'll walk right into it."

"Make it so!" the machine chimed.

"And Eva?"

"He'll have her close. I'll find her. We just need Milo out of the picture first."

Dumas gave a deep sigh and then a firm shake of his head.

"*Je suis désolé, Felix.* But this has got nothing to do with me. Not anymore."

"You're a government agent, J-P. It's got everything to do with you."

"Ex-government agent. They fired me, remember?"

"They only suspended you. This could help get you back in."

"I don't want to get back in. I just want to be left alone."

"She'll die, J-P. She'll die and Milo will walk away with the *Mona Lisa.* And we're the only ones who can stop him."

A pause, as Dumas considered this.

"What do you want from me?" he asked eventually.

"An introduction. Philippe Troussard."

"Troussard?" He grimaced. "Why do you want to see that *imbécile*?"

"He's the Louvre's new head of security. Got appointed last year."

"We were at ENA together," Dumas conceded.

"I know," Tom smiled.

"I slept with his girlfriend and came top of the year." Dumas grinned for the first time since Tom had arrived. "I'm not sure which annoyed him more."

"That was a long time ago. You could still get us in to see him."

"*Peut-être.* But it would take time. I need to shave first. I need to get some sleep."

"Today," Tom said firmly, levering him out of his chair by the elbow. "You'll get us in today."

Behind them the man swore and smacked the glass angrily as the ball disappeared down one of the outlane drains.

"Someday, you'll learn to play pinball," the machine cackled.

CHAPTER TWENTY-ONE

RIAD AL SINAN, MARRAKECH, MOROCCO

20th April—2:47 P.M.

The air was still and heavy, the washing, strung along the neighboring rooftops like a brightly colored kite's tail, barely twitching in the dusty heat. In the middle of the courtyard below, scattered rose petals drifted lazily across the surface of a shallow pond. At its center stood a graceful white marble fountain, the delicate piano play of water echoing off the terracotta-colored walls.

A late lunch had been prepared in the shadow of a drooping orange tree, condensation coating a jug of iced lemon water. Pulling a chair up to the table, Milo pushed the food out of the way and snorted the tramlines of coke that had been prepared for him on a silver dish. When he was done, he wet his finger and drew it deliberately over the dish's mirrored surface, rubbing the crumbs across his top gum, pink and fleshy.

For a moment he was still, his green eyes glittering unblinkingly as if in a trance, his tongue flickering across his teeth like a lizard perched on a rock, sniffing the air. The dappled sunlight played across his angular face, somber pools forming under the sharp ridge of his cheekbones and darkening his already tanned complexion, his curly black hair, slicked back with some sort of oil, glinting like a beetle's shell.

He allowed his mind to roam beyond the city's rooftops, across the cobalt sea, to France's gold-tipped shores. At his side, his right hand twitched unconsciously, like a gunfighter poised to draw, his long elegant fingers drumming against the folds of his suit trousers. He was close now. Soon there would be no going back.

The muffled echo of someone knocking at the front door broke the spell. Laurent Djoulou was ushered in, his boots squelching on the diamond-patterned floor. Milo rose with a broad smile, casting a skeletal shadow on the ground. The two men hugged and then kissed each other on each cheek, before Djoulou broke away and snapped his right hand into a salute.

"It's good to see you again, *mon colonel.*"

Tall and solid, his deep-set dark brown eyes blazed behind sunglasses, a ridge of perspiring muscle bulging at the base of his bald skull. Three parallel scars marked both of his fleshy cheeks like freshly turned furrows in a field—tribal markings from his village. He wore a black T-shirt and jeans that both looked a size too small for him. Part of his left ear was missing.

"There's no need to salute." Milo dismissed the gesture with a generous wave of his hand. "Not anymore."

He spoke in French, his words chosen carefully and delivered with the precision and force of a sniper's bullet.

"I prefer the old ways, sir," Djoulou countered in a rhythmic West African lilt. "It avoids any confusion."

"Always the soldier." Milo nodded slowly, and then saluted. "It's good to have you back, *Capitaine.*"

"I'm glad you asked me."

"Bored with Africa?"

Djoulou puffed out his cheeks.

"Things have changed since you left. Less money. More charity workers. It's hard to find an honest fight anymore."

"After this job, you won't need to," Milo reassured him with a smile. "Where are the men?"

"At the port loading up the gear. They'll meet us there tomorrow."

"I've got another piece of cargo I need shipped. Human."

"Cargo you want lost overboard on the way?" Djoulou guessed with a smile.

"It's the forger's daughter. We picked her up yesterday in Seville. I want her kept alive."

"You think she could still be useful?"

"She's insurance. Kirk was with her."

Djoulou frowned.

"Where have I heard that name before?"

Milo gave a rueful smile and poured himself a glass of lemon water.

"From me. He used to work for the CIA. Industrial espionage. When they tried to bury the whole program, Kirk included, the French secret service helped him escape in return for a few favors. Dumas put us together for a few jobs after I quit the Legion. It didn't last."

"Is he going to be a problem?"

"By the time he works out what we're up to, it'll be too late," Milo said with a dismissive shrug.

"If he was with the girl in Seville, how did he get away?"

"Excellent question, *Capitaine*." Milo nodded approvingly. "And one that you can perhaps help me answer."

He beckoned for Djoulou to follow him to the fountain at the center of the courtyard. There, previously hidden by the orange-glazed plant pots and green shrubbery, were two men lying gagged and bound against the rim of the shallow pool.

"It seems that Kirk, despite being unarmed and outnumbered, managed to overpower and kill one of my men, shoot Collins here, and then escape." He pressed his heel into the bullet wound in Collins's shoulder, triggering a muffled scream.

"You should have sent me," Djoulou growled. "I'd have killed him before all this started."

"Kirk's not to be killed," Milo insisted quickly. "There's a debt between us, a life. I intend to honor it."

"What do you want to do with them?" Djoulou nodded impassively at the two men staring up at them with fearful, teary-eyed gazes.

Milo crouched down, gently stroked each man's head, then stood up.

"These two you *can* lose overboard."

Stepping forward, he rolled both men into the pond with the tip of his shoe. They landed facedown with a splash, their hands still taped behind their back, their ankles strapped. Immediately they kicked out, trying to wrestle their heads above the surface, the water boiling and crashing over the pond's edges like an angry sea striking a rocky cliff. Djoulou and Milo stepped back so as not to get wet. A minute passed, maybe more. The struggling slowly subsided, the water cooling and flattening as if a fierce wind had dropped, until the only sound was the fountain's gentle chime, rose petals weaving through the men's drifting hair.

"I prefer the old ways too," Milo observed pensively. "When everything had its price. Even failure."

CHAPTER TWENTY-TWO

TWO HUNDRED MILES EAST OF NEWFOUNDLAND, CANADA

20th April—2:47 P.M.

In the end, things had gone surprisingly smoothly. Green had called back within the hour to confirm that she was good to go. A car had materialized on the street outside to take her to the airport. The tickets had been on the back seat. Business class.

Not that she had been surprised. After all, this trip presented Green with an elegant solution to the conundrum of how to keep her out of Lewis's way without being seen to be bowing to media pressure. And, as she had suspected, it had also met with an enthusiastic response from Lord Hudson, useful in dispelling any of Green's remaining doubts.

The *Fasten Seatbelt* sign pinged off. Almost immediately a man several rows in front leaped from his seat and bounded up to her. It was Benjamin Cole, or Ben as he'd told her to call him.

"I thought that was you in the lounge." He beamed.

"I didn't know you were going to Paris too." She smiled, pleasantly surprised.

"Usual PR bullshit. You know, press the flesh, give a speech, do some photos, have dinner, fly home."

"Actually I don't know." She laughed.

"No, I guess not. It's a crazy life. Mind if I join you?" He sat down in the empty seat next to her before she could answer. "So I guess this means the NYPD backed down over the Chagall?"

"You heard about that?" She was surprised. Cole was clearly better plugged in than she'd thought.

"Green called, wanting me to negotiate access to the paintings we're holding in Paris," he explained.

"You agreed."

"It makes sense. But last I heard, the NYPD weren't playing ball."

"Usual interagency bullshit," she said with a rueful smile. "You know, first they cite jurisdiction, then they emphasize the risk of a vital piece of evidence from an active homicide investigation going missing . . ."

"Actually, I don't know." He laughed.

"Director Green had to okay it with the Commissioner and the D.A." She rolled her eyes.

"And Razi?"

"No problem. His Gauguin was crated up and loaded on to the plane without a whisper."

"That surprises me." Cole frowned.

"Why?"

"I've met Razi a few times. Looked like the sort of guy who would want to keep a fairly tight leash on his property."

"Not this time. According to Lord Hudson, his main concern is to try and secure a sale as soon as possible."

"Why the hurry?"

"I'm not sure." Her first thought had been that he must need the money, although he certainly hadn't seemed to be short of cash. She'd already made a note to take a closer look at his finances when she got back.

"Well that's his business." Cole shrugged. "Did you get the details of the forensic expert?"

"Yes, but they didn't say which museum he works for."

"That's because he works for himself."

"Oh." She frowned. "Wouldn't it be better if we could get the Louvre or the Musée d'Orsay to authenticate them?"

"Sure, if you could convince them to do it." He laughed. "These days they're all too scared of getting it wrong and being sued. Anyway, believe me, Henri Besson is the go-to guy."

"That's what Lord Hudson said too." She nodded, still not convinced.

"He used to be an art forger himself. Specialized in old masters. Would still be doing it now if someone hadn't rolled over on him. He spent ten years inside and when he came out decided to switch sides. Just as well. He knows every trick in the book."

"I've got an appointment to see him first thing in the morning," Jennifer confirmed. "I'll let you know how it goes."

"Good." He stood up. "I'm going to try and catch some Zs before we land. We could share a limo into town, if you like?"

"Sure. Thanks."

"Sweet dreams," he said with a wink, then made his way back to his seat.

Reclining her seat, Jennifer closed her eyes, hoping that she too would be able to get a few hours' sleep before they landed. But she found her mind wandering.

There was no question that suggesting this trip had been the right move from the case's perspective. And yet, she couldn't help wondering if there hadn't been an underlying, more self-interested, motivation too. After all, she had powerful memories of her previous visit to Paris during the Double Eagle case. Despite the dangers she had faced then, it had been a happy time for her. And there was no denying that, when the idea of making this trip had first come to her, a small part of her had jumped at the opportunity to relive some of those memories, however fleetingly. Even if, this time, she would be on her own.

She gave a rueful shake of her head. There was no point in dwelling on the past. Hers especially. Instead she thought of the two crates strapped into the hold and the paintings encased within them. She thought of Hudson and Cole pacing around Falstaff's stall. She thought of Razi's purple suit and Hammon's bloodied tongue skewered to his chest. She thought of Lewis and his lying camera and his twisted smile.

She thought of proving him, and all those people who were so quick to doubt her, wrong.

CHAPTER TWENTY-THREE

SECOND FLOOR, DENON WING, MUSÉE DU LOUVRE, PARIS

20th April—4:33 P.M.

I'm sorry, but can you say that again?" Philippe Troussard asked, his head cocked slightly to the left. A large French tricolor, tipped with a golden spearhead, stood guard next to him, its pregnant folds brushing the parquet floor.

"You heard him first time, Philippe," Dumas said sharply. "He's serious."

Troussard switched his stony gaze back to Dumas. The two men were similar in age, although Troussard certainly looked the better for it, with a healthily tanned face, clear hazel eyes and a full head of curly steel-gray hair. Wearing an expensive blue suit, pale blue shirt and colorful Gucci tie, he projected a confident and determined presence, although Tom detected a certain instinctive arrogance in the way he peered at people over the top of his half-moon glasses, narrowing his eyes when they spoke as if silently scoring them. Judging from his skeptical expression, Tom guessed they were still in the low single digits.

Dumas, by contrast, was having difficulty masking the self-wrought ravages of the past few months, despite having sobered up, shaved and pulled his hair back into a neat ponytail at Tom's insistence. The clear bell of his voice was cracked, his skin weathered and gray, his hands trembling and uncertain. The only clean clothes in his apartment had been a crumpled T-shirt and jeans, which he had insisted on wearing with a black leather jacket, giving him the appearance of an aging rock star.

"How are you, Jean-Pierre?" Troussard's brow furrowed with concern. "Not too bored with civilian life, I hope? How's your wife? Oh, I'm sorry, I forgot."

"They're planning to steal it," Tom insisted in fluent French before Dumas could react. "We're here to help."

"Did you hear that, Cécile?" Troussard sneered. "They're here to help."

Cécile Levy, the Curator of Paintings at the Louvre, stepped forward and fished anxiously inside a well-worn red Kelly bag for a pack of Marlboro Lights. Extracting one, she placed it between her lips, fumbling with her lighter until she managed to strike a flame on the fourth or fifth attempt. Clearly the *No Smoking* signs that littered the museum applied to everyone except Louvre staff members. She inhaled gratefully, a dark silhouette against the gold lettering that speckled the leather spines of the books behind her like stars in a clear night sky.

The nicotine seemed to calm her and Tom wondered whether she was naturally nervous, or whether the pale dent on her ring finger hinted at the still-tender bruising of a recent divorce? Perhaps both. Either way, she looked younger than her forty-five years, with her jet-black bob held off a pale face by the Chanel sunglasses perched on top of her head, thick mascara coating her eyelashes, a slash of red across her lips.

"What is it you think you know, exactly?" she asked Tom, her curious tone in stark contrast to Troussard's studied indifference.

"I know that a man's been killed. A friend of mine," Tom replied. "I know that he left me some files: blueprints of the Louvre, guard rotas, passwords, alarm systems . . ." He'd printed off some of the files at Dumas's apartment and he arranged the pages on Troussard's desk as he spoke. "He was working for someone called Milo."

"Milo did some covert work for us a few years ago," Dumas confirmed. "Believe me, he's more than capable of pulling something like this off."

Troussard uncrossed his legs, leaned forward and ran a skeptical eye over the documents, before sitting back with a shrug.

"We had a small security breach about six months ago. An employee was selling access to some of our intrusion-prevention and detection measures. We had to overhaul the entire system. These documents are out of date."

"If they got hold of them once, then they can do it again," Dumas warned him.

"How do you know it's *La Joconde* they're after?" Levy, still standing, used the French name for the *Mona Lisa*.

"My friend was an art forger. Along with the files, he left me a painting," Tom explained, "a forgery of the *Mona Lisa*. A good one. Knowing Milo, my guess is that he was planning to get in here somehow and swap it. As far as I know, he still is—as soon as he can get hold of another copy."

"Your *guess*?" Troussard laughed, as he placed his hands behind his head and kicked back in his chair. "That's all you've got? A few out-of-date guard rotas and a vague gut feeling, and you expect me to hit the panic button?"

"You think we're making this up?" Dumas countered.

"I don't know." Troussard fixed him with a blank stare. "Are you?"

"It's not that we don't appreciate you coming here," Levy reassured them gently, stubbing her half-finished cigarette out, scarlet lipstick glowing on the filter. "But you have to realize that barely a week goes by without some lunatic threatening to steal, burn or blow up *La Joconde*."

"Is that what you think we are? Lunatics?" Dumas asked indignantly.

"My point is, she attracts artistic stalkers," Levy continued. "The sort of people who write in telling us that they've discovered some incredible relationship between the painting's dimensions and Léonard's birth date, or that *La Joconde* is not actually a woman at all but Léonard's gay lover."

Léonard. Even though they were all speaking French,

something in Tom instinctively objected to the Frenchification of da Vinci's name. It seemed at best affected, at worst a painfully clumsy attempt to appropriate him as one of their own. The rest of the world called him Leonardo. Why did the French always insist on being different?

"Conspiracy theories," said Troussard with a dismissive toss of his head. "I blame the Americans."

No surprises there, Tom thought to himself. This seemed to be the *Lord's Prayer* of the French governing classes: When in doubt, blame the Yanks.

"So it's no surprise to us that someone is planning to steal *La Joconde*," Levy continued. "Someone, somewhere, always is. It's part of what makes her what she is."

"They can plan all they want, as far as I'm concerned," sneered Troussard. "She lives under twenty-four-hour armed guard in a purpose-built room. She's the best-protected woman on the planet. She's not going anywhere."

"There's no such thing as perfect security," Tom said firmly.

"You asked us up here because you *know* there's a risk," Dumas added. "Small, maybe, but a risk nonetheless. All we're asking is that you look into it."

"I asked you up here because I wanted to see for myself if the stories were true." Troussard got to his feet and marched around the desk, looming over Dumas. "That you'd lost it. Gone off the rails. Well, they were wrong. You're twice as fucked up as I ever thought you'd be. Look at you. You're a disgrace. No wonder they kicked you out."

With a flourish, he threw the plans that Tom had laid out on the desk into Dumas's lap. Dumas shot out of the chair and squared up to him, but Tom immediately stepped between them.

"Let's go," he said, steering Dumas toward the door. "We've done what we can."

"I think that's probably best," Levy agreed, laying a hand on Troussard's quivering shoulder.

She waited until the door had closed behind them and then turned on Troussard with a reproachful look.

"Was that entirely necessary?"

"What do you mean?" He jutted his chin at her defiantly.

"I mean, what's the story with you and Dumas?"

"There is no story," he retorted a little too quickly and forcefully to be convincing. "Apart from the one he just spun for us. He's a drunk, for God's sake. I could smell it on him. A plot to steal the *Mona Lisa*? Pah! He probably dreamed the whole thing."

"He seemed pretty convinced to me," she reflected. "His friend too. Why would they make it up?"

"What else has he got to do all day? He probably thinks it's funny to have people like me running around in circles. Probably makes him feel more important."

"I think I'm going to mention it to Ledoux all the same. Just to be safe."

"There's no need to involve him." Troussard frowned in annoyance. "Not based on what we've heard today. I can deal with this."

"I can't risk being wrong." Her face blanched at the thought. "He's the Museum Director. Let him decide."

"He'll only make me change the guard rotas and walk through the security set-up again," Troussard huffed.

"Do you think we should tell the police?"

"If we called them every time we heard a story like that, we'd never get off the phone," he insisted. "Besides, security is my responsibility, no one else's. I don't need anyone interfering. Certainly not the police."

CHAPTER TWENTY-FOUR

JARDIN DU TUILERIES, PARIS

20th April—5:02 P.M.

The round pond was encircled by trees. As arranged, Archie was sitting on one of the park benches sheltered under their swaying branches. Here and there gravel paths led off from this central area like spokes, cutting through the formal parterres. Another pond lay at the end of the wide, unbroken vista that ran along the garden's main axis, and beyond that rose the granite spear of the ancient obelisk in the Place de la Concorde, deliberately positioned close to the site of one of Revolutionary France's most active scaffolds.

"How did it go?" Archie asked as they slumped on the bench beside him. A pile of discarded cigarette butts at his feet suggested he'd been waiting a while.

"Imbéciles," Dumas swore, producing a hip flask from his jacket and taking a swig.

"Idiots," Tom agreed with a sigh, grabbing the flask off Dumas and downing a mouthful himself.

"How bad?"

"They laughed."

"That's bad." Archie grinned, the gold identity bracelet on his left wrist glinting in the sun. "Well, I told you. They're up their own arse, that lot." He jerked his head in the direction of the Louvre. "Always have been."

"It's Troussard." Dumas shook his head, his jaw set firm. "*Petit salaud.* He's never forgiven me for . . ." He completed the sentence with a small hand gesture. "Well now, my life's in the gutter. He's finally won. The only reason he saw me was to rub it in."

"What about the police?" Tom suggested. "We could try them."

Dumas dismissed the idea with a wave.

"First thing they'd do is call Troussard. He'll just laugh at them the way he laughed at us."

"So what do we do? We can't just sit back and watch Milo walk in and take it."

"Assuming he *can* take it," Dumas observed. "Troussard was right about one thing. The security back there is bullet proof."

"You were right too. There's a risk. Whatever systems they've got in place, you can be sure that Milo's figured out some way around them. I would if I was going in for it."

In front of them, a couple of children leaned over the pond's rounded edge and placed a small sailboat on to the water. The wind caught its handkerchief-sized yellow sail and gently propelled it across the pond's dark waters. The children jumped up with an excited shout, running around the basin to keep up as it accelerated toward the opposite side.

"Maybe you *should* go in for it," Archie suggested as the children's laughter blended into the sound of a South American pipe band that had started up somewhere on the Rue de Rivoli.

"Sure. Let's just wander over there now." Tom laughed.

"I'm serious. If we had the painting, we could swap it for Eva."

"You *are* serious!" Tom exclaimed.

"Well, I'm not," Dumas spluttered. "We can't steal the *Mona Lisa*."

"Why not?" said Archie.

"*C'est impossible!*"

"Milo's planning to," Archie reminded him.

"That's different."

"Not really," Archie said evenly. "The way I see it, either we walk away, or we beat him to it and then trade it for Eva."

"Trade the *Mona Lisa*?" Dumas snorted, his tone both disbelieving and outraged.

"Not the real one," Archie explained. "A forgery . . ." He didn't need to finish the sentence for Tom to see where he was heading.

"We'd have to steal the real thing for Milo to believe that we had it to trade," he said slowly. "But if we traded Rafael's forgery for Eva, instead of the real painting, Milo wouldn't realize until it was too late. We'd be playing him at his own game."

"The painting's been nicked before," said Archie, his eyes glinting. "We could do it again."

"That was in 1911," Dumas reminded him. "A lot's changed since then."

"Maybe, maybe not," said Tom, turning to Archie. "How did they do it?"

"A guy called Eduardo de Valfierno was behind it," Archie explained, lighting another cigarette as he spoke. "An Argentinian conman. They say he once managed to sell the Eiffel Tower as scrap to some gullible punter."

"A Belgian, I expect." Dumas laughed.

"Valfierno teamed up with a forger called Yves Chaudron. The plan was to pinch the *Mona Lisa*, have Chaudron knock out and shift as many copies as possible while she was missing, and then drop her back at the Louvre so that the cops would call off the hunt."

"An art forger?" Tom said slowly. "Like Rafael?"

Archie locked eyes with Tom and nodded.

"Exactly like Rafael."

"So that's his plan." Tom gave a low whistle. "Steal the original, make some copies and sell off as many of them as you can while it's missing. Milo's pulling the same stunt as Valfierno tried to."

"It's a great con," Archie conceded. "The buyers can hardly go to the cops if they get suspicious. And he can always let them think they've got the real thing by telling them that he handed a fake back to the Louvre."

Tom nodded slowly, part of him almost wishing he'd thought of it himself.

"*Bravo, Milo.* Very clever. But I would still like to know how Valfierno got the painting out of the Louvre without getting caught," Dumas insisted.

"He signed up Vincenzo Peruggia, a carpenter who worked at the museum," Archie continued. "Peruggia and two other blokes went in one Sunday posing as tourists and then stashed themselves in a storeroom overnight, knowing that the museum was shut the next day. The following morning they lifted the painting off the wall, cut it out of its frame and walked out dressed as maintenance men, cool as you like. When they saw it was gone, the guards assumed it had been taken to be photographed. It wasn't until over a day later that anyone twigged that it was missing.

"They say it was the first ever truly global news story," Tom added. "There was a massive manhunt. It took them a week just to explore the Louvre. The French shut their borders and searched every ship and train leaving the country. The newspapers hyped it endlessly. Rewards were offered. People were arrested and released. If you ever wondered why the *Mona Lisa* is the world's most famous painting, it's got nothing to do with her enigmatic smile. It's because she was stolen."

"Where did they find it in the end?"

"Peruggia had it all along," Archie said with an appreciative smile. "All Valfierno wanted was the story in the papers long enough for him to shift his six forgeries. Once the news broke, Peruggia never heard from him again. A few years later, he tried to sell the painting to a dealer in Florence. The dealer tipped off the Uffizi. When the police nabbed him, they found that he'd been stashing it in a specially built trunk with a false bottom."

"So, based on that, all we need to do is hide in the Louvre overnight, take it off the wall and walk out." Dumas grinned. "What are we waiting for?"

"What do you mean, 'we?' " Tom frowned. "You've done

your bit, J-P. You got us in to see Troussard. Archie and I will take it from here."

"*Non,* you're not freezing me out now, Felix." Dumas's eyes flashed defiantly. "I was quite happily drunk in that bar until you dragged me out. Now that I'm sober, you're stuck with me until the end."

"You're a government agent, J-P," Tom insisted. "Archie and I know what we're getting into. This isn't your thing."

"What is my thing now, Felix? I've got no job. No wife . . ."

"Archie, you tell him," Tom pleaded.

"We'll need the extra muscle," said Archie with a shrug.

"He's a spy," Tom reminded him. "You hate spies."

"Ex-spy," said Archie. "Same as you. Besides, I've always thought J-P would make a good villain, if he put his mind to it."

"*Merci.*" Dumas winked. "Anyway, if by some miracle you actually do manage to steal the *Mona Lisa*, someone needs to make sure you two don't accidentally decide to hold on to it."

"You see, he's a natural crook," Archie said solemnly. "He doesn't trust anyone."

CHAPTER TWENTY-FIVE

AVENUE DE L'OBSERVATOIRE, 14TH ARRONDISSEMENT, PARIS

21st April—9:02 A.M.

The elevator was enclosed in a black wire cage that rose like a scorched tree up the central core of the winding stone staircase. Hauling open the concertina-style gate, Jennifer stepped inside, allowing it to spring shut behind her. The date on the brass control panel, almost polished away over the years, indicated that it had been installed in 1947. It seemed older.

She pressed five and, after a few moments' reflection, the cabin lurched skywards with an ominous clunking and shrieking noise. The floors crept past like rock strata, and she had the sudden sensation of being hauled up the side of a cliff in a wicker basket.

Henri Besson, the forgery expert Cole had hooked her up with, was standing waiting for her on the landing. At least she assumed it was him, the elevator rising to reveal first bare feet, then brightly patterned knee-length shorts and finally a loosely buttoned Hawaiian shirt sprouting silvery chest hair. He held out his hand, his greeting immediately dispelling her doubts.

"Mademoiselle Browne? Enchanté. Henri Besson à votre service."

He had the tan to match his clothes, his dark blue eyes twinkling out from an unshaven and surprisingly youthful face, given he was fifty or so years old. Only his curly hair, graying at the sides and thinning on top, gave some indication of his true age.

"Good morning." She smiled. "Thank you for doing this at such short notice."

"The larger the client, the less warning they give you."

He gave a disconcertingly lopsided smile and it took her a few moments to realize that the entire left side of his face was paralyzed. One cheek was slack and heavy, the other firm and dimpled; one eye drooping, while the other twinkled. She guessed that he'd had some sort of a stroke.

"Come in, please. The others are already here."

Hudson and Cole had both insisted that somebody from their respective Paris operations should be on hand to witness the initial examination in person. Partly this was to ensure that the tests were conducted to their mutual satisfaction, but she suspected there was also an element of cold-war style politics to it as well. Neither superpower was willing to concede the slightest potential advantage to the other.

Ushering her into a small office dominated by a floor-to-ceiling gilded mirror, Besson introduced her to Miles King and Caroline Vernin, representatives from Sotheby's and Christie's respectively. Both were young and sharply dressed and had the same hungry look she had seen in realtors when first trying to rent an apartment in Manhattan.

"The paintings arrived safely?" she asked, noting the teetering piles of auction catalogues on the far side of the room and the assortment of ash-filled wine glasses balancing on top of them.

"We delivered ours yesterday afternoon," Vernin confirmed.

"I made sure that the paintings that were on Agent Browne's flight were shipped straight from the airport as soon as they'd cleared Customs," King immediately fired back.

"Everything is ready," Besson reassured her. "Now, tell me, have you ever taken part in something like this before?"

"Is it anything like an autopsy?" she asked with a smile. "Because I've done plenty of them."

"*Précisement*!" Besson clapped his hands. "An artistic autopsy. Only no one has died."

The memory of Hammon's gaping eye sockets and the bloody gash of his open mouth flashed into her head and for a moment she thought of correcting him. Someone had died, and it hadn't needed an autopsy to explain the cause of death.

"*Venez*. I'll talk you through it."

He opened a set of double doors and led them from the office into a large room, the damage caused by his stroke further betrayed by his shuffling limp and the unnatural splay of his left foot.

It was dark, sunlight peeking in around the edges of the metal shutters. Even so, Jennifer could make out the elaborate nineteenth-century plaster cornicing that suggested this had once been the main sitting room. Not that there was any furniture now. Instead, the room was almost entirely taken up by a large chamber constructed from heavy-duty plastic sheeting, leaving only a narrow path around its perimeter. It reminded Jennifer of the forensic tents erected around a crime scene, except here the plastic was clear, not white. A pale inner glow was projecting various dark shapes against the translucent material as if it were a screen.

"It's a clean room," Besson explained, sensing the question she was asking herself. "It allows me to maintain the air purity, temperature and humidity at the right level."

He pulled on a white lab coat that reached just below his shorts and then pushed his feet into a pair of bright yellow boots of the type Jennifer had seen in abattoirs and mortuaries before. It certainly explained why he was barefoot. He handed each of them a similar coat and a set of elasticated overshoes.

"Please don't touch anything," he warned, as he pulled on a set of surgical gloves and then looped a pair of square-framed reading glasses around his neck.

As soon as they were all dressed, he located a split in the chamber wall and held it open for them. They stepped into a small anteroom and then pushed through a heavy curtain of overlapping clear plastic strips into the chamber itself, the temperature dropping noticeably. Motion-sensitive lights blinked on overhead, their ultraviolet filters radiating a faint blue wash.

The center of the chamber, Jennifer could now see, was dominated by a large circular table. All four paintings had been removed from their frames and mounted in steel cradles that allowed them to be moved and rotated without having to touch the canvas.

Seeing them side by side for the first time, she had to admit that, of the two artists, she preferred the Chagall. There was passionate energy there, an almost childish abandon of color and movement that she instinctively connected with, compared to the Gauguin's rather self-conscious sense of control.

On one side of the table a fearsome array of mechanical arms, bristling with cameras, lights and other unidentified appendages, hung down menacingly over the canvases, as if the paintings were patients sitting nervously in a dentist's chair. Meanwhile the edges of the chamber were lined with various unidentified pieces of electronic and analytical equipment that gave off a low hum as LED lights of different colors flashed wildly.

"Authentication typically requires two types of analysis—" Besson put his glasses on as he turned to face Jennifer, the explanation clearly aimed at her—"forensic and Morellian."

"Morellian?"

"In simple terms: Does it look right? Is it consistent with the preferred themes, style, composition and technique of a particular artist? To be honest, that's often enough. You just look at it, and you know."

"I think we'll need the full set of tests on this one," Vernin cautioned him. "If I have to go back to my clients with bad news, they're going to want to see everything."

"Mine too," King added quickly.

"Then I'll have to take samples."

"Only swabs," insisted Vernin.

"That rules out AAS and ICPS," he warned her.

"But you can still do X-ray, infrared, UV and TXRF," she pointed out. "That should be enough."

"TXRF?" Jennifer frowned.

"Total reflection X-ray fluorescence spectrometry," King explained. "Just don't ask me what it means."

"It means you take swabs from the painting's surface and then examine the trace elements under X-ray," Vernin said impatiently.

"AAS and ICPS tests involve scraping off actual paint chips and then burning them to analyze their resins," Besson said as he busied himself around the main computer. "Most people won't allow them. But it's always worth asking."

One of the robotic arms sprang into life, lowering itself over the first Gauguin canvas and then tracking across its surface. Jennifer watched silently as, with metronomic sweeps of the cursor, the scanned image of the painting began to take shape on the computer screen. When it was finished, the table rotated automatically until the other Gauguin was in position. Then it too was scanned in.

As soon as both paintings had been captured, Besson called up the images on another set of screens, leaving the computer to scan in the two Chagalls behind him. Adjusting the magnification until it was possible to see the individual brush strokes, Besson tracked across the surface of the first painting, switching at various points to the equivalent section of the other painting to compare them.

"Any joy?" King asked hopefully after fifteen or so minutes.

Besson, ignoring the question, crossed to the table and tilted the two paintings upright. He stood for a few minutes in front of each one, his left arm across his stomach, the other supporting his chin as he contemplated them. Finally, with a nod, he went to the right-hand Gauguin and placed his hand on the top of the canvas.

"This one."

"What?"

"It's not right."

"In what way?" queried Jennifer.

"It's good. Excellent. But the confidence of the brush strokes, the layering of the paint and the colors are far more consistent in the other painting with Gauguin's style at that time. This one is a bit . . . soulless."

King stepped forward and glanced at the painting's identification label before giving Vernin a triumphant grin.

"One of yours. Unlucky."

Jennifer nodded to herself. Hudson had been right, after all. Razi's painting was the genuine one.

"I'll want those tests," Vernin instructed Besson in a stern tone, "And a second opinion."

"Of course," he nodded. "I suggest the Wildenstein Institute. Sylvie Ducroq is the Gauguin expert there."

"What about the Chagall?" Jennifer reminded him.

Besson set about repeating the exercise he had run through previously. This time, however, it only took half as long.

"No question that this is the original," he announced, indicating the painting to his right. "The other one hasn't got the right aging. The colors are too fresh, too new. It's not as good an attempt as the Gauguin. I expect it was done in China. They still teach traditional oil techniques out there."

"Fifty euro says that one's yours too," King challenged Vernin with a smile.

"You're such a child," she sighed as she stepped forward to examine the label before looking around with an anguished look.

"Just not your day, is it?" King crowed.

Jennifer wasn't listening. She was trying to understand the significance of both forgeries ending up in the hands of Christie's Japanese client.

"The full forensic tests will take one or two days," Besson observed, pulling his gloves off with a loud thwack. "I'll email them through as soon as they're done. I suggest you hold off talking to your clients until then."

"Agreed," said King cheerfully, barely able to contain himself. This was clearly the art world equivalent of the Battle of Chattanooga. "Thanks for your help on this one, Henri." He shook his hand enthusiastically.

"We'll see ourselves out," Vernin said curtly, casting off

her protective white coat and striding toward the opening in the chamber's plastic folds.

"I'll arrange for the paintings to be returned as soon as I've finished," he called after them, before turning back to Jennifer. "Presumably you would like the ones you brought over to be sent to your hotel, Mademoiselle Browne?"

"The George V," she confirmed. "Thank you."

She shook Besson's hand and then turned to follow King and Vernin back to the office.

"*Mademoiselle Browne. Un moment, s'il vous plaît,*" Besson called her back, removing his glasses. "I didn't want to mention it in front of the others," he said in a low voice, "but there's something else you should know about these paintings, the Gauguin in particular."

"Go on."

"These aren't just forgeries. They are perfect copies."

"What do you mean?"

"I mean that whoever painted them must have had direct access to the originals. The Gauguin is certainly the better executed of the two, but they both combine small details that the painter would only have been aware of if they had the original in front of them. Maybe he or she has been a little too clever?"

Jennifer gave a pained sigh. Far from simplifying the case by allowing her to focus on the two forgeries and their history, she now had no choice but to include the originals in her investigation as well. She was right back where she'd started.

"Not the answer you were looking for?"

"That would have been too easy." She smiled ruefully.

He escorted her to the front door but as she stepped out on to the landing, she paused, suddenly remembering that she had one more question for him. Pulling a slip of paper from her handbag, she asked, "Does this mean anything to you?"

Besson put his glasses back on and studied the number she had copied down from Hammon's fax machine.

"It looks like a Louvre accession number." He frowned. "Usually accession numbers have the date of acquisition followed by a serial number, but the Louvre has its own system.

They like to be different. I'm not sure what it's for, though. Would you like me to find out?"

She hesitated for a moment. If it was a Louvre number she was keen to go there in person. On the other hand, there was no guarantee anyone would be available to see her.

"That would be great."

"Can I keep this?"

"Of course. Just let me know if you come up with anything."

Closing the door behind her, Besson stood for a few moments in the hallway, flicking his fingernail against his teeth.

"So, was it her?" he asked in French, sensing someone walking up alongside him.

"Yeah," Tom sighed. "It was her."

CHAPTER TWENTY-SIX

10:32 A.M.

Let me get this straight," Besson laughed, as he poured the coffee. "You and the FBI agent . . ."

"It wasn't like that," Tom protested.

"No?"

"Well, not exactly," he conceded in an awkward tone. "It was complicated. I was helping her . . . She blackmailed me into it, really. Anyway we were in Paris together and things sort of just . . . happened. It was over before it began. You know what it's like."

"Actually, no." Besson grinned. "In my day we didn't sleep with cops, even the beautiful ones."

"In your day, all the cops were men."

"What did Archie say?"

"Not much." Tom ran a hand through his hair.

"Liar!" Besson laughed again. "We both know how he feels about anyone with a badge."

"He didn't trust her," Tom conceded. "Not at first, anyway. But later, when she followed through on what she'd promised, when she fought in my corner with the FBI, he realized she was different."

"They didn't have an ass like that, for a start," said Besson appreciatively.

Tom smiled, but he was only half listening. He'd thought it must have been a coincidence when Besson had mentioned Jennifer's name. Even when he'd seen her walk through the door from his vantage point behind the two-way mirror in the office, he'd not quite believed it. But it was her. Here in Paris.

It was a strange feeling. First the sharp pinch of recognition as someone he'd relegated to the back of his mind suddenly surged to the fore of his consciousness. Then the spark of a broken connection being mended, of all those dangers they had faced and overcome together being jolted into vivid relief. Finally the uncomfortable blend of attraction and anger that had settled in his stomach like oil floating on water.

Attraction, as he gazed at her soft, inviting lips and at her long toned legs and reminded himself of those few sultry summer nights together almost a year ago now. Anger that the defenses he had so carefully erected to partition away his memories of that time had been so easily washed away. Now certainly wasn't the time to get distracted.

"What did she want?" he asked.

"Help identifying a couple of forgeries. Some case she's working on over in the States where there are four paintings but only two certificates of authenticity."

"Let me guess—" Tom smiled "—the certificates are with the forgeries."

"Exactly. And no surprise either that they've turned up in Japan." A pause. "You going to let her know, or shall I?

"She's smart. She'll work it out," said Tom. "Anything else?"

"She wanted to know what this was—" He held out the piece of paper that she had given him. Tom glanced at the number written on it and then locked eyes with Besson, his concern overriding his surprise.

"But that's . . ."

"I know."

"What did you tell her?"

"That I'd look into it."

"Well, hold off for now," Tom instructed him. "We've got enough to deal with without involving the FBI too." Tom's words sounded hopeful even to him. The FBI were clearly already involved, even if Jennifer didn't know it yet. He needed to make sure it stayed that way as long as possible. Until this was over, at least.

"By the way, the fake Gauguin she just had me look at—it's one of Rafael's."

"Are you sure?"

"Pretty sure. There aren't many people who can knock out something that good."

"You can," Tom reminded him. "Or could, if you hadn't retired."

"Except, according to you, I haven't." Besson gave a wry smile as he picked up Rafael's forged version of the *Madonna of the Yarnwinder* that Tom had carefully placed between them.

"Well? Will you do it?"

"Of course I'll do it. It just seems a bit of a shame."

"It's an insurance policy."

"What do you want done?"

"Use your imagination."

"And this?" Besson picked up the porcelain obelisk Tom had unwrapped and placed on the kitchen table.

"A present from Rafael before he died."

"Mind if I borrow it?"

"What for?" Tom asked with a frown.

"Inspiration. It's given me an idea."

"You can't paint what you like. It just needs to be convincing."

"Maybe I'd be more convincing if I knew what it was for."

"Do you really want to know?"

"You're right," Besson grinned. "It's better if I don't. It's for you. That's all I need to know."

"No," Tom shook his head, suddenly serious. "It's not for me. It's for Rafael. It's for Eva."

CHAPTER TWENTY-SEVEN

QUAI DE JEMMAPES, 10TH ARRONDISSEMENT, PARIS

21st April—12:01 P.M.

The room was empty. Milo was alone, standing to one side of the window so he couldn't be seen from the street below, his hands folded behind his back. It was busy outside, a narrow boat chugging merrily along the Canal St. Martin, cyclists and lunchtime joggers negotiating the cobbled tow-path, tourists ambling obediently wherever their guidebooks led them. Over the rooftops, he could just about make out Sacré Coeur's white-breasted dome at the top of Montmartre. Every time the sun reappeared from behind the clouds it winked at him like a distant lighthouse.

It was a while since he had been in Paris. Although part of him felt glad to be back, he was well aware of the risks posed by his return. Still, he'd always known that, if he was going to pull this job off, he'd have to be here in person. And by the time they realized what had happened, he'd be long gone.

There was a knock. He adjusted his tie and pulled half an inch of shirt cuff out from under each sleeve, then turned to face the door.

"Come."

Djoulou strode into the room, a gun tucked into his waistband.

"She's here, sir."

"Well, show her in, Captain," he barked impatiently.

Djoulou stepped aside and pulled Eva into the room. She was blindfolded and walked unsteadily, one arm in front of her, the other gripping Djoulou's sleeve. He stopped her in the middle of the room, under the bare wires that dangled down from the central light fitting like loose veins.

"Some guy called Axel's just showed up too."

"Tech support. Help him get set up in the basement," Milo ordered. "We'll have a run-through tonight."

With a nod, Djoulou slipped out of the room. Milo let a few moments pass before advancing toward Eva, the herringbone parquet betraying each step with an arthritic creak.

"What do you want?" she demanded, turning her head to the noise. Milo remained silent until he was standing directly in front of her.

"You can take this off now," he said, carefully removing her silver bracelet and flinging it across the room as if it was scorching his fingers.

"Is this really necessary?" she insisted.

"Absolutely," he smiled, placing his hands around her waist. Without prompting, she lifted her arms around his neck and pulled him to her, her mouth parting as she felt for his tongue, her breathing quickening. They stumbled to the wall, him pressing into her, his hand squeezing her right breast and then gliding between her legs and making her moan.

He suddenly snatched his head back, the blood welling from his lip.

"That's for having your performing monkeys force a rag down my throat." She snatched her blindfold off and licked the palm of her hand as if she was trying to get rid of a bad taste.

"You said it had to look convincing," he reminded her, angrily sucking the blood from where she'd bitten him.

"You said Kirk would be too busy chasing the *Yarnwinder* to even know that Rafael was dead." Her dark eyes flashed defiantly. "Wasn't that the whole point of nailing that stinking cat to the wall?"

"Well, now he's looking for you instead. That works just as well."

She glared at him for a few seconds before conceding with a small shrug of the shoulders that he had a point.

"He thinks that message Rafael left on the well means that you killed him."

"Of course he thinks I killed him. He wants to think I killed him. It suits him to think I killed him. But you and I both know I didn't."

There was a pause. Their eyes met, his resolute, hers questioning.

"What happened between you two?"

"Nothing. It's just that neither of us like losing."

"Did you know Rafael had been over to London to see him a few weeks ago?" She went to the mirror and carefully applied some lipstick, pressing her lips together and then wiping away a small smear with her little finger.

"He must have slipped across when he made that last trip to Paris," Milo guessed. "So much for agreeing not to step out of line in case something happened to you."

"It was a wasted journey," she reassured him, smoothing her hair back under her white Alice band. "Tom was away."

"So they never actually spoke?"

"Apparently not."

"So how does he know?" he probed, looking into her eyes.

"Know what?"

"Everything. He turned up at the Louvre yesterday with Dumas and tipped them off."

"That's impossible," she said disbelievingly.

"Somebody must have talked. If not Rafael, who?"

"Somebody talked?" she shot back angrily. "A year's worth of planning gone like that because somebody talked?" She snapped her fingers to emphasize her point.

"Don't worry, nothing's changed." Milo's tone was firm. "They laughed him out of the building. If anything, we can turn this to our advantage. After all, we've still got one big factor in our favor. One button we can press to keep Kirk exactly where we want him."

"And what's that?" Her bottom lip was jutting out in a way that suggested she thought this extremely unlikely.

"You." He stooped to kiss her on the forehead, as if trying to smooth her frown away. "Now help me with this."

He stepped over to the wooden crate on the floor next to the fireplace, picked up two screwdrivers and handed one to her. Together they levered the crate open one corner at a time. Reaching in, he carefully scooped out the packing straw and placed it in the grate, gradually revealing a woman gazing attentively, some might even say fearfully, at the naked child perched on her lap. The child's attention, however, was almost entirely consumed by the small wooden rod that he was clutching with both hands. A yarnwinder.

"When did it get here?" she asked excitedly.

"This morning."

"Did you know that Rafael made a copy before he died. He hid it in his workshop. Tom found it last night."

"Rafael is proving to be far more full of surprises now he's dead than when he was alive," Milo said in a tone that hovered somewhere between admiration and anger. "But Kirk's welcome to it. It's of no use to anyone. Have you got a light?"

She reached into her back pocket and threw him a box of matches. He struck one and then held the flame against the packing straw in the fireplace. It caught light almost immediately, hissing and spitting as its orange glow snaked across the grate.

"Get the shutters!" he ordered. "You never know who's watching."

As soon as the room was dark, Milo carefully lifted the painted wooden panel out and angled it so that the flickering firelight skated across its varnished surface.

"This is how a work like this should be seen . . ." He spoke in an uncharacteristically gentle, almost reverential tone. "Electricity robs a painting of its mystery by revealing it in all its deliberate artifice. But a naked flame softens it, masking the small blemishes and worry lines of time and infusing it with a strange, dancing glow that makes the skin blush and eyes sparkle until they almost seem alive. Magic is best done in the dark."

"We could keep it," she suggested, the fire giving her dark hair and eyes a lustrous sheen as she gazed at it hungrily.

"Too risky." Milo's tone hardened once more. "The plan stands."

With a final, almost wistful look, he turned to the fireplace and carefully placed the painting in the grate. For a few seconds it sat there, untouched, the flames seeming to part respectfully around it like a retreating tide. But then, inexorably, they rolled back in, clawing with increasing insistence at the infant's naked flesh and tearing at the delicate folds of the Madonna's robe.

The painted surface darkened, smoke rising off its surface in narrow coils until a sudden surge of heat engulfed the two figures, their skin blistering and the wooden panel buckling forward, as if in agony, before splitting. Slowly the figures melted away completely, until all that remained was the faint outline of a few of the rocks in the background and the occasional tongue of green fire as the paint burned off.

"Did you see the color of the flames?" Milo asked thoughtfully as he prodded the blackened panel with a poker, breaking it up into smaller pieces that settled on to the embers with a splutter of sparks. "That's from the pigments in the paint they used to use."

"Then at least we know it wasn't a copy." She smiled.

"It's a bit like the old witch trials," Milo agreed, suddenly pensive.

"What do you mean?"

"Suspected witches used to be weighed down with stones and then thrown into the river. If they drowned, they would be declared innocent, but if they survived they would be killed anyway for being in league with the devil."

"What does that have to do with the *Yarnwinder*?" she asked with a frown.

"Sometimes, you can only find out if something really is what it claims to be by destroying it."

CHAPTER TWENTY-EIGHT

FIRST FLOOR, DENON WING, MUSÉE DU LOUVRE, PARIS

21st April—4:23 P.M.

Tom had long wondered whether he would ever really be able to experience a museum in the same way as everyone else. It wasn't that he couldn't appreciate what was on display; his years as a thief had, if anything, honed the passion for art that his parents had instilled in him from childhood. But no matter how hard he tried to concentrate, he was only half-looking at what was on show. The art retreated into the background of his consciousness like expensive wallpaper, becoming an almost incidental part of his visit, rather than its main purpose.

Instead, he found his attention irresistibly drawn to studying the security set-up—the number of guards, the location of the cameras and alarm panels, the positioning of the doors and windows, the thickness of the emergency shutters. These, not the skill with which an artist had captured the delicate play of light across silk or carved the smooth muscle tone of a flexed shoulder blade, were the elements that resonated as he walked around. And every detail, however small, was stored meticulously away.

It was only when he found himself standing opposite the *Mona Lisa*, that he realized he had no real recollection of anything else he'd seen along the way. Not that he had needed to concentrate on where he was going, the storm surge of tourists having carried him like driftwood toward her—up the stairs, right at the *Winged Victory of Samothrace*, through the first three rooms of early Italian paintings, right again into the Grande Gallerie, and then, about halfway down, a final right turn into the newly refurbished Salle des Etats.

He stood toward the rear of the room, Veronese's magnificent *Wedding Feast at Cana* towering colorfully behind him, the *Mona Lisa* hanging opposite him on a specially erected freestanding wall. A semi-circular wooden barrier held the crowd back at a respectful distance, the number of people ebbing and flowing according to the arrival and departure times of the phalanx of coaches parked outside. They gazed up in awe, a congregation of all faiths momentarily drawn to this high altar, their fleeting silence marking the completion of an artistic Hajj. A devout few even circled back around behind it for another look, their rapt faces orbiting like planets around a sun.

Tom looked on silently, struck, as ever, by how small the *Mona Lisa* was—only about thirty inches high and twenty across. She seemed distant too, maybe even a little lonely. Alone on the wall, sheltering behind her bulletproof glass and cracked varnish, she gazed down at him with a sad, almost lost smile.

"You shouldn't have come here." A female voice suddenly broke into his thoughts.

Tom looked around and recognized Cécile Levy at his side. He wondered how long she had been following and watching him. Probably since the security cameras picked him up at the entrance.

"Has Troussard sent you to do his dirty work?" he replied in French.

"I volunteered. I convinced him you'd leave quietly if I asked you."

Tom considered her for a few moments. She seemed so fragile to him, her face made up like a china doll's, her delicate ballerina-style shoes perfectly coordinated with the white piping on her classic Chanel jacket. Her hand was buried in her jacket pocket, the rectangular outline of the cigarette packet visible through the material. Tom wondered what she would give to be able to light up right there and then.

"How can you both be so sure that Dumas and I are wrong about what Milo is planning?" he asked.

"We're sure that Dumas has a drink problem. If we're going to follow something up, we need solid evidence from *credible* sources," she explained, her tone firm and yet faintly apologetic. "You provided neither."

"The only evidence you'll get is when you come in one day and find a blank space on the wall," Tom observed coldly.

"Troussard's no diplomat, but he knows what he's doing," she insisted, although there was again the hint of an apology in her voice, which Tom took as a tacit admission that she too found Troussard difficult to deal with. "Besides we took the precaution of alerting the Museum Director. He's approved some additional security measures."

"Then you've got nothing to worry about, have you?"

There was a long pause, punctuated only by the sound of rubber soles squeaking on the wooden floor and the occasional bark of the guards as they spotted a camera or someone chewing gum.

"Perhaps you should walk me to the exit," she suggested tentatively. He didn't argue. He'd seen everything he needed to.

They walked back out into the Grande Gallerie and toward the staircase. Tom was lost in his own thoughts, but as the seconds ticked past he sensed Levy growing increasingly uncomfortable at his side. He guessed that, being of a nervous disposition anyway, she found the silence rather disquieting. Sure enough, a few paces later she spoke up in an artificially casual tone.

"You know Léonard took her everywhere with him. They say that he never really finished her."

"Whoever she was?"

"Vasari was pretty clear she was Lisa del Giocondo." She seemed relieved that he'd taken the bait and that the awkward moment had passed. "You don't agree?"

"Who knows?" He shrugged. "I've heard it said that she's

Isabella of Aragon. Others have claimed that *she* is actually a *he*—da Vinci himself, or one of his lovers."

"She does look slightly androgynous," Levy conceded. "But then the fashion at the time was to pluck out your eyebrows."

"To be honest, I'm not sure it really matters," he sighed. "*Mona Lisa, La Joconde*—it's just a name. It doesn't change what it is."

"You don't actually like it, do you?" Her tone conveyed a mixture of curiosity and disbelief.

"It's not a question of not liking it. It's just that sometimes I wonder if she isn't the Paris Hilton of the art world. You know, famous for being famous. The problem is that the painting comes with so much baggage that it's impossible to appreciate it objectively anymore. In fact, I'm not even sure you can like or dislike it. It just is."

"You have to be careful what you say around here," she said with a grin as they made their way down the main staircase into the Greek sculpture hall. Her smile suited her, Tom thought, certainly more than the nervous, thin-lipped grimace that she usually deployed. "Léonard is local royalty."

"I know, they used to guillotine you for less." Tom laughed.

"I don't think people fully appreciate how far ahead of his time he was." Her voice grew more animated and confident. "The use of foreshortening and perspective to create an illusion of depth. The sensuous curves and subtle *sfumato* shifts of tone and color. The sense of balance and harmony. Hopefully we will change all that soon."

"What do you mean?"

"Didn't you see the signs?"

He shook his head.

"The painting's warped a little over the past few years. We've asked the Center for Research and Restoration to stabilize it and we're taking the opportunity to run a full set of forensic tests at the same time. The first it's ever had."

"Ever?" He found this rather unlikely.

"Well, we've run some basic analyzes before, of course—X-rays and the like. But nothing like this. The Louvre has always been too worried about it being damaged. But with modern forensic techniques we can safely strip away Léonard's genius for all to see and understand. It's being taken off display tomorrow and moved up to the restoration rooms."

They had arrived back in the main entrance area under the glass pyramid, its soaring walls amplifying the persistent drone of eager feet and agitated voices to a frenzied roar.

"Would I be wasting my time if I told you not to come back?" she asked, her tone more hopeful than anything.

"Probably."

"Troussard thinks you're a troublemaker. My own view is that you're someone who attracts trouble rather than causes it. Either way, neither of us really want you in our museum. Today it's me walking you out. The next time, believe me, Troussard will take great pleasure in having you thrown out."

"I understand." Tom shook her outstretched hand. It felt brittle and cold, like porcelain. "You won't see me here again."

"Good." She had reverted to the grimace again. "And don't worry. As long as she's here, she's in safe hands."

Tom nodded but he wasn't listening, already reaching for his phone as he headed for the exit.

"Archie, it's Tom. The painting's being moved tomorrow night. Up to the restoration rooms on the second floor."

"That's it then. That's when Milo's going to make his move." Archie's conclusion echoed Tom's own thoughts. "It don't leave us much time."

"You need to find us a way in. A way of getting close. Call in whatever favors you can."

"I'll get us in. The question is, how will you get us out?"

"I'm still working on that. Just see what you can do. It's possible that—Archie, I'll call you back."

Tom killed the call, his eyes narrowing as he assured himself that the face he had just seen ahead of him, heading for the exit, was indeed who he thought it was. At least this time he had been half expecting to see it. And maybe, just maybe, it had given him the glimmering of an idea.

He glanced around and saw a Polish tourist struggling to

make himself understood at the information desk. A slim leather briefcase was at his feet, resting against the base of the counter. Tom went to stand next to the man and, picking his moment, reached down, grabbed the briefcase and walked briskly toward the exit.

Luckily, it wasn't monogrammed. Just as well, or it would have made it that much harder for Tom to pass it off as his own.

CHAPTER TWENTY-NINE

COUR NAPOLÉON, MUSÉE DU LOUVRE, PARIS

21st April—4:49 P.M.

Jennifer stepped out into the Cour Napoléon and paused. The day seemed caught in a curious in-between moment, pale ribbons of light unfurling through occasional breaks in the dark clouds that glowered overhead, creating a strange half light that gave people's faces a ghoulish quality. The pyramid hovered silently behind her, the Louvre's scrolling façade broken into a thousand triangular pieces where the glass panels had carved it into neat equilateral sections, the stone pale and drawn.

She set off toward the Champs Elysées, but stopped almost immediately. A man was sitting on the edge of one of the granite fountains in front of her. He had a leather briefcase between his legs and was studying a piece of paper intently, looking up every so often at the buildings around him.

"Tom?" His name was out before she even realized it.

Tom looked up, a guilty look washing across his face as he shoved whatever he was reading inside his briefcase. For a moment she almost wondered if he'd been waiting for her, whether this was some sort of elaborate set-up. But there was no way he could have known she was in Paris, let alone at the Louvre. Besides, what was there to set up?

"What are you doing here?" she exclaimed. He looked well, handsome even, with those striking blue eyes and confident, controlled manner. More handsome than she remembered him.

"What are *you* doing here?" he asked, rising to his feet. Rather than curiosity, there was the hint of an accusation to Tom's voice, as if she was somehow intruding. She was suddenly glad that she'd been too surprised to try and hug or kiss him hello.

"I'm on a case. They needed me over here for a few days."

"Great."

She waited, but that was it. That was all he had to say. No, "I'm so glad to see you" or "You should have let me know you were coming." Just "great" and a twitched smile.

"You . . . ?" she asked eventually.

"Visiting some friends."

"Great."

There was a long pause. However many times Jennifer had played out their reunion in her mind, it had never gone like this. Whatever might have happened over the last year, they'd had a connection once. The sort of spark that wasn't easily forgotten. Maybe that was the problem. Maybe he was embarrassed. Maybe that was why he was acting as if he'd been cornered by an unloved aunt at a family funeral. How very English. She coughed for no reason, wondering if she should just walk away and pretend she'd never seen him.

"Chagall?" he quizzed.

"What?"

"The case you're working?"

"How . . . ?"

Tom pointed at the book peeking out of her bag.

"Yeah. Sort of," she conceded sheepishly.

"I like Chagall." Tom gave a deliberate nod. "Have you seen the ceiling in the Opéra Garnier?"

"Should I?"

"Everyone should." He fixed her with a searching look. "It's beautiful, but at the same time . . . demonic. If you stare at it long enough, it feels like you've been lifted into a dream world. A nightmare. A lurid, spinning, drunken nightmare."

For a moment she saw a glimpse of Tom as she remembered him—the sharp mind and jealously concealed passion. He snatched his eyes away, as if suddenly realizing that he had given her a more personal insight than he wanted to.

"What's the case?"

"You know I can't . . ."

"Come on, Jen," he cajoled. "Who am I going to tell?"

"That's not the point."

"The point is I might be able to help." He sat down again, the water shearing off the fountain's surface behind him into a deep trough, like sheet steel spooling out from under a rolling mill. "Besides, what else are we going to talk about?"

She hesitated, torn between what she knew Green would say and her selfish instinct not to let this moment pass without making some attempt, however futile, to get Tom to warm up a little. Besides he was right. He might be able to help. She sat down next to him, placing her bag between them.

"We've had a couple of forgeries show up in New York," she began, thinking hard about what she could and couldn't tell him.

"A Chagall . . ." Tom eyed the pigeon foraging around his feet as she spoke, his right arm draped around his briefcase.

She nodded. "And a Gauguin. We got tipped off when both the original and the copy were put up for auction at the same time—one in New York, the other here in Paris. Same story with the Chagall. We figure there are probably more."

"Hmm . . ." Tom reflected for a few moments. "Good forgeries?"

"That's why I'm here. To try and identify the originals from the rip-offs."

"And they're valuable?"

"Valuable enough."

"Any certificates of authenticity?"

"One in each case."

"With the fake, right?"

"Right." She frowned. "Does that mean something?"

"Sounds like a Scotch and Soda." He made eye contact again.

"A drink?"

"A coin trick. You ask someone to hold a silver dollar tight in the palm of their hand, but when they open their fingers, it's turned into a nickel." He illustrated this with a coin that he made vanish under her nose only for a smaller one to reappear moments later. "Put it another way. You buy an original Gauguin with a certificate of authenticity, get a copy made, and then sell that on with the certificate. The buyer thinks they're holding the silver dollar, but they're squeezing it too tight to notice you slipped them the forgery. Even when they open their hand to take a look, the certificate fools them. When you're ready, you resell the original and double your money. More, if the market's moved the right way. The internet's making it harder to pull off, but if you know what you're doing, there's no one to stop you. It's pretty simple really."

"It's pretty effective too," she breathed excitedly. If Tom was right, it would certainly explain how the two copies had come into existence and why they were so accurate. It also placed Razi even more firmly at the center of the case. He owned the original Gauguin. What if he'd once owned the Chagall as well? Maybe he'd sold the original to Hammon and a forgery to the same Japanese company that he'd sold the forged Gauguin to. If Hammon had found out, it would be reason enough for a fight. And if Hammon had threatened to speak up and blow the whole scam, reason enough for a murder too.

"I gotta make some calls," she said, getting up hurriedly.

"Sure," he shrugged, getting up with her.

"This has been really useful, thanks."

"Always happy to help the FBI." He was joking, but in his smile she sensed the hint of an apology for his earlier manner.

"It's been good, Tom—good to see you again, I mean. If I'd known you were going to be in Paris, I'd have called."

"You too," he agreed with a nod.

She turned to leave and then paused.

"You know, I'm around later if you want to meet up," she said in what she hoped was a casual tone.

"Thanks, but . . ." He shifted his weight uneasily on to his other foot.

"We could meet early if you need to get away?" she suggested.

"It's not that easy," he blustered. "I'm seeing this guy and until he calls me . . ."

"Fine," she snapped, now regretting having even asked him. He was clearly wishing that this little encounter had never happened. So much for reliving some of her Paris memories.

"Look, I'm sorry." He gave an apologetic shrug. "It's not that I . . . I guess I'm just a bit surprised to see you, that's all. But you're right, it would be great to meet up. That is if I haven't scared you off." He smiled. "You can reach me here—" He jotted his number down on the inside cover of her Chagall book. "Call me in an hour and I'll know when I'll be free."

"It'll be fun," she reassured him.

With a smile, she floated off. Tom waited until she had disappeared through the arches leading on to the Rue de Rivoli before pulling his phone out of his pocket.

"Archie, it's me again. You're not going to like this, but I think I've just found us our way out."

CHAPTER THIRTY

QUAI DE JEMMAPES, 10TH ARRONDISSEMENT, PARIS

21st April—6:41 P.M.

I thought I asked for the Commando variant?" Milo kicked open a crate and pulled out one of the ten blackened FA-MAS G2 assault rifles it contained, noting that the barrel was slightly longer than he'd wanted for the close-quarter combat situation they were likely to face.

"You did." Djoulou had stripped down to his trousers, his slab-chested torso glistening with the effort of unloading the gear. A rare genetic condition had caused his ebony skin to lose its pigment in various places, and pale pink blotches were spattered across his body like acid thrown on to a canvas. He reached into another crate. "But the standard model doesn't need a separate under-barrel grenade launcher. It's one less thing to go wrong."

He tossed a grenade to Milo, who snatched it out of the air with an approving nod and fitted it to the end of the barrel.

"We're in," Eva called from the adjacent room.

They marched through and found her sitting next to Axel in front of a large screen sub-divided into about sixteen smaller images.

From the little he had revealed about himself, Axel seemed to live a twilight existence, caught somewhere between the real world and the online one he spent most of his time immersed in. The adoption of his hacking username in everyday life was just one further example of how far his realities appeared to have merged. To Milo he looked faintly ridiculous, dressed entirely in black apart from his peroxide blond hair, drawn back into cornrows, but then he did what he was asked, when he was asked and without too many questions. Putting up with his dress sense and gum habit was a small price to pay, given how good he was.

"The good news is that the Louvre cameras are all on a wireless network," Eva explained, "It avoids them having to lift the floors to lay the cables."

"It's encrypted, just not very well." Axel pushed his gum to the corner of his mouth as he spoke.

"There she is—" Eva pointed excitedly at one of the feeds showing the *Mona Lisa* high on her wall. The room was empty, the museum having shut at six, apart from two guards positioned on either side of the painting and another three at each entrance to the room. "I think she just smiled at me."

"Can you override the network?" Milo asked.

"The surveillance system is a piece of cake," Axel confirmed. "But the alarm is a no-go. It's a stand-alone network hard-wired to the cops, probably housed in armored cables sunk into about three feet of concrete. We'd need to get inside and try and hack in through one of their service terminals to have any chance."

"We haven't got time for that," said Milo impatiently. "Besides, there's no need. They'll have to deactivate everything anyway when they transfer it upstairs to the lab."

"Which is when?"

"Tomorrow at six fifteen exactly."

"There will be five men on each floor to make sure she gets in and out safely. Maybe more," Eva noted. "But only two, maybe three, can fit in the elevator with the painting itself. It'll take them five minutes to get the painting off the wall and into the car, then fifteen seconds from the moment the doors shut on the first floor to when they open on the second. That's when we'll hit them."

"Eva and I will be waiting here until we lower ourselves

on to the roof," Milo nodded, touching the image showing the top of the elevator shaft. "So we'll need you to make sure they can't see us." Axel took careful notes while keeping his eyes fixed on where Milo was pointing.

"Do you want to loop it or just lose the picture?" asked Axel.

"Lose it," Milo confirmed. "We'll fold the hatch back, deal with the guards, grab the painting and then jump back on to the roof before the doors open. So far, we've got it down to thirteen seconds." He nodded toward the replica elevator cabin in one of the other rooms.

"We can do it in eleven." Eva gave a determined nod.

"As soon as we're out, we'll set off the incendiary charges here and here." Milo pointed to two locations at either end of the Grande Gallerie. "That's your cue to cut the rest of the feeds."

"The fire alarms will bring down the security barriers," Eva continued. "By the time they put the fire out, get their system up and running, and work out what's happened, we'll be gone."

"We need the helicopter there exactly two minutes after we drop on to the elevator. That'll give us enough time to make it back out on to the roof."

"Any problems, I'll have the boys parked nearby," said Djoulou. "We'll come in and get you."

"Is everyone clear on what they're doing and when?"

Djoulou nodded.

"I want to run through it again," Axel suggested, folding a fresh piece of gum into his mouth. "Just to be sure."

"Good." Milo grabbed his hair and yanked his head back. "Because if you screw this up, I'll saw your head off with a blunt pocket knife."

CHAPTER THIRTY-ONE

LA FONTAINE DE MARS RESTAURANT,

7TH ARRONDISSEMENT, PARIS

21st April—8:17 P.M.

"Let me see that list again."

Tom motioned toward the printout. Jennifer watched him as he leafed through the pages, his brow creased in concentration. She remembered the last time they had sat together like this. Also in a restaurant. Also in Paris. So much had changed since that initial, suspicious encounter, and yet here they were again, perhaps even more suspicious and wary than then. Was that the heavy price of their fleeting intimacy, she wondered. Unsustained, the barriers had come up twice as high as before.

If nothing else it explained why he was so keen to focus on her case—this way he didn't have to risk talking about anything more personal.

"Look at the buying patterns—" he traced a finger over the page. "Your friend Razi is buying some good stuff here—Klee, Laurencin, Utrillo, even a Renoir or two. But he's buying a lot of rubbish too. Similar period, but rubbish all the same."

"Meaning what?"

"If you're looking to forge something, one of the hardest

things to fake is canvas age," he explained. "But with access to paintings like this, you wouldn't have to. All you need to do is clean them off, paint whatever you want in its place and nobody would be any the wiser."

"And that's what you think he was doing?"

"Apart from the period broadly matching, his buying is pretty indiscriminate. It certainly looks to me like he was just in it for the canvases," Tom confirmed. "I'd be amazed if the sellers didn't know exactly what he was up to."

"Even if they thought he was using them to make forgeries?"

"He was doing them a favor by taking them off their hands. Ask around. The clue will be when everyone tells you what a great guy he is," Tom said with a rueful sigh.

"That's exactly what happened!" she exclaimed, thinking back to her unpleasant meetings with Wilson and the other members of the Upper East Side art-dealing fraternity.

"You've got to be pretty brave to finger someone for fraud. Especially in the States with its trigger-happy approach to litigation. That's why Razi focused on the mid-market. No one was going to risk calling his bluff, or the cops, over a couple of hundred thousand bucks. He flew right under the radar."

"And like you said before, the certificates of authenticity helped convince the Japanese buyers that they were getting the real thing."

"The Japanese don't have ready access to the types of experts we have over here who can spot a fake at fifty feet. And they're not going to bother flying one over for a half a million dollar painting. The certificate is all they've got to go on. In fact, often they're more interested in that than the painting itself. You know what the Japanese are like with labels."

"I know they don't like to talk when they discover that they've been ripped off," she said, thinking of her ongoing and so far fruitless struggle to get someone at Takano Holdings to talk to her.

"They probably don't want to lose face," Tom guessed. "That's the clever thing about this scam. Razi turned the frailties of the art market to his own advantage. The Japanese thirst for certificates and their shame complex. The American fear of lawsuits from a misplaced accusation and their willingness to back a perceived winner, however bad the smell." He slid the printout back across the table. "It's impressive."

A waiter appeared at their table and took their order. Tom, refusing his offer to deposit his briefcase in the cloakroom, placed it instead between his feet. Jennifer smiled. Even thieves, it seemed, worried about theft.

"By the way, you never did say what you were doing at the Louvre?" she asked, pouring him some wine and then helping herself.

"Killing time." He shrugged. "You?"

"I had an appointment there to see someone. They had to cancel."

"About your case?"

"Sort of." She wasn't about to share details of Hammon's murder and what she had found there without clearing it with Green and the NYPD first. "How's Archie?"

"Bored." Tom smiled. "Sometimes I worry it's all he can do not to jump off the wagon straight back into his old life."

"He's not with you then?"

"No, he's in London. Hates traveling."

They paused as the waiter served the first course.

"What about you?" Jennifer asked between mouthfuls. "Have you been tempted to jump back in? Do another job?"

"Would you care?"

"Of course."

"Why?"

"I don't know." She frowned. "Because you said you wouldn't. Because it's wrong."

"Jennifer Browne." Tom laughed. "The voice of my conscience. Anyway, what would you do? Rat me out?"

"If I knew you'd done a job?"

"Or thought I was going to."

"Maybe. It would depend."

"What on, the weather?"

"Lots of things."

"Well, luckily I can save you that dilemma," Tom placed a

reassuring hand on hers. She left it there, not wanting to break his flow now that he finally seemed to be talking. "I've been a good boy."

"Not a single job?"

"You almost sound disappointed."

"I'm just surprised you've never been tempted."

"I never said I hadn't been tempted." He grinned.

"Were you ever tempted to reply to my emails?" She tried to sound indifferent, but from the way Tom immediately drew his hand away and flicked his eyes to his plate, she knew she'd failed.

"I didn't want things to get complicated."

"It was just an email, Tom. 'Hello. How are you?' The usual thing. Even if you don't like me, you don't have to ignore me."

"Of course I like you," he shot back.

"Then what was it?"

There was a long pause and Tom seemed to be searching for the right thing to say.

"Look, I'm not very good at . . . I didn't mean to upset you or anything. I just thought . . . I just thought it was easier that way."

"For you?"

"For both of us. We live on different sides of the world. We have totally different lives. And in case you'd forgotten, you're a cop and I'm a thief."

"Reformed thief," she reminded him.

"You know what I mean," he said with a shake of the head. "What did you think was going to happen between us?"

She gazed at him for a few moments and then gave a resigned shrug, his words dousing the final few embers that remained from her memories of their time together the previous summer.

"Nothing." She sighed. "You're right."

"I mean, life's complicated enough, right, without, you know . . ." He gave a short laugh.

"I think we make it more complicated than it needs to be." She summoned up a smile, the arrival of the waiter to collect their plates providing a welcome break in the conversation for both of them. She didn't really agree or even necessarily follow his reasoning, but it seemed pointless to dwell on it. That was then. Maybe he was right and her expectations were unrealistic. Maybe they both just needed to put it all behind them.

The evening wore on, Tom loosening up as they drifted through slightly calmer water over the main course, dessert and coffee. Jennifer's family and what they were up to. Some of Tom's cases and the people he'd dealt with. A trip he'd taken to St. Petersburg. Byron Bailey, a young FBI agent they'd both come across over the last few months.

During the course of this she was struck by how little she really knew him, or indeed had ever really got to know him the last time they had been together. Then again, she wondered if Tom ever let anyone get close enough to know any more than he wanted them to.

"So, how long are you staying?" Tom helped her on with her coat as they stepped out on to the street, the night warm and still.

"Another day, two at the most. You?"

"The same."

There was an awkward pause and then Tom went to kiss her on the cheek while she held out her hand. They both laughed. Then she leaned forward and pressed her cheek to his lips.

"Just hold that!" A voice rang out, accompanied by the flash of a camera. "Beautiful!"

Jennifer snatched herself away from Tom and looked over to where the voice had come from.

"Lewis," she gasped in a strangled voice.

"*Bonsoir,* Agent Browne," Lewis smirked, a cigarette dangling from his bloodless lips, his tape recorder appearing from inside a faded jeans jacket. "Or do you mind if I call you Jennifer? I feel like we're really getting to know each other now."

"How the hell . . . ?"

"Didn't you hear? You're big news back home." He limped toward them, the loose skin under his chin swaying gently. "Our circulation was up fifteen percent for my 'Black Widow' piece. Did you like the photo, by the way?" He winked. "Anyway, my editor wants me to run with it. Get to know the woman behind the badge. The girl behind the gun. Good thing for me your concierge is saving for dental work or I'd never have found you."

"Who is this idiot?" Tom stepped between Lewis and her, shielding her from the photographer who was still clicking away.

"No one," she breathed, too surprised to be angry.

"Leigh Lewis, *American Voice*," Lewis introduced himself, tobacco-stained fingers snaking over Tom's shoulder bearing a dog-eared business card. "I don't believe we've met, Mr.—?"

"Leave her alone," Tom ordered him.

"The American people have a right to know why they're paying for a federal agent to take her boyfriend out to dinner," Lewis proclaimed grandly, his eyes bulging hungrily.

"As a matter of fact, I paid," Tom said tersely. "And I'm not her boyfriend."

"Of course not." Lewis winked. "Just be careful if you're screwing her, okay, buddy? Her bite's pretty deadly."

"Why don't you just fuck off?" Tom took a step toward Lewis, who stood his ground defiantly. A small group of curious onlookers had gathered at a safe distance.

"Don't, Tom," she warned him. "You'll only make it worse. This is my problem, not yours."

"You want to watch out for her temper," Lewis cautioned him. "She's killed one man already and attacked me just a few days back. I'm thinking of suing."

"If you want to sue someone, sue me."

Tom's fist caught Lewis on the side of his chin and threw him on to the hood of the car behind him, his lit cigarette tracing a fiery circle as it was sent spinning out of his mouth.

A woman behind them screamed. Someone else mumbled something about calling the police. With a low moan, Lewis slid down on to the ground in a rubbery heap. The photographer cursed and sprinted off down the street.

"Shit," Jennifer swore. After the trouble she'd just had with Green, this was the last thing she needed.

"Shit," Tom agreed, as if he'd realized that he'd made a mistake the second his fist had connected with Lewis's face. "I didn't mean . . ."

"You have any idea how bad this will look?" she said with a despairing shake of her head.

"I'm sorry," he said, looking chastened. "He just really . . . I guess I wasn't thinking. I just wanted to make him shut up."

She gazed at him silently for a few seconds. It was difficult to be angry with him, when all he'd been doing was standing up for her.

"It's okay," she sighed. "He had it coming. I'm sure we can explain . . ."

"No," Tom insisted quickly, glancing nervously back up the street. "I'm not explaining anything to anyone."

"What do you mean?"

"I can't risk the police pulling me in on this, Jen."

"Why? What's wrong?" She frowned, his suddenly furtive manner fueling her suspicions.

"Nothing," he insisted.

"It can't be nothing."

"No," he admitted, looking somewhat sheepish. "It's just that I had some trouble with the law here a few years back. Nothing serious, but if they finger me for this . . ."

His voice petered out. She looked at him blankly, hoping that her expression made it clear he was going to have to volunteer a bit more detail.

"You want me to spell it out, fine," he said, running his hand through his hair impatiently. "I broke some guy's arm in a fight. If they pick me up on another assault charge, they'll make me do six months for the first guy and another six for Lewis."

"You got a suspended prison sentence?" She didn't know how the French legal system worked, but that sounded harsh for a first-time offense.

"I broke it in three places." His face broke into a grin at the memory. "And his nose. And three ribs."

"Jesus, Tom," she remonstrated. "What had he done?"

"I can't even remember. And right now, it doesn't matter. I just want to get out of here before the police show up."

"Then go," she conceded with a weary shake of her head. "I'll deal with it."

"I need you to hold on to this for me—" He held out his briefcase with a pleading look. "Just in case the cops get lucky and pick me up."

"Why, what's in it?" she asked with a curious frown.

"Paperwork. Details of cases I'm working and people I know. People who are happy to help me, but who wouldn't want the cops knowing about them or what they do."

"Fine," she said, taking the briefcase from him. Tom was rapidly using up all the goodwill that standing up for her just now had earned him.

"Thanks. I appreciate it." Smiling, he leaned forward to kiss her on the cheek. "Maybe we can meet up tomorrow when things have died down so I can get it back?"

"I'll call you in the morning," she agreed.

"And I'm really sorry about this—" He nodded at Lewis's slumped and moaning body. "I hope you don't get into too much trouble."

"So do I." She pursed her lips ruefully, already knowing how Green would view this latest turn of events.

With a final wave, Tom took off toward the river. She shook her head at his retreating back. This wasn't exactly how she'd pictured the evening ending: a fight and Tom on the run.

"I'll sue you for this," Lewis groaned as he staggered to his feet, supporting himself against the car. "You and your boyfriend. I'll sue you both."

For one glorious moment, Jennifer seriously considered hitting him again.

CHAPTER THIRTY-TWO

RUE DE CHARENTON, 12TH ARRONDISSEMENT, PARIS

21st April—11:02 P.M.

Dumas had found them this place, a small end-of-terrace house, its render sloughing away like dead skin from the dry brick walls underneath. It overlooked the railway, and the sound of the trains was ever-present, a clanking shriek of metal and sparks that flowed down the broad scar formed by the rusty tracks. From the top floor it was even possible to see the gleaming outline of the Palais de Bercy sports and music arena rising uneasily above the festering streets and leaking chimneys that encircled it, as if it knew it had no right to be there.

"You been scrapping?" Archie grabbed Tom's arm accusingly as he stepped through the front door. Tom glanced at the split on his knuckles where they'd connected with Lewis's unshaven chin.

"Don't start," he muttered. "J-P here?"

"You just try and keep him away." Archie winked, gesturing toward the rear of the house.

They made their way through to the kitchen. A floor plan of the first floor of the Louvre had been pinned to a couple of the pine-effect wall cabinets. Dumas was sitting with his feet up on the chipped melamine table, smoking.

"What happened to coffee back at her place then?" he growled disapprovingly.

"This wasn't about that. Besides we've got work to do."

"Beautiful girl. The city of light . . ." Dumas sniffed. "You wouldn't get far in French politics with an attitude like that."

"I'm trying to play her, not sleep with her."

"Why not do both?" Dumas insisted.

"She's got the briefcase. That's all that matters."

"What did you do? Ask her to look after it for you?"

"Pretty much," said Tom, not yet quite sure how to tell the others about punching Lewis.

"We were just wondering what Milo's take might be on a job like this," Archie mused distractedly.

"Depends how many copies Rafael did for him," said Tom, grateful for the change of subject. "Eighty, a hundred million each?"

"Fuck me!" Archie swore. "That much?"

"The original was insured for a hundred million bucks when it went on loan to the States in 1962," Tom pointed out. "Adjusted for inflation, that's six or seven hundred million today. If you ask me, a hundred million's cheap."

"What about the security set-up?" Archie rinsed a glass, helped himself to some wine and accepted a cigarette from Dumas.

"State of the art, as you'd expect," Tom said with a sigh, holding his own glass out for Dumas to fill. "Getting into the building is easy. The problem's going to be getting close to the painting itself. Even if we go in at night, there are cameras here, here and here—" he pointed out the locations on the floor plan. "With laser trip wires all the way along the Grande Gallerie, not to mention at least ten guards on random patrol patterns."

"And the room where the painting is?" Archie pressed.

"Even worse." Tom tapped the relevant section of the floor plan. "It's been purpose built to house the *Mona Lisa,* and they haven't missed a trick. Two cameras on each door, three on the painting itself." Again, he traced their location on the map. "Titanium gates. All the windows alarmed and bolted. And don't forget the two, maybe even three, armed guards."

"So you're saying that, even if we do get close to it, we'll be trapped as soon as we try to take it off the wall?" Dumas said with a mournful shake of his head.

"Pretty much," Tom agreed.

"That's why Milo will have to make his move when they shift it up to the lab," Archie explained. "All those systems will count for shit once it's off the wall."

"Systems can be fooled. The trick is getting close enough to fool them," Tom observed.

"I can get you close. In fact I can get you within touching distance. But I don't see how that's going to help get it out," Archie said in a cautious tone.

"What do you mean 'close?' "

"The display case."

"What case?" Dumas frowned.

"The *Mona Lisa* sits in a bulletproof plexiglass case," Archie explained.

"A gift from the Japanese when it went on tour to Tokyo in the mid seventies, right?" Tom recalled.

"Yeah, 1974," Archie confirmed. "It's designed to maintain a constant temperature of sixty-eight degrees Fahrenheit and fifty-five percent humidity to stop the wood cracking."

"There'll be an infrared grid around it," Tom said slowly. "And it'll be alarmed and secured to the wall."

"That doesn't sound good," said Dumas.

"It isn't." Archie smiled. "The good news is that the case has a built-in air-conditioning unit. They service it once a year, every year. It takes a couple of hours. You can even book tickets to watch it happen."

"And this is happening tomorrow?" There was a spark of excitement in Tom's voice.

"No," Archie sniffed. "It's not due for a few months."

"Then I don't see . . ."

"The air-conditioning unit is remotely monitored by an outside firm. It's got some fancy internal diagnostic system that tells them when there's a problem. As soon as a fault is detected they get on the blower and arrange to come in."

"What's the response time?"

"Thirty minutes. An hour max."

"And to allow them to work on the unit, the Louvre would have to switch off the alarm systems and let them into the case," Tom guessed. "You're right, it does get us close."

"What about the cameras and the guards?" Dumas reminded them.

"We could cut the video feed." Tom dismissed his objections with a wave of his hand. "And the guards could be distracted, even disabled if necessary."

"Disabled?" Dumas shot him a concerned look.

"Gas. Tranquilizer darts. Don't worry, J-P, I'm not planning to kill anyone. I leave all that to Milo."

"But we still don't have an exit," Archie reminded him.

"We don't need one," Tom smiled. "Because we won't even be inside."

"You've lost me." Dumas, clearly confused, shook his head.

"You and me both," Archie agreed.

"Get me a plan of the sewerage system that runs under the Louvre, and I'll show you exactly what I mean."

CHAPTER THIRTY-THREE

FOUR SEASONS HOTEL GEORGE V, 8TH ARRONDISSEMENT, PARIS

21st April—11:33 P.M.

Jennifer had been on hold for almost fifteen minutes before Green came on. Judging from the delay and the muffled background noise, she guessed that he was on a plane.

"Browne, I've got three minutes so make it quick."

"It's Razi, sir. I'm almost sure of it. He's been buying paintings, making copies and then selling them in the Far East, before reselling the originals through auction houses in Europe and the U.S. He's probably been at it for years."

She ran through the details of the scam as Tom and she had discussed it. The use of certificates of authenticity, the targeting of Japanese buyers, the code of *Omertà* that seemed to blanket the New York dealer community.

Green took a deep breath.

"We're going to have to go through every major Impressionist auction over the past ten years and check it against whatever Razi's bought and sold in that same period." She smiled; like her, he sensed that the net was closing. "There could be millions of dollars at stake here. Hudson and Cole will go nuts."

"But that still leaves Hammon," she continued. "I don't see how he fits."

"Maybe Razi got greedy and Hammon threatened to talk."

"Or maybe it's something else altogether. Something that involves the Louvre accession number we found on that piece of paper in his office."

"I thought you were going to speak to someone there?"

"I had an appointment, but they blew me out. I'll try again tomorrow."

"You should feed all this back to the NYPD. They might have a view." His tone suggested he thought this highly unlikely. "Well done, Browne. It's too bad—"

"There's one other thing, sir," she interrupted. "Lewis."

"What about him?" She sensed his voice harden. He certainly wasn't going to make this any easier for her.

"He's in Paris. He followed me here."

"You've got to be kidding!" Green exploded.

"I wish I was. The problem is . . ."

"You just steer clear of him, you hear?" Green barked. "You don't speak to him, you don't even look at him. If he walks in the room through one door, you walk out through the other. That way there won't be any problem. In fact, I want you on the next flight home, just to be sure."

"It's a bit late."

"A bit late for what? Please tell me you didn't hit the guy again."

"I didn't hit him, sir." She paused, sensing that the conversation had reached its tipping point but knowing that she was too far along now to turn back. "But Tom Kirk did."

"Kirk?" If Green was holding a drink, she guessed from his tone that he'd probably just dropped it in his lap.

"The guy who helped us on the Double Eagle case."

"I know who he is, Browne," he replied icily. "What the hell has he got to do with this?"

"It was a coincidence," she explained, glancing over at Tom's briefcase, which she'd placed on the bed. "I ran into him at the Louvre. We got talking and I thought he might be able to help on the case. We carried on over dinner."

"Dinner! Christ, this just gets worse."

"Lewis was waiting for us when we came out. He picked up where he'd left off in New York. Tom . . . Kirk, I mean, punched him. Knocked him to the ground."

There was a long silence from the other end of the phone. When Green eventually spoke, it was in a strangely calm and measured voice. She'd preferred it when he'd been angry.

"You understand that this doesn't look good, Browne? The optics, I mean."

"Yes, sir, but I've not done anything wrong."

"You think Lewis cares about right or wrong? He just wants a story. And whether you meant to or not, you've given him another headline."

A long silence. Much as she hated to admit it, he was right.

"What do you want me to do?" she asked, her stomach turning over as she sensed all her good work over the past few years slowly unraveling.

"I want you to take that vacation we spoke about the other day. A couple of weeks. Maybe a month. Just long enough for us to calm this whole situation down before it gets totally out of control."

"What about Razi?" There was a hint of desperation in her voice now.

"That's what I was about to tell you." Green's voice was breaking up. "Razi caught a flight to Grand Cayman this morning. Then took the shuttle to Cuba. We're too late for him now." A pause before he added, almost as an afterthought. "I just hope it isn't too late for you."

CHAPTER THIRTY-FOUR

GINZA DISTRICT, TOKYO

22nd April—1:22 P.M.

The edges of the room were wreathed in darkness, the center weakly illuminated by parallel strips of sunken LEDs running down the middle of the ceiling like landing lights on a runway. Leo waited until he was summoned forward, the dining table stretching fifteen, maybe even twenty feet in front of him, a shimmering ebony bridge across the cherrywood floor. The Dobermans, flanks scarred from fighting, eyed him disdainfully from their vantage points on either side of the room's only chair, their silky ears pressed flat against their skulls.

The bald-headed figure seated in the chair glanced up from the shadows at the far end of the table and called him over with a flick of his chopsticks. As usual, he was dressed in a black suit with a crimson lining, black shirt and crisp white tie that seemed to bisect him down the middle like the flash of a sword blade.

The food and plates had been meticulously laid out in front of him, each colorfully glazed dish and bamboo basket a precise distance from the next as per his written instructions and hand-drawn table plan. He was nothing if not a creature of habit and his staff had learned not to disappoint him.

"Takeshi-San," Leo began. "A delivery from America. From New York."

He held out a small white box secured with a black velvet bow.

Takeshi looked up, placed his chopsticks down on their porcelain rest, pressed a crisp napkin to his lips, replaced it in his lap and held his hand out with a click of his long fingers. Holding the box carefully in both hands and bowing deeply, Leo gently placed it on to his palm and then stepped back.

Takeshi looked up at him with a questioning frown, the smooth skin on his forehead creasing, his contracting muscles sending small ripples of movement back along the length of his polished skull like a pond shivering as a fish swims just below its mirrored surface.

"It's cold."

"It came in a refrigerated container," Leo explained.

Takeshi stared at him, his green eyes unblinking and glowing in the gloom like two small lanterns released into the night sky. Leo lowered his gaze, knowing that it would be disrespectful to hold his stare for more than a few seconds.

With a nod, Takeshi unraveled the black bow and removed the lid. Peering inside, his face relaxed into a smile. He picked up his chopsticks, reached into the box and removed a small object that he held up.

For a moment Leo thought it was an oyster or scallop, but a sudden flash of color and the thin web of capillaries coating its glistening surface made him swallow hard. It was an eyeball, the trailing muscle tissue and nerve endings bunched up under it like jellyfish tentacles.

"An eye for an eye. Isn't that the expression?" Takeshi said unsmilingly.

"The art dealer?" Leo guessed.

"The lawyer," Takeshi corrected him. "I gave orders that they be cut out before he died. So he could understand what I see when I look at the pictures he sold me."

"You heard that we found the other one?"

"In Paris, yes," said Takeshi.

"The men are flying there today."

A pause.

"I think I'll go with them."

"Sir?" Leo made no attempt to hide his surprise. Takeshi hadn't been off the 53rd floor of this building in over six years.

"The video's never as good as the real thing."

"No," Leo agreed, still reeling.

"Besides, maybe the trip will do me good."

"Yes."

"We'll take the jet."

"Of course."

Leo turned to leave, but then remembered something.

"Do you want me to get rid of those?" He nodded at the box.

"No need."

Takeshi flicked the eyeball he was holding to the floor in front of the dog to his left. Then he delicately extracted the other one with the chopsticks and tossed it to his right. Both animals watched him unblinkingly, their heads slightly tilted, ears erect, thick fronds of slaver swinging from their jaws.

Takeshi clicked his fingers. The dogs leaped forward, one snuffling flex of their jaws popping each eyeball open like a ripe egg, the watery yolk exploding through the gaps in their creamy teeth.

CHAPTER THIRTY-FIVE

LES ULIS, SUBURBS OF PARIS

22nd April—7:03 A.M.

"Who is it?"

Archie nodded at Tom's phone vibrating noisily on the dash.

Tom glanced at it, then looked away.

"Jennifer. She probably wants to arrange a time to return my briefcase."

"You going to answer it?"

"Not until Henri's spoken to her."

The phone fell silent. Then a few moments later it started ringing again.

"She's persistent," Archie noted.

"Maybe she wants to talk about what happened last night."

"What did happen last night?" Dumas leaned forward in the gap between the two front seats and grabbed Tom's left wrist, examining his knuckles.

"There was a journalist—" Tom snatched his hand away, realizing that he wasn't going to get away without an explanation. "A real low-life. He'd flown here to follow up on some shitty little story he's writing. She was upset. Stupid bastard wouldn't shut up. So I hit him."

"You're my hero, Tom," Archie mimicked a woman's voice and then laughed, Dumas joining in.

He'd never admit it to these two, but he'd really felt for Jennifer as Lewis's barrage of steel-edged questions had bitten into her. He'd wanted to make that startled, lost look on her face go away.

"I think she was more upset than grateful," he argued.

"Not too upset to take the briefcase," Dumas pointed out. "You must have cooked up a hell of a good story." He winked.

"You're actually enjoying this, aren't you?"

"Why, aren't you?" Dumas fired back.

"Jennifer's a good person. Who knows, in another life the two of us . . . I just don't like using her like this."

"It was your idea," Dumas reminded him.

"I know. That just makes it worse," Tom said glumly.

"Break it up, girls, I think we're on."

Archie pointed excitedly toward the man opening the gates to the low-slung warehouse on the other side of the road. A sign to the left of the main door indicated that this was the head office of Lacombe et Fils, the firm responsible for maintaining the *Mona Lisa*'s air-conditioning unit.

"You got a signal here?" Tom nodded at the laptop balancing on Archie's knees.

"Seems okay."

Tom and Dumas got out of the car and made their way through the gates into the courtyard. Some tires had been stacked precariously in the far corner, next to an old motorbike that had been stripped for parts until only its rusty skeleton remained. A blue Renault van was parked on the other side of the cobbled area, the firm's name and phone number emblazoned down the side.

The reception was deserted. Two low plastic chairs flanked an empty watercooler. Posters illustrating half-naked women draped awkwardly over air filters and air-conditioning power plants adorned the drab and peeling walls.

"Anybody home?" Dumas called in French, before pinching his thumb and forefinger together, placing them against his lower lip and giving a sharp whistle.

"Can I help?" A man appeared, wiping his hands on his trousers, the sound of flushing water echoing behind him.

"Who are you?" Dumas barked.

"Marcel Dutroux." The man frowned.

"Dutroux. Marcel." Dumas made a show of carefully writing the name down. "My name is Alain Gueneau. This is my colleague Marc Berger. We'd like to talk to the duty manager about a matter of national security." He flashed him an out-of-date secret service badge that he had dug out of one of his drawers at home.

"Th-that's me," the man stammered, pushing his glasses up the bridge of his nose. "I'm the only one here until eight."

"Excellent." Dumas gave him a tight smile. "Dutroux, we have reason to believe that terrorists may be planning to use air-conditioning units to spread poison gas through government buildings."

Tom suppressed a smile. Dumas was well aware that there was nothing like the T-word to grab people's attention. Besides, unfortunately, these days it wasn't quite as fanciful an idea as it might once have been.

"Poison gas?" Dutroux's eyes bulged.

"That's right. We understand that you have maintenance contracts with a number of government agencies and organizations. We need to know exactly what measures you have in place to safeguard against someone tampering with your units."

"Of course." Dutroux nodded furiously. "Follow me."

He lifted the counter and then ushered them through into the back office. The overhead strip-lights flickered on, revealing an open-plan room with twelve desks arranged in three pods of four. One of them was garlanded with cards and balloons, perhaps indicating a recent birthday.

"All our units are remotely monitored here—" Dutroux indicated one of the workstations which, unlike the others, was free of clutter. "Any unauthorized tampering would automatically get flagged on the system and then trigger a site visit."

"Show me," Dumas ordered.

With a nod, Dutroux entered the password and unlocked the machine.

"Here, you see—" he pointed at the screen. "Every unit we manage . . ."

As Dutroux launched into a detailed explanation of how the system worked, Tom quietly stepped away and approached the large whiteboard that had been screwed to the far wall. It showed the various jobs for the week and which team had been allocated to each. He studied it quickly, making a mental note of a couple of the itineraries and roughly where each vehicle could be expected when.

"Berger, you okay to wait here for a few minutes?" Dumas called from across the room. "Monsieur Dutroux has offered to give me a quick tour of the facility."

"Sure," Tom called back.

Dutroux ushered Dumas out of the room toward the warehouse, still loyally expounding the virtues of his company's system. Tom waited until their footsteps had faded, then ran over to the computer they had just been consulting. Dutroux had sensibly gone to the trouble of locking it, although this was a slightly redundant precaution given that Tom had been able to read his password over his shoulder as he had typed it in. He grabbed a CD from his pocket. Loading it into the computer, he located the program it contained and then ran it, his eyes flicking nervously to the door, mindful of the risk of Dutroux returning at any moment. A few agonizingly long minutes later, his phone rang.

"Archie? Can you see it?"

"Yeah. It's just popped up now."

"The password's 'Belmondo.' "

Tom heard the sound of approaching voices. There was silence from Archie.

"Come on," Tom urged.

A door squeaked open and then slammed shut, their footsteps perilously close now.

"Archie!"

"I'm in. Go!"

Grabbing the CD out of the tray, Tom locked the screen again and sprinted over to a Pirelli calendar which he was staring at intently by the time Dumas and Dutroux walked back in.

"Ready?" Dumas arched his eyebrows into a question.

"Just about," Tom nodded, slipping the CD into the back pocket of his jeans.

"Monsieur Dutroux, you have been extremely helpful." Dumas shook his hand enthusiastically. "I commend you for your vigilance. On behalf of France, thank you."

For a moment, Dutroux looked like he might pass out with pride.

CHAPTER THIRTY-SIX

FOUR SEASONS HOTEL GEORGE V, 8TH ARRONDISSEMENT, PARIS

22nd April—8:21 A.M.

Jennifer stepped out of the elevator and turned toward the Le Cinq restaurant. Her discussion with Green had led to a fitful night's sleep. A proper breakfast and plenty of coffee was her only chance of surviving the day in one piece; certainly of making her flight home.

"Mademoiselle Browne?"

A voice called over from one of the chairs arranged in front of the reception desk and a man stood up.

Jennifer looked over and smiled in recognition.

"Monsieur Besson."

If Besson's surfwear had looked slightly inappropriate when she had seen him yesterday, then here, amidst the glistening chandeliers, ornate ormolu clocks and hand-polished marble floors, it verged on the offensive. That certainly seemed to be the opinion of the concierge, who was eyeing him with unconcealed disdain.

"Is everything okay?" she asked with a frown.

"I'm sorry to bother you here . . ." He seemed strangely agitated, compared to the last time they'd met. Or rather one half of his face appeared agitated; the other remained as impassive and inscrutable as ever.

"Is there somewhere we can talk?" He glanced furtively at the concierge.

"Yes, of course." She led him away from the front desk to a sofa positioned squarely underneath a gaudy tapestry of the Annunciation. "What is it?"

"Your number, the Louvre accession number you showed me."

"What about it?"

"Did you ever find out what it was?"

"I had an appointment to see someone at the Louvre yesterday," Jennifer replied. "They had to cancel. I was going to call them when I got back to the States."

"You're going home?" He sounded surprised.

"I have a flight this afternoon."

"Then I'm glad I caught you."

"You've found out what the number is?" she guessed, sitting forward in anticipation.

"I called in a favor," he said, glancing nervously around the lobby. "Someone who has access to the Louvre's cataloguing system. And . . ." His voice petered out, as if he was unsure whether he should continue.

"And?" she encouraged him.

"And it seems that what you gave me is the accession number for the *Mona Lisa*."

"The *Mona Lisa*?" She shook her head in disbelief.

"By Leonardo da Vinci."

"I know what the *Mona Lisa* is," she said curtly, a little riled that Besson had mistaken her astonishment for ignorance. Then again, most Europeans seemed to assume that American appreciation of foreign culture didn't extend far beyond Mexican food and Cuban cigars. "I'm just surprised."

"To be honest, so was I." Besson gave an excited cough. "Can I ask where you came across it?"

"You can ask, but I'm afraid I can't tell you."

"No, of course," he said hurriedly. "Anyway, I thought it best not to leave a note at reception." He snatched another apprehensive look at the glowering concierge.

"You did the right thing. I really appreciate you coming over."

"My pleasure, Mademoiselle Browne." They stood up and shook hands. "Good luck with your case."

Jennifer slumped back on to the sofa, alone with her thoughts, as Besson shuffled toward the entrance, the concierge ushering him outside with a contemptuous glare. Why would Hammon have been sent the *Mona Lisa*'s accession number? What did the $100 million refer to? The *Mona Lisa*? Was someone offering to sell the *Mona Lisa* to him? That made no sense at all. The *Mona Lisa* was safely in the Louvre. How could you sell something you didn't have? Unless . . .

She paused, struck by a sudden, terrible thought. A thought that she dismissed almost as soon as it occurred to her. No. Surely not? Even he would never dare . . .

But she had to be certain.

She raced across the lobby and into the elevator, leaping out on the fourth floor and letting herself into her room. Tom's leather briefcase was in the wardrobe where she'd placed it the previous night. She snatched it up and set it on the bed, her mind racing, hating what she was thinking but unable to stop herself.

What had Tom been doing at the Louvre yesterday? What had been on that piece of paper he had been studying so intently and then guiltily hidden away? Why was he being so evasive and vague about what he was up to in Paris? What had prompted that rather strange discussion about what she would do if she found he was involved in a job? Why had he really taken off last night the moment someone had mentioned the police?

And most pertinently, as she gazed down at it, what was prompting him to carry this briefcase around with him all the time, clutching it to his side like a child grasping a favorite toy?

This last question, at least, was one she could answer now.

She removed a safety pin from the complimentary sewing kit provided by the hotel, opened it and then trapped it in the minibar door until she had bent it into a small hook. Inserting it into the lock, she carefully moved it around until she felt it catch against the mechanism. With a flick of her wrist, the lock clicked open.

The briefcase contained a thick sheaf of paper which she removed. As she examined each one in turn, she felt herself being gripped by a growing sense of disbelief and horror. A list of the Louvre guards, their ages and addresses. A schematic of the main alarm system. The layout of the underground service tunnels and sewers. The location of all the cameras and their cycle times.

It's not possible, she said to herself. There must be another explanation, another reason why Tom had these. But however hard she tried to discount what she was seeing, each new document removed another barrowful of earth from under the crumbling wall of Tom's presumed innocence.

So much so that, when it came, the final document was almost something of a relief, the exhaustion of resisting wave after wave of marauding attacks finally replaced by a surge of instinctive anger as the final ramparts of his honesty came crashing down. It was a blank page with a single number on it. A number she recognized instantly.

The *Mona Lisa*'s accession number.

CHAPTER THIRTY-SEVEN

RUE CHRISTINE, 6TH ARRONDISSEMENT, PARIS

22nd April—11:37 A.M.

The one-way street was blocked by a car, hazard lights blinking. The van slowed to a halt, its driver sounding his horn impatiently.

"What's going on?" a muffled voice called from behind him.

"Some idiot's double-parked," the driver yelled back, craning his head through the open window. "Come on!" he shouted, the horn again echoing down the narrow street.

Still, the car didn't move, although the engine appeared to be running.

"Michel?" He smacked the leg of the man snoozing to his right, who woke with a start. "Go and tell that moron to move his damned car. I've got better things to do than sit here all day."

"That won't be necessary," said Tom, appearing at the open window, a gun in his hand. "Out. Both of you."

Their eyes bulging, the two men slipped and stumbled out of the driver's side door, their eyes locked on the squat barrel aimed at their chests. Archie, meanwhile, opened the passenger door and climbed in. Ahead of them, Dumas turned the car's hazard lights off and eased away.

His gun concealed in his coat pocket, Tom led the men around to the rear of the van. A small queue of traffic had already built up behind them.

"If you say a word, I'll kill you," Tom hissed, waving apologetically at the waiting cars to indicate that they would shortly be moving on. Tom had no intention of shooting anyone, of course. In fact the gun wasn't even loaded. But for this to work, they needed to believe he might.

"Get in," he ordered.

They did as they were told, surprising a third person who appeared to be in the middle of an early lunch.

"What's this?" he mumbled, his mouth full.

"Shut up," said Tom as he climbed in after them and pulled the door shut. "Get over there," he directed, waving the gun in the direction of the bench that ran down the right-hand side of the van. "Let's go," he shouted, banging the roof and swaying gently as the van pulled away.

"What do you want?" one of the men asked fearfully.

"We don't carry any cash in the van," another cautioned. "Everything's on account."

"Your clothes," Tom said with a smile. "We just want your clothes."

CHAPTER THIRTY-EIGHT

POMPIDOU CENTER, 4TH ARRONDISSEMENT, PARIS

22nd April—12:20 P.M.

A narrow slice of the Pompidou Center was framed between the two gray buildings ahead of Jennifer, the childishly bright reds, greens and blues making it seem unreal, almost cartoonish. It was only as she drew closer that she could see that the colors defined an erupting, tangled mass of pipes and escalators—the structure's veins and arteries—all encased in a white, skeletal frame. It was almost as if the building had been turned in on itself, like a glove.

The piazza in front of the main entrance was still relatively quiet, a small crowd having formed around a fire-eater, a couple of kids practicing skateboarding tricks alongside the ever-present caricature artists and hair-braiders.

She made her way up the escalators to the second floor and then paused on the landing, wondering if she might be able to see Tom arriving and, if so, whether he was alone. Sure enough, about five minutes later, Tom stepped out of a blue van that had pulled up just off the piazza.

"Can I borrow that for a second?" she asked the tourist standing next to her. "Police business."

With a puzzled frown, the man lifted his camera off his

neck and handed it to her. Adjusting the telephoto, she zoomed in first on the van, making a mental note of the name painted on its side. Then she panned across and saw Tom make his way into an adjacent toyshop, emerging a few minutes later with a small bag that he tossed to the driver. Her eyes narrowed as she recognized the man behind the wheel. Archie. So Tom had lied about him not being in Paris too.

Gritting her teeth in anger, she handed the camera back to the bewildered tourist and made her way up to the viewing platform on the top floor. From there she could make out the squat mass of Notre Dame, the delicate spider's web of the Eiffel Tower and, between them, the gilded dome of Les Invalides. It was there, little more than a year ago, that Tom had repaid her faith in him by saving her life. How misguided that faith seemed now.

"Sorry I'm late."

Tom stepped off the escalator.

"No problem."

"And I'm sorry about last night too." He gave an embarrassed shrug. "I guess I lost my temper."

"Is this what you came for?"

She held out his briefcase, her face unsmiling, her voice hard.

"Yeah." He reached for it, smiling gratefully, but as he went to take it, she pulled it away.

"What's going on, Tom?"

"What do you mean?"

"I've opened it." She pointed at him accusingly. "I know what you're planning."

He snatched it off her angrily.

"You had no right . . ."

"The Louvre? The *Mona Lisa*? Are you fucking insane?"

"Keep your bloody voice down," Tom hissed, grabbing her by the elbow and steering her toward a deserted part of the viewing platform.

"You said you were out," she said, wrenching her arm free.

"It's not that simple," he insisted.

"You're planning to steal the *Mona Lisa*. That sounds pretty simple to me."

"I've got no choice. I tried to warn the Louvre, but they didn't believe me."

"Warn them about what?"

"That someone else is planning to take it. A thief called Milo. I'm going to stop him."

"You mean you're going to steal it instead?"

"I'm going to give it back."

"Oh please." She rolled her eyes and gave a sarcastic laugh. "You really expect me to buy that? You and Archie are back in the game, aren't you? That's why he's here with you. All that bullshit about giving up, about never being tempted. You were just telling me what I wanted to hear. You've got it all worked out."

"Milo's kidnapped someone. A girl called Eva. A friend of mine." There was a desperate edge to Tom's voice now. 'I don't care about the painting. I just need it as a bargaining chip. Milo's planning to go in tonight. I've got to make my move first. If I don't, he'll kill her."

Jennifer shook her head, drilling him with a disbelieving look.

"You lied to me, Tom."

"Only because I knew what you'd say," he pleaded. "I knew you'd try and stop me."

"You're damn right I'm going to stop you."

"Why does everything have to be so black and white with you?" he countered angrily.

"Not black and white: right or wrong."

"The right thing is to do what I can to save Eva. The right thing is to trust me."

"How the hell do you expect me to do that after this?"

"That's something you're going to have to figure out for yourself," Tom shot back. "Just don't get in my way."

Jennifer's eyes blazed as Tom retreated down the escalator. The funny thing was that even now, angry as she was, despite everything she'd seen, a small part of her wanted to believe him. But it was hard to overlook the documents in his briefcase or the piece of paper in Hammon's office that looked for all the world like an offer to sell the *Mona Lisa*.

And harder still to believe that Tom, despite all his protests, could ever really change who or what he was.

CHAPTER THIRTY-NINE

RICHELIEU WING, MUSÉE DU LOUVRE, PARIS

22nd April—4:02 P.M.

"Can I help you?" the security guard challenged them as they approached through the main works entrance.

"We're from the architects." Milo held out two fake badges and a forged letter from the firm responsible for the renovation project currently underway in this section of the Louvre. "Apparently they're thinking of changing the entire Phase Two design. We need to rework all our measurements. As if we didn't have enough on our plate!"

The guard studied the documents carefully, then nodded at the site foreman who was slouched over his paper, Gauloise in hand, to indicate they checked out.

"I'm on a break. You know your way around?" he asked hopefully.

"Straight up and don't get too close to the edge," said Eva. "Don't worry, we know the drill."

"Just watch out for the bird shit," the foreman warned them with a grin. "It's like a bloody ice-rink up there."

A bright yellow elevator had been temporarily erected up the front of the building to ferry people and supplies between the floors. Stepping into it, Milo shut the safety gate behind them and then hit the button for the roof.

"Can you see us?" he radioed a few moments later as they stepped on to the gently sloping galvanized zinc surface under a video camera's watchful gaze.

"Yeah, I got you," Axel radioed back. "Love the hard hats."

"Ready?" Milo asked Eva.

She stretched up and kissed him.

"Ready." She smiled.

"Let's go."

They set off, Axel killing the feed for a few seconds until they reached the base of a large chimney that he had identified as being concealed from both the camera they were running away from and the one they were running toward.

"We're there," Milo panted.

"Okay. First camera's back up. Next one's down. Go."

Guided by Axel's barked instructions, they repeated this process six or seven times, sprinting in zig-zagging bursts from one camera blind spot to another, until they eventually reached the top of the elevator shaft on the other side of the building.

"You're clear," Axel reassured them. "Security have just radioed through a possible electrical fault. But no one saw you."

They stripped off their civilian clothes to reveal the black combat fatigues and bulletproof vests that they had been wearing underneath. Then they armed themselves with weapons, ammunition and night-vision goggles. Finally they packed everything they weren't now wearing or carrying back into their packs. The less clues they left for the police to work on, the better.

Milo approached the steel door that opened into the top of the elevator shaft and sprung it open.

"Now what?" Axel radioed uncertainly as first Milo, then Eva, stepped inside.

"Now we wait."

CHAPTER FORTY

CONTROL ROOM, BASEMENT, DENON WING,
MUSÉE DU LOUVRE, PARIS
22nd April—4:32 P.M.

She had to admit it was an impressive set-up. Camera feeds from all over the museum displayed on a wall of monitors, eight across and five high. Six full-time operators in constant radio contact with hundreds of security personnel. A detailed schematic of the entire complex that showed the status of all the security devices on each floor. A bank of computers to control lighting, heating, the elevators, and the doors. Little, if anything, had been left to chance. She swallowed hard. Tom had no idea what he was up against.

"You did the right thing," Cécile Levy, standing to her left, reassured her with a smile.

Jennifer nodded but said nothing. If she was doing the right thing, why did it feel so wrong?

She glanced at the other people in the room, the lack of windows and dimmed lighting dappling their features with a thin gauze of shadow. As well as Levy she had been introduced to Philippe Troussard, the museum's head of security, Antoine Ledoux, the Museum Director and Serge Ferrat, the police liaison officer who was coordinating the extra cover that had been drafted in to help.

She herself had been introduced as a special agent from the FBI. As far as she knew, this was still an accurate title, despite the previous evening's conversation with Green. Not that she'd been able to confirm this with him, as he'd proved strangely elusive all day. In the end she had been forced to dictate a message to a switchboard operator up at Quantico, detailing what she had discovered and the steps she was proposing to take.

"I still don't understand how they think they're going to get away with this," Ledoux sniffed.

He was at least sixty, Jennifer guessed, although he had done what he could to make himself appear younger by cropping his thinning white hair and opting for a pair of bright red rectangular-framed glasses that matched his socks. His black suit, too, was an ultra-fashionable cut, a dark gray shirt and tie combination making it difficult to see where one item of clothing ended and the next began. But there was no disguising the loose skin on the back of his hands or the fissures that lined his cheeks like the cracked mud of a river that had run dry, despite the pale glow of bronze foundation which had left scuff marks on his collar.

"You say you saw this man Kirk in a Lacombe van, Agent Browne?" he continued. "But they're not due here for months. I don't see how that will help him."

As if on cue, a small section of the museum displayed on the wall flashed yellow and a warning message popped up on one of the computer screens.

"There's a fault with the air-conditioning unit inside the case," Troussard breathed, staring incredulously at the screen and then glancing up at the others. "He must have hacked into Lacombe's system."

Jennifer shook her head and allowed herself a grudging smile. Tom's ingenuity was impressive if nothing else.

One of the phones in the control room rang. Troussard nodded at the operative on his right to answer it.

"Contrôle . . . Oui on l'a vu aussi . . . Vingt minutes?" He looked questioningly at Troussard who nodded. *"Okay. Je previendrai les gars en bas de vous attendre."*

"They'll have someone here in twenty minutes," Troussard

explained for her benefit, although that was probably the one part of the conversation she had understood.

"He must have patched into the phone system to make that call." Ferrat, a short, grossly overweight man with a curly mass of lacquered black hair that had an almost synthetic sheen, gave a firm nod. "Clever. But nothing to worry about." He sketched a grand sweep with his pudgy hand. "I've got fifty armed men positioned around the building. Another thirty in reserve who can be deployed in forty-five seconds. Once he's in, he won't be getting out." He beamed confidently, his small eyes bulging like a bullfrog's, a ruff of loose skin spilling over his collar.

"We're not worried," sniffed Troussard, his tone suggesting that, far from being reassured by Ferrat's presence, he rather resented it. Then again, the look he had given Jennifer when she had been introduced suggested that he resented anyone straying into his territory. "If your men fail to deal with him, we have our own contingency plan."

"Oh, they'll deal with him," Ferrat huffed, fiddling with the silver buttons on his uniform so that they all pointed the same way up. "They'll deal with all of them."

"What contingency plan?" Jennifer queried.

"Hopefully, we won't need it," said Troussard curtly, refusing to volunteer anything further.

Ten, then twenty minutes went by, filled mainly by false sightings of Tom wandering around the museum and an animated account by Ledoux of the previous, successful attempt on the *Mona Lisa* by Valfierno's gang in 1911. Eventually, however, Troussard jabbed his finger triumphantly against the screen.

"Here they come."

It was the same van that Jennifer had seen Tom get out of earlier, or at least it looked the same: dark blue with white lettering down the side. She followed it as it made its way down the road that ran between the Louvre and the Seine, disappearing off the left-hand edge of one screen only to reappear on the right-hand side of the one below as another camera picked it up.

As it drew closer, Jennifer was filled with a growing sense

of dread. She had been so sure of herself earlier; that she was doing the right thing; that Tom had left her no choice. But now, with the van drawing inexorably closer, the faces next to her straining hungrily toward the screen like a pack of hyenas circling a wounded gazelle, the doubts she had previously so deliberately ignored came crashing against the crumbling cliff of her conscience.

Rightly or wrongly, she'd delivered Tom straight into a trap. And now it was too late to do anything about it. Too late to do anything other than watch as the animals prepared to feast.

CHAPTER FORTY-ONE

22nd April—4:49 P.M.

They've stopped," Ledoux pointed at the screen. The van had pulled up about two hundred yards short of where it should have turned into the museum.

Troussard stepped closer, frowning.

"What are they doing?"

"Checking their equipment?" Ledoux suggested.

"Maybe." He sounded unconvinced.

"What do we do?" Asked Levy.

"We wait." Ferrat was firm. "Whatever they're doing, it won't last long. Besides, so far all they've done is steal a van. They need to be inside before we can arrest them."

The minutes ticked by. Five, then ten. Still no movement. Nothing apart from the occasional sway of the van as the traffic swooshed past.

"*C'est ridicule*," Ledoux spluttered, removing his glasses, furiously polishing them on the end of his tie, and then jabbing them back on to his nose. "How long are we going to stand here? We need to do something."

"Not while they're in that van, we don't," Ferrat countered.

Jennifer stared at the screen, her lips pursed as she pondered what Tom was playing at. She knew him. He never left anything to chance. If he'd stopped there, it was for a reason. The question was what? She ran back through their discussion that morning to see if there had been any clue there. She thought back to their dinner the previous evening. She tried to picture what she'd seen in his briefcase—alarm systems, floor plans, maps.

"Oh my God!" she exclaimed as one map in particular suddenly leaped to the front of her mind. "They're not in the van."

"Of course they're in the van," Ferrat snorted. "We've been watching them the whole time."

"They're in the sewers," she insisted, "He had a map showing the layout of all the sewers under the museum. I saw it."

"The sewers lead right inside the building," Ledoux said fearfully.

"I'm going up," Troussard announced.

"I'll come with you," said Jennifer, falling in behind him.

He punched the exit switch and the door slid open. She could hear Ferrat frantically radioing for back-up as the door closed behind them. They sprinted up the stairs and into one of the large internal courtyards. Two police vans gunned past them as they ran out onto the street through a set of heavy iron gates and slewed to a halt on either side of the blue van, blocking its path in both directions. Eight armed men jumped out of each one, their sub-machine guns drawn. They wore the blue uniform of the CRS, the French riot police, and full body armor.

Jennifer and Troussard held back. Ferrat suddenly appeared at her shoulder, gasping for breath as he signaled for the men to move in. The first team threw the front doors open, jabbing their guns inside the cabin. It was empty. Simultaneously the second team wrenched the rear doors apart, two men jumping inside with a shout. A few moments passed. Then three men, bound at the wrists and naked except for their socks and underwear, emerged blinking into the sunlight, visibly terrified.

"Is that them?" Ferrat turned hopefully to Jennifer, chest heaving, all his buttons askew.

"No." She shook her head, a grim expression on her face. "I expect you'll find they work for the air-conditioning company."

"Then where are they?" Troussard sounded slightly hysterical.

Ferrat led them over to the rear of the van and they all climbed inside.

"Look," he pointed.

A neat hole had been cut in the vehicle's floor. Peering through it, Jennifer was able to make out the gaping throat of an open manhole and a rudimentary ladder that disappeared into the gloom. For a second, she was sure she could hear the echo of Tom's laughter.

"Where do these come up?" Jennifer asked.

"Everywhere." Ferrat sounded panic stricken.

"So he could be inside?"

"You heard what Ledoux said."

"You don't know where he is, do you?" Troussard hissed. "So much for taking care of things. So much for not worrying."

"He's in the sewers, not the museum," Ferrat countered.

"You had your chance," Troussard insisted. "Now it's my turn."

He snatched Ferrat's radio out of his hand. Jennifer recognized the voices on the other end as first Levy and then Ledoux, but wasn't able to follow what they were saying. A sullen-looking Ferrat chipped in once or twice, but mostly he was silent. Tom's ruse had clearly taken him by surprise.

"Come on." With a satisfied nod, Troussard jumped down from the van and turned toward the museum.

"What's going on?" Jennifer demanded.

"Contingency plan," he explained over his shoulder as they ran back through the gate into the inner courtyard. "We have a secure facility just north of Paris. The security protocol calls for the painting to be evacuated if we can no longer guarantee its safety on site."

In her haste to follow Troussard out on to the street, Jennifer hadn't noticed the convoy of vehicles in the courtyard, their engines running. Two police motorcycles were followed by a police van, its sliding side doors jammed open to reveal two officers squatting inside wearing helmets and bulletproof vests, hefting their machine guns. Then came a gleaming white Brinks armored lorry, followed by another police van and two more motorcycles bringing up the rear. Given the situation, it was a reassuring sight.

The doors at the top of the curved staircase that led down into the courtyard suddenly flew open. Ten or so armed policemen ran out and took up defensive positions, scanning the rooftops and the windows around them. Seemingly happy that the coast was clear, two men carrying a flat metal box were waved forward. They made their way carefully down the stairs and toward the back of the van. As they approached it, the rear door opened and they handed the box over.

The door slammed shut and the convoy roared into life. Engines racing, sirens blaring, lights flashing, it shot through the gate and out on to the street.

"There," Troussard breathed a sigh of relief as the noise retreated into the distance. "He can't get to her now."

CHAPTER FORTY-TWO

DENON WING, MUSÉE DU LOUVRE, PARIS

22nd April—5:09 P.M.

"We've got a problem."

Milo pressed his hand to his ear, the noise of the elevator mechanism above him making it hard to hear what Axel was saying.

"What sort of a problem?"

"They've opened the case. They're moving it."

"They're early."

"They're not early," Axel explained, panic in his voice. "This is something else. There are cops everywhere. Fuck knows where they've come from. The whole wing's been shut down. There's some sort of armed convoy in the courtyard below. They've locked the painting in a metal container. It looks like they're transferring it somewhere."

"*Putain de merde*," Milo swore.

"They're on to us," Eva, sitting opposite him at the top of the elevator shaft, whispered anxiously.

"No," Milo snarled. "It's Kirk. He's panicked them into moving it."

"They're taking it down the stairs," Axel relayed what was happening in real time. "Out the door . . . it's inside the armored van . . . they're leaving."

"Captain, you picking this up? Where's the helicopter?"

"It can be there in two minutes, *mon colonel*," Djoulou's voice crackled over the radio. "Can you make it back up on to the roof?"

"I don't want it for us. I want it following that convoy. I need to know where they're headed."

"What about you?"

Milo paused as he considered their options.

"We could go back the way we came," Eva suggested. "Across the roof and back down the service elevator."

"Not enough time," he said with a shake of his head. "We need to get down on to the street, fast. The quickest way is straight down and out through the courtyard."

"You're right," she agreed.

"Captain, we're going to fall back to the side entrance," Milo radioed through to Djoulou. "Meet us there in three."

"Roger," Djoulou confirmed.

Milo pulled his mask down on to his face and then looked up at Eva.

"Ready?"

She leaned across and kissed him before cocking her gun and pulling her own mask down.

"Let's go."

Pushing off from the ledge where they had been perching, they rappelled noiselessly down the shaft, landing with a gentle thud on the elevator's roof. With Eva positioned to take out anyone inside, Milo flipped the trapdoor open. The cabin was empty. They jumped down and then pressed the button for the ground floor.

The doors pinged open. Two cops were standing with their back to them. Eva took out the one on the left with two shots in the back. Milo dropped his partner to the marble floor with a single shot to the head as he turned toward them, his mouth gaping in surprise.

"Blow the charges," Milo ordered.

Above them they heard the dull boom of two explosions as Eva set off the detonators. The building shook, and was then swallowed up by the shrill call of the fire alarm.

"This way!" Eva threw open the door to the courtyard.

There were fifteen or twenty people gathered there, but they scattered like startled fish as Milo opened fire indiscriminately to clear a path across the courtyard toward the gate.

"How the hell did they get here so quickly?" Milo snarled as the CRS out on the main street, alerted by the shooting, took cover behind a van and began returning fire, stone chips shattering off the doorway where they had taken shelter.

"Grenade!" Eva warned as she stepped out and fired one into the nearest CRS van. It exploded on impact, launching the gray vehicle into the air on an angry fist of flame, scattering bodies across the street.

A powerful car burst through the pall of smoke and fire, its tires tracing a broad black arc on the tarmac as it skidded to a halt alongside them. The doors flew open.

"Get in," Djoulou screamed.

They both dived inside and the car screeched away, Eva smashing the rear window with the butt of her weapon and providing a murderous volley of covering fire.

"Where's the convoy?" Milo barked, ripping the mask off his face.

"About two miles ahead."

"And the men?"

"On their way."

"Good. I want that van stopped. Nothing's changed. In fact, this should make things even easier."

CHAPTER FORTY-THREE

INTERNAL COURTYARD, DENON WING,
MUSÉE DU LOUVRE, PARIS
22nd April—5:12 P.M.

You hurt?" Jennifer helped Troussard to his feet, wiping the dirt from her hands and knees where she had dived for cover behind the staircase's stone balustrade.

"I don't think so." He was shaking, his face blanched with fear. Blood was dripping from a deep gash on his forehead.

Jennifer glanced around at the incongruously hellish scene amidst the Louvre's serene splendor, her ears still ringing from the sound of the gunshots. At least five people were dead, their bodies twisted into strange, inhuman shapes, the ancient cobbles spattered with blood. Perhaps another seven or eight were badly injured, their low moans and shrieks of pain combining with the muffled sound of sirens and the persistent scream of the fire alarm into an anguished symphony.

This wasn't Tom's work, surely. Not the Tom she'd known. A thief, yes. A criminal, undeniably. But not someone who would fire indiscriminately into a crowd of people. Not a killer. Not unless he'd changed far beyond anything she'd ever suspected.

"*Mon Dieu*, the paintings!" Troussard gave a pained cry at

the sight of flames surging from one of the upstairs windows and licking the stonework. "I need to help."

"You need to get yourself stitched up." Jennifer grabbed Troussard's arm and steered him roughly toward what she assumed was the sound of approaching ambulances and police cars. "That's a bad cut and . . ."

She tripped, cursing loudly as she lost her balance and landed heavily on her hands and knees. She struggled to her feet and looked to see where she had caught her foot. It was a raised manhole cover. Or rather, a manhole cover that had been lifted and not replaced properly.

The sight gave her a sudden, terrible thought.

"I need to see the video footage again," she ordered Troussard.

"What?"

"The video footage," she repeated. Troussard looked at her blankly, his eyes wide and staring. He was in shock. "Sit here." She eased him to the ground and pressed his head between his knees. "Wait for some help."

She sprinted to the other side of the courtyard and made her way downstairs. The control room looked as if it had been ravaged by a violent tropical storm; the digital floorplan was flashing like lightning, alarms thundering, tempers boiling over as people ran this way and that like ships that had been ripped from their moorings and carried out to sea. Levy was cowering in the corner, her face in her hands, crying. In the center of the room stood Ledoux, a look of utter panic etched on to his face. Still and silent, he was at the eye of the hurricane that was raging around him.

Jennifer fought her way through the swirling gale of people and grabbed him by the arm.

"I need to see the tapes."

"What?" he shouted over the noise.

"The courtyard where the convoy was. I need to see the tapes."

"Why?"

"Because I think Kirk may be on that van."

He eyed her blankly for a few seconds and then with a nod led her to the bank of video screens.

"Bring up the internal courtyard," he ordered the operator. The sudden energy in his voice suggested that he welcomed the opportunity to focus on anything other than what was happening outside.

"When from?"

"When did the convoy get here?" Jennifer asked.

"About an hour after you," Ferrat answered breathlessly, having rejoined them. "What's going on?"

"She thinks Kirk may have been in the armored van," Ledoux explained, his eyebrows raised skeptically.

"Impossible," Ferrat snorted.

"Play it back," Jennifer instructed the operator. With a nod, he brought up the footage of the courtyard from just before the convoy arrived. She stepped forward and studied the picture.

"Stop. Can you zoom in here?"

He nodded and focused on the manhole cover she had tripped over. A few seconds later it disappeared from view as the police vehicles and armored van parked up next to the steps.

"We need to see the other side," she said impatiently.

"This is the only angle of the courtyard we have," he explained.

"Then roll forward to just after the convoy left and show me that same shot again."

He forwarded the tape, stopping it just as the vehicles moved off. This time when he zoomed in, however, the manhole cover was raised at one end. It had been moved.

She turned to face the two men, a resigned look on her face.

"That manhole is no more than ten feet from where the convoy was parked. Kirk must have let himself into the sewers, come up into the courtyard and crawled under the armored car."

"What are you saying?" Ledoux shook his head, confused.

"I'm saying that if you don't get the *Mona Lisa* off that van now, you'll never see her again."

CHAPTER FORTY-FOUR

RUE DE RIVOLI, 1ST ARRONDISSEMENT, PARIS

22nd April—5:12 P.M.

Tom wasn't sure when the idea had first occurred to him. Perhaps when he had realized that his only real chance of stealing the *Mona Lisa* was to somehow get it beyond the safety of the Louvre's protective walls. Or when he had read through the security protocols that had been included with the files Rafael had left him, indicating the circumstances in which the painting might be evacuated from the museum. Or, more likely, when he'd caught sight of Jennifer at the Louvre and conceived that the museum staff were far more likely to listen to her than to him.

Not that he was feeling particularly pleased with himself at the moment. Not when he was suspended from the bottom of an armored van in a makeshift cradle that swayed wildly every time it went around a corner, the road surface barely a foot beneath him and his ears ringing with the whine and mewl of sirens and screeching tires.

Of course he'd always known that getting close to the van itself would be relatively easy. The sewers below the Louvre, which were rarely patrolled, led directly from the manhole outside up into the courtyard, with only a few padlocked gates to tackle on the way. The convoy had stopped predictably close to the steps, and no more than ten or so feet from the closest of the three or four manholes that dotted the cobbled area. He'd had to pick his moment, of course, but luckily all the vehicles were parked so close together that once he'd managed to slip under the police escort vehicle nearest to him, it had been simple enough to crawl forward until he was under the armored van.

His first task, once he had secured himself in place, had been to patch into the van's internal CCTV system. According to Archie, who had identified Brinks as the Louvre's primary contractor for this type of operation, this could be located via a small maintenance hatch about three feet in front of the right rear wheel arch. As Archie had predicted, the tamper-proof sensor had been pretty rudimentary, and within a few minutes Tom's pocket-size video display was simultaneously relaying pictures from inside the van and recording the footage. As usual, it had a three-man crew—two in the front and one in the rear.

The vehicle itself was based on a Mercedes chassis and had been custom built for Brinks by Labock Technologies. Engineered to BR6 protection levels, it had been equipped with bulletproof glass, gun ports and a computer-controlled entry system complemented by pneumatic doors.

And yet despite this rather formidable pedigree, it had, according to Archie, an Achilles heel. For reasons of weight and cost and the belief that no one could possibly be so stupid as to even try, the underside of the vehicle had not been fully armor plated. At one point in particular, not only was the metal a mere three inches thick, but nothing mechanical or electrical lay between the underside of the floor and the inside. This was something they could work to their advantage.

Tom checked his watch, a vintage Panerai Marina Militare. He didn't have much time. Reaching for his drill, he carefully made a small hole up through the van's floor, the sound masked by the noise of the engine and the hand towel he'd wrapped around the housing. As he approached the red tape he'd fixed to the drill to indicate the precise thickness of the metal, he slowed the chuck speed down. A few seconds later, he felt the tip nudge through.

He paused, waiting for the van to slow or for an angry shout from above as the hole was discovered. But none came, and the image on his small screen showed the guard in the back reading a newspaper and sipping coffee from a thermos flask. He breathed a sigh of relief. So far so good.

With a flick of a switch on his video display, he replaced the live feed being broadcast into the front compartment with a continuous loop of the previous few minutes' footage that he had just recorded. Now only he could see what was really happening in the rear of the van.

He reached for a small bottle of compressed gas, inserted the nozzle into the hole and turned it on. It took a couple of seconds, the guard's eyes drooping first, then his head sagging on to his chest and his newspaper fluttering to the floor as the gas took effect.

With a smile, Tom jammed the radio and the phone connections.

CHAPTER FORTY-FIVE

CONTROL ROOM, DENON WING, MUSÉE DU LOUVRE,

PARIS

22nd April—5:18 P.M.

Ferrat and Ledoux stared at her blankly, and Jennifer realized that, after what had just happened, they were going to need a proper explanation.

"He's fooled us. Me more than anyone."

"What do you mean?"

"It was a set-up. He acted suspiciously so I would start asking questions. He gave me his briefcase, guessing that I'd go through it. He allowed me to see him stepping out of that van, knowing I'd see the name of the air-con company. He even admitted what he was planning, trusting that I'd come here and tell you everything and that you'd believe me."

"He knew you'd betray him?" Ferrat frowned in surprise.

"He was counting on it," she said, frustration at her own naivete tempered only by her growing anger with Tom. He'd used her. From the moment they'd met outside the Louvre, he'd played her. She felt almost dizzy as the past few days rearranged themselves in her mind, as all her bearings were suddenly swept away. "He was counting on me believing that he was going to break in here and steal the *Mona Lisa*. He was counting on me telling you."

"You mean he wasn't planning to steal it?" Ledoux looked confused, the foundation coating his face cracking under the stress of the past few hours.

"Oh, he was planning to take it, just not from here. The whole time all he really wanted was to scare you into moving the painting to a different location. He must have known about your contingency plan, about the armored convoy. He knew you would listen to me. He must think he's got more chance out there than he has in here."

"Then what do you think we should do?" Ledoux looked first to Jennifer, then Ferrat, who shrugged helplessly.

"Get the convoy to turn around and come back here," Jennifer suggested. "The Louvre is the safest place for it."

With a nod of agreement from Ferrat, Ledoux crossed to the radio. He tried it once, twice, then looked up, his jaw clenched.

"I can't get through."

CHAPTER FORTY-SIX

PORTE MAILLOT, 16TH ARRONDISSEMENT, PARIS

22nd April—5:18 P.M.

There was only one way inside the van—through the floor. Fine in theory, since the carbide-tipped hardened steel blade of his small circular saw was capable of cutting through six-inch steel plate in less than twelve seconds, while the van's floor was only three inches thick at his point of entry. Slightly more tricky in practice.

Quite apart from the difficulty of safely manipulating a saw underneath a moving vehicle, there was the constant risk of the sparks being seen as they sprayed to the ground. Not to mention, of course, the danger of being heard, the blade shrieking like a deranged cat as it clawed away at the metal.

The solution to the sparks had been to seal a small hammock-like structure of fire-resistant material around the area where he was cutting to capture the glowing shards before they fell to the ground. It wasn't perfect, but so far it seemed to be holding up well. As for the noise, here Tom was trusting in the meaty whine of the van's diesel engine and the armor plating to soundproof his activity.

His eyes smarting from the exhaust, his throat burning with the tang of hot oil, and his arms aching from holding them over his head, it took ten precious minutes to fashion a hole big enough to fit though. It felt much longer.

He pushed the section of floor he'd cut free back into the van and placed his arms inside. Then, using his elbows, he levered his head and shoulders through the gap. The gas had cleared but the guard was still slumped in the seat to his right. A series of lockers lined the left-hand wall.

Tom inched along the cradle, hauling himself in until he was able to sit up. Then he leaned forward and swung his legs out and behind him so that he was lying on his stomach. Finally he pulled himself forward, his feet momentarily catching on the road before he gratefully snatched them away and lifted them inside. He rolled on to his back, gasping, the sweat stinging his eyes and soaking his clothes. A year out of the game had clearly taken its toll on his fitness, although his time away had sharpened his enjoyment of the sharp punch of adrenaline that was coursing through him like electricity.

He checked his watch again. The Louvre's secure facility was located near St. Germain in northwestern Paris, a journey of twenty-five to thirty minutes at most when you didn't have to worry about traffic or stopping at the lights. That gave him less than fifteen minutes to locate the painting and get out.

He scrambled over to the guard and unclipped the key ring from his belt. The slim metal case was in the third locker he tried. He slid it out and placed it gently on the floor. It was secured by an electronic lock operated by a standard numerical keypad. Reaching into one of his pockets, he extracted a small device and clicked it into place over the number pad. Flicking it on, he pressed a button and immediately the LED display on the box lit up as the device began to test every combination between 0000 and 9999. In this case, at least, Tom mused as the numbers scrolled across the screen, there was no danger of the box spraying purple dye over its contents if it was tampered with, as would happen with a cash shipment.

It stopped sooner than he'd expected, the box unlocking with a muffled click. Tom smiled as he saw the number flashing on the display: 1519. The year of da Vinci's death. He probably could have guessed it if he'd tried. He placed his hand on the box, took a deep breath, and carefully opened the lid.

There she was. The *Mona Lisa. La Joconde. La Gioconda.* Gazing up at him with a curious, vulnerable smile. He wondered how many people over the years had been alone with her as he was now. Unchaperoned, free to gaze, even to touch. Not many. Not recently, at any rate. She seemed even more delicate and petite now than she had in the Louvre and Tom was almost afraid to lift her.

"Don't worry," he whispered. "I'm here to help."

He unstrapped the small padded container that he had been wearing across his chest and ripped open the Velcro seals. It didn't have the climate controls of this specially designed transportation box, but Tom wasn't planning on going far. He removed his outer gloves, revealing another clean white pair that he was wearing underneath. Then, he delicately lifted the painting out of the metal box and placed it in the padded container.

Pausing only to place a small black object inside the metal box, he shut its lid, removed his electronic opening device and then scrambled the code. Checking that it was securely locked, he slid it back inside the locker and then fastened the door, replacing the keys on the guard's belt.

The van suddenly braked, throwing Tom off his feet and almost through the hole in the floor, the road beneath him a dizzying blur of stained concrete. He struggled to his feet with a worried frown as they slowed to a halt, his left wrist throbbing where he'd taken the brunt of the fall. What was going on? They had to be at least three miles from where he had planned to jump out. Had they hit traffic?

Then he heard the unmistakable sound of gunfire.

CHAPTER FORTY-SEVEN

ST. CLOUD, NORTHERN PARIS

22nd April—5:34 P.M.

There it is!" Djoulou, sweat beading his brow, pointed at the convoy ahead of them as it bulldozed through the early-evening traffic, cars leaping out of its way as if they'd been stung.

"We need to get ahead of them," Eva urged.

"There's a tunnel up ahead." Milo pointed calmly at the sat-nav display. "Get the chopper to land on the other side. We'll come up behind and trap them."

"You want them to land on a road?" Djoulou gave him a questioning look.

"Is that a problem?"

The tunnel entrance reared up ahead of them like the barrels of a shotgun, two wide openings that burrowed deep into the side of the steeply rising hill. Djoulou radioed the helicopter tracking them overhead. A few moments later it broke to the right and swooped out of view.

"Now let's even up the odds—" Milo pointed at the two outriders bringing up the rear of the convoy.

With a nod, Djoulou stamped on the gas, the car lurching forward as it bore down on the motorcyclists. As they drew level, one of the policemen caught sight of them and ordered them back with an angry wave of his hand. Grinning sadistically, Djoulou jerked the wheel, sending the car swerving across the carriageway and sweeping both motorcyclists into the central reservation.

"*Bravo, Capitaine*!" Milo grunted his approval as the bikes disappeared behind them in a jagged cartwheel of metal, sparks and flailing limbs.

A few moments later they swept inside the tunnel, the rumble of the engines and the hum of the tires echoing around them, a growling bass note overlaid by the rhythmic rise and fall of the siren's harsh treble in the distance.

"Get closer," Milo ordered as the tunnel's orange lights flashed hypnotically past, "The exit's not far."

"The traffic's slowing," Eva pointed out. "They must have landed."

The roof of the tunnel suddenly glowed red as if a fire had been lit at the far end, the glow advancing in a steady ripple toward them as the cars ahead applied their brakes, like a field of corn bending under a sudden gust of wind.

"Get past them," Milo instructed.

Djoulou obediently carved across on to the hard shoulder, fizzing past the slowing cars. Ahead they could see the semicircular outline of the tunnel exit and, silhouetted against it, the helicopter parked across the opening, its rotors still shredding the air.

They arrived just as the convoy came to a halt. Milo opened fire, catching both lead motorcyclists before they knew what had hit them. Eva meanwhile took out the driver of the first police van with a well-aimed burst that had him dancing in his seat as if he'd been electrocuted.

Milo rolled out of the door and took up a position behind the hood of a small Renault. The woman inside screamed at the sight of his gun and, rather pointlessly, wound up her window.

"Get down," Milo shouted. It wasn't that he minded hitting civilians. He just didn't want them getting in the way. Eva and Djoulou threw themselves next to him.

A van pulled up alongside them and disgorged the rest of

Milo's men. The five remaining policemen jumped down and fired toward them as they too ran for shelter.

"Spread out and move in," Milo ordered. "Drive them toward the helicopter."

CHAPTER FORTY-EIGHT

22nd April—5:37 P.M.

The tunnel's access hatch was no more than five feet away, but with the sound of spent cartridges pinging off the tarmac around Tom and tiles shattering overhead, it seemed like fifty. So much for Archie engineering a temporary stop at a secluded point where he would be able to slip unobtrusively into the trees. Anyway, five yards or fifty, all he knew was that he needed to get as far away from this van as he could before Milo cracked it open. Assuming it was Milo, of course. But then, who else could it be?

With a deep breath, he crawled out from under the van and scrambled over to the hatch. Yanking it open, he rolled inside and pulled it shut behind him with relief. He found himself in a central service corridor that ran between the two main tunnels. It was dimly lit by an intermittent series of sodium lights that stretched into the distance, their orange glow revealing a damp floor and calcified concrete walls.

Rather than turn right toward the nearest exit, however, Tom set off toward the door at the far end of the tunnel, the narrow walls amplifying the sound of his breathing, his feet splashing through long stretches of standing water. He wanted to get as far away from Milo and his men as he could.

A few minutes later there was a muffled boom, the ground

shuddering underfoot. He guessed that they must have blown open the back of the van. For a fleeting moment he allowed himself to picture Milo's reaction on opening the case and seeing the little gift he'd left him. It would almost have been worth the risk of staying behind to see that.

The tunnel ended at a solid metal door fitted with a bolt encased in glass that was, according to the sign above it, only to be broken in an emergency. As far as Tom was concerned, this qualified on several counts. He shattered the glass with his elbow and then threw back the bolt, the door swinging open. But before he could step outside, a shot rang out and a bullet buried itself in the wall just a few feet to his left.

He immediately guessed that someone must have seen him escape into the tunnel and followed him. Judging from their rangy stride, they were tall and clearly prepared to shoot first and forget the questions altogether. Right now, that was all Tom needed or wanted to know.

He dived outside, slamming the door behind him. To his left the traffic had already backed up for nearly a mile behind the carnage at the far end of the tunnel, but to his right it was still flowing smoothly. Tom vaulted the crash barrier and carefully picked his moment to sprint across to the far side of the road, cars and trucks marking his stuttering progress across the lanes by angrily sounding their horns as they flew past.

Behind him the door crashed open and his pursuer tumbled out. The gunman took aim, but thankfully the traffic seemed to be moving too fast to give him a clear shot. Cursing, he holstered his weapon and set off toward Tom, negotiating one lane, then a second.

Tom waited until the man was almost halfway across the road before calling out to him. The gunman looked up, momentarily confused, perhaps worried that Tom might also be armed. It was only a slight hesitation but it was enough for a small car to appear out of the tunnel's darkness and plow into him with a futile squeal of its brakes.

Tom turned away so that he didn't have to watch the man be catapulted through the air only to have his back broken when he landed under the wheels of another car.

CHAPTER FORTY-NINE

22nd April—5:37 P.M.

Djoulou turned to his expectant men and gave them a series of punched hand signals. With a nod, they split into pairs and then fanned out in a wide semi-circle. Using the civilian cars as shelter, they moved forward in a classic cover-and-shoot formation, firing in accurate short, controlled bursts. Several people screamed. Most huddled, terrified, in the foot-wells of their cars as the bullets pinged and fizzed around them, the tunnel echoing with the sharp crack of gunfire, the shriek of broken glass and the crash of shredded metal.

The police fired back and for a few minutes it even seemed that they had gained the initiative. One of Milo's men was caught in the neck and sent spinning to the ground, blood arcing through the air. Another writhed, screaming, his knee-cap shattered, until a comrade hauled him to safety.

But outnumbered and outgunned, it was only a question of when, not if, the police would admit defeat. Eventually, with three of their colleagues dead and surrounded on all sides, the two survivors threw down their weapons and lay flat on their stomachs. Milo's men rose slowly out of the smoking wreck-age and in seconds the two men had been frisked and cuffed, face down.

"Status?" Milo barked, holstering his weapon.

"One dead, two injured," Djoulou replied.

"Three injured," Eva corrected him, her arm limp, blood dripping from her fingers.

"You okay?" Milo eyed her with concern.

"Fine." She nodded, seeming more annoyed with herself than anything. "It's a flesh wound."

"Schmidt's gone after someone he saw escaping down the service tunnel," Djoulou informed them.

"Get him back here," Milo insisted impatiently. "Whoever it is, we don't need them."

Milo stepped over one of the dead policemen toward the front of the armored car. The driver and his colleague were still sitting in the front cabin, their faces clenched with fear behind the bullet-chipped and debris-strewn glass.

"Open the door," Milo ordered.

They shook their heads—small, nervous, barely noticeable movements.

"Open it up, or we'll execute them," Milo insisted, his tone ice cold.

Eva stood over one of the surviving policemen and cocked her gun. The two guards glanced at each other and then shrugged helplessly.

"Eva," Milo called.

She emptied two shots into the back of the policeman's skull, his face disintegrating onto the road.

"Open the door," Milo blazed as Eva hauled the remaining policeman to his feet. She pressed her gun to his temple, the muzzle branding his skin with a faint fizz of burning flesh that made him yell out.

"We can't," a voice, distorted by a loudspeaker, rang out. "We've tripped the safe mode. It can only be opened by a supervisor back at the depot."

"We'll see about that," Milo breathed through clenched teeth. "Djoulou?"

With a nod, Djoulou stepped around to the rear of the truck and placed several small charges against the hinges and lock area. Then he ran back and handed the detonator to Milo, who had taken cover with Eva and the rest of the men behind a small truck.

Milo pressed the switch. There was a massive flash and then a deafening boom as the armored car lurched into the air. A burning hot wind washed over them, followed by a thick curtain of smoke that slowly cleared to leave the cloying smell of hot metal and melted rubber.

"You think it's all right?" Eva asked anxiously as she followed Milo to the rear of the van. Both rear doors were hanging off their hinges.

"These cabinets are bomb-proof," Milo reassured her as he stepped up into the van and forced the first locker open, eventually finding the metal box he was looking for in the third one he tried. "Here we go."

He kicked what remained of the guard who had been inside the van out of the way and then laid the box down on the floor.

"They cycle the code between dates that have something to do with da Vinci or the painting," he explained with a smile. "This week, it's 1519—the year he died."

He keyed in the numbers and the lock clicked open.

"The police backup is on its way. We need to be out of here in sixty seconds," Djoulou warned them.

"Don't rush me," Milo retorted. "I've waited too long for this."

"What's that?" Eva pointed with a frown.

"That's . . . that's not possible," Milo half whispered, his eyes widening as he saw the small hole that had been cut in the van's floor. He suddenly realized that he was too late.

He threw the lid back. The container was empty. Empty apart from a small black cat.

"Kirk!" he screamed, grabbing the stuffed toy. In the intermittent flash of the blue lights on top of the bullet-riddled police van, it almost seemed to be winking at him.

CHAPTER FIFTY

RUE DE CHARENTON, 12TH ARRONDISSEMENT, PARIS

22nd April—10:55 P.M.

"Who wants another drink?"

Archie had a wild, exultant look on his face that Tom hadn't seen since he'd pulled a straight on the river card at a poker game a few years before.

"Fill her up," Dumas ordered, thrusting his glass under the whiskey bottle. Holding it there until it overflowed, he then downed half of it as Archie cheered him on. Tom smiled—he could see it was going to be a long night.

"Tom, mate?" Archie turned to face him expectantly. "You in?"

"All the way." Tom held his chipped mug out, Archie and Dumas having laid claim to the only two glasses in the house.

"Cheers." Archie clinked the bottle against the mug and then stood up unsteadily on a chair. "Here's to us," he slurred, his gestures increasingly expansive and uncoordinated. "Here's to Tom and a job bloody well done. One of his best. Perhaps the best ever."

"Here's to Rafael." Tom raised his mug, but his heart wasn't in it. It wasn't that he wasn't pleased with how things had gone. It was just that this was all for nothing unless they got Eva back. Because he'd made a promise. Because he hadn't forgotten that she knew something about his father; something he was determined to hear. "Here's to Eva."

"Look. We're famous!" Dumas tugged on Archie's leg and pointed at the television.

The program had been interrupted by a news flash. Even though the volume was turned down, the headlines across the bottom of the screen told the grim statistics of the day—twelve dead, twenty injured, twin explosions at the Louvre, a gun-battle with police in a tunnel outside Paris, the assailants still at large.

"Turn it up," Tom said.

The newsreader handed over to a reporter at the scene. The picture switched to footage of the inside of the tunnel. Shattered glass and blood on the road, emerald blankets over bodies, a disco-beat of blue lights reflecting off the tunnel roof, the scorched wreckage of the Brinks armored van, the twisted shell of a burned-out civilian car caught up in the explosion. Interestingly though, Tom noted, no mention of the *Mona Lisa*. Not yet, at least. That would come when they'd worked out their story. Covered whatever expensively clothed backsides needed protecting.

"Tom?"

Besson called him over from the doorway, his face troubled, a white lab coat worn over his Hawaiian shirt and shorts.

"Where have you been?" Tom jumped down from the worktop.

"Can we talk?" Besson's right eye twitched nervously.

"What's up?" Tom frowned. It wasn't like Besson to pass up on a drink.

"It's better if I show you," he insisted in a low voice.

"Sure," Tom nodded.

He followed him upstairs into the front room. The *Mona Lisa* was in a large Perspex box and Tom crouched down to peer at it, half anxious, half disbelieving, like a new father gazing at a premature baby in an incubator. She was really there, safe and well, her smile serene now and at peace.

On the other side of the room, Besson had assembled a

small makeshift lab complete with a portable X-ray machine and electronic testing devices.

"You said you only wanted to take a quick look at it," Tom reminded him, surprised by the amount of equipment crowded into the small room. "Not run a full set of tests."

"This is a once-in-a-lifetime opportunity," Besson insisted. "You'll thank me later."

"Not if you damage it, I won't."

"It wouldn't matter if I did." Besson shook his head, an apprehensive look in his eyes. "It's not the real painting."

"What do you mean, it's not real?" Tom laughed. "They took it straight down from the Salle des Etats to the armored van."

"Oh no, it's the *Mona Lisa*," Besson reassured him. "At least, the *Mona Lisa* as we have come to know it. See here—" he put his glasses on and indicated some close-up photos of the lower half of the portrait, his finger circling a small area where the surface of the paint was very faintly different from the rest. "This is where it was restored following the acid attack in 1956. And this here is from when a Bolivian student threw a rock at it later that same year."

"Then what are you saying?" The amusement in Tom's voice had been replaced by a growing sense of concern. If Besson was kidding around, he wasn't getting the joke.

"Look at these . . ." Besson's initial apprehensiveness seemed now to have given way to a nervous energy as he shuffled over to an upturned box on which he'd arranged more photos. "I took some X-rays."

Tom studied the images that Besson thrust eagerly into his hands, the *Mona Lisa*'s rich, sensuous colors reduced to clinical, monochromatic shades of gray and black, her eyes cold and dead. He looked up, puzzled. If there was something there, he certainly couldn't see it.

"Is this meant to be telling me something?"

"Nothing!" Besson exclaimed triumphantly. "It's telling you nothing. That's exactly my point. There's nothing there, apart from the painting itself."

"Well, what else would there be?"

"Da Vinci was very experimental in his approach. He

would sketch out initial designs, move things around, add in a detail one day only to take it away the next. X-rays of his work show evidence of this underpainting. But this painting has none."

"What does that prove?" Tom challenged him. "Maybe he didn't need any for the *Mona Lisa*."

"Then it would be the only work he ever painted where he didn't," Besson scoffed. "Besides, that's not the only problem. There's the pigments too."

"The pigments?" Tom's head was spinning.

"I ran some TXRF tests . . ." Besson was barely able to contain himself now, the words tumbling out of his mouth. "I found trace elements of Prussian Blue."

"And that's bad?"

"Very bad." Besson nodded emphatically. "Prussian Blue wasn't invented until 1725."

"But that's two hundred years after da Vinci died."

"Exactly." Besson's face and tone neatly reflected both his excitement at what he had discovered and his fear at its implications.

"So what are you saying? That it's a fake?"

"It depends what you mean by fake. This is the same painting that has hung in the Louvre for at least the last two hundred years. This is the *Mona Lisa* that we have all come to know and admire . . ." he paused. "But it wasn't painted by Leonardo da Vinci."

PART III

This way for the sorrowful city,
This way for eternal suffering,
This way to join the lost . . .
Abandon all hope, you who enter

DANTE, *The Divine Comedy*
(Inferno III.i)

CHAPTER FIFTY-ONE

HOTEL CLICHY, 17TH ARRONDISSEMENT, PARIS

23rd April—7:32 A.M.

Leigh Lewis wedged the phone against his shoulder and dialed room service. He let it ring, one minute, then two, gingerly exercising his bruised jaw, before stabbing the hook switch angrily and dialing reception.

He had only been out of the States once before. Well, twice if you included Niagara Falls for his honeymoon, which he didn't. Canada didn't count.

He remembered it well. It had been London in the fall of 1977. A two-week holiday with his girlfriend of the time who was crazy about the Sex Pistols and, by extension, anything else British. When the Pistols split up after a final performance at the San Francisco Winterland Ballroom in 1978, she had told him tearfully that rock and roll had died that night. Personally, he'd been happy to see them go. The relationship had fizzled out soon after Sid murdered Nancy that fateful night in the Hotel Chelsea.

He hadn't enjoyed the trip. Sure Big Ben and Buckingham Palace had been swell. He'd ridden in a bright red double-decker bus, had his photo taken with a real "Bobby" and seen the punks loitering along the King's Road. But it had rained non-stop, their B&B had been small and dirty, and the food—

and this was what he couldn't forgive or forget—had been shit.

Not that Paris was shaping up much better. Browne had given him the run-around yesterday, and so far all he had to show for his trouble was a bruised face, a couple of blurred photos and a hangover.

As for his hotel, it was in the middle of the red-light district. His tiny airless room had one window which gave on to a dingy alleyway that the local prostitutes used for sex and tramps for pissing in. Needless to say, there was no air-con, forcing him into an impossible choice between the stench and intermittent groaning from the street below or sweating through the unseasonably warm nights. The paper was picking up the tab, of course, but that was hardly the point. It was no excuse for the hot water running out by eight in the morning or food not being served after nine at night. It was certainly no excuse for his phone calls going un-answered when all he wanted was a goddammed cup of coffee.

He slammed the phone down and pulled on a pair of jeans and a Georgetown sweatshirt—his cousin's son had left it at his place a few summers ago. Grabbing his key, he marched out into the hall as fast as his bad hip would let him, and made his way down the staircase, the carpet rough and covered in invisible bits of dirt under his bare feet.

"What the hell kind of operation are you clowns running here?" he raged as he rounded the corner that led to the small ground-floor reception area. "I've been trying . . ." He tailed off. There was no one there. Nor was there anyone in the small, chaotic office that lay beyond the reception desk. The switchboard was flashing on about six lines. Where the hell was everyone?

Frowning, he retraced his steps to the foot of the staircase and paused. A door at the end of the passage ahead of him was ajar, the flicker of a television and the faint hum of voices seeping from within.

He nudged the door open and found himself in what he guessed, from the battered lockers and overflowing ashtrays, was the staff room. A small TV set had been fixed high on the far wall and gazing up at it, open-mouthed, were the receptionist, bellboy, chef and kitchen porter. They had also, judging from the way they were dressed, been joined by a couple of the girls who worked the neighboring strip of sidewalk.

His curiosity stifling his indignation, Lewis stepped into the room. On the screen above him he could make out a reporter standing in front of the Louvre's glass pyramid.

"What's happened?" he asked no one in particular, the few words of Spanish that he relied on to get his shirts laundered of little use now.

The receptionist looked up at him with mild surprise and then shrugged helplessly, his English clearly not up to the task either.

"*La Joconde*—the *Mona Lisa*," one of the hookers explained in a thick accent without looking round, "she's been stolen." The girl standing next to her nodded mournfully and Lewis thought he could see a tear running down her cheek.

"Stolen? When?"

"Yesterday afternoon. But the police only announced it a few hours ago."

"Who do they think took it?"

"Him—" The girl pointed with a thin, ring-encrusted finger.

Lewis snatched his eyes back to the screen, and flinched at the grainy image staring back at him.

"Him?" he choked. "Are you sure?"

"*Oui*," said the girl, a hint of anger in her voice.

Lewis didn't wait to hear any more. Sprinting back out into the corridor, he took the stairs two at a time, the pain from his hip all but forgotten. Pausing breathlessly outside his room to unlock the door, his key skated nervously across the surface of the lock before finally sliding home. He flung the door open and leaped over to the bed, kneeling next to it. Brushing the discarded whiskey miniatures and soiled tissues to one side, he feverishly spread out the pile of black-and-white photographs on the floor with both hands so that he could see them all.

"There—" He snatched one up triumphantly. "I knew it!"

This was pure gold; the break-through story he'd always

dreamed of. The *New York Times.* The *Washington Post.* He'd have his pick of them all. He switched his phone on and dialed without even listening to his waiting messages.

"Editorial," a voice chirped.

"Marcie, it's Leigh. You're still there. Good."

"Leigh, where the fuck have you been?" the voice barked. "We've been leaving messages all over for you. The biggest story since Jesus breaks and the only guy we have in Paris goes fucking AWOL . . ." A pause. "Are you sober?"

"Relax, Marcie, I'm already on it," Lewis reassured her. "In fact, I'm all over it."

"Why, what have you got?" She didn't sound convinced.

"Oh, nothing much," Lewis said nonchalantly, holding the photo up with a smile. "Just a shot of the prime suspect kissing Special Agent Jennifer Browne the night before the heist. Let's see the Bureau try and shake this one off."

"Leigh," she breathed, "I think I love you."

CHAPTER FIFTY-TWO

RUE DE CHARENTON, 12TH ARRONDISSEMENT, PARIS

23rd April—8:42 A.M.

Archie's rasping voice, the overspill of ash on the floral tablecloth and the two empty bottles of Laphroaig were the only reminders of the previous evening's interrupted celebrations. Besson's discovery had instantly derailed the party atmosphere.

Not that Tom was entirely sure what it was he had discovered. After all, how was it possible that the painting the Louvre had carefully nurtured all these years was a forgery? Hadn't they known?

"Is that the best shot of your ugly mug they could get?" Archie sniffed as Tom's face filled the TV screen yet again. He had flipped the chair around and was sitting with his arms folded and resting on the chair back.

"Copied it from the Louvre security cameras, I expect," Tom yawned, having slept only fitfully. "To be honest, I'm surprised they waited until this morning before putting it out." He swung the window open to let some air in and try and wake himself up.

"It's taken until now to circulate it to every policeman, soldier, border guard, ticket inspector and check-in clerk they can get their hands on," Dumas explained, swilling some whiskey dregs around a glass, hesitating, and then putting it down with a pained grimace. "Until we give the painting back, you need to stay out of sight."

"We're not giving anything back until we've got Eva," Tom reminded him sharply.

"Are you sure it's still Eva you're worried about?" Dumas asked.

"What do you mean?"

"I'm just wondering if this is really about you and Milo? About not letting him win?"

Tom snorted dismissively. "No. And even if it was, what does it matter as long as we get her back?"

"It matters because the painting isn't a toy for you and him to fight over," Dumas insisted. "I won't let anything happen to it."

"You think all this is a game?" Tom squared up to Dumas unsmilingly.

"You two were always fighting when you worked for me," Dumas retorted, eyeing him defiantly. "Nothing changed after you both left. Why should it be any different now?"

Besson interrupted them with a cough.

"I want to take the painting back to my place and run some more tests there."

"Fine."

Tom sat down with an angry shrug. The truth was he didn't want Milo to win. Wouldn't let him win. But surely that didn't make saving Eva any less important or mean that they should just give up?

"Take J-P with you, since he's so worried about looking after it. And don't forget the *Yarnwinder*."

"I'm almost finished," Besson reassured him.

Tom's phone rang. He gave a wry smile and then answered it.

"Are you calling to congratulate me?"

"We need to talk," Milo countered, his voice cold and businesslike. "Top of the Arc de Triomphe. You and me. Ten a.m."

He rang off.

"We got a meet?" Archie went to light a cigarette, found

that the pack was empty and crumpled it into a ball in disgust.

"Just the two of us."

"How did he sound?"

"Annoyed." Tom grinned.

CHAPTER FIFTY-THREE

FOUQUET'S, 8TH ARRONDISSEMENT, PARIS

23rd April—8:50 A.M.

"Do you mind if I join you?"

Jennifer looked up from her paper, squinting into the sun despite her sunglasses.

"Commissaire Ferrat?" Her tone registered her surprise. "I thought we'd said midday?"

"We did."

He sat down at her table and ordered an espresso. His small brown eyes looked sore and tired. Two men were leaning against the hood of the unmarked car parked opposite, watching them carefully. Ferrat's escort, she guessed.

"What are they saying?"

He nodded at the selection of late-edition English-language newspapers that Jennifer had scattered in front of her and on the chair to her left. Each was emblazoned with a shouted headline: *Mona Lisa Missing; Da Vinci Masterpiece Snatched; La Gioconda Stolen—Again.*

Invariably, this was followed by five to six full pages of detailed coverage with pictures of the painting and the carnage in the tunnel. A train crash in the Punjab killing two hundred people and a suicide bombing at a primary school in the Middle East had been relegated to the seventh and eighth pages respectively.

"They're saying that you're heading up the investigation." She smiled. "Congratulations."

"For now." He took a deep breath and placed his hat on the table, arranging it so that the badge was square on to him. "Twelve dead. *La Joconde* missing. The Louvre bombed. A gun battle on the streets of Paris . . ." He paused, as if suddenly struck by the enormity of the previous day's events. "A case like this demands results. Immediate results. Or . . . *Bonjour Madame Guillotine.*" He brought the edge of one hand down on to the open palm of the other in a chopping motion.

"Is that why you're here now?"

"I'm just here to talk."

"Then I need to call the Embassy."

She had, of course, been expecting to be interviewed. How could she not? After all, she was the one who had tipped them off about Tom in the first place. It was just that she had agreed with the duty officer at the Embassy not to speak to anyone without having one of the staff lawyers there with her. Then again, the duty officer had agreed to get Green to call her, and that hadn't happened yet either.

"This isn't a formal interview, just a . . . conversation between colleagues," Ferrat reassured her. "It's all off the record."

"Nothing's ever off the record," she observed dryly.

"Well, I'm not writing anything down and it's just you and me." A pause, while he polished his hat's shiny peak with his fingertip. "It's up to you, but it would help."

Jennifer gave a deep sigh. She already felt bad enough about what had happened yesterday, without Ferrat spooning on the guilt.

"The papers said there was a hole in the bottom of the armored van. Is that right?"

"There was a hole, yes," he confirmed.

"And yet the doors were blown off as well? Doesn't that strike you as strange?"

"You have a theory?"

"Tom mentioned someone else. A thief called Milo. He said that he was only taking the painting to stop Milo getting to it first."

"We know Milo and we know what he's capable of," Ferrat confirmed. "What's your point?"

"My point? Two thieves. Two jobs. One comes up underneath, the other blows the doors off."

"It's possible." Ferrat nodded, Jennifer guessing from his expression that this was a scenario that he had already considered.

"I know Tom. There's no way he was behind what happened at the Louvre or in that tunnel. There must have been someone else involved."

"I've got a forensic team working every centimeter of both crime scenes. If either of them were there, we'll know about it."

"The question is, who got to the painting first?"

"That's one question," he agreed, his eyes meeting hers. "The other involves you."

"Me?"

"You know Kirk, don't you?"

"Yes, of course."

"How did you meet?"

She shook her head. "I'm sorry, but that's classified." Even off the record, she wasn't prepared to go into the details of how she had met Tom on the Double Eagle case. Not without permission.

"You are friends." It was a statement.

"No," she insisted, the sting of Tom's betrayal still smarting.

"No?"

"Once, maybe," she relented. "More acquaintances now."

"And yet you had dinner with him just two nights ago?"

Ferrat had clearly done his homework and she wasn't sure she liked the way the conversation was heading, or the slight hardening of his tone. She knew that she needed to tread carefully.

"I already told you—" she kept her voice level and matter-of-fact—"we bumped into each other. He offered to help with my case. We hadn't seen each other for a while. I suggested dinner to talk things over. I didn't know that he was setting me up."

A pause.

"Do you know someone called Leigh Lewis?"

She crossed her arms and sat back in her chair. This was hardly shaping up to be the gentle conversation Ferrat had promised and she certainly wasn't fooled by his casual tone and the way he was picking invisible hairs from his uniform as if barely listening.

"You know I do."

"He called my office this morning. He certainly has an interesting perspective on your relationship with Kirk."

"I don't have a relationship with Kirk," she shot back. "And Lewis is a liar who'll say anything for a story."

"He claims to have photographs of you . . . kissing Kirk."

"Kissing!" She snorted. "If he thinks that's a kiss he's got more problems than I thought. We were just saying good-bye. Nothing more. What you need to understand about Lewis is that he always makes things look worse than they are. That's his job."

"And what you need to understand, Agent Browne," Ferrat sighed, locking eyes with her, "is that, the more I hear, the worse it looks. We've circulated a description of both Kirk and Milo, but so far all I know for certain is that a man fitting Kirk's description hijacked a van belonging to an air-conditioning company. A van that was later used to gain entry to an inner courtyard of the Louvre. A courtyard where, thanks to your intervention, an emergency convoy was preparing to remove *La Joconde* to safety, should the need arise. And that need arose. Now, with the painting missing, I find that you and Kirk had dinner the evening before the robbery, with photographs suggesting that you were, shall we say, more than just acquaintances. Do you want me to go on?"

"Not until I call the Embassy." Jennifer's face hardened, her eyes never having once left his. "We can continue this *conversation between colleagues* when they have sent someone over."

"Excellent idea." Ferrat waved his two men over to the table. "Why don't you tell them to meet us at the station."

"The station?"

Ferrat slid a pair of handcuffs across the table toward her, the left cuff framing the *Mona Lisa*'s troubled smile as she gazed out from the newspaper. Ferrat's men appeared at Jennifer's sides, blocking any possible escape.

"Jennifer Browne," Ferrat intoned, "I am arresting you on suspicion of complicity in the theft of *La Joconde*."

CHAPTER FIFTY-FOUR

ARC DE TRIOMPHE, PARIS

23rd April—9:58 A.M.

There was a Napoleon quote that Tom vaguely remembered, something about the sublime being only a few steps from the ridiculous. Nowhere was that sentiment more appropriate than here.

The Arc de Triomphe was, after all, a magnificent structure. Standing square and squat, like a gorilla resting on its knuckles, it had a daunting, brooding presence. It spoke of victories carved out on distant battlefields, of the thunder of hooves and marching feet, of the intoxicating opium of absolute power, of blood and sacrifice. And at its heart, sheltering under the sharp snap and tumble of a giant tricolor, the tomb of the Unknown Soldier, the sweet and fitting sacrifice of war captured in the blue hiss of an eternal flame.

And yet it was by the same token an outrageous memorial to the vanity of one man. Napoleon, like a latter-day Ozymandius, had carved his name and that of his victories in stone, in the futile hope that they would not be shrouded by the sands of time. It was in truth a monumental folly, executed on an epic scale in a doomed attempt to emulate the martial grandeur of ancient Rome. And today, reduced to the role of central bollard at the heart of Europe's biggest roundabout.

Tom, wearing sunglasses and a faded baseball cap as a rudimentary disguise, took the first elevator of the morning up to the top of the viewing platform. He had been joined by a group of Japanese tourists dressed in matching yellow Mickey Mouse plastic ponchos, despite the bright sunshine. Milo came up in the next elevator, Tom guessing that he had waited to see him go inside before following. He appeared to be alone, although there was no guarantee that none of the other people spilling out of the elevator with him weren't on his payroll.

"Hello, Felix."

"Milo." Tom nodded.

"Magnificent view, isn't it?"

Milo stopped about five feet in front of him, both his hands thrust deep inside his black overcoat. It had been a long time since Tom had seen him. He looked a little thinner in the face, the lines more pronounced around the corners of his eyes and across his forehead, perhaps, his hair slightly thinner. But otherwise he had changed startlingly little. His green eyes still glittered like ice in the sun, his bloodless lips drawn into a thin, almost mocking smile, his shoulders confidently thrown back. Certainly he'd made no attempt to disguise himself, but then, why should he? His wasn't the face gracing news bulletins around the world.

"It's only from up here that you can really appreciate Paris's unique symmetry, the Champs Elysées on one side running like a swollen river toward the Arche de Triomphe du Carousel, the Avenue de la Grande Armée on the other marching up toward the Arche de la Défense."

Tom caught a glimpse of Milo's watch as he stretched his arm to the horizon, a rare 1950s IWC Mark 11, originally designed for and issued to the British Air Force. Milo's model, Tom noted, was the "No T" variant, hastily discontinued by the British authorities after they realized that its luminescent Radium dial markings were slightly radioactive. Although unusual, it seemed to Tom, at least, an entirely appropriate choice, combining Milo's precision, elegance and refinement with an undercurrent of danger and violence; maybe even death.

"Shall we cut the small talk?" Tom sniffed dismissively.

"What do you expect me to say? Congratulations? Fine, well done," Milo snapped. "Breaking into a moving van was a new one, even to me. Now, give me my painting back."

"You can have it, as soon as I have Eva."

"Quintavalle's little bitch?" Milo laughed incredulously. "Is that what you want?"

"I want proof of life," Tom demanded. "Now."

Milo gave a grudging nod and reached for his phone.

"Put her on," he ordered, before passing the handset to Tom, eyebrows raised expectantly.

"Eva? Eva, is that you?"

"Tom?" She sounded weak and frightened and Tom's initial elation at the sound of her voice was short-lived.

"Are you okay? Has he hurt you?"

"Help me, Tom. Do what he says and help me," her voice collapsed into a sob.

Milo snatched the phone back and cut the call.

"As you can hear, she's alive, although I wouldn't go so far as to say well."

Tom could feel the rage building in his chest.

"If you've hurt her, I'll—"

"I don't know why you're even bothering," Milo interrupted him with a dismissive laugh. "I heard you ran out on her. Broke her little heart. You think she'd be here for you if I'd locked you away instead?"

"I made a promise," Tom countered, Milo's jibe hitting home. He had let her down before—that's why he wouldn't do it again. "You wouldn't understand."

"Probably not."

"What's she to you, anyway?" Tom challenged him.

"An insurance policy. All I want is the *Mona Lisa*."

"What for? The theft is in the news. That's all you need to sell the forged paintings Rafael made for you, isn't it?"

Milo nodded slowly, his expression confirming Tom and Archie's guesswork about what he was planning.

"Yes. But there's only one way to ensure that their authenticity is never put in doubt."

"You need to destroy the original," Tom breathed in sudden realization.

"The type of clients I have lined up will not tolerate any sort of uncertainty," Milo confirmed. "Especially given the prices they are paying. I have to be certain that the Louvre's *Mona Lisa* will never go on display again."

"Well, you can roll it up and smoke it for all I care," Tom snapped. "All I want is Eva."

"In that case there's a place I know. An industrial park. We could do the exchange there tonight."

"Sure," Tom laughed. "Somewhere quiet and out of the way where you can pick me off nice and easy in the dark. No, we're going to do this in daylight and out in the open. Do you know the Voie Georges Pompidou?"

"On the river? Of course." Milo nodded.

"We'll make the exchange there. Midday. I'd tell you to come alone, but I know you won't. Just remember that we can both come out of this with what we want. No one needs to get hurt. There doesn't always have to be a winner."

"Agreed." Milo stretched out his arm. "I haven't forgotten that there's a debt of honor between us, a blood debt. You have nothing to fear from me."

Tom, reluctantly, shook his hand.

Unseen by either of them on the other side of the platform, a uniformed elevator attendant spoke into his phone.

"Hello. Are you dealing with the Louvre case? Good. I need you to get a message to Commissaire Ferrat. Tell him I think I've spotted one of the men you're looking for."

CHAPTER FIFTY-FIVE

CENTRAL POLICE STATION, 1ST ARRONDISSEMENT, PARIS

23rd April—10:31 A.M.

Looking around, it struck Jennifer that, no matter the country or culture, all holding cells looked pretty much the same. A narrow room—window optional. A steel door complete with viewing/feeding slot. A bed with a thin, flameproof mattress. The unrelenting glare of an overhead light that was never turned off. Even the choice of colors had consolidated around different shades of blue or green, generally held to have a pacifying effect on the cell's potentially unstable or violent inmates.

Not that she was of a mind to cause trouble, despite Ferrat's heavy-handed treatment. Not yet, at least. As soon as the Embassy representative turned up and word got back to the FBI, he'd have to back off and go through the proper channels. She had nothing to hide and had done nothing wrong. He was the one who would have to learn to play by the rules.

She'd spent her time in the cell thinking about Tom and the events of the last forty-eight hours. The more she'd learned about what had really unfolded at the Louvre and in that tunnel, the more she'd been struck by the uneasy sensation that Tom had probably been telling the truth about what had driven him to steal the *Mona Lisa*. It didn't excuse what he had done, of course, or the way he had used her to get to the painting, but it did at least explain why he had done it and who had really been responsible for the killings. Given all that, she couldn't help but feel guilty at having rolled over on him quite so quickly. The fact that he'd known she would—had counted on it, in fact—only made it worse.

Her head flicked to the door as the viewing slot snapped open and momentarily framed a set of brown eyes and the bridge of a nose. It slammed shut as the tinkle of keys and creak of the lock announced that someone was there to see her. Finally.

Her relief was short-lived. Far from despatching the cavalry, the Embassy seemed to have sent a boy scout. The ginger-haired man standing nervously in front of her, thin face covered in acne scars and razor burn, looked as if he was barely out of college. He jumped as the door clanged behind him, glancing fearfully at the lock as it crunched shut, then at the single naked bulb overhead. She guessed this was probably his first time inside a cell. Great.

"Er . . . Agent Browne?" he stuttered, fidgeting with the strap of his briefcase. "Bill Kendrick. I'm from the Embassy."

"You certainly took your time."

"We're . . . er . . . a little short-staffed at the moment." She took this as an explanation for both his tardiness and his obvious inexperience.

"You've come to get me out?"

"It's not that easy." He gave her a weak smile.

"All it takes is a phone call. It doesn't get much easier than that."

"It's complicated."

"Not to me." She gave an exasperated shake of her head.

"The theft is all over the press. You can't switch on the TV or pick up a paper without reading about it," he sounded almost excited. "Today's *American Voice* is going to claim that you and Kirk were lovers. There are photos apparently."

"Lewis has a personal grudge against me. The photos prove nothing. I already explained all this to Ferrat, but he doesn't want to listen. He just wants to be able to show his bosses that he's making progress. Well, he's wasting his time. There are protocols in place, for God's sake. And none of them involve serving FBI agents being arrested and held on a hunch."

Kendrick gave an awkward cough before answering.

"The State Department is coming under pressure from the French government to cooperate with their investigation. Wire taps, stop-and-search powers, satellite imagery. Needless to say, this also extends to the questioning, and if necessary detainment, of U.S. nationals."

"Have you even spoken to the FBI?" Jennifer was growing tired of Kendrick's evasive manner. "Ask for Director Green. He can vouch for me."

"Unfortunately I have not been able to reach FBI Director Green."

He gave an apologetic shrug, his eyes flicking to the ground as if steeling himself to say something. Jennifer suddenly had the sickening realization that Kendrick hadn't been sent to secure her release at all. He'd been sent to give her a message. Green, ever the politician, was distancing himself, scenting a scandal.

"I spoke with Deputy Director Travis instead. According to him, not only have you been on vacation since the evening of April twenty-first, but your approach to the Louvre wasn't sanctioned by the FBI."

"I had orders to talk to Director Green and Director Green only," she protested, the cell beginning to spin around her. "He wasn't available, so I left a message. What did they expect me to do—stand by and do nothing?"

"From the FBI's perspective, therefore," Kendrick continued as if he hadn't heard her, "you have been in Paris as a private citizen since the evening of April twenty-first. Your intervention with the Louvre was, as a consequence, a personal matter of which they had no prior knowledge or involvement."

"They're cutting me loose?" Jennifer's voice was disbelieving.

"The Embassy will of course provide you with all the help and assistance we would give any U.S. national implicated in a police investigation," he intoned. From the obvious comfort he took in legalistic phrasing, Jennifer guessed that he was a law school grad. "However, given the high-profile and politically sensitive nature of the case, it would not be appropriate for us or the French authorities to extend any preferential treatment to you. I suggest you continue to cooperate fully with the investigation. Hopefully this will all be resolved soon."

"*Hopefully*?" Jennifer nailed him with a withering look. "They sent you all the way here to tell me to click my heels and think of home?" She gave a despairing shake of her head. "Anything else I should know?"

Kendrick paused, and then let his mask momentarily slip.

"Look, I probably shouldn't say this, but the French want to see some heads rolling and, from the case Ferrat is building, it looks like you're going to be first on the scaffold. So if I were you, I'd get a good attorney. You're going to need one."

CHAPTER FIFTY-SIX

VOIE GEORGES POMPIDOU, PARIS

23rd April—11:59 A.M.

He's here!" Dumas pointed at the Range Rover turning on to the ramp that led down to the Quai, the sound of its tires on the cobblestones echoing across the water.

"Who's with him?" Tom didn't want to get too close until he knew what he was dealing with.

"One car on the bridge. Another one parked on the road above," Archie radioed back from his vantage point on the Allée des Cygnes, a finger-shaped island in the middle of the river opposite Tom. "Two men in each."

"That sounds about right." Tom gave a rueful smile. Milo had never been shy of loading the dice in his favor. One time in Macau, quite literally. "Okay, I'm going in."

Tom edged the throttle forward and pointed the speedboat toward a gap between two houseboats where the car had stopped, the powerful engine spluttering its disdain at the low revs. He neared the bank and slipped back into neutral, the Seine rolling gently underneath him as he waited. The front passenger door opened and Milo got out.

"New toy?" he called.

"Just borrowing it."

He'd come by boat because it afforded him the option of a

quick escape if Milo tried anything. He noticed now, however, that Milo was being careful to stay close to the open door in case he needed to dive back inside. Not for the first time, it occurred to Tom that sometimes the similarities between them were more striking than the differences. What was it that had led them both to choose such divergent paths, despite their similar beginnings in the business? Upbringing? Circumstance? An intuitive sense of right and wrong, of where to draw the line? It was impossible to say, but it did make Tom wonder how close he had come to following a different, and in his view, darker path.

"Where is she?"

The rear passenger door swung open and Eva half climbed, half-fell to the ground. Milo hauled her roughly to her feet and then grabbed the hair at the back of her head to hold her still. She was wearing the same clothes she'd had on the other day, only these were now ripped and dirty and she had her left arm in a sling. One of his men climbed out of the other door and made his way to Milo's side.

"What have you done to her?" Tom called, his expression and voice caught between his instinctive anger at Milo's indiscriminate brutality and concern for Eva, who appeared lost and in pain. Certainly, looking at her now, her shoulders cowed in defeat, lips trembling like autumn leaves in the wind, it was hard to believe that this was the same fiercely proud woman he'd last seen in Seville. His cheek burned with the sudden memory of how she'd slapped him only a few days ago. Now Tom suspected that if she were to raise her arm, it might snap like a branch that had been bent back on itself.

"It was an accident." Milo shrugged. "She'll live."

Tom nodded slowly, his eyes brimming with black fury. There was little he could do now other than get Eva back and hold her close and promise never to let Milo get to her again. But he made a silent pledge that one day, he would make Milo pay.

"Is that the painting?"

Tom held out the protective metal case containing Rafael's copy of the *Mona Lisa* and nodded.

"Send Eva over."

"Show me it first," Milo insisted. "I need to see more than just a box."

Tom nodded and nudged the boat forward until its prow was bobbing just a few feet from the bank.

"I'll hold her here," he said to Dumas in a low voice, the engine idling. "Just bring Eva back in one piece."

With a nod, Dumas grabbed the case and clambered unsteadily over the padded sun beds that lined the stern, before jumping down on to the bank.

"Wait," Milo called. The man next to him stepped forward and searched Dumas thoroughly before letting him pass.

"That's far enough," Tom called. "Show him."

Dumas flicked the catches on the case and held it up against his chest as he opened it. A smile teased the corners of Milo's mouth.

"It looks like we have a deal."

Dumas snapped the case shut and placed it on the ground next to him, before taking a step back. Milo shoved Eva toward Dumas—she stumbled on the uneven surface, almost losing her balance. Then he too, took a step back. The strange choreography of all this wasn't lost on Tom—an elaborate ballet played out against an unheard and yet instinctively understood melody.

"You've got company," Archie's voice suddenly crackled. "Get out of there."

"Get back to the boat!" Tom shouted.

Dumas reached for Eva but the air was suddenly split by the sound of sirens as three unmarked police cars shot down the ramp toward them. At the same time a helicopter soared over the rooftop of the neighboring building and swooped down.

With an angry shout, Milo pulled his gun and advanced on Dumas, snatching up the case and grabbing Eva by the wrist. The man next to him swung a sub-machine gun out from under his arm and emptied a full clip into the window of the lead police vehicle, which swerved into the wall and then flipped on to its side as it caught the curb. The car behind it fired back, bullets pinging around their feet. Milo suddenly gave an anguished shout and held the case up. Three loose shots had ricocheted off the ground and carved neat holes right through its silver hide.

"You need to get out of there," Archie urged him over the radio.

"I can't leave Eva."

"It's too late for that now, mate. Get out while you still can."

"Damn." Tom punched the wheel.

Retreating toward his car, his gun still trained on a bewildered-looking Dumas, Milo threw the case through the open door before bundling Eva in after it and jumping in. The car immediately leaped away with a screech of rubber, the helicopter setting off in pursuit with a dip of its rotors.

"Let's go," Tom shouted at Dumas over the noise.

Dumas turned and sprinted toward him, a stream of police vehicles flowing over the neighboring bridge and disgorging their uniformed occupants. A siren echoed up the river. Tom turned to see a police launch bearing down on him from the right, armed officers lining the stern rail. They had even less time than Archie had suggested.

"Come on," he urged. Dumas was now no more than ten feet away. But even as he spoke, shots rang out, splintering the ground around Dumas's feet. He stumbled and then fell heavily, groaning as the air was knocked out of him.

"Get up!"

"I've been hit," Dumas shouted back, clutching his leg. "Go. Find Milo. Don't let them get you too."

Tom hesitated, desperate not to compound the loss of both Eva and the painting by leaving Dumas behind. A renewed fusillade from the fast-closing police launch ripped across the stern, sending clouds of stuffing from the sun beds twirling through the air like snow.

"Go," Archie urged over the radio. "Go now before they have to fish you out."

Grim faced, Tom dumped the throttle into reverse, the prow dipping as he retreated from the bank, then rising as he throttled up again, the boat yawing to port as he straightened up. He glanced over his shoulder as he pulled away; the launch was bearing down on him, something indistinguishable being shouted over the loudhailer. Out of the corner of his eye he saw Dumas being surrounded and handcuffed, the bank swarming with armed officers.

The revs climbed, the hull clawing its way out of the water as Tom adjusted the trim to keep the propellers submerged. The increasing speed transformed the water's previously lazy embrace into a hard smack that vibrated up through the wheel in time with the rise and fall of the engine's thunder. Over the noise he heard the rattle and fizz of police gunfire as the bullets buried themselves in the water around him like hot coals being flung angrily into a pond.

He suddenly caught sight of a police car on fire on the riverbank ahead of him. Another one lay on its side, windows shattered, its inert passengers hanging out through the half-open doors. Milo's ever lethal handiwork.

"Find out where they're taking J-P," Tom radioed Archie.

"What for?"

"So I can go in and get him."

"Don't be daft!"

"We can't just leave him. Besides, it's the last place they'll be looking for me."

"You need to dump that boat first."

"I know. Meet me at the Pont de l'Alma. South side."

As Tom reached the apex of the Allée des Cygnes he swung the boat to the left, rounding the tip of the island in a wide, keeling arc that sent a fan of water crashing over him. Just for a moment, he was frozen under the imperious gaze of the small Statue of Liberty that stood there. Then he accelerated away, shaking the water from his face as he doubled back on himself on the other side of the island. He glanced over his shoulder and saw that he was pulling away from the chasing launch. Good. The important thing now was to put as much distance as he could between them.

The gardens of the Parc Citroën flashed past, then the Bir-Hakeim Bridge and, to his right, the elegant thrust of the Eiffel Tower and the sparkling windows of the parked tourist coaches. He knew he could outrun them in this boat, but for how long? Reaching into the storage hatch in front of him, he found a flashlight, an empty beer can and a piece of rope. More than long enough for what he needed.

He carefully fixed one end of the rope to the wheel and then, as he hugged the bend and pointed it toward the open stretch of water ahead of him, secured it against the throttle lever. Glancing behind, he saw that, as he had hoped, the pursuing launch had momentarily disappeared behind the natural curve of the river. With a final tweak to the boat's steering, he stepped up on to the side and dived in.

A few seconds later, the police launch roared into view and shot past, Tom barely visible in the shadowy waters that lazed under the Alma Bridge. The surging wash swept Tom closer to the bank and, as the engine noise faded, he hauled himself out of the water.

"Nicely done," Archie panted as he made his way down to him. "Let's get out of here."

"Did you find out where they've taken J-P?"

"The central police station for the first arrondissement. Apparently that's where they're coordinating the entire investigation from."

In the distance, a sudden flash and the momentarily delayed boom of an explosion told them both that the boat had finally ran out of river.

CHAPTER FIFTY-SEVEN

CENTRAL POLICE STATION, 1ST ARRONDISSEMENT, PARIS

23rd April—1:33 P.M.

Jean-Pierre Dumas, DST," Tom lied.

The duty officer, a phone pressed against one ear and an old woman complaining about the noise from a neighboring flat monopolizing the other, barely glanced at the pass as he buzzed Tom in. It was just as well, because although he had dressed in Dumas's usual camouflage of black leather jacket and jeans complemented by a baseball cap, a closer inspection of the outdated ID that Dumas had left in his jacket would have quickly revealed the deception.

Inside, uniformed and plainclothes officers swarmed anxiously through the corridors. Some were on their phones, others were ignoring the *No Smoking* signs, their ties loosened and shirts hanging out of their trousers. The frantic pitch of the constant buzz and drone of their conversations and snatched phone calls suggested that the afternoon's events had served as another sharp kick against the hive. Tom found an empty office and grabbed a stack of case files and a radio from the desk to round out his disguise before heading out again.

"Where are the holding cells?" Tom intercepted an officer as he hurried past.

"Who are you?" the man shot back suspiciously.

"Dumas. DST," Tom lied again, flashing his badge and making sure that the officer also saw the police radio shoved into his jacket pocket, broadcasting static.

"You must be here to see the FBI agent. Lucky you!" He winked.

"What FBI agent?"

"The woman. She's in Interview Room 2. We thought we'd let her stew in there for a while until we interrogate her again. You know, soften her up."

"Oh, her." Tom flicked open one of the files and pretended to read from it, careful to conceal his surprise. "Jennifer Browne. Yeah, she's cute." He smiled at the officer and snapped the file shut.

What the hell was Jennifer doing here? Had she been arrested? Did they think she was involved somehow? He felt a sudden stab of guilt.

"What about the guy you just pulled off the riverbank," he asked hopefully.

"We shipped him out about fifteen minutes ago," he said gleefully. "The bastard took two slugs in the leg, but your lot want to question him over in Rue Nelaton before they let him go to the hospital. Said the pain would help jog his memory."

Tom's heart sank. Rue Nelaton was the DST headquarters over in the fifteenth. There was no chance he'd be able to get in there. At least not without a fight. But in the meantime there was still Jennifer.

"Where are the interview rooms? I might go down and see if Agent Browne is as hot in the flesh as she looks in her photo," Tom asked with a wink.

"Down there and on the right. Take your time. She's not going anywhere. Not for the next twenty years, I'd say." He laughed.

Tom set off in the direction he had indicated, trying to remain inconspicuous as he negotiated his way through the bustling corridors, although in truth everyone seemed far too distracted to notice him. Interview Room 2 was at the far end of the building, next to a fire exit.

The technician working the video and recording equipment jumped up as Tom announced himself, stubbing out his cigarette.

"Jean-Pierre Dumas," Tom flashed his badge but kept toward the back of the darkened room, the only light coming from a small lamp angled over the main control panel. "Can she see us in here?" He nodded toward Jennifer, who was sitting at a small table on the other side of a glass wall, her head resting in her hands.

"Not while it's switched on." The technician grinned. "Electrochromic glass. The current makes it darken."

"And she can't hear me either, right?" He removed his jacket and placed the files down on the desk in front of him.

"Not unless you turn the mike on here first." He pointed at a switch, a puzzled frown creasing his face. "It's a standard set-up. Where did you say you were from again?"

"I didn't," Tom said firmly, picking up a half-empty bottle of mineral water and swinging it against the side of the man's head, the glass echoing with a hollow clunk as it connected with his skull. He fell back in his seat, out cold.

Wheeling him out of the way, Tom turned the microphone on, hesitated, and then spoke.

CHAPTER FIFTY-EIGHT

23rd April—1:43 P.M.

Jennifer lifted her head, her eyes incredulously searching the room before settling accusingly on the mirrored panel set into the wall.

"Tom?"

"Yes."

"How did you get in here?"

"What are you doing here?"

"What the hell does it look like I'm doing here?" she shot back angrily, her surprise evaporating. "They think I was in on it with you."

A pause.

"I'm sorry. I never thought that they would . . ."

"Save it," she cut him off, and stepped toward the glass, "the only person you thought about was yourself. You used me, Tom. You used me to make them move the painting."

"They didn't believe me," Tom's voice echoed back. "I had no choice."

"Except now I'm the one stuck in here being asked the same dumb-assed questions again and again."

"What about the Bureau? Why haven't they got you out?"

"Good question." She gave a sad laugh. "They're saying I acted wihout their agreement and that it's not their problem.

And the French are kicking up too much of a shitstorm for the Embassy to get involved beyond the standard handholding." Her anger was replaced by a sudden melancholy. "I'm on my own."

"No you're not."

"Why are you even here? You've got the painting. That's what you wanted, wasn't it?"

"The cops caught Jean-Pierre. I was hoping to break him out."

"Dumas is in on this too?" she spluttered. She'd met Jean-Pierre Dumas with Tom last time she'd been in Paris. It hadn't been a pleasant experience, Dumas having threatened her with arrest for trespassing on a crime scene and then more or less ordering her out of the country. She wasn't sure, therefore, if her outrage stemmed from this tainted memory or her shock at a French government agent having crossed over to Tom's side.

The glass suddenly went clear. Tom was standing directly in front of her, no more than a foot away.

"I could get you out instead."

"Oh, that's a great idea," she snorted, stepping back. "Let's go on the run together. That should help clear things up."

"We don't have much time," he urged her. "You want to take your chances with the French legal system, fine. Or you can leave here now and help me figure out what the hell is going on and how to put it right."

"What are you talking about?"

"Milo's still got Eva. I tried to make an exchange with a forged version of the *Mona Lisa* today but the police must have been following him. That's how they caught J-P."

"So you've still got the one you took from the convoy?" she asked with relief.

"Yeah. Except it's a forgery too."

"That's impossible." She snorted disbelievingly. "They lifted it off the wall and took it straight down."

"Henri ran some tests on it. He says—"

"Hold on," she interrupted with an angry shake of her head. "Besson is working with you too? Since when?"

"Right from the start."

"Has anyone been straight with me since I got here?" she fumed.

"He thinks that at some stage in the last couple of hundred years, it's been switched." He quickly ran through Besson's findings concerning the discrepant X-rays and paint pigment. "Unless I can prove what Milo's up to, they'll pin the whole thing on me. Dumas will go down for it. You, too, from the look of things."

"It's got nothing to do with me." She sat down heavily in the chair.

"Really? Then where did you get that Louvre accession number?"

"That's none of your business."

"It had something to do with your case, right?"

"I can't tell you," she insisted.

"The FBI have thrown you to the wolves, Jen. You owe them nothing. Where did you get that number?"

She stared at him blankly.

"They could send somebody down any moment now to continue the questioning," he reminded her. "Every second counts."

She shrugged and then gave a heavy sigh. He was right. Besides, what possible difference could it make anymore? She quickly told him about Razi and Hammon and the piece of paper they'd found on his fax.

"How was it signed?"

"It wasn't. It just had an M with a circle . . ." She tailed off, the significance of that letter only now dawning on her.

"Milo," Tom confirmed what she had just guessed. "Don't you see? We've been working the same case from different angles. Hammon must have been acting for one of Milo's buyers."

"Then why did he kill him?" she asked.

"Once you're free we can figure that out together. But we need to leave now."

"The FBI will—"

"The FBI don't give a shit about anyone other than themselves," he cut her off impatiently. "There's no one to help you now apart from me."

"But if I run now, they'll think we were working together."

"They think that already," he retorted.

"Yeah, but if I stay put, there's a good chance this will work itself out," she said firmly, wondering if she was trying to convince him, or herself.

"A good chance? Are you really willing to roll the dice with the next twenty years of your life?"

"That's not what I—"

"Look, I listened to you once Jen," Tom pleaded. "I listened to you, and I was right to do so. Now you need to do the same for me before someone comes and it's too late."

"That was totally different," she shot back, even though she could sense her resistance flagging.

"Why? Because then I was the thief and now you're the one in a cell? We're both looking for the same answers. Milo's the key to everything. If we stop him, we'll both be in the clear."

She hesitated, knowing he was right and that it came down to a simple choice: Wait here and trust the system, or get outside and force the issue. In the end, the decision was easier than she might have expected. She'd never been the trusting type.

"Even if I say yes, how are you planning to get me out of here?"

Tom grinned with relief.

"Straight out the front door."

He disappeared from the other side of the glass. A few moments later, the cell door buzzed open.

"Put these on." He tossed her a pair of handcuffs and slipped his baseball cap back on.

"You must be kidding."

"You got a better idea?"

She shook her head sullenly and held her arms out in front of her with a sigh. An FBI agent being cuffed by a thief. It wasn't exactly how she'd seen this case playing out when she'd first taken it on.

"This place is crawling with people from about five different agencies. No one knows anyone anymore," Tom explained as he snapped them shut. "We can use that. Just keep your head down. Everyone will assume you're being moved to a different cell or interview room." He cracked the door open an inch and peered into the corridor. "Okay. Let's go."

He led her back toward the entrance. As he had predicted, no one gave them a second glance. Reaching the security barrier, he signed Jennifer out and then pushed her roughly ahead of him through the revolving gate.

"Does Ferrat know you're transferring her?" The same officer that Tom had questioned earlier stepped into their path just as they were about to exit on to the street.

"What do you think?" Tom shot back irritably.

"Just checking." The man held his hands up apologetically and stepped aside.

Tom steered Jennifer toward where Archie was waiting for them, the engine running.

"Wait a minute . . ." The officer had followed them out on to the street. "Don't I know you from somewhere?"

"Keep walking," Tom whispered to Jennifer as he turned to face him. "I don't think so."

"Yes . . ." A look of shocked realization spread across the officer's face. "You're . . ."

Tom threw the radio at him before he had a chance to finish his sentence, catching him on the side of his head and sending him reeling to the floor.

"Run!" he shouted, shoving Jennifer toward the waiting car as the officer staggered to his feet and raised the alarm.

"What the hell is she doing here?" Archie exclaimed angrily as they leaped inside. "Where's J-P?"

"Can we do the explanations later?" Tom nodded toward the pack of officers loping toward them.

"They'd better be good," Archie insisted, putting the car into gear and pulling away. They stalled with a sudden lurch.

"Archie!" Tom exclaimed as the officers reached them and tried the doors.

"French piece of shit," Archie fumed as he started the engine again. "Clutch is shot to bloody pieces."

The window nearest to Jennifer shattered as one of the

policemen swung his torch against it. Another man leaped on to the hood and reached for his gun.

"Whenever you're ready," Tom shouted as he leaned across to help Jennifer fight the man off.

With a roar, the car suddenly swung out and accelerated away, sending the man on the hood spinning to the ground. Meanwhile a well-aimed kick from Jennifer dislodged the officer who had forced his upper body through the window.

The remaining men gave chase for about five hundred yards before giving up.

"You'd better be right about this." Jennifer glared at Tom.

"You'd better hope I can get those handcuffs off," he smiled.

CHAPTER FIFTY-NINE

AVENUE DE L'OBSERVATOIRE, 14TH ARRONDISSEMENT,

PARIS

23rd April—2:17 P.M.

How long have you known Besson?" Jennifer asked Tom as he closed the gate behind them and pressed five.

"Almost since I got started, really. He's been clean for years, but that didn't stop him helping out here and there."

"He's a handy bloke to know," Archie confirmed, having calmed down a bit now that Tom had explained exactly how it was that he'd gone in for Dumas and come out with Jennifer. Even so, Tom sensed that Archie was already taking a perverse pleasure in her tasting life on the other side of the law.

"He's a convincing liar," she retorted as the elevator shuddered and scraped its way up the shaft.

Tom wasn't surprised by her resentful tone. No one liked having the wool pulled over their eyes, least of all Jennifer, who from what he'd seen, already suffered from a slight tendency to think that everyone was out to get her.

"Don't hold that against him," he urged her. "He didn't lie to you about your case. Anything else he did or said was to help me and Eva. It's nothing personal."

Besson greeted them warmly until he caught sight of Jennifer and stopped in his tracks, peering out beyond her into the corridor with a worried frown that pulled one half of his face into a question mark.

"Where's Jean-Pierre?"

"The police were on to us," Archie explained. "Someone must have followed Milo from the meet this morning. J-P got pinched."

"And her?" Besson asked as if she wasn't there.

"Ask Tom." Archie shrugged.

"We're all in this together now," Tom said firmly. "Jennifer's got as much at stake as the rest of us. Maybe even more."

Besson glanced at Archie as if trying to enlist some support, but Archie, beyond raising his eyebrows, refused to be drawn.

"Where are they keeping Jean-Pierre?"

"The DST are questioning him," Tom answered. "I'm guessing they'll move him to a hospital once they've finished."

"He's hurt?"

"Took two in the leg," Tom said with a rueful nod.

"He'll live." Archie shrugged impatiently. "Where's the painting?"

"Back here."

Shuffling awkwardly, Besson led them through to the small office next to his lab. Stopping in front of the large mirror, he pressed against the bottom right-hand corner of its frame. With a click it swung open, revealing a small hidden room.

"There," Besson smiled, pointing at the painting, safely housed within a plastic case.

"Two-way glass," Tom explained to Jennifer, placing his hand on the other side of the mirror so she could see it. "This is where I was hiding the day you first came here."

"It's come in useful over the years." Besson gave a knowing smile. "There's even a way out through to the neighboring building. Luckily I've never had to use it. Anyway, we'd better leave her to rest." He closed the mirror again. "She's had a busy day."

"You've been running some more tests?" Jennifer asked.

"Tom told you what I found?"

"He said you think it's a forgery." She didn't sound convinced.

"I date it to the late eighteenth, early nineteenth century," he confirmed. "But what's really strange is that when *La Joconde* was recovered after the Valfierno theft, many people didn't believe they'd got the real one back. So the Louvre released a set of X-rays to prove it was the original. And they showed underpainting."

"That's impossible," Archie snorted. "How could their X-rays have underpainting and ours none?"

"The Louvre could have faked them," Tom speculated, finding himself gravitating inexorably toward the most logical explanation, even though he knew it was unlikely. "Maybe they knew even then that they had a forgery."

"They know something," Besson agreed, turning to Jennifer. "Do you remember what I told you about your Gauguin and Chagall paintings? About how the copies were almost too good, that they must have been painted from the original?"

"Of course."

"Well, I could say the same about Rafael's copy of the *Mona Lisa*. It's identical to the one Tom stole. He must have had access to it."

"Then somebody owes us an explanation." Tom was grim faced, realizing now that there had perhaps been more to Dumas's and his frosty reception at the Louvre the other day than personal grievances and their lack of evidence. "And I think I know exactly who to ask."

"I'm coming with you," Jennifer insisted. "From now on, you don't make a move without me being there too." Tom nodded in agreement. That seemed a fair price to pay for the risk she was taking. Besides, chances were he could do with the help.

"What about Milo?" asked Archie.

"When he realizes we gave him one of his own forgeries, he'll be back in touch," Tom guessed. "Only next time he'll want to run proper tests before handing Eva over."

"You mean *if* he realizes we gave him a forgery," Besson corrected him. "I meant to tell you: Rafael added underpainting. In my opinion, the copy Milo's got now is better than the Louvre forgery we took. He might think he's got the real thing and just disappear."

"Then we need to find him," Tom said to Archie. "We need to find him before he decides he has what he came for and that he doesn't need Eva anymore."

CHAPTER SIXTY

J. EDGAR HOOVER BUILDING, WASHINGTON, D.C.

23rd April—9:05 A.M.

You're saying she walked out of there voluntarily?" Green eyed the conference phone warily.

"She was handcuffed, yes, but she walked past at least ten of my men without even trying to call for help," Ferrat's voice squawked back. "And she didn't walk. She ran to the car."

"It doesn't make any sense." Green banged his hand down on the table in frustration.

"With respect, Director Green, it does make sense if she was working with Kirk," Ferrat suggested gently.

"With respect, Commissioner Ferrat, I've worked with Browne. Sure, she's stepped out of line a few times; she tends to act on instinct without always thinking the implications through. But then so do a lot of good agents and, believe me, Browne's a good agent. It sure don't make her a criminal."

"Then why did she run?" Ferrat pointed out. "Why didn't she just stay and cooperate?"

"Maybe she felt like she had no choice. Maybe you should have listened to her side of the story before arresting her."

"Maybe you should let me decide how to run my own case," Ferrat shot back.

There was a pause and Green looked first at Deputy Director Travis and then at Jim Stone, who'd been dispatched from the State Department to listen in on this call. One rolled his eyes, the other shrugged. Like him, they just wanted all this to go away and go away fast.

"What do you want from us, Commissioner Ferrat?" Green's tone was brisk.

"Access to your DNA database. Several members of the gang were hit in the tunnel. We have blood and tissue samples. You may have a match."

"Anything else?"

"Browne's file. Fingerprints. Known acquaintances. Details of her past involvement with Kirk."

"Absolutely no way," Green snorted. "You want help IDing your unsubs, fine. But we don't just hand over top secret information . . ."

"Hold on, Jack—" Stone pressed the mute key. "We have to play ball on this one. The French are calling in all their favors."

"I didn't think they had any left in this town."

"We don't have a choice," Stone insisted unblinkingly.

"'Allo?" Ferrat called.

With a heavy sigh, Green took the phone off mute.

"I'll see what I can do."

"Thank you," Ferrat acknowledged. "Believe me, I also hope Agent Browne had nothing to do with this terrible business. I hope, but I have to be sure."

"I hate the French," Travis swore as soon as Ferrat had rung off.

"The good news is, they hate you right back," Stone reassured him with a smile.

"This wouldn't have happened if we'd cut her some slack," Green observed angrily. "Instead we cut her adrift. What choice did we leave her but to strike out for shore on her own?"

"We couldn't let the actions of one agent compromise the Bureau or the Administration," Stone reminded him. "She's already caused us enough problems with the Press. Imagine if Lewis got wind that you were trying to fix things with the

French. You need to play this one by the book or it'll come back and bite us all in the ass."

"She could take us all down with her if it turns out she's involved and we've tried to help her out," Travis agreed. "And even if she's not involved, what the hell's she doing playing Bonnie and Clyde? I know it's none of my business, but think what a potential donor would say?"

"You're damn right it's none of your business!" Green shot back angrily. "I don't give a shit about donors. Right now, I just want her found. Get the boys up in Langley involved if you need to. I don't care anymore. If she really is in on this with Kirk then, believe me, I'll gift-wrap her and hand her over to the French myself. But if there's something else going on, an angle that she's working, I want to know about it."

CHAPTER SIXTY-ONE

RUE DE CHARONNE, 11TH ARRONDISSEMENT, PARIS

23rd April—3:10 P.M.

Tom paused in Cécile Levy's bedroom, the noise of the shower and a thin gauze of steam creeping around the edges of the bathroom door. Her dress lay coiled on the floor where she had stepped out of it. The bed was unmade, the *Mona Lisa* smiling suggestively from the cover of the French newspaper casually thrown there.

The open wardrobe door revealed two shelves of handbags, each carefully wrapped in their protective cloth pouches. Beneath them was row upon row of shoe boxes, each with a Polaroid photo of their contents taped to the front. Above them, her clothes hung in the plastic wrappers supplied by the dry cleaners.

In contrast to this deliberate orderliness, the random paraphernalia of Cécile Levy's everyday life lay scattered next to the bed—cigarettes, sunglasses, keys, lipstick, mobile phone, a half-empty bottle of gin, a small photo of her with her parents taken on a beach when she was still a kid.

Tom wondered which was a better reflection of Levy's current state of mind—the wardrobe's cold military precision, or the emotional chaos of her bedside table? Perhaps both?

Maybe the cigarettes and alcohol allowed her to bridge the two, or more likely, veer from one to the other.

He pocketed her phone to stop her trying to use it and then padded over to the bathroom door and slowly edged it open. As the steam billowed out, Tom was just about able to make out Levy's shape on the other side of the shower curtain. He reached in and turned the sink's hot tap on. A few moments later, she swore and hurriedly shut off the water. Pulling the curtain back, she reached for a towel and then screamed as she caught sight of Tom holding one out for her. She clenched the curtain against herself fearfully.

"Get out," Tom ordered, throwing her the towel. "We need to talk."

A few minutes later Levy emerged nervously into the sitting room where Tom and Jennifer were waiting for her. She was wearing the same dress Tom had seen lying on the floor earlier and her glistening hair was yet again held back off her face by a pair of sunglasses. Tom sensed that she drew some small comfort from the thought that at any moment she could lower them on to her face and cover her eyes.

"What do you want?" She stood with her back pressed to the wall, her eyes flicking hopefully toward the front door. She had brought her cigarettes with her and she lit one now, the trembling in her hand subsiding as she took a first, long drag. She wore no make-up, giving her face a slightly washed out, blank look.

"You remember Agent Browne?" He nodded toward Jennifer.

"So, Ferrat was right." She gave a tight-lipped, almost bitter, smile. "You tricked us."

"I was the one who was tricked," Jennifer corrected her, glaring at Tom.

"We can do the hows and the whys later," Tom insisted. "Right now, we just want some information."

"What sort of information?" she asked in a sullen, defensive tone.

"About the *Mona Lisa*. About what the Louvre really knows."

"Ferrat's told us nothing."

"I'm not talking about the case, I'm talking about the painting being a forgery. I'm talking about how, all these years, the Louvre has been passing off a nineteenth-century reproduction as an original da Vinci."

"What are you talking about?" She lit another cigarette from the half-finished butt of the previous one, her hand trembling.

"We've analyzed the painting. We know."

"Is this another one of your tricks?" She laughed, although Tom detected a forced, perhaps even hysterical edge to her voice.

"Prussian blue in a fifteenth-century painting?" he challenged her. "Now that's a neat trick if you can pull it off."

"Clumsy restoration work." She shrugged, pinching her tongue as if she'd got a hair caught there. "People weren't always as careful as we are now."

"Oh, you're very careful now, aren't you? Careful to make sure that no one else gets close enough to examine the painting properly."

"You're imagining things," she tutted dismissively, opening the window that led out on to the narrow balcony, her pink nostrils blanching slightly as she took a deep breath.

"Am I? Was I imagining the X-ray of the *Mona Lisa* that the Louvre released in 1914? Or did I just make up the one that we took the other day with no underpainting at all."

This time she said nothing, her back to them as she faced the open window, teeth biting into her bottom lip, the cigarette wavering slightly in her pale fingers.

"Because I think that the Louvre has known all along that the painting was a forgery," Tom continued, stepping closer. "Only they couldn't admit it. Too many red faces on too many important people."

There was a long pause. Levy leaned forward and stubbed out her cigarette on the ashtray on top of the baby grand piano. Petals from a drooping vase of lilies lay sprinkled across the mirrored surface like autumn leaves on a pond.

"I always said someone would find out eventually." Her voice was clear and small, her eyes moist.

"How long has the Louvre known?" Jennifer asked.

"Since 1913. Since it was recovered after the Valfierno theft."

She quickly scanned the room and Tom suspected she was desperately searching out the bottle of gin he'd seen next to the bed. She'd struck him as highly strung the first time they'd met. Perhaps her nerves were even more brittle than he'd guessed.

"At first it was assumed that the thieves had substituted one of Chaudron's forgeries for the real *Joconde*," she continued. "But then they realized that it was the same painting we'd always had. It had just never really been analyzed properly before. That's when they guessed that the original must have been replaced."

"When?" Jennifer prompted her again.

"Sometime between the Revolution and the Restoration." She shrugged, the words now tumbling from her bloodless lips. It was strange, but Tom sensed that she was finding a strange release in talking to them, as if a burden was being lifted from her shoulders. "It was a chaotic time. Things were moved around. Records were destroyed."

"What about you, when did you find out?" he asked.

"A year after being made Curator of Paintings. Once they were sure that they could count on me not to talk." She looked up with a pained smile at the recollection.

"Who else knows apart from you?"

"A handful of people. Louvre employees."

"No one in government?" Jennifer asked in surprise.

"No." She gave a hollow laugh. "If you want to keep a secret, you don't tell a politician."

"But you had arranged to send the painting for forensic testing." Tom frowned. "Wouldn't the secret have come out then anyway?"

"We've always resisted pressure to subject it to a proper analysis. But when we noticed the warping, the Ministry of Culture forced our hand. We had to play along."

"Even though that would have revealed the truth?"

"You don't understand, do you?" She gave a rueful, almost mocking laugh. "It was never going to make it upstairs. That was the whole point."

"The point of what?" Jennifer said sharply.

Levy shook her head vehemently, turning to face the open window again.

"I've said too much already."

"Please," Jennifer insisted. "We need to know."

"What for?" Levy looked out over the rooftops with a distant, glazed look. "If you keep it, they'll think you stole it. But if you hand it back, the Louvre will just claim that you switched it for a forgery. It's too late for you. It's too late for all of us."

"Not if we can prove what's really going on," Jennifer insisted.

"It's like a terrible curse . . ." Levy spoke in an almost dreamlike voice, her words directed at no one in particular, "A burden handed down through the generations, the lie growing as each year goes by, as each new person is drawn into the circle of deceit."

She stepped out on to the balcony, her black hair sashaying across her cheeks, the sunglasses on her head glinting like an extra set of eyes.

"Now I'm the last one. It will all fall on me. They'll say it's my fault. The whole world will be looking. Accusing. Blaming."

She turned to face them, her back to the railings, and slowly slipped the sunglasses down on to her face.

"Well, I won't let them," she said defiantly. "I won't give them that pleasure."

She leaned back against the railing and, before they had time to register what was happening, tipped herself over the edge.

There was an awful moment of paralyzed silence. Then a scream and the screech of skidding tires from the street below. Tom and Jennifer rushed to the balcony and peered down in horror. Levy had landed on her back, her left leg twisted under her so that her foot almost reached her shoulder like a doll thrown to the ground. Blood was pooling beside her shattered head. The first few passersby reached her and instinctively looked up.

Tom, his face pale, yanked Jennifer away from the edge. She was trembling, her breathing ragged.

"Are you okay?"

"Why did she have to . . . ?" she eventually mumbled.

"She didn't."

"We drove her to it. We could have stopped her." She glanced resentfully at the balcony, as if it was also partly to blame for not having grabbed at Levy's ankles as she had gone over.

"It wasn't our fault," Tom insisted, although he had the sudden, sickening realization that she might have a point. Levy had clearly been on the edge. Had they pushed her too hard? He could feel an indigestible cocktail of shock, disgust and guilt settling in his stomach.

CHAPTER SIXTY-TWO

SAINT-OUEN, PARIS

23rd April—3:10 P.M.

It must have been ten years since Archie had been up to the flea market. Not much had changed. The day-traders still lined the route from the Metro like fly-paper, each hoping that a few of the jostling passers-by would stick to them as they spilled off the trains and flitted past.

Initially the stalls mostly contained designer rip-offs, carved African statues and cheap tourist trinkets, but it wasn't long before they gave way to more quirky traders, their wares carefully arranged on stained blankets or heavily patched plastic sheeting. Roller skates, an old Snoopy, a radio missing its volume knob, miscellaneous keys, odd crockery, a dog-eared book. If ever there was a place that proved that everything had a value, then this was it. The trick was finding who it was of value to, of course, and how much it was worth to them.

Archie walked through the gates of the main market itself and headed toward the center, gambling not only on his memory being reliable but that Ludo wouldn't have moved. All in all, it was a relatively safe bet. Ludo was a man of habit. Fish on a Friday. Two sugars in his coffee. Sports pages before the news.

He recognized the shop immediately, the window bulging with an eclectic assortment of items—a set of red velvet cinema seats, a scale model of a sailing boat, a wastepaper bin made from an elephant's foot, a bird cage shaped like a hot-air balloon, a crucifix wrestled from a deconsecrated grave, oversized spectacles that had once hung over an opticians.

Archie pushed the door open, a bell tinkling overhead. Ludo looked out from behind a case containing a stuffed vulture, his face breaking into an immediate, gap-toothed smile. He was even fatter now than Archie remembered him, his stained red tie cascading down his front and riding up and over his stomach like water flowing down a cliff, his short legs forced apart by the girth of his thighs, his chocolate eyes peering out from the heavy cowling of his brows and fleshy cheeks.

"Archie, *quelle surprise*!" To Archie's barely concealed discomfort, Ludo hugged him, his soft gut pressing against him, before leaning across the void and kissing him on both cheeks. "Good to see you again."

"You too, mate." Archie shrugged off the embrace as politely as he could, silently vowing to lay off the biscuits when he got home. "No change here, I see."

"That's what I like about this business. I sell the past. There's no need to change."

"You still selling information too?"

"For the right price, I'll sell anything." Ludo grinned, unconsciously wetting his lips with his tongue. "Why, what are you looking for?"

"Not what, who," Archie corrected him. "I need to find someone. I need to find someone now."

CHAPTER SIXTY-THREE

AVENUE DE L'OBSERVATOIRE, 14TH ARRONDISSEMENT,

PARIS

23rd April—4:01 P.M.

"Did she date the Louvre's *Mona Lisa* before she . . . ?" Besson left the sentence unfinished as he turned away from the stove where he was boiling a pan of water. Tom and Jennifer were sitting on opposite sides of the kitchen's small, semi-circular table.

"She said that it had probably been replaced sometime between the Revolution and the Restoration. So that's what . . . ?" Tom gave a questioning shrug. "About 1789 to 1814, right?"

"That's consistent with what I thought too," said Besson.

"Does it matter?" Jennifer seemed distracted. Having emptied a packet of matches on to the table, she was now dropping them one at a time back into the box.

Tom wondered if she was still reliving Levy's final moments—her ashen face, the pale cigarette in her trembling fingers, her fragile voice, the way she had carefully slipped her sunglasses on before jumping, as if she had known that her eyes would otherwise betray the violent end she had in mind for herself.

He, for one, was forcing himself not to dwell on that final, arresting image. He wasn't being unfeeling, just pragmatic. They couldn't help Levy now, but they could still help themselves.

"It matters if we're going to find the original," he reminded her.

"Get real!" she snorted impatiently.

"I'm serious. You heard what she said. Even if we give the painting back, the Louvre will accuse us of returning a fake. We haven't got any choice."

"You think pinning all our hopes on finding a painting that's been missing for two hundred years is a choice?" She gave a hollow laugh.

"No one's ever known it's been missing before. No one's ever really looked for it before," Tom insisted. "Maybe if we go back through the painting's history. See who's owned it, where it's been, then we . . ."

"*Plutôt facile*," Besson broke in. "*La Joconde* is one of the least-traveled paintings in history."

"What do you mean?"

"Da Vinci never actually delivered it. They say he liked it too much. He took it everywhere with him until he sold it to François I, just before he died. The painting was installed at Fontainebleau and then transferred first to Versailles and then to the Louvre during the Revolution. It's hardly ever moved from there since."

"But it has moved?" Jennifer asked.

"A few times," he conceded. "Apart from the Valfierno robbery, there was a brief evacuation during the Franco-Prussian war and tours to the U.S. in the 1960s and Japan and Russia in the 1970s. And of course Napoleon borrowed it for a few years, but as he was only living next door in the Tuileries, I'm not sure that counts."

"Napoleon?" Tom looked up sharply. "Napoleon borrowed it?"

"*Oui*. They say he hung it over his bed."

"Shit!" Tom clasped his hands behind his head and squeezed his eyes shut. "I've been such an idiot."

"What?" Jennifer frowned.

"Henri, you remember I told you Rafael left me a message . . ."

"A message?" Besson looked at him blankly.

"He wrote something just before they killed him. Three letters in a triangle." He grabbed a pen and a piece of paper and drew them out. "An F for me—Felix. Then Q for Quintavalle. And an N, which I assumed was an unfinished M—you know, thinking he must have been interrupted before being able to complete the final downstroke. An M for Milo, to tell me that that was who had killed him. But what if it really *was* an N? An N for Napoleon."

"You mean that Milo didn't kill him?" Besson, looking confused, scratched the side of his face.

"Maybe. Or maybe he was trying to tell me something he felt was more important. Something to do with the *Mona Lisa* and Napoleon. Where's the porcelain obelisk I left here?"

"In the office. It's been modeling for me."

Tom ran next door only to reappear a few moments later holding a large object wrapped in a white cloth.

"What's that?" Jennifer asked.

"Rafael came to see me in London before he died. He left me this," Tom explained as he unwrapped the obelisk and placed it on the table between them. "It's a piece of the Sèvres Egyptian dinner service. It was made for Napoleon."

She carefully picked it up.

"You think that it's got something to do . . ."

"I don't know," said Tom. "I've been so caught up in stopping Milo that I haven't even thought about it until now. But he must have taken it for a reason."

"The date certainly fits," Besson observed. "The painting was in the Tuileries, out of the Louvre's control. Napoleon's word was law."

Tom nodded slowly.

"Maybe he decided to keep it."

CHAPTER SIXTY-FOUR

23rd April—4:14 P.M.

Jennifer turned the obelisk over in her hands, studying each side carefully. Tom noted that, for now at least, her curiosity seemed to have provided her with a welcome distraction from the shock of Levy's death. She had even dropped the slightly distant, accusing tone that had colored most of their conversations since she'd left the police station with him.

"Do these actually mean anything?" She indicated the dense web of hieroglyphics that decorated each of the obelisk's sides.

"No." Tom shook his head. "They're random. The service was made in 1810, but hieroglyphics weren't decoded until much later."

"Not until 1836," Besson confirmed. "That's when Champollion published his Egyptian grammar."

"Did he leave anything else with it?"

"Just this—" Tom held out the envelope endorsed with Rafael's distinctive script. "It was empty. I thought it was some sort of a joke. That's why I called him up. That's how I found out he'd been killed."

"Did he post all this to you?" she asked in surprise.

"No, he dropped it off in person," Tom replied, thinking back to what Dominique had told him.

"So why is there a stamp on the envelope?" She pointed at the top right-hand corner. "An Egyptian stamp."

"She's right!" Besson peered excitedly at the stamp through his glasses, before looking up. "Take it off."

Tom held the envelope over the pan of boiling water, careful to keep his hand out of the steam. A minute or so later, he carefully lifted the corner of the stamp and then gently peeled it back.

"There's another stamp underneath it," Jennifer breathed as it came away. "French this time. A woman's head."

"It's the Marianne," Besson explained. "The female symbol of France."

"Maybe we should steam that one off too," Jennifer suggested.

Nodding, Tom again held the envelope over the pan and then slowly peeled the remaining stamp away.

"You're right. There is something here," he said.

They all crowded around, trying to make out the faint pencil marks.

"*Tajan*," Tom read, "*23 April*." He looked up at the others. "That's today."

"Tajan? The auction house?" Jennifer inquired.

"Must be. What's this number at the bottom? Sixty-three?"

"Sixty-two," she corrected him.

"If there's an auction tonight, I'll have the catalog next door," Besson volunteered. "I can't afford anything, but they still send them."

They followed him through to his office and he knelt down next to one of the piles of catalogues stacked up against the far wall.

"Here we go." He pulled one out from the middle of the stack, just catching the wine glass balancing on top of the listing pile before it toppled to the floor.

"Sixty-two must be the lot number," Jennifer guessed as Besson thumbed his way through it.

"*Lot number sixty-two*," he read. "*Volume One of the Imperial Edition (1809) of the* Description de l'Égypte, *the monumental scientific description of ancient and modern*

Egypt completed following the Emperor Napoleon's Egyptian campaign between 1798 and 1802."

"Napoleon and Egypt again," Tom commented. "It all fits."

"We need to get hold of that book," Jennifer said slowly. "Whatever we're looking for, it must be in there somewhere."

"Why didn't Rafael write all this down rather than have us chasing shadows?" Besson sighed.

"He did," Tom said, remembering something Gillez had told him in Seville. "He burned something just before he died. A small notebook. He didn't want Milo to learn what he'd discovered. He was hoping that I'd be able to follow the clues he'd left me. Only I haven't even bothered to look at them until now."

The phone rang and Besson reluctantly went to answer it, leaving Tom and Jennifer to read through the rest of the catalogue entry.

"It's Archie." He held the receiver out for Tom, who took it off him with a nod.

"Archie?"

"I've got a fix on Milo. Ludo had to call in a few markers, but it's looking sound. A block of flats over near the canal."

"Let's split up," Tom suggested. "Jen and I will head over there. You and Henri can check out the auction."

"What auction?"

"Rafael was on to something. Something that might just tip the game on its head."

CHAPTER SIXTY-FIVE

QUAI DE JEMMAPES, 10TH ARRONDISSEMENT, PARIS

23rd April—6:01 P.M.

This time tomorrow there'd have been no one here." Tom handed the binoculars to Jennifer, pointing at where two men were loading a large crate into the back of a van in front of the building's entrance. "They're shipping out."

They had parked on the opposite side of the canal a couple of hundred yards up from the address Archie had given them. The building's façade was ice gray under a low, windless sky, the windows glinting like sheet steel.

"How many of them are there?"

"Two people guarding the van. Another two doing the heavy lifting. All armed. There could be more inside."

A young couple walked past the car. Tom shielded his face and looked away. No point in risking someone recognizing him from their morning paper or the hourly news bulletin that every major channel had been running on the Mona Lisa theft since yesterday.

"Do you think Milo's with them?"

"I doubt it," he said, accepting the binoculars back off Jennifer and training them on the building's entrance. "After what happened today he must figure his cover's blown. It would be too risky to come back here. Then again, it might depend on what they're moving."

"Or who. He could have Eva in there."

"True."

A pause.

"You haven't really told me much about her."

Tom shifted in his seat. For some reason, he felt awkward talking to Jennifer about Eva. Perhaps because of what had happened between them. Perhaps because of the slightly pointed edge to her voice.

"What do you want to know?"

"She's a friend of yours, right?"

"Yeah." He kept the binoculars pressed to his face.

"A good friend?" she probed.

"Used to be."

"How good? I mean, did you two used to date or something?" she asked with a laugh.

"A long time ago," he admitted, realizing that he was only going to regain her trust by being honest. The way her smile faded, however, immediately made him regret his decision.

"So is that what this is all about? Rescuing your girlfriend?"

"She's not my girlfriend. Not for a long time now." Still he kept his binoculars trained on the building opposite; any excuse not to actually have to meet her accusing gaze.

Another pause.

"How did you meet?"

Tom wasn't sure, but thought he detected a hint of petulance in her voice. Was she annoyed that he'd not told her the truth about Eva before? Possibly, but then she'd never asked. Was she jealous? He didn't see how she could be, not after the way he'd used her over the past few days. Maybe this was less about her than it was about him. Maybe he was the one imagining her strained tone because part of him wanted her to be annoyed about Eva. Perhaps part of him wanted her to care.

"Does it matter?"

"If she's the reason I'm risking Milo sticking a gun to my head, it matters."

"Fine," he put the binoculars down and turned to face her. "She's Rafael's daughter. We dated. It didn't work out. I left her. She was pissed off, but life went on. End of story."

"Oh, so this is really all about you?" She gave a knowing smile. "You let her down once and you don't want to do it again."

"You want to play shrink, you go ahead," he snapped, annoyed at being read so easily. The truth was she was right, or at least partly right, although not for the reason she had suggested. If Tom had his own selfish motivation for pursuing this case, it was less about assuaging his guilt for having let Eva down before than it was in understanding her final words to him in Seville. Even now they echoed in his head. *There's something you should know. Something Rafael told me about your father. About how he died.*

He may well have first been drawn into this case by his sense of loyalty to Rafael and Eva and by his pig-headed refusal to let Milo win. Now, however, he wondered if his own powerful urge to grasp at the truth Eva had hinted at had grown into a far more powerful motivating factor. Not that he would ever admit it.

"Right now, I'm more interested in the second-floor window. The one with the balcony." He handed her the binoculars again.

"What about it?"

"It's open."

"You told me that we were staying put until Archie and Henri show up."

"That was before we found out they were shipping out," Tom argued. "If Eva is inside, this could be our only chance to get to her before Milo disappears."

"But there's only two of us," she reminded him.

"One. I need you to stay here."

"That's not the deal," she said firmly. "We stick together."

"What about if they drive off? One of us has to be able to follow them."

"This is crazy," she countered. "If they see you, they'll—"

"Then I'll have to make sure they don't," Tom cut her off.

"They won't be expecting me, so that evens the odds up a little. Besides, it's not like I'm going in empty-handed." He patted the gun on his lap.

There was a pause.

"Okay," she finally conceded with a resigned shrug. "How can I help?"

"Distract the guards."

"How?"

"You'll think of something. All I need is a couple of seconds. I'll signal when."

Burying the gun inside his jacket pocket, Tom got out. Jennifer shuffled over into the driver's seat and then lowered the window.

"You've got ten minutes. After that you either come out, call me, or I'm coming in."

"Is that ten minutes from now or from when I'm inside? Because really that would only be seven or eight, depending how long it takes me to get in."

"Just go." She smiled for the first time since Tom had broken her out of the police station. "And be careful."

Tom turned and walked across the bridge, burying his face in his collar so as not to be recognized. In the distance, the sudden wail of a siren made his heart skip a beat, even though he could tell it was moving away from him. They were out there, he knew, thousands of police officers and informers and agents, all of them looking for him. The thought only increased his resolve. He had to find out what he could before the net finally closed in.

Milo's building was just beyond a sharp left-hand curve in the canal, creating a blind spot that allowed him to get within thirty or so feet of the van without being seen. When he had got as close as possible, he glanced across to Jennifer and nodded. Lowering the binoculars, she set off.

Tom readied himself. A few moments later there was the sound of squealing tires and then the tortured yell of bent metal and shattered glass. He immediately sprinted around the side of the building to find that, as he had hoped, all Milo's men had turned toward the opposite bank where Jennifer had slammed the car into a large metal bollard.

Tom leaped up and grabbed the drainpipe, hauling himself up it hand over hand, his feet flat to the wall as if he was walking up it. Muttering and shaking their heads, Milo's men turned back just as Tom disappeared from view and vaulted over the railings on to the second-floor balcony.

The window ahead of him was still open. The room was empty. He was in.

CHAPTER SIXTY-SIX

DROUOT AUCTION ROOMS, 9TH ARRONDISSEMENT,

PARIS

23rd April—6:26 P.M.

Archie liked this place. Compared to the sleek, sanitized efficiency of the larger auction houses, there was something reassuringly authentic and informal about Drouot. Not that it was lacking in history, its salesrooms having operated on the site since 1852. It was just that, because the auction facilities were rented by over seventy different firms of various shapes and sizes, there was a raw, entrepreneurial energy about it that was missing from the faceless conglomerates that had evolved out of the traditional auction aristocracy.

There was no need for ties or below-the-knee hemlines here, no canapés or white-gloved waiters, no photographs for the society pages of whoever happened to be sitting in the front row. This place was about the deal—the bid, the raise, the strike of the gavel, the ready camaraderie of the chase, whatever the outcome. People were even allowed to smoke, their nervous anticipation snaking from quivering lips and compressed fingers and mushrooming across the ceiling for all to see, fanning the tense atmosphere still further. It was the way things used to be, until the suits had taken over.

There seemed to be a peculiar, nervous energy tonight,

especially. The theft of the *Mona Lisa* was on everyone's lips, Archie catching fragments of scattered conversations as he elbowed his way through the crowds, people speculating about the painting's likely fate, the identity of whoever had ordered the theft and what the authorities could and should have done differently. Interestingly, their reactions seemed to be a mixture of distress and excitement, as if the people here, considering themselves to be members of the extended art fraternity, felt somehow implicated in the previous afternoon's bloody events.

"I thought Tajan were based over in the Eighth?" Archie struggled to make himself heard over the noise.

"They are," Besson confirmed, "But they still use Drouot for some of their smaller sales. There's always lots of people . . ." He paused, looking up uncertainly at the signs fixed to the wall ahead. "What room did I say?"

"Two." Archie pointed to his left.

The auction was already well underway and Archie and Besson slipped in unnoticed, eventually finding a space in the far corner that gave them a good vantage point from which to observe the rest of the audience.

"Recognize anyone?" Archie asked as the lots steadily climbed through the high fifties.

"Lots of people." Besson nodded. "But no one who stands out. *Ah, finalement.*"

"Lot number sixty-two," the auctioneer declaimed, the polka-dot handkerchief in his breast pocket fluttering as he rocked excitedly backward and forward on his heels, his hands gripping the sides of the podium. "A superb first edition of Volume One of the *Déscription de L'Egypte,* the definitive study of ancient and modern Egypt completed by the group of scientists and artists who accompanied Napoleon Bonaparte on his Egyptian Campaign."

To the left of him, a white-gloved attendant held up a leather-bound book open at the engraved title page and displayed it to the room.

"Hitler may have had a Napoleon complex, but Napoleon had an Egyptian complex," Besson whispered. "He was obsessed by the place. The full set runs to twenty-three volumes of text, engravings and maps. It even came in a specially made display case."

"This particular volume, printed in 1809, is the sole surviving volume from the set of the *Déscription de L'Egypte* owned by Doctor Francesco Antonmarchi, Napoleon Bonaparte's personal physician during his final years in exile," the auctioneer continued. "I'd like to start the bidding at twenty thousand euro." A man in the front row waggled his catalog. "Thank you, sir."

Immediately two other people joined the chase, the price rising in three thousand euro increments as the auctioneer circled between them, one of the bidders coming back immediately each time with a higher offer, another reflecting carefully before nodding. At thirty-five thousand, the price stalled, the initiative resting with a short round man with a waxed mustache who smiled nervously as the ivory hammer was raised over the ebony gavel.

At the last possible moment, a telephone bidder came in, offering forty thousand. The mustachioed man offered forty-five and then, with a sad shake of his head, declined at fifty.

"Going once to the bidder on the phone," the auctioneer warned. "Come now, ladies and gentlemen, this is a unique opportunity to acquire a definitive work with a unique pedigree. Going twice . . ."

"Seventy thousand," someone called from the back of the room, the audience giving a low murmur of surprise as they turned in their seats toward the voice. Archie strained forward and looked along the line of people standing to his right, but whoever had spoken was masked by those standing around him.

"Seventy thousand! Thank you, sir." The auctioneer beamed. "Seventy thousand at the back of the room. Now, do I hear seventy-five?" He eyed the woman on the phone to the telephone bidder hopefully, but without any real conviction.

"She'll drop out," Besson predicted. "Fifty thousand is right at the top end. Seventy is crazy."

Studiously avoiding any form of eye contact or sudden gestures, the woman spoke urgently into the phone, then listened for a few moments before looking up and giving a firm shake of her head.

"It's with the gentleman at the back of the room at seventy thousand . . ." announced the auctioneer. "Going once . . . going twice . . ." A final pause. "Sold to Monsieur Ledoux for seventy thousand euros." He cracked the hammer down. "Thank you, sir. It's an honor to have you here."

"Ledoux?" As the crowd broke up with a muted round of applause to reveal an elderly-looking man in bright red glasses and a black suit, shirt and tie, Archie turned to his companion. "Is he famous or something?"

"Paul Ledoux." Besson frowned. "The Director of the Louvre. What's he doing here?"

"More to the point, why does he want that book?"

CHAPTER SIXTY-SEVEN

QUAI DE JEMMAPES, 10TH ARRONDISSEMENT, PARIS

23rd April—6:21 P.M.

She'd only been doing about ten miles an hour when she hit the barrier post, but from the noise and the damage, you'd have thought it had been sixty. A large bite had been taken out of the front left wing, the headlight exploding in a fine spray of glass. As for the post itself, it had almost been uprooted, the paving slabs around its base lifting like loose earth around the roots of a tree blown over in a storm. It was sobering to think that these formed the only protective barrier between the road and the canal below.

Jennifer drove off before the concierge of the neighboring building, alerted by the noise, was able to make good on her angry threat to call the police. She wasn't sure if Ferrat would have issued a description of her yet, but she didn't want to wait around and find out.

There was no sign of Tom by the time she'd circled back to where they had parked before and she guessed he'd managed to make his way inside. The minutes ticked by, Jennifer nervously running her thumbnail through the small gap in her front teeth and intermittently sweeping the binoculars across each window and the men still loading up the back of the van as she waited. She checked her watch again. Still only five minutes gone.

She hated sitting here like this, a spectator, unable to help or do anything. But rather here than inside a police cell, meekly awaiting her fate. She had that to thank Tom for at least. Whatever her previous relationship with him, this girl Eva was clearly in danger. And if Eva wasn't here, then maybe there was something in this book Archie had gone to look at that would help stop Milo and get her back.

She scanned the entrance to the building again and noticed that the two guards had suddenly taken up defensive positions at either end of the van, their hands shoved tellingly under their jackets. The other two men, meanwhile, had emerged on to the street carrying a crate which they gingerly lifted into the back of the van and then covered with blankets. A crate just like the two she'd brought over from the States. A crate designed to house a small painting.

She sat up with a start. If Tom's theory was right, these could be the forged versions of the *Mona Lisa* that Milo had commissioned Rafael to paint. Perhaps he had been storing them in this building along with the rest of his equipment? If so, they'd just been handed a gilt-edged opportunity to abort Milo's plan at birth. She went to dial Tom before suddenly realizing with a grimace that the noise might give him away. Whatever she was going to do, she was going to have to do it alone.

She stepped out of the car and opened the trunk. There was a tool kit in a side pocket, and she grabbed a screwdriver and a heavy wrench, slipping them inside her coat. Turning, she jogged over the bridge just as they were bringing out a second, identically sized crate which they also placed in the back of the van before plunging back inside. Slowing her pace, she approached the rear of the van and nodded at the guard stationed there. He eyed her suspiciously as she walked past.

The second guard was standing in front of the hood, smoking, his jacket falling open to reveal the gun tucked in the waistband of his black jeans.

"Cigarette?" she asked hopefully, positioning herself out

of sight of the first guard and gesturing with her hands. Looking her up and down with a smile, he nodded, reaching into his back pocket. His eyes only dipped for a second, but that was all the time Jennifer needed to lash him across the side of the head with the wrench. With a grunt he fell forward into her outstretched arms. She lowered him gently to the street and then rolled him out of sight as best she could under the front of the van.

Pausing to check that no one had seen or heard her, she sidled around to the driver's side door. It was open and she slipped inside, crouching in the footwell to hide from the first guard who she could see quite clearly now through the open rear doors. The other two men came out, placed a third crate in the van and then slammed the doors shut.

Sensing her opportunity, she forced the screwdriver into the ignition slot and then turned it hard. The mechanism snapped with a muffled crack. Then she clambered into the back of the van, making her way over to the three crates. Easing the tip of the screwdriver under the lid, she quickly prized the first one open and scooped out the packing straw.

There she was. The *Mona Lisa*. Strangely incongruous in these somber, airless surroundings, with only packing boxes, crates and the thick stench of diesel for company, but unmistakably her. The strange thing was that, even though she knew it was a forgery, it was still infused with an almost spiritual quality that gave it a strange, magnetic draw. It felt somehow wrong to mutilate that delicately sensuous face and soft smile. And yet she knew that was exactly what she had to do.

She raised the screwdriver above her head like a dagger, but before she could plunge it into the wooden panel, the rear doors suddenly snapped open.

"I knew I recognized you," the first guard snarled, a cold look carved on his face as he grabbed her wrist. "You're the same dumb bitch who just crashed your car opposite."

"Raoul's out cold," one of the other men yelled from the front of the vehicle.

"Check the van," the guard ordered.

The other man climbed into the driver's seat.

"She's taken out the ignition."

"Start it from the engine bay," the guard called back, hauling Jennifer out and pinning her to the inside of the open door. "I want this shipment out of here ASAP."

The driver popped the hood and then jumped down. The guard pressed his gun to her temple.

"Start talking."

Jennifer stared back at him defiantly. With a thin smile, he smacked the butt of the gun into the side of her head, opening up a deep gash on her temple and knocking her to the ground.

"You've got three seconds," he warned her, hauling her to her feet and cocking the gun. "One . . . Two . . ."

A shot suddenly rang out and with a choked gurgle he collapsed to the ground. She looked up. Tom was standing in the doorway, his gun smoking.

"Get over here," Tom shouted, taking cover as one of the other men, sheltering behind the vehicle, returned fire. The engine suddenly burst into life, the hood slamming down with a clang.

"Come on," he urged her. She hesitated and then shook her head. She couldn't let the paintings get away.

Gripping the screwdriver between her teeth, she dropped to the ground and then crawled under the van. Locating the petrol tank, she stabbed it repeatedly, the oily liquid spraying on to her arms and the street.

The two remaining men, still firing at Tom, clambered through the passenger door, stamped on the accelerator and roared away, the vehicle lurching as they ran over the guard still lying on the street where Jennifer had left him, snapping his neck.

"Are you okay?" Tom ran over and pulled her to her feet. Although he sounded angry, he looked worried by the sight of the gash on her head. "What the hell were you doing? We agreed ten minutes."

"You were right." She leaped over to the guard and felt for his matches. "Milo has had copies made. Three of them. And they're in the back of that van."

She lit a match and dropped it on to the shimmering trail

of petrol from the ruptured tank. It caught light immediately, a pale blue flame, barely visible in the daylight, that raced along the street in pursuit of the speeding van.

They watched, fascinated, as it skipped over the cobblestones, flushing orange in one place and yellow in another, irresistibly drawing closer and closer until, with a final effort, it leaped toward the underside of the vehicle. For a moment nothing happened. Then there was a flash and a sudden explosion as a fireball ripped through the van. It veered to the left and smashed into a tree, its tires on fire, the roof bent back like a half-opened tin can, thick smoke spilling out of every orifice.

Through the open rear doors, Jennifer could just about make out the outline of the three crates, burning like bodies on a funeral pyre.

CHAPTER SIXTY-EIGHT

QUAI DE JEMMAPES, 10TH ARRONDISSEMENT, PARIS

23rd April—7:27 P.M.

The heat had scorched the tree trunk and formed a semicircular dent of shriveled leaves in the otherwise luxuriantly green branches directly above the van's blackened carcass.

"What's the damage?" Ferrat turned from the smoldering wreckage that the fire brigade were still hosing down with foam, and strode back toward the main crime scene.

"Another six bodies."

Gallas had been foisted on him by the chief of police, supposedly to help, but in reality reporting back on his every movement. That was half the problem. Everyone was so busy covering their own backsides that no one was actually focusing on solving the case. No one apart from him.

"Six? I was told four—two on the street and two in the van."

"They just found another two inside the building. Looks like they let them bleed to death rather than risk taking them to a doctor."

"I can't turn around on this case without tripping over another stiff," Ferrat sighed.

"If it's any consolation, they've been dead a day or so."

"It's no consolation whatsoever," Ferrat snapped. "What about the prints we found over at Levy's?"

"The lab just called. Browne was definitely there."

"But no match with the blood found in the tunnel yet?" Ferrat checked.

"No, we're still waiting to see if the FBI get a hit. Our guys could tell one of them was a woman. They just couldn't say who."

"Let's see what the Americans come up with. One thing's for sure: if Browne was at Levy's, the man seen with her must have been Kirk."

"But why would they have killed Levy?"

"Maybe she was in on it with them?" Ferrat speculated. "Maybe they had nothing to do with it in the first place. To be honest, none of this makes any sense anymore." He gave a wild sweep of his arm to emphasize his confusion.

Gallas's radio crackled as a voice broke into their conversation.

"Sir, there's a witness here who swears she saw Browne here, too."

Ferrat grabbed Gallas's radio off him before he could answer.

"What have you got?"

"I'm with the concierge of one of the blocks across the canal from you," Ferrat and Gallas looked over to where a uniformed officer was signaling to them. "She's adamant that someone matching Browne's description collided with this barrier post and then drove off." He pointed to a post that had been ripped out of the pavement.

"I don't suppose there's any chance she took a note of what car this woman was driving?" Ferrat asked hopefully.

"Make, model and registration number." The officer triumphantly waved a small piece of paper.

"We've held off as long as we can," Ferrat sighed. "It's going to annoy our American friends, but let's get a photo and description of Browne out to the media. Someone must have seen her. There can't be that many black female FBI agents running around Paris."

"What do you think she was doing here?" asked Gallas as Ferrat handed him his radio back.

"I think we've walked into a war and she's part of it." Ferrat pinched the top of his nose wearily. "Milo and Kirk both have something the other wants and they're going to carry on killing until one of them wins. And we just get to pick up the pieces."

CHAPTER SIXTY-NINE

FONTAINEBLEAU, FRANCE

23rd April—8:43 P.M.

It was a fifty-minute drive from the underground garage where Tom and Jennifer had met Archie and swapped cars to Ledoux's house in Fontainebleau.

"So there was no sign of Milo?" Archie asked, still grinning at Tom's description of how Jennifer had destroyed the forged paintings.

"No," said Tom. "But I found this."

"Eva?" Archie guessed, as Tom held up a silver bangle.

"I gave this to her when . . ." His voice tailed off as his eyes caught Jennifer's. "She was wearing this when Milo's men captured her in Seville. It was in one of the rooms."

"What about you?" Jennifer asked Archie in a brittle tone. "Did you see who bought the book?"

With a nod, Archie told them about Ledoux and his last-minute knock-out bid.

"According to Henri, Ledoux never usually shows his face at Drouot," Archie continued. "Rough crowd, apparently. He must have really wanted it."

"You've met Ledoux," Tom turned to Jennifer. "What do you think he's up to?"

"Levy told us there was some deal to make sure the *Mona*

Lisa never made it up to the lab for testing," she reminded them. "Ledoux must have known that the painting was a fake. Maybe they were working together."

"That still doesn't explain how he knew about the book," Archie pointed out.

"Where is Henri?" Tom frowned. "Didn't he want to come along tonight?"

"He had to finish up the alterations you wanted to Rafael's *Yarnwinder* forgery," Archie explained. "By the way, he said to tell you that J-P's been transferred to some hospital over in the thirteenth. Pity something."

"Pitié Salpêtrière." Tom nodded, recognizing the name. "Is he okay?"

"Yeah, he's fine. But he's not going anywhere. Bars on the window and armed guards outside in case he tries to make a run for it. Right, this is it." Archie turned down a narrow lane and killed the engine.

"Where?" Tom peered into the gloom. There seemed to be nothing but fields and the occasional winking light from a distant farm.

"Back there," Archie pointed.

"Be quicker if I go alone. You okay to wait here?" Tom asked Jennifer hopefully.

"Sure." She shrugged. "Just make it quick."

Tom nodded. At least Jennifer no longer felt the need to police his every move. Perhaps the afternoon's events had gone some way to restoring her shattered trust. Either that or the headache from where she had been hit earlier was worse than she was letting on.

"I'll be in and out," he reassured her.

Tom made his way back to the main road. It was a windy night, a constant breeze bending the long grass sprouting along the verge, the occasional wild gust changing the pitch of the leaves fluttering above from a low whisper to a deep roar.

Ledoux lived in a rambling old mill house at the end of a winding gravel drive. A narrow river flanked the property, the rusting metal fixtures protruding over the silted mill race showing where the water wheel would once have hung.

Scaling the ivy-clad wall, Tom kept to the shadows of the trees that lined the riverbank until he reached the house. Then, keeping below the windows, he ghosted his way past the front door to the far corner and made his way around to the back.

Ledoux was sitting at a desk in a room Tom took to be his office, although it had clearly once served as the library. The shelves that lined each wall had been stripped of books and filled instead with a large and varied collection of modern sculpture. Lighting installed at the rear of each shelf illuminated the different shapes and colors of the sculptures, some fluid and flowing and made of colored glass or stone, others sharp and twisted and made from untreated steel or recycled plastic.

Peering through the gap between the fastened shutters, he could see that Ledoux was wearing a purple silk dressing gown over an open-necked black shirt, his red glasses pushed up on to his head as he bent forward over an open book. He was holding some sort of steel instrument in his hand, and appeared to be gingerly probing the inside cover.

The sound of a bell echoed through the house. Ledoux glanced up in annoyance, but ignored it. A few moments later the bell rang again and this time, swearing under his breath, he stood up, his dressing gown momentarily gaping open and revealing that he had removed his trousers but not his socks. He closed the book and placed it carefully in the desk drawer which he then locked, slipping the key into his pocket.

As soon as he'd left the room, Tom slipped the blade of his knife through the gap in the shutters and lifted the latch. The window eased open noiselessly and he lowered himself in. The rudimentary lock on the desk drawer only resisted him for a few seconds. Inside, together with an unpaid parking ticket and a men's contact magazine, was a thick book embossed in gold. Pausing only to confirm that it was the right one, he slipped it into his backpack and then padded over to the open window.

As he climbed out, the sound of raised voices echoed through the house's low corridors toward him. He paused.

There was something about one of these voices that sounded very familiar. And very unexpected.

He stepped back inside and crept over to the doorway. Through the crack, he could see Ledoux standing in the main hallway, arguing feverishly in French with another man. Arguing with Milo.

"We'd agreed you wouldn't come here," Ledoux said angrily, toying with the tassels on his dressing-gown belt. "They could be watching me. It's too risky."

"We'd agreed that the painting was to be moved up to the laboratory," Milo retorted, his voice measured and calm. "That didn't happen either."

"I've told you, that wasn't my fault." Ledoux's dressing gown slipped open and he fumbled with the belt as he fastened it around himself again. "Everything was set up exactly as we'd agreed. But Kirk made them panic. I couldn't stop them moving it without implicating myself. As soon as the convoy left, I sent you the combination to the box it was being transported in. I did what I could."

"Of course you did." Milo tilted his head slightly to one side. "If you hadn't, you'd already be dead. That's not why I'm here."

"It's not?"

"The forgeries have been destroyed."

"Destroyed . . . How?" Ledoux stammered.

"That's irrelevant." Tom couldn't help himself from smiling at the black rage that momentarily engulfed Milo's face.

"Your forgeries are nothing to do with me," Ledoux insisted nervously, trying to preempt any move by Milo to implicate him. "All I wanted was the painting out of the museum. That's what I paid you for."

"And you got what you wanted," Milo countered icily. "Well done." He stepped forward until they were almost touching. "But where does that leave me?"

"That's not my fault." There was a desperate edge to Ledoux's voice.

"There's hundreds of millions of dollars at stake here. It's somebody's fault."

"I thought you told me that you got the original back

when Kirk tried to swap it for the girl. You can just use that to paint some more," Ledoux suggested hopefully.

"That wasn't the original, it was another forgery." Milo gave a hollow laugh. "Quintavalle must have made an extra copy and left it for Tom somewhere. Anyway, the police put three holes in it when they ambushed us. It's no use to anyone."

"That's not my—"

With a sudden jerk, Milo smashed his forehead into the bridge of Ledoux's nose. The director screamed as it broke, blood streaming between his fingers as he clutched his face, his eyes filling with tears.

"I'll tell you if it's not your fault or not," Milo hissed in his ear.

"What do you want?" Ledoux sobbed, his voice muffled. "It's not my . . . I can't help you any more than I already have."

Milo stepped back and considered him for a moment with a curious smile, before holding out a crisp white handkerchief.

"You can help me understand something that's been puzzling me," Milo asked as Ledoux accepted the handkerchief and pressed it to his nose. "This job is worth millions, yet you've never asked for anything. Not once."

"So?" Ledoux shrugged sullenly.

"My father once told me that I should never trust a man who didn't drink," Milo reflected, circling him slowly. "He was wrong. What he should have said is that you should never trust a man who isn't interested in money. It makes them impossible to read. Difficult to predict."

"This was never about the money to me," Ledoux insisted. "This was about safeguarding the Louvre's reputation."

"Lie to me again and I'll kill you." Milo grabbed a handful of hair and yanked Ledoux's head back so that the sharp angle of his adam's apple bulged out of his neck. "Don't tell me that this was some selfless act. I don't buy it. There's no such thing."

"What do you want from me," he gurgled.

Milo loosened his grip on Ledoux's hair and pushed him away.

"I want to know what you were doing at Drouot's this evening."

"There was a lot there I was interested in," he explained falteringly. "A book."

"What's it for?"

"N-nothing," he stammered.

"You spent seventy thousand on nothing?"

"No, not nothing. Research."

"Do you take me for an idiot?" Milo stood in front of him again. "It's not even your period."

"I . . . I . . ." Ledoux began to edge away from him.

"Let me tell you what I think," Milo said softly, taking his gun out of his pocket, checking the magazine and then slapping it home. "I think the reason you never asked me for a cut was because you'd already figured out another way to cash in. And I think it's got something to do with that book."

Ledoux said nothing, transfixed by the gun glittering in Milo's hand and the silencer that he was carefully screwing on.

"Now I'm only going to ask you once. What's the book for?"

"I'm not sure," he muttered.

"Guess." Milo cocked the gun.

"Ask Quintavalle. He knows. He knows everything."

At the sound of Rafael's name, Tom strained to make out Ledoux's babbled words.

"What does he know?"

"He found something when he was doing his research. Something that involved that book."

"Where is it?"

"In my desk—" Ledoux gestured toward the office, but Milo's gaze didn't waver.

"What did he find?"

The question went unanswered as a sudden gust of wind blew the shutter Tom had opened against the wall with a clatter. Milo's eyes snapped around to the office door. Tom snatched his head out of the way just in time.

"Who's in there?" Milo demanded.

"No one."

"I asked you who's in there." Milo aimed his gun at him.

"No one," Ledoux insisted.

"I warned you about lying to me!" Milo snarled as he pressed the gun against Ledoux's chest and fired, blood spattering the walls as his back erupted.

Tossing him to the ground, Milo stepped toward the office.

CHAPTER SEVENTY

23rd April—9:01 P.M.

The door swung open. Milo carefully edged his gun and then his head around the frame. The room was empty.

He stepped inside. The desk was to his right, a small sofa and coffee table taking up the other side of the room. One of the windows was open, the wind teasing the curtains and playfully swinging the rusting shutters from side to side.

He stepped cautiously over to the window, checked that there was no one there and then locked it shut. Becalmed, the curtains dropped, a sudden hush settling over the room as he wiped his blood-spattered sleeve on the dark green material.

He flicked the desk light on and then tried the drawers, all of them opening easily and revealing a mixture of old bills, business cards, loose photos and various newspaper articles that had been carefully cut out. All, that is, apart from the central drawer.

Holding his arm in front of his eyes, Milo placed the gun against the lock and squeezed the trigger. The shot splintered the front of the drawer and this time it slid out easily.

But the book wasn't there.

He looked up at the window accusingly and then sprinted through to the front door, opening it just in time to hear a car accelerate into the distance.

"Who was that?" Djoulou asked, stepping inside.

"Kirk!" Milo slammed the door.

"You sure?"

"It was him."

"What happened?" Djoulou had just caught sight of Ledoux's crumpled body.

"He lied to me," Milo sniffed disdainfully as he stepped over the corpse and back into the office.

Sitting down heavily at the desk, he began to sort through some of the books that Ledoux had piled there, each with pages turned down or marked with a piece of paper. Various histories of da Vinci and the *Mona Lisa*. Biographies of Napoleon. Accounts of the Louvre's history.

"What was he looking for?" Djoulou frowned.

"I'm not sure."

"Maybe you should have asked him before you killed him?" Djoulou observed.

"Maybe you should shut the hell up, Captain!" Milo hissed. "Your men's incompetence cost me close to three hundred million dollars' worth of merchandise today. Luckily for them, they're dead. Don't make me look for someone else to blame."

His anger masked the fact that he knew Djoulou was probably right. The loss of the paintings had worn his temper to breaking point. Ledoux's insolence had pushed him over the edge.

With a shrug, Djoulou picked up a notepad and leafed through the first few pages. A rough chronology had been sketched out on one of them—a series of dates from 1505 until just last year. Two were circled in red: 1800 and 1804. Next to them a small comment: *La Joconde moved to Imperial apartments.* Below it a large question mark.

"What do you suppose this means?"

Milo studied the page, his eyes narrowing and then relaxing into a smile as he guessed at its meaning. So this was what Quintavalle had found. This was what Ledoux was looking for in the book he'd paid so much to secure. Evidence that the real *Mona Lisa* had survived. A clue as to its present location. Perhaps there was a way of salvaging something from this after all. He reached for his phone and dialed a number.

"Eva?"

"Did you get it?" she asked hopefully.

"Kirk was here before us."

"How did he . . . ?"

"Never mind that. I'm more interested in where he's going next."

"What do you mean?"

"Your stepfather discovered that Napoleon swapped the *Mona Lisa* for a forgery. Kirk thinks the original is still out there somewhere. That book is the key to where."

"Then we need to get the book back before he finds it," she exclaimed.

"Do we?" Milo sniffed. "He's been one step ahead of us right from the start. Why not use that? Why not just let him lead us straight to it?"

"We need to find him to follow him," she pointed out.

"That's easy," Milo smiled. "There's only one place he can go now."

CHAPTER SEVENTY-ONE

23rd April—9:01 P.M.

Tom surged out of the darkness and rapped his knuckles against the glass. They both jumped.

"Let's get out of here," he said breathlessly as he climbed in.

Archie immediately dropped into first and accelerated back on to the main road toward Paris.

"Did you slip?" Jennifer grinned at his dripping shoes and trousers.

"I jumped," Tom explained with a rueful smile. "It was the only way past Milo's men."

"He was there!" She glanced back through the rear window in concern.

"Turned up just after me," Tom confirmed. "Ledoux's working with him. Or rather, he was. But I heard enough to know that, whatever Rafael was on to, this is definitely the key."

He pulled the book out of his backpack, checked it was still dry, and then handed it to Jennifer. She turned it over in her hands, rubbing the leather binding appreciatively before flicking through some of the pages.

"Either of you know anything about books?" she asked hopefully.

Tom's eyes met Archie's in the rear-view mirror. Archie nodded.

"Not enough to figure this one out. But there's someone we know. He works in the business too. He can help."

"Where's he based?"

"You wouldn't believe me if I told you." Tom smiled.

They settled back into silence for the remainder of the journey, the darkness fading as they hit a main road and the orange streetlights lit their path back toward the city.

At least now they knew why Rafael's forgeries were so accurate, Tom reflected. Ledoux had paid Milo to steal the *Mona Lisa*. Part of the deal must have been to give Rafael direct access to the original painting, or rather the painting that the Louvre had passed off as the original. Ledoux must have helped him with his research too, locating any relevant documents or contemporary descriptions. And somehow, during the course of this work, Rafael had uncovered something. Something that Ledoux had then picked up on. Finding the real *Mona Lisa* would have been worth far more to Ledoux than money. He should have guessed that Milo would never have let him live long enough to enjoy the moment.

He glanced across at Jennifer. She was thumbing absentmindedly through the book, her thumbnail flicking the small gap in her front teeth, her dark hair falling forward across her pale brown face. It was funny, but the deeper they got, the more relaxed she seemed to become. Perhaps she realized now that she, like Tom, had been caught up in something bigger than either of them had initially realized. Perhaps she had grasped that their chances of solving this were much greater if they worked together rather than alone. Certainly he was glad to have her there. He wondered if she felt the same.

About an hour later they parked up near the northern end of the Avenue de l'Opera, next to the Metro, and got out.

"Let's take the obelisk," Tom suggested, grabbing his backpack out of the boot. "The cops may be looking for the car."

A blast of warm air tinged with the smell of rubber and disinfectant rushed up to greet them as they stood at the top of the Metro steps, two streetlights arching gracefully above them, like branches weighed down with ripe fruit.

"We'll meet you back here in an hour," Archie told Jennifer firmly.

"I don't think so," she said with a dismissive shake of her head. "I want to hear whatever this guy has to say."

"Tom?" Archie appealed.

"She's right," said Tom, his voice muffled by the scarf he was using to mask his face from passersby. "We're in this together."

"You know the rules. If he twigs, he'll go ape. He'll never let us in again."

"You mean he might never let us out." Tom grinned. "It won't come to that. She'll behave. Won't you?"

"I might, if you two would stop talking like I'm not here," she retorted. "Or if I even knew what you were talking about."

"It's simple. You can never tell anyone this place," Tom instructed her.

"What place?"

"You'll see."

CHAPTER SEVENTY-TWO

PALAIS GARNIER, 9TH ARRONDISSEMENT, PARIS

23rd April—10:10 P.M.

They crossed the road, Jennifer noticing that Tom was keeping his gaze lowered so as not to make eye contact with anyone they crossed. She did the same, certain that by now Ferrat would have released a photo and description of her, turning the entire city into his eyes and ears. Only Archie, who the police still knew nothing about, walked with his head held high.

The Palais Garnier opera house loomed ahead of them at the apex of the wide avenue, its ornate façade lavished with statuary and opulently decorated with multicolored marble friezes and columns. Far above, two gilded winged horses framed a copper dome. Behind this, the sharp, angular silhouette of its main roof fell away toward the cobbled street below.

Tom led them around to the left of the building, the posters outside the main steps indicating that the evening's performance of *Il Trittico* was sold out. Stopping about halfway down, he nodded toward a small metal door, perhaps five feet high and three across.

"In here?" Jennifer frowned. She didn't like being kept in the dark and Tom was being uncharacteristically cryptic.

"If he'll see us," said Tom, pointing at the video camera pointing toward them.

"Who?"

"He's called Ketter. Markus Ketter."

"Just don't make any sudden movements," Archie warned her. "He's a nervous bastard at the best of times."

Unprompted, the door suddenly swung open and they stepped inside. As the door locked itself shut behind them an overhead light automatically flickered on, revealing a small chamber, empty apart from the narrow stone spiral staircase that coiled steeply toward the shadowy heavens.

"I hope you've got your comfortable shoes on," Tom warned her with a smile.

The light from the chamber soon faded behind them, the steps rising in a dark, dizzy corkscrew that left Jennifer feeling increasingly disorientated and nervously pressing her right hand to the rough stone walls to keep her balance and guide her feet. The air felt thick and heavy too, the sound of their footsteps and strained breathing echoing through its dense, suffocating embrace as if it couldn't escape. But then, almost imperceptibly at first, a more gentle sound filtered down to them. A woman's voice.

"Listen," Tom said, suddenly stopping. Jennifer could hear the voice quite clearly now, a pure, crisp sound that rose and fell like the swell of the sea. "We're lucky, they don't put *Il Trittico* on very often. It's made up of three one-act operas. Sounds like they've just started *Gianni Schicchi*. Come on, I want to show you something."

A little further on the darkness suddenly lifted where one of the stones in the wall had been replaced with a small metal grille. The light from the massive central chandelier was leaking through it.

"This staircase runs behind a false wall. We're right up in the gods here." On the stage far below a young woman was seemingly pleading with her father. Tom pointed up at the ceiling. "Look, do you remember the Chagall painting I told you about?"

She did remember his rather breathless description back at the Louvre, though it seemed a lifetime ago now, rather than just a few days. He'd portrayed the ceiling then as being somehow slightly demonic. Now that she was able to see it for herself, however, she wasn't sure she agreed. The dizzying, intoxicating carousel of bright colors and wild shapes seemed more like a dream to her; a warm, slightly drunken dream that you might never want to wake up from. She gazed at it longingly, sensing Tom smiling at her, sharing in her wonder.

"It's beautiful."

Again they climbed, the music accompanying them all the way, until a solid brick wall suddenly loomed ahead of them, blocking the top of the stairs. Jennifer frowned, wondering how they were going to get past, until she noticed a small steel panel set into the bricks at about waist height. The panel suddenly snapped open and a gun muzzle appeared through the rectangle of light it had revealed, aimed straight at Tom's stomach.

"Who is it?" A muffled voice intoned in clipped, precise English.

"You know who it is, Markus," Tom chided him. "You've got infrared cameras the whole way up that staircase."

"Half the planet is looking for you, Felix. If you've led them here . . ." The accent was hard and unfeeling. German perhaps, or possibly Scandinavian.

"If I had, you wouldn't be talking to us now," Tom said nonchalantly.

"Who's she?" The gun swiveled to point at her.

"She's with us."

"She moves like a cop."

"Old habits die hard. She's running with us now."

There was a pause.

"What do you want? You know I don't like surprises."

Tom held the book out. The gun was slowly retracted and a white gloved hand reached out and grabbed it. There was a long silence. Then the hiss and release of a hydraulic pump as the entire wall slowly rose into the roof like a giant portcullis. They stepped inside and the wall immediately lowered itself behind them.

Ketter emerged out of the darkness, shifting his weight

warily from foot to foot. Dressed entirely in white, from his patent leather shoes to his tie and white cotton gloves, his willowy figure stood out from the surrounding gloom like a candle flame in the night.

"Come," he ordered them, turning on his heel before she could get a good look at his face.

"Shoes there. Lighters and matches here. Wash there." Ketter pointed first at a low shelf, then at a large dish and finally at a white porcelain surgeon's basin complete with elongated tap handles to allow people to turn the water off with their elbows rather than use their hands again.

"What's with the outfit?" she whispered.

"So he can see the dirt," Tom explained as he turned the taps on and squeezed some soap on to his hands. "In fact the only thing he hates more than dirt is fire."

"Why fire?" she asked.

"You'll see," Archie hissed, shaking his head as he dropped his lighter into the dish, making it ping.

"Look," Jennifer mouthed. Ketter was sealing a thin plastic sheet over their shoes. Sensing their eyes on him, he stood up and smoothed his suit down self-consciously.

She could see now that he was in his late fifties, with deep vertical lines carved into his sunken cheeks and pink grooves on the bridge of his nose from wearing glasses. He was also tall, and would have seemed even taller if it wasn't for the way he pulled his shoulders up into his neck as if he was flinching. In fact, there was something slightly elephantine about him, his hands and feet almost comically oversized.

Satisfied that they were done, Ketter led them up a narrow set of stairs to a steel trapdoor set into the low ceiling. Unlocking it, he nodded at them to step through and then bolted it shut behind them, muttering to himself as he opened and shut the lock several times to check it was secure.

A cloying red tint from a couple of filtered overhead lights gave the room an apocalyptic, almost satanic feel. Ketter's suit, for one, had been transformed into a blood-red velvet and even his thinning brush of white hair had burst into a crown of crimson flames.

He found the switch and flicked it on, a cool wash of light

revealing the dome's graceful roof soaring high above them, the walls covered in white rectangular tiles whose beveled edges glinted in the light. But her eye was instinctively drawn to the regimented lines of shelves that stretched the length of the circular room as if on parade, their height rising and falling with the arch of the dome like a bulging muscle.

It was an impressive and unexpected sight and she breathed in sharply, just catching Tom staring at her out of the corner of his eye. It was strange, but he seemed to be taking a rather perverse pleasure in bringing her here, in initiating her into some of the secrets of his world. Perhaps this was his way of opening up, of convincing her that she really could trust him again.

"What is this place?" she whispered as Ketter led them down one of the narrow corridors formed by the rows of bookcases, suddenly understanding the reason for Ketter's dislike of fire.

"A library." Tom smiled. "A library of stolen books."

In truth it seemed less of a library to Jennifer than a morgue—the walls covered with white tiles, the books laid out on the metal shelves towering on either side like corpses on gurneys. And the whole time the opera's distant echo rose from the stage below, the words half-formed and indecipherable but strangely compelling.

"A first edition *Don Quixote*." Tom pointed at the gilded spine of one of the books wrapped in a protective wrapper on the felted shelves. "And here, a full set of the *Blaeu-Van der Hem Atlas*."

"Don't touch," Ketter warned them without looking around.

"All stolen?"

"Markus finds them a new home, gives them a new lease on life."

There was a break in the shelving to their right and Ketter led them through it, crossing several aisles until he came to a small clearing. To the left was a narrow bed, meticulously made, and a spotless kitchen and eating area. To the right was a workshop, complete with desk and an array of tools, magnifying glasses, scanners, glues and other binding materials.

Ketter sat down and placed the book in front of him on a

type of foam pillow that supported its spine. His hunched shoulders seemed to relax as he arched forward over the book, as if adopting a familiar and comforting position.

"What do you want?"

"An opinion," Tom answered.

"On what?"

"We're not sure," Tom conceded. "Anything unusual."

"The standard consultation fee is five thousand dollars."

"Put it on our account," Archie suggested.

Ketter glared at him unsmilingly.

"It's a joke, Markus," Archie reassured him, raising his eyebrows at Tom and Jennifer. "I'll make sure you have it in the morning."

"Good." Apparently satisfied with this, Ketter took a fresh tissue and opened the book to the title page. "Volume One of the Imperial edition of the *Description de L'Egypte*," he intoned. "Published 1809. Condition . . . acceptable. I've seen better. It's rare, yes, but without the rest of the set and in this state . . . not particularly valuable. From the library of . . ." He glanced down at the bookplate on the inside front cover and then looked up with a toothy smile, the first he had given. "Well, you certainly didn't waste any time."

"What do you mean?" Jennifer asked.

"This was in tonight's sale at Tajan, wasn't it? I saw it in the catalog a few weeks ago. What did it go for in the end?"

"Seventy thousand," Archie volunteered.

"Too much." Ketter shook his head. "Forty, forty-five at the most."

"Ledoux bought it," Tom informed him.

"Ledoux?" He seemed genuinely surprised. "That's interesting . . ." He looked down at the book again with a frown. "I wonder why he . . . ?" His voice tailed off as he switched on a desk light that had a magnifying glass built into it and held it over the signed bookplate. "This has been tampered with," he said slowly, pointing at where one of the corners had been lifted.

"Ledoux was prodding it with some sort of scalpel," Tom confirmed, thinking back to what he had seen through the window in Fontainebleau.

Ketter reached for a bottle in front of him and moistened a cotton wool bud. Then, gripping the raised corner with a large pair of tweezers, he rubbed the bud against the underside of the plate. Little by little it lifted, the chemical dissolving the glue, Ketter proving himself to be surprisingly dextrous despite his ungainly hands.

"There's something there," Jennifer exclaimed as a spidery shape emerged from under it. "A word."

"A name," Tom corrected her as the scrawl became clearer, underlined by a wild swish of black ink. "A signature. Napoleon."

CHAPTER SEVENTY-THREE

AVENUE DE L'OBSERVATOIRE, 14TH ARRONDISSEMENT,

PARIS

23rd April—10:27 P.M.

There. It was done. Besson placed the canvas in the crate, flicked the light off and shut the mirror behind him. He'd rarely worked as hard or as fast to get something finished on time. Especially something as unusual as this. He just hoped it was what Tom wanted.

The sound of the front doorbell trilled through the apartment. Besson checked his watch with a frown. Maybe they were back early. Good. He was as intrigued as the rest of them to learn exactly what Ledoux had been hoping to find in that book. He unbolted the door and swung it open with an eager smile.

"Henri Besson?"

A Japanese man was standing on the landing wearing jeans and a thigh-length brown leather coat. He had a square, flat face and a broad scar across the bridge of his nose that looked as if it was still healing. The point of his chin was covered with stubble into which he had shaved a narrow vertical bar, separating the two sides of his face. A large purple birthmark covered his left cheek as if a bottle of ink had been carelessly spilled across him and then left to dry.

To his left stood another man, bald and dressed entirely in black apart from a spotless white tie. Even though his face was concealed by a white surgeon's mask hooked behind each ear, Besson could still make out his eyes, pale green and cold as a mountain spring. His smile faded.

"Who are you? How did you get in here?"

"My name is Leo. I represent Mr. Asahi Takeshi," the man announced, bowing slightly in the direction of the masked man at his side. "He is here about a painting."

"Then he can call me in the morning like everyone else," Besson said impatiently.

"He is here about one of your paintings," Leo continued calmly. "*La Nappe Mauve*? Perhaps you remember it?"

"*La Nappe Mauve* was painted by Chagall," Besson said warily.

"Not the version my employer was sold." Leo's voice hardened. "As you know, that was painted by you."

Besson slammed the door shut and threw the deadbolts home. But before he could move, the wood around the lock splintered in three, then five places, the muffled whisper of a silenced gun just about audible. Transfixed, he watched as a couple of firm kicks sent the mechanism spinning across the floor. A hand reached in through the hole, felt for the bolts and loosened them. The door swung open, framing the two men. Takeshi's hands were clasped behind his back and, even though he still had his mask on, Besson was almost certain he was smiling.

Four men streamed through the doorway and grabbed Besson. He struggled as far as he could with his good arm, but it was more for show than with any real hope of escape. He'd seen this game played out more times than he cared to remember. He could only hope it ended quickly.

"In here—" The man who'd introduced himself as Leo led them toward the clean room. A butterfly knife danced into the hands of one of the men as he gouged a jagged tear in its plastic walls. The others stretched the folds open and dragged

Besson through. He noticed that two of the men were missing the little fingers on their left hands.

"Tie him down."

Besson felt himself being lifted on to the inspection table and his wrists and ankles being zip-locked to the metal fixings. They'd come prepared for whatever was about to happen. They'd planned his death. A light snapped on, searing the gloom. Besson turned his head to it, blinking. A video camera. He swallowed hard.

Takeshi stood behind his head so that Besson was staring straight up at him, the surface of the mask rippling every time he breathed, his bald head blocking out one of the overhead lights like a large moon that had passed in front of the sun.

"Did you really think you would escape?" Leo's voice echoed from the other side of the room.

"All I did was paint what they told me to," Besson insisted, his eyes still locked fearfully on Takeshi's.

"That's what Quintavalle said."

"That was you?" For a fleeting moment, Besson's surprise drowned out his fear and he raised his head, straining to see Leo at the foot of the table. "You killed him because of a painting?"

"We killed him because he stole from Mr. Takeshi."

"I killed him because, like you, he made me look a fool," Takeshi spoke for the first time, the words delivered in a measured, controlled tone that was at once soothing and coldly menacing. Besson lay down again.

"What are you going to do to me?" he asked Takeshi resignedly.

"Me? Nothing. I'm just here to watch."

Takeshi stepped back with a nod and two of his men approached. One of them was holding a wooden spoon which he forced between Besson's lips, pressing his tongue flat to the floor of his mouth and making him gag. The other was holding a tin of red enamel paint that he opened with the blade of his knife.

Besson felt his head being tilted back so that his throat was lifted and exposed. The second man placed the edge of the tin against his bloodless lips and, like a priest giving communion, carefully poured the paint into his open mouth.

He felt the thick liquid glooping over his teeth and sliding to the back of his throat. He felt the wooden spoon pressing his tongue out of the way so that the paint could flow unimpeded down his throat and up along his nose and, when he could hold his breath no longer, into his lungs.

He felt it hardening like concrete.

CHAPTER SEVENTY-FOUR

PALAIS GARNIER, 9TH ARRONDISSEMENT, PARIS

23rd April—10:35 P.M.

Ledoux's no idiot." Ketter looked as though he might actually laugh. "This is one of Napoleon's personal copies. It's worth double what he paid."

"That's not why he bought it," Tom said confidently. "There must be something else."

"I've got a couple of other examples here," Ketter volunteered. "We can compare them, if you like."

He shuffled off toward the bookshelves, reappearing a few moments later carefully carrying a similar-looking book under his arm.

"This is from a set with an impeccable provenance. If your version is different in any way, this will reveal it."

He placed the books side by side and slowly leafed through them looking for any differences in the text, font or layout, again using a fresh tissue to turn the pages. It was a painstaking process, the silence filled by the opera's distant echo, but one that Ketter pursued with unwavering concentration, pausing only to sip water from a small glass that he kept on the floor so as not to risk spilling it over one of the books.

"It's a match," Ketter eventually announced with a weary

sigh. "Of course there are some forensic tests I could do to be certain, but these will take . . ."

He tailed off as he bent forward over the leather cover, then reopened the book and examined the spine carefully.

"This has been rebound," he said slowly.

"It's not original?" Jennifer asked.

"It's all original," he reassured her. "But the leather binding has been taken off and reattached. I hadn't noticed before, but you can see here and here, that the stitching is slightly different and that the paper has been lifted and then stuck back down."

Tom studied the places Ketter had indicated on the inside cover and across the top of the spine, but to him they looked no different from the other book.

"Take it off," he instructed him.

"Are you sure?" Ketter glanced up uncertainly. "This is an extremely valuable book. Personal items of Napoleon's hardly ever come up for auction."

"I don't care what it's worth. In fact you can keep it when we've finished," Tom insisted impatiently. "Just take it off."

"As you wish." Ketter shrugged.

Delicately gripping a scalpel between his thumb and forefinger, he made a series of incisions along the inside cover, the blade slicing through the downy paper with a faint rasping noise. Once released, he gently peeled the leather binding away from the rest of the book, hacking through a few sinewy strands of cotton which clung stubbornly to the pages. Shorn of its cover, the book looked strangely naked to Tom; a shivering mass of white paper exposed, like a newborn baby, to the cold light of the world for the first time.

"Look—" Ketter pointed to a small strip of paper, perhaps an inch across and six inches long, which had been glued to the inside of the spine. Ketter glanced up at them excitedly, his impassive demeanor momentarily, at least, forgotten.

"What does it say?" Archie moved around the table to get a better look.

"Don't touch it," Ketter cautioned anxiously. "It could tear."

"Can you open it?" Tom asked.

"I can try."

Ketter picked up his tweezers and slowly lifted one edge where it had been folded down. This in turn uncovered another flap that he also delicately folded back.

"What are they?" Tom frowned at the faded ink drawings that had been revealed.

"They're symbols," Jennifer breathed. "Hieroglyphs." She quickly counted them. "Twenty-six in all."

"It's a key," Tom guessed. "One for each letter of the alphabet."

Jennifer nodded. "So an owl must be an A. The snake a B. The hand a C. Look—"

She grabbed a piece of paper and jotted down the letters of the alphabet and then roughly sketched the corresponding symbol set out on the small piece of paper.

"There are hieroglyphs on the obelisk," Archie reminded them.

"What obelisk?" Ketter frowned.

"It's better you don't know," Tom answered as he unhooked his backpack from his shoulder and retrieved the obelisk from inside, placing it on the table.

"The symbols repeat themselves," Jennifer said slowly, as she examined the obelisk's decorated surface.

"What's the first one?" Tom asked.

"A sort of semi-circle."

"That's an L," Tom confirmed from the list Jennifer had laid out.

"Then an owl. That's an A."

"Then a hand," Archie volunteered.

"C," read Tom.

Slowly the words took shape, although it was often unclear where one ended and the next one began.

"It's French," Tom informed them, before reading the message back slowly. *"La clé au sourire vie a l'interieur de chacun."*

"The key to the smile lives inside each of us," Ketter translated with a frown.

"Oh, very deep." Archie rolled his eyes.

"The smile?" Jennifer said slowly. "Do you think it's referring to the *Mona Lisa*'s smile?"

"Is that what this is about?" Ketter looked slightly faint.

"Maybe it's saying her smile means different things to different people," Archie suggested, less flippant now.

"Or something even simpler." Tom picked the obelisk up and carefully felt its weight. "If the key lives inside each of us, why not in this too?"

"In the obelisk?" Jennifer gave a half laugh. "You're kidding, right?"

With a shrug, Tom lifted the obelisk above his head and flung it to the floor. It smashed into three pieces like the mast of a stricken ship dashed on the rocks, hundreds of small fragments of porcelain skating across the concrete.

"What the hell are you doing?" Archie cried disbelievingly. "If Raf nicked that, it wasn't so that you could . . ." He tailed off as Tom bent down and then triumphantly held out a small bundle of material about the size of a box of matches that he had retrieved from inside the obelisk's square base.

Ketter was silent, his eyes bulging, although Tom wasn't sure if that was surprise at what he had just witnessed or the mess on his floor.

He placed the package down on the desk and carefully unwrapped it. It came open to reveal a small key decorated at one end with a gilded N surrounded by laurel leaves.

"The key to the smile," Jennifer breathed excitedly.

"Forget the key. Take a butcher's at this—"

Archie smoothed out the material that the key had been wrapped in, tilting the desk light so they could all see the faint lines and occasional words that had been drawn on to it.

"It's a map of Paris," said Tom after studying it for a few seconds. "Look, there's the Seine and the Ile St. Louis."

"And this must be where we need to get to—" Jennifer pointed at a spot that had been circled in red.

"The *Autel des Obelisques*," Tom read the words underneath it. "The Altar of Obelisks. It certainly fits."

"It can't be Paris," Ketter said with a firm shake of his head. "None of these roads exist."

They gazed at the map uncertainly, the steadily increasing

pace and volume of the echoing music suggesting that, far below, the opera was reaching its climax.

"You're right," Tom said with a frown. "Either we've got the wrong city or . . ." He paused, struck by a sudden thought.

"Or what?"

"Or we're looking in the wrong place."

"Where else is there to look?" Archie frowned.

"Underground," Tom suggested excitedly. "This is a map of the Paris catacombs."

"If it is, I can introduce you to a guide," Ketter offered. "Lives down there now, as far as I can tell."

"I don't want to get lost," Tom agreed. "Can you try and set something up?"

"When for?"

"Now."

As Tom and the others pored over the map, trying to work out exactly how it related to the streets above, Ketter dialed his contact and made some brief arrangements.

"Somebody called Franzy will meet you over at the Place du Trocadéro at eleven," Ketter announced. "Apparently there's an entrance near there. He'll find you. But she can't go." He pointed at Jennifer accusingly.

"What do you mean?" Tom sounded annoyed.

"No cops, no weapons. Those are the rules," Ketter insisted.

"There's no way . . ."

"That's fine," Jennifer nodded. "You two go."

"I thought we'd agreed to stick together?" Tom reminded her. He'd made a deal and wanted to stick to it.

"We need to know what's down there. This is the only way," she explained.

Tom shook his head but said nothing, knowing that she was probably right. He felt for her though. Ketter was cutting her no slack, despite the risk she had taken by coming with them.

"That's decided," Ketter nodded. "Good. I will see you out. You haven't got much time."

Covering his desk with a white cloth, Ketter led them back

through the bookshelves, down through the trapdoor, past the washbasins where they recovered their shoes and Archie his lighter, to the false wall. He paused to check the video monitors positioned to the left of the door and then pressed a switch. With a hiss, the wall lifted into the roof and Tom, Jennifer and Archie stepped out into the staircase.

Ketter watched as the wall clunked shut, then retraced his steps to his office. He sat at his desk, gazing at the dismembered book lying in front of him. A dark shape emerged from the shadows.

"You see? I told you they would come." Eva smiled, tying her hair back. "I'm glad I stayed."

"You need to leave if you don't want to lose them," Ketter said sullenly.

"Why bother, when you're going to tell me exactly where they're going?"

"That wasn't what we agreed," he insisted angrily.

"The deal's changed." She shrugged, flicking her Zippo open and striking a light.

Ketter gazed fearfully at the guttering flame, then at the books slumbering obliviously on the shelves behind her, and nodded.

CHAPTER SEVENTY-FIVE

23rd April—10:49 P.M.

By the time they made it down on to the street the curtain had come down and a few members of the audience were already being chased down the front steps by the sound of muffled applause. Several were humming snatched fragments of the closing aria.

"We need to shift if we're going to meet this bloke by eleven," Archie pointed out.

"I'll head over to Henri's," Jennifer suggested. "Bring him up to speed."

"You okay with that?" Tom asked, his tone making it clear that he suspected she wasn't.

He was right. She was annoyed with Ketter's instinctive distrust of her, of being excluded. But then it was a feeling she knew only too well. She'd always had to walk an uneasy line between her white mother's South Carolina farming background and her city-dwelling father's Haitian heritage. Caught between two colors, two cultures, immigrant and settler, city and country, North and South, she'd never been fully accepted by either. It was the same now, the police pursuing her as a criminal, the criminals treating her with the distrust and contempt they reserved for the cops. She was trapped in a strange twilight world where she belonged everywhere and yet nowhere at once. Only Tom, it seemed, was making an effort to bridge the gap, to give her a sense of belonging, however temporary.

"It's not like we have much choice," she said with a resigned shrug. "Why don't we meet at, say, one?"

"The Place St. Michel," Tom agreed, flagging down a passing taxi for her. "And you'd better take this—" He slipped her his gun.

"Shouldn't you . . . ?"

"You heard Ketter. No cops, no weapons. You'll need this, too. It's the entrance code to the door downstairs." He jotted down a four-digit number on a piece of paper and handed it to her. "Henri said he was finishing my painting tonight, so he should be in."

"Be careful," she warned them, stuffing the paper into her pocket.

"Aren't we always?" Tom grinned.

The taxi's radio was tuned to a lively phone-in debating how good a painting the *Mona Lisa* actually was and whether its theft wasn't actually a blessing in disguise. The driver made a half-hearted attempt to draw Jennifer into a similar conversation, but with her hat pulled down low and her face buried in her collar so she couldn't be recognized, she pretended to have fallen asleep. He gave up, leaving her to reflect on the day's events.

It was hard to believe only fourteen hours had passed since Ferrat had snapped a pair of cuffs on her wrists over breakfast. So much had changed in that short period. Not only in her mounting excitement at the discovery of clues that might lead them to the real *Mona Lisa*, but also in what she felt about Tom. She believed him when he said he was sorry and that he hadn't known she would be implicated in all this. She believed him when he said he was trying to help her. That didn't mean she could entirely trust him, of course, but then did she entirely trust anyone?

The traffic was light and it took them less than fifteen minutes to make their way south through the Place de la Bastille and over the river to Besson's apartment. She punched in the entry code and the front door clicked open, giving her access to a vaulted passageway and a second, glass door. She located Besson's buzzer on the wall to her left and pressed it. A few moments later the door buzzed open. She frowned. Last time he'd checked who it was. Maybe he'd guessed that, at this hour, it could only have been her or Tom.

A few minutes later, the elevator jerked to an unsteady halt on the fifth floor. She got out, half expecting Besson to be there to greet her. But the hall was empty and the front door ajar, a faint glow running the length of the narrow gap where the streetlights were shining through the apartment's uncovered windows. She knew instinctively that something wasn't right.

She took out the gun Tom had given her and cocked it, noting the splintered lock as she stepped warily inside. Someone had forced their way in.

"Henri?" she called. There was no answer.

Carefully checking behind her every few steps, she slowly made her way through the office to the lab, its sealed plastic chamber glowing like a Chinese lantern. With a growing sense of dread, she saw that one of its walls had been slashed open.

She carefully stepped through the opening and then stopped, her gun dropping. Besson had been strapped to the inspection table by his wrists and ankles, a single light illuminating him as if he were a painting on a gallery wall. She ran to him, but there was no mistaking the unexpected symmetry of his face, the right-hand side now mirroring in death the flaccid, hollow-eyed, slack-cheeked paralysis of the left, blood trickling from his nose and the corners of his mouth. Except, she suddenly realized as she leaned closer and placed her gun down next to him, it wasn't blood at all but paint, congealed into thick red clots and veins like candle wax.

She stepped back as a sudden, terrible question flashed into her head. If Besson was dead, who had buzzed her in? Instinctively, she reached for the gun, but a cloth was pressed to her face before she could even consider an answer.

CHAPTER SEVENTY-SIX

PLACE DU TROCADÉRO, 16TH ARRONDISSEMENT, PARIS

23rd April—11:03 P.M.

The two squat wings of the Palais de Chaillot loomed like sullen guard dogs on either side of them, each protectively framing the sparkling thrust of the Eiffel Tower on the other side of the river.

"Do you think we missed him?" Archie asked.

"I hope not," Tom sighed, gazing out on the series of stepped terraces and cascading fountains that led to the bridge at the base of the hill below them. "I don't want to have to find this place on my own."

"Why not?"

"Sudden cave-ins, flooding, hidden drops into natural wells, exposed electricity cables. Not to mention the risk of getting lost."

"We've got a map," Archie reminded him. "It can't be that hard."

"They're over three hundred kilometers long," a voice answered. "I'm Franzy. You're late."

Franzy's head looked too small for the rest of him, his eyes so close together that the resulting permanent squint disguised which direction he was looking in. He had long dark hair that he'd bleached blond at the tips, and piercings through his nose, tongue and left eyebrow. And although it was hard to tell in the dark, it seemed he was wearing eyeliner to match his black jeans and Ramones T-shirt. The tell-tale white headphones of his mp3 player were wound around his thin neck, one bud still lodged in his ear, the other dangling free and broadcasting a tinny hiss of drum beats and shrieked vocals.

"We got here as fast as we could," Tom apologized. "Did Ketter tell you what we needed?"

"You need Blanco." Franzy nodded, spitting his gum into the air and deftly volleying it over the parapet with his right foot. "You got nothing else to wear?" He nodded skeptically at Archie's mustard-colored suspenders and pinstripe suit.

"Problem?"

"Not if you don't mind fucking your clothes up."

He led them down the hill away from the esplanade and then paused. Glancing to make sure no one was looking, he crouched and hauled the manhole cover at his feet open with a small metal implement.

"Get in," he urged them.

Tom climbed down the ladder fixed to the wall of the vertical shaft. Archie followed right behind him with Franzy dragging the cover back into place as soon as he too was inside. It settled with a solid thump that echoed around them.

"This way." A flashlight materialized in Franzy's hands as he led them off down a narrow passage. "And watch your heads," he added as a large pipe suddenly crossed the void at about chest height, forcing them to scramble underneath it.

They continued in silence, the ground dry and uneven, the temperature dropping, until a few minutes later they came to a large blue tarpaulin that had been stretched drum-tight between the tunnel walls. Tom translated the large sign fixed to it for Archie's benefit.

"Building site. No access."

Franzy lifted one corner of the tarpaulin and indicated that they should crawl through the small gap. On the other side a video camera mounted on a small desk bleeped into life as soon as Tom stood up.

"Motion sensitive, so we can keep track of who's been through here," Franzy explained. From behind him the sound of angry barking echoed up a tunnel lit with what looked like a salvaged set of Christmas tree lights.

"Ignore the dogs," he sniffed, brushing away the long hair that was constantly falling across his eyes. "It's a recording. To scare the tourists away."

"Tourists?" Tom queried.

"Kids mainly. Looking for a place to get high or fuck. This is our world. We try and keep our distance."

"Who's 'we?' "

"Up there they call us *cataphiles*. But we don't like to label ourselves. It's too limiting. We want to be free."

They arrived at a large door which opened as they approached it.

"They're with me," Franzy explained to the two unsmiling men who came out to greet them. They were each patted down and then waved through with a grunt, the tunnel angling down into the hill.

"Keep your voices down," Franzy told them as the passage leveled out and they approached a thick black curtain. "The film's still on."

"Film? What film?" Archie frowned.

Franzy swept the curtain aside with a flourish. They stepped cautiously through and found themselves in a cavernous amphitheater lit by a flickering image being projected on to a painted stone wall. Tom recognized the movie—*The Bicycle Thieves*.

Facing the screen were several shallow terraces carved into the rock, crowded with people, some gazing rapturously at the screen, some kissing, some passed out. A few mismatched sofas and armchairs were arranged in the space between the terraced seating and the screen, people smoking and drinking as if they were slumped in front of their TV at home. A small group was gathered around a candle on the far side of the chamber, the sallow light revealing their haunted, hungry faces as they prepared to shoot up, a dark liquid bubbling in the spoon they held suspended over the dancing flame. Witches around a cauldron.

"We excavated this place," Franzy informed them proudly. "We run a cinema club every few nights."

"Where do you get the power?" Tom shook his head in amazement. It was hard to believe that this shadow world revolved unnoticed beneath the feet of the one above. Franzy laughed, and Tom wondered whether bringing outsiders here allowed him, briefly at least, to see this place almost as if for the first time, to overcome the anesthesia of familiarity.

"We siphon it off the grid," he giggled. "Just like we use water from the fountains above to flush the toilets. Come on. Blanco's this way."

He led them past the terraced seating. A few people glanced at them disinterestedly before turning back to the film, their partner, or whatever it was they were trying to inject or ingest at the time. Stepping into a narrow passage, he lifted another heavy black curtain.

This time they found themselves in a much smaller chamber filled with mismatched tables and chairs that Tom assumed had been snatched from outside various restaurants and cafés. To their left, two tables housed a rudimentary bar and a makeshift cooking area. The sound of laughter and clinking crockery from the twenty or so people finishing dinner washed over them.

"We have six or seven similar restaurants all over Paris," Franzy boasted.

"Who else knows about this?" asked Archie, clearly as surprised as Tom.

"Not many. It's been illegal to come down here since the fifties. The *cataflics*, the cops who patrol the catacombs, fine you if they catch you. But since Blanco joined, they tend to leave us alone. He used to be one of them."

He steered them over to a table at the back of the room. A man was sitting there, picking over the remains of a meal, a joint in one hand. He wore a red headscarf tied into a knot in the nape of his neck and colored beads tied into his straggly beard. Both his ears were pierced all the way along their edge and each lower lobe had a plastic insert embedded into it, designed to stretch a hole in the skin. His neck was tattooed with a star, although it wasn't clear if it was meant to be a pentacle or a Star of David. A narrow steel bar, tipped with sharp points, pierced the soft skin between his eyes where his nose met his forehead. What struck Tom most of all, however, was not Blanco's tribal body decoration but that under his holed tracksuit he had the lean, sharp-edged physique of an endurance runner. Whatever he did to amuse himself down in the Stygian darkness of these tunnels, it clearly kept him fit.

"Blanco . . ." Franzy seemed suddenly nervous. "These are the people I told you about. The ones Ketter vouched for."

"Sit," the man instructed them in a raspy voice, pale eyes glowering under dark eyebrows. "Not you, Franzy. You can piss off." Franzy grimaced and scuttled off to the bar where he ordered a drink and eyed them sullenly from a distance.

"Franzy pretends to be one of us," Blanco growled. Tom wondered if his strange, almost American accent, was a deliberate affectation or more likely the result of watching too much imported TV. "But he hasn't made the leap yet. He still lives up top; only comes down here when he feels like it. I don't like agnostics. Either you believe or you don't . . ." He paused to pick something out of his yellowing teeth. "Which are you?"

"We're just passing through. Ketter said you could help."

"I could. I still haven't decided if I will," he said unsmilingly.

"We'll pay," Tom ventured.

"What do you think your money buys you down here?" He gave a dismissive shrug. "If I help you, it'll be because I choose to." He removed his headscarf and pulled his bleached hair back into a ponytail that he fixed into place with an elastic band.

"We're looking for something," Tom explained. "A place down here called the *Autel des Obelisques*."

"Never heard of it."

"We have a map."

Tom cleared the plates out of the way and smoothed the map out. The sight of the faded cloth seemed to trigger a flicker of interest in Blanco. He put his joint down and leaned forward.

"How old is this?"

"About two hundred years."

He gave a low whistle, his tongue stud clinking against his teeth.

"Most of these passageways are still intact . . ." He traced a path along some of the lines on it. "This is where we are now—" he indicated a spot on the map. "But there are other places on here I've never even heard about."

"When we've finished, you can keep it," Tom offered, guessing from his interest that this might sway him. "All we need is for you to take us here and back." He pointed at the spot circled in red. "Do you know it?"

"I know where it is," Blanco nodded, "But it doesn't exist. The tunnel ends here—" He indicated a point some way short of the circle. "I'll take you if you want, but it's a long walk for not very much."

"How long?" Archie sounded concerned.

"Near the Luxembourg Gardens."

"We could drive," Archie suggested hopefully.

Blanco fixed him with a hard stare.

"I've not been on top in five years. I'm not about to start now."

CHAPTER SEVENTY-SEVEN

AVENUE DE L'OBSERVATOIRE, 14TH ARRONDISSEMENT, PARIS

23rd April—11:54 P.M.

She couldn't move—her hands were tied behind her back, her ankles lashed to the chair legs. Worryingly though, although blindfolded, she wasn't gagged. Not a good sign. It meant they didn't care if she screamed for help. It meant they knew that no one would hear, that no one would come to help. She was on her own.

She heard a voice, but didn't recognize the language. Korean? Japanese? Thai? Something like that. Was this Milo's crowd? Had he somehow figured out that Henri was helping them? The blindfold was ripped from her head.

"You're awake. Good."

Blinking, she saw two Asian-looking men standing on either side of a snowing TV screen. The man on the left—short, stocky and dressed in a black suit—was totally bald. He had no eyelashes or eyebrows either, which, taken together with his white surgical mask, gave him a strange, almost alien appearance that seemed at once permanently surprised and disconcertingly expressionless. His skin had a pale, luminescent quality too, almost as if it had been smoothed on like wax. The man to the right was dressed more conventionally and stood a good few inches taller, with a square head and jagged scar across the bridge of his nose. He was holding a butterfly knife that he was flicking open and shut in a rhythmic blur of blackened steel.

Although Jennifer recognized a slight theatricality in the scene, she had to admit that it was working—she was scared.

"Who are you?" she mumbled, her throat dry and sore. "What do you want?"

"Watch," the man with the knife said, nodding at someone behind her.

The TV flickered and then burst into color, the screen filled with a close-up of Besson's terrified face. Two sets of hands, both missing their little fingers, appeared from the sides, one clutching a wooden spoon, the other grasping a tin of paint. Red enamel paint. She looked away, horrified, but immediately felt someone grab a fistful of hair and force her head back around. She screwed her eyes shut, the fleeting glimpse of Besson's bulging eyes and blue lips making her stomach turn over.

"Watch," the voice came again. "Watch, or we'll cut your eyes out too."

She looked up. Besson was convulsing now, but she focused on a point on the horizon beyond the screen so that all she could see was a strangely beautiful kaleidoscope of shifting shapes and colors. And she tried to block out Besson's choked gurgling by focusing her mind instead on deciphering what the man had just said—"We'll cut your eyes out *too*." Did that mean these were the people who had killed and mutilated Hammon?

The video ended. The screen began to snow again, filling the room with a strange yellow light as if a storm was about to break. The man on the left stepped forward and spoke through his mask, the material riding up on his nose.

"Fifteen years ago I bought two paintings . . ." Each word appeared to have been carefully measured and then delivered with precision. "A Chagall and a Gauguin."

"You're Asahi Takeshi?" she guessed, suddenly relating his baldness to the story she had heard about him having survived radiation poisoning by a Triad gang.

"One was painted by Rafael Quintavalle, the other by Henri Besson," he continued without answering. "I'm sure you can guess who sold them to me?"

"Hammon." She nodded. No wonder Besson had been able to identify the forgeries so quickly the other day, she thought to herself. He'd painted one and his old friend Rafael the other.

"When I tried to sell them, I was told they were forgeries. That I had been stolen from. Humiliated. So one by one I found those responsible and made them pay. Now only Razi is left. The coward won't long outlive the others. I don't forget and I don't forgive."

They'd been wrong, she realized now. Milo had had nothing to do with Hammon or Quintavalle's deaths. This was revenge. Brutal revenge for a scam committed fifteen years ago and then forgotten by everyone. Forgotten by everyone except the person they'd ripped off.

"Killing me won't help."

"None of this helps. I do it because it pleases me. Because I can."

He nodded at the man next to him, who locked his knife into the open position and stepped toward her.

"Wait," she called, her eyes fixed fearfully on the approaching blade. "I can help."

"How?" he sneered.

"Your paintings—the real ones. They're in a safe in my hotel. I can give you access to them."

The man holding the knife paused, waiting for some instruction from Takeshi who appeared to be considering her offer.

"Go on."

"You'll have the certificates and the originals. The auction houses will have no choice but to sell them as planned. How could they refuse? No one will ever know about the forgeries you bought." She felt no guilt about this. Hammon was dead and Razi had fled the country. Neither would miss the paintings and, given the circumstances, she wasn't sure she had much choice.

Takeshi nodded, but before he could speak, another of his

men gave a panicked shout. A steady blue pulse could be seen through the kitchen window rising from the street below like steam. The police had arrived. Somehow they had found this place too. And even though she couldn't see his face under his mask, from the steely look in Takeshi's eyes and the way his men were already checking their weapons and ammunition, she guessed that not only were they hopelessly outnumbered, but that they had no intention of going quietly. Not unless she showed them how.

"There's something else I can help you with," she offered quickly. "A way out."

CHAPTER SEVENTY-EIGHT

THE CATACOMBS, PARIS

24th April—12:01 A.M.

Tom had been right about needing a guide. Archie was finding that his normally reliable sense of direction had been totally scrambled by a bewildering maze of intersecting passageways and corridors. It was only when their flashlight beams pierced the cloying darkness and occasionally revealed a name daubed or carved into the limestone, that he got some fleeting indication of what street lay above. Down here, Blanco, for all his dismissive surliness, was indispensable.

As well as being disorientating, it was hard going too, the ground rising and falling through a series of subterranean hills that followed the contours of the rock strata. And while in some places they were able to stand up straight, in others protruding pipes and low-hanging cables forced them to crawl through centuries of rubble and dirt and wade across stagnant pools formed by the sweating ceilings overhead. Not that anything seemed to break Blanco's confident, loping stride.

One constant throughout the changing terrain, however, was the graffiti. In places this amounted to nothing more than crude tagging and the occasional political slogan, but in others surprisingly colorful and accomplished murals stood out garishly against the anemic, dusty walls. It was a broad human tapestry, depicting on the one hand a grinning skeleton, two cartoon characters chasing each other with an axe and an oversize marijuana leaf, and yet on the other a Mayan sun god, a commemoration of the American moon landing and the fall of the Berlin Wall. Down here, there seemed to be no distinction necessary between the trivial and the momentous. This world set its own priorities.

Blanco paused next to a brick wall to let them catch up. An uneven hole had been punched through it with a sledgehammer.

"The *cataflics* brick the tunnels over, we break them down," he explained. "They try to fence us in like cattle, but the tunnels aren't theirs to control. They don't understand that this is frontier country. We make the law down here."

"How old are the tunnels?" Archie panted as he wearily checked his watch and saw that they'd been down here for an hour already. So far this seemed to be the only topic that Blanco willingly engaged in and the longer he kept him talking, the longer he got to rest.

"They are mostly Roman-era limestone quarries," Blanco answered, "People have been coming down here ever since. Look."

He shone his flashlight at the wall. Amidst the kaleidoscope of spray-painted graffiti, Archie saw a carved name and below it a date—1727.

"Aristocrats fled here in the Revolution. Peasants took shelter during the Commune. The Resistance hid here during the war. Now it's our time."

To Archie's dismay he led them off again in silence, their footsteps echoing around them, their flashlight beams carving narrow tubes of light through the darkness. Another forty-five minutes evaporated away.

"Good. We're at the bunker," Blanco suddenly announced. "Not far now."

"The bunker?" Archie panted, his hands on his knees.

"The Nazis built an air-raid shelter under a school near the Luxembourg Gardens." Blanco shone his flashlight at a corroded steel door with a wheel-shaped handle that looked like it had been salvaged from a submarine. It was off its hinges and resting against the wall next to the sturdy brickwork of the blast doorway.

Archie peered inside and saw a sign in German high on the opposite wall: *Rauchen verboten.*

"Smoking forbidden," Tom translated.

"Just as well," Archie wheezed. "A fag now would finish me off for good."

"The arrows point to different entrance points." Blanco aimed his flashlight at a section of wall beneath the sign where colored arrows had been painted on to a white background. "The black ones lead back up to the street," he said, turning away impatiently. "Let's keep moving. You get a lot of kids in this section and the *cataflics* are never that far behind them."

Blanco vaulted over a pile of earth and stone caused by a partial collapse in the roof above. Tom and Archie followed him through the narrow gap and then continued a short way, until Blanco suddenly stopped ahead of them.

"You see, I was right," he announced, pointing his flashlight ahead of them and revealing a solid wall. A large skull had been painted on it in reflective paint and it leered at them tauntingly.

"Are you sure?" Tom approached the wall. "Maybe we took a wrong turn."

"I don't make wrong turns," Blanco said testily. "It just ends here."

"Then what's this?" Archie shone his flashlight at one of the bricks. Beneath the paint, a small hieroglyph of a scarab had been carved in the skeleton's left eye.

CHAPTER SEVENTY-NINE

AVENUE DE L'OBSERVATOIRE, 14TH ARRONDISSEMENT,

PARIS

24th April—12:07 A.M.

Through here—" Jennifer rubbed her wrists as she ran from the kitchen, her fingers tingling as the circulation returned.

She stopped in front of the mirror and then pressed on the bottom right-hand corner of the frame as she remembered Besson doing. It swung open. From the stairwell came the sound of heavy footsteps and the whine of the elevator rising toward them. Takeshi barked an order and his men climbed through the hole into the small room. Jennifer swung the mirror shut just as the shadow of the first policeman crossed the threshold.

She held her finger to her lips. Takeshi nodded and glared at his men to stay quiet. A six-man hostage rescue team armed with night-vision goggles and sub-machine guns entered the apartment and fanned out in pairs to secure the apartment. At each room they came to, one of them took up a cover position at the entrance, while their partner, weapon cocked and safety off, swung inside and ensured it was empty. Besson's body was in the last room they checked and its discovery elicited a sudden shout. A few minutes later, Ferrat and a squad of five uniformed policemen appeared at the front door and were escorted straight to the lab. Ferrat soon reappeared, swearing and giving orders. Somebody, presumably at his instruction, found the light switch and turned it on.

It was strange to be watching them like this, as if this was all being played out on a huge screen. Takeshi, especially, seemed transfixed, his eyes barely blinking, beads of sweat breaking out across his forehead. Ferrat approached the mirror, still yelling instructions as he straightened his uniform buttons and centered his hat. Jennifer found herself holding her breath, Ferrat's eyes seemed to bore straight into hers, until he eventually looked away, distracted by the forensic team that had just jogged into the picture.

"Besson told me there was a way out of here," she whispered. "An escape route."

"Where?"

"I'm not sure," she admitted, checking behind a box to her left. "I just know there is one."

She pulled another few boxes away from the wall and then pointed triumphantly at a previously concealed opening in the left-hand corner just about large enough to crawl through.

"Where does it lead?" Takeshi asked skeptically as he crouched down next to her.

"Away from here—" Jennifer nodded toward the mirror. "Right now, that's all I care about."

"Then you go first," he said unsmilingly.

"Fine." She dropped to her stomach and began to crawl inside the opening before stopping, having suddenly remembered something. "Is there a painting on one of those shelves?"

"What for?"

"It belongs to a . . . a friend of mine. He asked me to get it for him. It's of no use to you."

Takeshi eyed her for a few moments, then muttered something to one of his men. They reappeared a few seconds later clutching a small crate. In the top right-hand corner she could see that it had been marked with a large F. F for Felix.

"That's it," she said, turning back to the opening.

The passage was perhaps fifteen feet long and just wide

enough for her to pull herself through on her elbows. It was filthy though, covered in dust and cobwebs and mouse droppings. She doubted it had ever been used. It ended in a small grille that a firm shove sent spinning out of sight. She peered out, first down, then up, snatching her head back just in time.

"It's an elevator shaft," she called as the car shot past. "There's a door just beneath us on the other side. I think I can make it across. Hold on to me."

Checking that the elevator had stopped, she rolled on to her back and pulled herself forward until she was leaning right out into the shaft. With Takeshi holding her legs, she stretched for the steel cable that connected the top of the cabin to the motor somewhere in the roof.

"Got it," she called, grabbing on to it gratefully and pulling her legs free.

"You need to press the switch to release the door," Takeshi instructed her.

With a nod, she reached with her foot for the trip switch he had pointed out. The door buzzed open.

"Climb in," Takeshi called.

She slid a small way down the cable to get to a better height, the metal cable searing her palms, and then jumped across through the open doorway, landing in an awkward crouch and immediately grabbing the sides so as not to fall back.

"Your turn," she called.

Helped by the man behind him, Takeshi carefully climbed across on to the cable and then copied her by sliding down to a better height.

"Jump," she urged him.

He nodded but didn't move, and she suddenly realized from his bulging eyes and strained breathing that it was all he could do just to hold on. Maybe all those years of seclusion and lack of exercise had weakened him more than he'd thought.

He slid down another few feet on the greasy cable, taking him below a height at which he could easily jump down through the open doorway. She lay down on her stomach and reached out.

"Grab on to me."

He nodded and this time launched himself across the narrow gap, his hands grasping on to hers tightly.

Beneath them the elevator began to rise with a mechanical mewl. Jennifer quickly braced herself against the doorway and hauled him inside, his legs flicking through the doorway just as the empty cabin flashed past.

"Thank you." He stood up and gave her a small bow as he patted his forehead down with a pristine white handkerchief. Then, having clearly paused to reflect on it, he removed his mask and smiled, his teeth narrow and growing across each other at odd angles. "I don't easily forgive. But nor do I forget."

CHAPTER EIGHTY

THE CATACOMBS, PARIS

24th April—12:50 A.M.

Do you carry any tools?" Tom asked Blanco hopefully, rubbing his fingers across the carved hieroglyph.

Blanco nodded and extracted a lightweight hammer and piton.

"In case I need to rope across something," he explained as he handed them to Tom.

Tom set to work, chipping away at the pale mortar with the metal spike, the rhythmic ping of the hammer strikes echoing around them. Little by little, the stone loosened, until Tom was able to lever it out on to the floor next to him.

"What's behind it?" Archie asked, a dark square now visible where the stone had once been.

Tom leaned forward and plunged his arm into the void.

"Nothing." He grinned with growing excitement. "Give me a hand working some others free."

Archie knelt down next to him to help. Blanco, however, held back, prompting Tom to wonder if he perhaps resented a non-believer revealing this hidden corner of his underground realm.

As soon as they had cleared enough stones away, they crawled though the narrow gap and stood up in what was clearly the continuation of the tunnel they had just been in. Checking the map, this time Tom led them off. The passage veered away to the right and widened out, revealing a series of large, vaulted openings on either side of them. Openings brimming, Tom realized as he trained his flashlight on them, with human bones and skulls arranged into intricate diamond and cross-shaped patterns, like the parterres of a *Le Nôtre* garden. In a few places these arrangements had collapsed, the bleached bones spilling on to the ground like an avalanche across a valley floor. In others, the skulls had crumpled under the weight, their faces cracked in half.

"We must have come through into some hidden part of the ossuary," Blanco guessed, seemingly underwhelmed. Tom guessed he had seen this type of place before.

"What ossuary?" inquired Archie, clouds of dust rising off him as he disconsolately patted his ripped and stained suit.

"They moved human remains here from central Paris in the late eighteenth and early nineteenth centuries to try and stop the spread of disease," Tom explained.

"Eight million people," Blanco confirmed with a nod. "The entire city is built on empty graveyards."

The tunnel narrowed again, and then gave on to a wide, triangular chamber. They paused at the entrance, their flashlights revealing that a single passageway led off from the center of each side of the triangle, while opposite them, at the apex of the room, was a white shape.

"That's it," Tom breathed. "The Altar of Obelisks."

The tip of the triangle had been squared off and lined with white marble engraved with a dense web of hieroglyphs that glinted as they caught the light. In its center was a scrolled black marble plaque.

Directly below the plaque and flush to the wall was a simple altar, its top lip overhanging the base by a few inches and surmounted at each end by two large black obelisks, perhaps three feet high. The altar's base, meanwhile, was embroidered with a starkly symmetrical pattern of black marble roundels, each engraved with different Egyptian symbols—a pyramid, a sphinx, a scarab, even a profile of Anubis. Tom read the Italian words etched into the plaque in gold.

"*Per me si va tra la perduta gente* . . . This way to join the lost," he translated. "It's Dante. Part of the inscription at the entrance to hell."

"He's an old favorite down here," Blanco sniffed.

"I'm not sure about the gates of Hell, but this must open something," Tom observed, holding out the key recovered from inside the obelisk.

"Take a look at this—" Archie pointed at the front of the altar.

Squatting down, Tom saw what he meant. One of the black roundels was different from all the others. Instead of featuring an Egyptian symbol, this one was engraved with an N surrounded by a ring of laurel leaves. The same symbol they'd found on the key.

Tom tried to push it and then slide it first to one side, then to the other. It wouldn't move. Nor did it come loose when he attempted to lever it forward with the blade of his knife.

"Try twisting it," Archie suggested.

"What do you mean?"

"Like this—" Grabbing the edges of the roundel impatiently, Archie turned it as if it were a doorknob. It moved a quarter of a turn to the right and then came loose in his hands, leaving a circular hole.

"There's a lock," Archie exclaimed, shining his flashlight into the recess. "Give me the key."

Tom handed it to him and he slipped the key into the narrow slot and turned it, the mechanism initially resisting before reluctantly giving way.

Standing up, Tom grabbed the altar's edge and gave it a firm tug. It swung back easily, skating over the top of the steps, a large counterbalanced hinge on the left-hand side making the massive marble construction appear as if it had no weight at all. It revealed a small alcove sized to fit a coffin.

"*Putain*," Blanco swore in surprise from behind them, scrambling forward for a better look.

"It's not there," Archie said in a disappointed voice.

"Something's there," Tom corrected him as he reached in to retrieve the object he had caught sight of right at the back of the recess. He carefully lifted it out and then blew on it, the dust clearing to reveal a plaster cast of a human face.

"What the hell's that?" Archie frowned, his tone caught somewhere between surprise and disgust.

"It's a death mask," Tom replied. "They were popular as mementos back in the eighteenth and nineteenth centuries. I saw Dante's in the Palazzo Vecchio in Florence once." He gazed down at the mask's sunken cheeks, balding forehead and protruding nose. It struck him that there was a strange echo of weary despair in those silent, blanched features.

"That's not Dante." Archie gave a firm shake of his head. "That's Napoleon."

"Yes," Blanco agreed, stepping forward for a better look. "That's Napoleon Bonaparte."

He reached forward to touch the mask's powdery surface, but Tom suddenly grabbed his wrist, causing him to cry out in pain.

"What's up?" Archie called.

"Turn off your light," Tom said grimly. "Now look at his fingers," he nodded at the luminescent stains on Blanco's thumb and forefinger. "It's some sort of phosphorescent paint. He's been leaving a trail behind us."

Tom twisted Blanco's arm back behind him, pressing his face down against the altar. Then he searched through his pockets until he found a small tube of paint that was missing its lid.

"It takes a few minutes of contact with the air before the chemicals work," Tom explained, reading off the label. "That's why we didn't see him rubbing it on to the walls."

"I can explain . . ."

"Who's this for?"

"It's in case we got lost," Blanco protested.

"Bullshit. You could find your way out of here with a bag over your head. Who's paying you?"

"No one," he shouted angrily, writhing furiously to free his arm.

Tom pressed forward and with a sudden jerk, snapped his wrist. Blanco screamed and was suddenly still.

"Who?"

"I don't know his name." The words came in a jumbled whimper. "He turned up just before you. All I had to do was mark the way."

"Milo," Archie said through gritted teeth. "He must have found out we went to see Ketter and forced him to talk."

"How long have we been here?"

"Ten, fifteen minutes?" Archie guessed.

"Then we can't go back the way we came in," Tom said grimly. "He must be right behind us." He released Blanco's arm and pulled him upright. "We need a way out."

Clutching his wrist, Blanco fixed Tom with a hate-filled glare.

"I don't know these tunnels."

"Then you'd better get to know them fast, or I'll break more than your wrist."

Blanco stared at him angrily, then gave a sullen shrug.

"Let me see the map again." Tom laid it out on the altar and Blanco leaned over it. "We must be right next to the main ossuary," he said eventually. "We should be able to break through here. From there, we can follow the signs back up to the street."

"Which way?" Archie nodded toward the two passages that led off each side of the chamber.

"Left," Blanco muttered.

They sprinted into the tunnel, Tom pushing Blanco ahead of him past another series of skull-filled openings, until they arrived at a further dead end. As Blanco looked on, cradling his wrist, Tom and Archie attacked the wall, hammering and kicking and hauling stones out of their way until there was a large enough gap for them to squeeze through. Behind them, Tom could hear the sound of running feet and raised voices.

"Follow the black arrows," Blanco pointed at the wall once he was through. "The black arrows always lead to the exit."

They sprinted down a tunnel past yet more burial chambers, small plaques indicating which graveyards they had originally been removed from, until they came to a place where the tunnel ceiling had partially given way and been shored up by several wooden beams. Blanco pulled them back.

"Temporary repairs," he whispered. "Be careful. It doesn't take much to bring it down."

Tom edged around the narrow gap between the two beams. One of them groaned, a faint trickle of loose earth sprinkling to the ground like sand trickling inside an hourglass.

"Quick," Tom called, the voices behind them so close now that he could almost decipher their muted echo. "It could go any minute."

Archie dived through after him, but, as he squeezed pa his suit snagged on a nail. Struggling to free himself, he kicked out, only for his foot to inadvertently catch one of the beams and send it spinning to the ground.

"Shit!" he swore, then reached back for Blanco. "Come on."

Before he could move, the roof suddenly gave way with a pained roar and Blanco's face vanished in a billowing cloud of dust and stone.

"We need to get him out." Tom coughed, his eyes streaming as he pulled Archie clear of the rubble.

Archie shook his head. "He'll have to take his chances with Milo," he said, dusting himself down.

"That's not taking a chance," Tom said in a grim voice. "It's a death sentence. We can't leave him."

"We can't exactly go back in for him either," Archie pointed out. "Not unless you want to take your chances with Milo too."

There was a pause as Tom considered their options. In the end, he knew that Archie was right.

"Then let's just get out of here," he conceded.

They sprinted on through the tunnels, following the black arrows until they reached a gate. Tom sprung the lock, the bare earth and darkness suddenly giving way to smoothed concrete and electric lights.

"We must be in the section they open to the public," Tom guessed.

"You mean people pay to see this shit?" Archie shivered.

They came to another gate and then, a short way beyond it, a spiral staircase that led into a small room at street level.

The door there was also locked, but again Tom soon had it squeaking open.

They emerged gratefully on to the street. It had been raining; the pavements formed a shimmering black mirror under the streetlights, while a pair of carved lions dripped water from their frozen manes. A couple of taxis were waiting hopefully at a neighboring rank. Tom felt the tightness in his chest lifting as the fresh air hit his lungs and the night sky soared far above.

"Let's boost a car and get to the meeting point," he suggested. "We're late and Jen will be worried."

CHAPTER EIGHTY-ONE

THE CATACOMBS, PARIS

24th April—1:32 A.M.

Don't tell me. They got away." Milo's finger was angrily tapping his trigger, feeling the tight spring flexing slightly under his touch.

"They collapsed the roof," said Djoulou. "We haven't got the equipment to get through."

"Damn!" Milo spat in disgust. "How the hell did he know we were coming?"

"Maybe you should ask *him*." Eva threw Blanco to the floor, his wrist still clutched protectively to his chest.

"Kirk left him behind?" Milo crouched next to him and lifted his chin with the barrel of his gun. "That's unlike him. What did you do?"

"He saw the paint," Blanco protested weakly. "I didn't tell him anything."

"Not even a way out?"

Blanco's eyes flicked guiltily to the floor.

"Colonel, look at this—" Djoulou pulled on the altar and revealed the alcove behind it. "It's empty."

"Of course it's empty," Milo snapped without looking around. "What do you think Kirk's been doing down here? The question is what was in it?" Again, he lifted Blanco's chin until his eyes met his.

"A mask . . ." Blanco stammered. "A plaster cast of a man's face. Kirk said it was a death mask."

"Whose?"

"They said it was Napoleon," he replied hesitantly. "I only got a quick look, but it looked like him."

Eva frowned at Milo.

"A dead end, or another clue?"

"I'm not sure. Either way, we're not going to solve it down here."

"What about him?" Eva nodded at Blanco.

Milo paused, then nodded toward the altar.

"Since he likes down here so much, he can stay."

"No," Blanco wailed as Djoulou and one of his men dragged Blanco toward the altar.

"Please no!" he shrieked as they forced him into the narrow alcove, kicking his flailing arms and legs so that he would pull them out of the way.

"I'm begging you, no," he sobbed as they swung the altar shut.

The mechanism locked with a firm clunk, extinguishing his screams.

CHAPTER EIGHTY-TWO

PLACE ST. MICHEL, 7TH ARRONDISSEMENT, PARIS

24th April—2:01 A.M.

Jennifer stepped from the shadows of the doorway she had been sheltering in and signaled as they drew up.

"Sorry we're late," Tom called through the driver's window.

"I just got here myself," she replied as she stepped around to the rear passenger door, handed Archie the crate left for Tom by Besson, then climbed into the front seat.

"You been fighting?" Archie exclaimed, almost sounding impressed. Her clothes were covered in oil and dirt and her face and throat looked bruised.

"Have you?" She nodded at Archie's ripped suit and blackened shirt and Tom's filthy jeans and coat.

"We've just spent three hours crawling through all sorts of shit. You were meant to be taking it easy at Henri's," he reminded her.

"Where do you think this happened?" She indicated her battered face.

"But . . ."

"Henri's dead."

"Milo?" Tom guessed through clenched teeth, immediately wishing he'd insisted Besson come with them rather than remain alone. Her answer, though, surprised him.

"Takeshi."

She ran through her evening, starting with the discovery of Besson's body and culminating in her leading Takeshi and his men to safety through the secret room into the adjacent apartment block and from there out on to the street, well away from the massed ranks of police, ambulances and slack-jawed onlookers.

"So Milo didn't kill Rafael?" Tom said, frowning as he furiously retraced his steps and thoughts over the previous few days to try and work out exactly when and how he'd got that so wrong.

"You mean Takeshi got there first," Archie growled. "Milo would have offed him eventually to keep him quiet."

"Where's Takeshi now?"

"I told him that the originals of his paintings were at my hotel," she said. "I expect he's on his way there to collect them."

"Sounds like he owes you."

"I'm not exactly keeping score. I was just happy to get out of that place alive." She paused, then glanced around with a frown, as if looking for something. "What about you? Wasn't there anything down there?"

"Something was down there. We just don't know what it means," Tom said with a shrug. "Show her what we found," he added, nodding to Archie.

Archie carefully handed the mask to her and she turned it over in her hands, puzzled.

"Why would someone hide this there? Even if it is of Napoleon, it can't be what this has all been about?"

"I bloody well hope not," Archie agreed.

"Do you think it's rare?" she mused.

"It looks like the original, which makes it pretty much unique," said Tom. "Why?"

"Because the rarer it is, the easier it will be to track down," she pointed out.

"Track down how?" Tom pressed.

She pointed at an all-night café on the other side of the road. A blinking neon sign in the window advertised twenty-four-hour internet access. A few minutes later, they were huddled around a terminal with coffees on order, their backs turned to the bored-looking student manning the till so he couldn't see their faces.

Death mask, Napoleon, she typed in. "Here we go." She selected the second result of the three quarters of a million returned. "*There are several different versions of Napoleon's death mask in circulation*," she read. "*The original impression was taken by Dr. Francis Burton over forty hours after the emperor's death*." She skipped ahead. "Apparently Burton's cast was stolen, but a copy later turned up in the hands of Dr. Francesco Antommarchi."

"Who?"

"Antommarchi." She consulted the screen again. "Napoleon's personal physician. It seems he received permission from the French government to create bronze and plaster copies of—"

"Antommarchi?" Archie interrupted.

"That's right," Jennifer checked.

"That's the same bloke who owned the book," Archie exclaimed.

"Are you sure?"

"Of course I'm bloody sure," Archie insisted. "The auctioneer said it was from the personal collection of Dr. Francesco Antom-wotsit. It was on the book plate too."

"You're right," Tom breathed, his excitement building as yet another piece of the puzzle slotted into place.

"According to this, Antommarchi and Napoleon were pretty much inseparable during the last two years of his life," Jennifer continued. "He was with him when he died. He even helped carry out the autopsy."

"In which case, it's possible Napoleon confided in him when he knew he was dying," Tom suggested. "Perhaps even told him about the *Mona Lisa* and the catacombs and the map he'd had hidden in the Egyptian dinner service."

"You mean the painting *was* down there once?" Archie asked with a skeptical frown.

"How else did one of Antommarchi's death masks get down there?" Tom asked. "He must have swapped it for the painting and then bricked the tunnel up behind him."

"Napoleon would've had to tell him exactly where to find it and given him a different key to the one we found," Jennifer pointed out. "Otherwise he would have had to destroy the book and the porcelain obelisk to get to it."

"Either way, it don't help us much," Archie sighed. "It could be anywhere now."

There was a long silence as this point sunk in.

"What happened to him in the end?" Tom asked eventually.

"The doctor? Not sure."

She turned back to the computer and searched under Antommarchi's full name, then scanned through the first page or so of results.

"It says here he emigrated to New Orleans in 1834 and then moved to Cuba. Died four months later from yellow fever. He's buried in the Santa Ifigenia Cemetery in Santiago de Cuba."

"That's it?" Archie sniffed.

"Wait, this is interesting." She held up a hand to silence him as she read: "*Most of Antommarchi's possessions, including paintings, furniture and a copy of Napoleon's death mask, passed into the care of the Governor of Santiago de Cuba, who had let Antommarchi live in and work out of his home. These same possessions were later bought from the governor's descendants by Julio Lobo Olavarria, a Cuban millionaire, to add to his Napoleon collection which is now housed in a museum in Havana.*"

"I think they'd have twigged if they had the *Mona Lisa* up on the wall," Archie laughed.

"Not if there was something else painted over it," Jennifer insisted with a firm shake of her head.

"What do you mean?"

"Remember how Rafael had stuck one stamp over another on the letter he left for Tom?" she reminded them. "We didn't understand it at the time, but what if he was trying to tell us that the *Mona Lisa* had been hidden in the same way? Under another painting. Under one of Antommarchi's paintings. It could still be there now."

There was a long pause, filled by the sound of two Japanese

girls giggling as they uploaded pictures of themselves on to their blog. Archie gave a deep sigh, then shook his head.

"Well, I'm not going to bloody Cuba," he sniffed.

"Jen and I will go," Tom agreed. "I want you to stay here and keep an eye on J-P. If Milo gets desperate, he may try and make a move on him to flush me out."

"No one's going to Cuba," Jennifer pointed out. "Not unless we swim there. Ferrat will be watching the airports."

"Didn't you tell me Razi was in Havana?" Tom asked slowly.

"Yeah." She nodded. "We think they owed him for some scam he helped pull a few years back."

"Well, your new friend Takeshi owes you too. And I think he'd be pretty interested in finding out where Razi's hiding out," Tom said with a smile. "Maybe even interested enough to lend us his jet."

CHAPTER EIGHTY-THREE

HÔPITAL PITIÉ SALPÊTRIÈRE, 13TH ARRONDISSEMENT, PARIS

24th April—8:02 A.M.

He couldn't prove it, but Dumas was pretty certain the nursing staff had been ordered to ration his morphine. Either that, or they'd deliberately left the bullets in to spite him. How else to explain why the hot blade of pain embedded in his leg was being twisted and pushed faster and deeper with every passing hour. He certainly didn't buy the tired line that the doctor kept trotting out about how this meant he was getting better.

The lock turned on the door. Dumas looked up from his bed accusingly, ready to tackle the doctor on this point once again, before screwing his face into an angry scowl when he saw who had walked in.

"What the hell do you want?"

"Is it so wrong to want to visit an old friend?" Troussard shrugged, pulling a chair up to the bed.

"How did you get in here?"

"Those guards are there to stop you leaving, not me coming in," Troussard reminded him.

"Does Ferrat know you're here?"

"Ferrat asked me to come. He thought maybe we could talk."

"I've got nothing to say to you." Dumas turned away.

"You've got nothing to say to anyone," Troussard laughed. "That's the problem. I've told them it's a waste of time. That you're a drunk. That you probably can't remember which muscles to squeeze to piss or shit, let alone anything else. But they asked me to try all the same." He placed a hand on Dumas's arm and squeezed it encouragingly.

"If you touch me again, I'll show you I remember exactly which muscles control what," Dumas said through gritted teeth. Troussard snatched his hand away.

"Frankly I don't care if you talk or not," he sniffed. "The way I see it, the less you cooperate with us, the longer you'll go away for."

"What do you mean, 'cooperate with us?'" Dumas laughed. "Ferrat's not that stupid. He's not fool enough to let a clown like you get anywhere near his case."

"Well then, you're the fool," Troussard retorted. "Ferrat is circulating daily reports on his progress to a select number of senior Louvre officials, and I'm one of them."

"Oh, well done," Dumas applauded sarcastically. "Thirty years of brown-nosing and you're on a mailing list. I hope it's everything you dreamed it would be."

"The President himself receives the same report," Troussard said haughtily.

"Is that right? Then what's the latest from ground zero? What stunning breakthrough have you made today?"

"As if I'd tell you!" he snorted.

"More like you don't know." Dumas gave a mocking laugh. "You haven't changed. All flirt and no follow through."

"How's this for size, then?" Troussard shot back angrily. "One of Milo's gang is a woman."

"You really expect me to swallow that?" Dumas shook his head in disbelief.

"The FBI have confirmed her DNA sample," Troussard shot back triumphantly. "Eva Quintavalle. It confirms an eyewitness report that a woman executed one of the police officers in the tunnel. She was last seen six months ago in Tokyo visiting Asahi Takeshi, a Japanese businessman with strong links to the Yakuza. We think she may have been lining him up as a buyer . . ." He paused and then stood up, nodding slowly. "Oh, I see what you're doing. Very clever. But I'm not falling for it."

"Falling for what?" Dumas said innocently. "You're not going, are you? We were just getting started."

"You think you're so goddammed clever, don't you?" Troussard said through clenched teeth. "So much smarter than everyone else. Well, in case you hadn't noticed, I'm not the one under arrest."

"Believe me, I'd rather be in prison than have to listen to you harp on much longer."

"Is that what your wife said when she left you?"

Dumas was up in a flash, the pain in his leg forgotten, his forearm pinning Troussard to the wall by his throat.

"Don't you talk about her, you bastard. Don't you even think her name."

"Guard!" Troussard croaked, his eyes flicking despairingly toward the door. "Guard!"

Moments later, Dumas was being prized away by one uniformed officer while another was helping Troussard stagger back to his feet.

"Okay, okay," Dumas shook the guard off and got back into bed. "Just get him out of here."

The guards ushered Troussard toward the door. For a moment he looked as if he was gearing up for some parting remark, but a biting look from Dumas sent him scurrying from the room clutching his throat.

Dumas waited until he was sure they'd locked the door behind them before taking out the phone he'd managed to slip out of Troussard's jacket pocket. He dialed first one number and then, when that wasn't answered, a second.

"Archie, it's Jean-Pierre."

"J-P! You okay mate? Whose phone are you calling on?"

"Never mind that. Where's Felix?" he asked in an urgent tone.

"On his way to Cuba with Jennifer."

"The FBI agent?" Dumas frowned, confused. The last he'd heard, they were setting her up, not working with her.

"A lot's happened since you've been gone." Archie sounded weary.

"You can tell me everything later," Dumas said impatiently. "You need to get a message to Felix. You need to warn him about Eva."

"What about Eva?"

"She's working with Milo."

A pause.

"What have they got you on in there?"

"I'm serious," Dumas insisted. "I just had Troussard in here, showing off. He told me that the FBI had identified her from a DNA sample left in the tunnel. She wasn't there as a hostage. She was fighting alongside Milo."

"He didn't take his phone in case they managed to track it." There was a slightly despairing edge to Archie's voice.

"Then you need to get out there."

"How? I'm on Interpol's watchlist as one of Tom's known associates. I won't get past Duty Free."

"They managed it."

"They borrowed a plane off some Japanese mobster who owed Jennifer a favor. Asahi . . ."

"Takeshi," Dumas completed the sentence for him, his face set into a grim frown.

"You know him?"

"Archie, they think Takeshi is one of the buyers. Eva was seen with him a few months ago."

"They're walking into a trap," Archie breathed.

"If you can't go, you'll have to find someone else who can," Dumas said slowly. "And they'll need a plan."

CHAPTER EIGHTY-FOUR

MALECÓN, HAVANA, CUBA

24th April—10:12 P.M.

The girls were turning out along the Malecón, their lipstick glowing invitingly in the lights of the passing cars. Their skirts hitched, they patrolled narrow strips of pavement like lionesses pacing around a small cage, their pimps resting at a discreet distance against the sea wall, smoking or playing cards or both. Across the harbor's dark waters a buoy blinked red, its pulsing light seeming to serve more as an invitation than a warning to the passing ships.

Jennifer and Tom walked on silently, refusing the occasional offers of cigars smuggled out of the Partagas factory and the constant whistles of the bicycle taxis encouraging them to jump on. After ten hours on a plane catching up on the previous few days' sleep, both of them seemed to be enjoying the playful tug of the wind through their hair and the sharp tang of the sea.

"Do you really think it's in the museum?" Jennifer asked eventually as an antique scooter loaded with groceries chugged past.

"According to the catalog, they own four or five paintings that used to belong to Antommarchi," Tom reminded her.

"But until we get in there tomorrow morning, we won't know for sure."

"And if it's not?"

"Then we keep looking. There's no reason to think he would have destroyed it. Besides, what else can we do if we're going to prove our side of the story and try and get Eva back?"

A neon-blue '57 Chevrolet Bel-Air purred past, its tail-fins gleaming under the orange streetlights like the afterburn on a pair of booster rockets. The incongruous sight made Jennifer smile, bringing home the strange series of events that had led her here. A few days ago she'd been investigating a small-scale art forgery ring in New York. Now here she was wandering the streets of Havana with the prime suspect in the theft of the *Mona Lisa*, a fugitive from justice. However you spun it, it wasn't going to look good on her resumé.

Not that she regretted the decisions she'd taken. If she hadn't taken her chances with Tom, she'd still be in custody, forgotten by the FBI, a trophy for Ferrat to parade in front of his masters as if on a tumbrel on her way to the guillotine. She never would have known the truth about the *Mona Lisa* or the Louvre's role in attempting to cover up two hundred years of subterfuge. Tom had been right. Sometimes you just had to help yourself.

"Thank you," she said in a low voice.

"What for?" He gave her a puzzled grin.

"For convincing me to come with you."

She squeezed his arm. He tensed slightly under her touch. She let him go and glanced up. He had a thoughtful, almost sad look upon his face and she wondered if he was thinking of Rafael and Henri and Eva. The last few days must have been harder on him than anyone. It was sometimes easy to forget that he had feelings too.

A pause.

"I'm sorry I dragged you into all this," Tom said. "You were right, I didn't think it through. It was wrong of me."

"We've both done things we regret." She gave him an awkward look.

"You're probably right," he laughed.

They walked on in silence, the waves breaking gently against the sea wall, the wash occasionally leaping above the parapet like a performing dolphin in an amusement park. Eventually Tom spoke again.

"Do you think it's ever possible for people like you and me to . . ." he tailed off.

"To what?"

"Could we ever . . . Do you see that?" he interrupted himself suddenly, pointing at a large illuminated monument marooned in the center of the boulevard to their right. It featured two large cannons laid flat and pointing in opposite directions. Between them was an elaborate pedestal decorated with statues and surmounted by two Corinthian columns. "It's a monument to the USS *Maine*, a warship destroyed in the harbor here. It was meant as a permanent tribute to the friendship between Cuba and the United States, a reminder of shared ideals of liberty and sacrifice."

"And?" She frowned, not sure where this was leading.

"Now look over there."

On the other side of the road was a billboard showing a sinister-looking Uncle Sam squaring up to a determined Cuban soldier, Kalashnikov at the ready.

"*Dear Imperialists: We are not in the least bit afraid of you*," Tom translated the slogan that separated the two figures.

"What are you trying to say?" Jennifer pressed him gently, sensing that he was circling around a point that he wasn't quite sure how to make.

"Just that I wonder whether, sometimes, despite everyone's best intentions, things start off one way and finish another?" he said slowly, his eyes fixed at some distant point on the horizon. "I wonder if some things just aren't meant to be."

She turned to face him, drawing his gaze down to hers.

"Perhaps some things *are* meant to be, only we worry too much to let them happen," she suggested with a smile.

"Yes, that's probably it." He nodded. "But often I think it's better that way."

They walked on toward their hotel, the rise and fall of the waves and the frenzied beat of the city filling Jennifer's ears.

CHAPTER EIGHTY-FIVE

MUSEO NAPOLEÓNICO, HAVANA

25th April—9:55 A.M.

The Museo Napoleónico was located on the far side of the Universidad de la Habana. Students loitered on the steps outside its monumental entrance, some reading notes pulled from leather satchels, others gathered in small groups sharing cigarettes and stories, a few even turning to politics once they were certain they couldn't be overheard.

Tom and Jennifer made their way through the university's central square and past the library, mindful of the cyclists who waited until the last possible moment before furiously ringing their bells, as if it was somehow your fault that they were about to run you down. At the far side of the park they exited the compound through a small gate and found the museum at the top of Calle San Miguel.

Originally a private house, La Dolce Dimora, as the building was called, had been built in an ornate Florentine Renaissance style totally at odds with the rather more functional and dirty constructions that surrounded it. It was a small jewel of extravagance, its lush green gardens sprinkled with marble sculptures, glinting like an emerald washed up on a muddy riverbank.

"The museum has four floors," the girl on reception

proudly announced as they paid for their tickets. "The first three are dedicated to the different stages of the French Revolution, while the last floor houses the library and the Fencing Hall, with tiles from Valencia and . . ."

"Where do you keep the death mask?" Tom inquired, reminding Jennifer of the tourists at the Louvre who she had observed bypassing the untold richness of the rest of the collection for a few snatched minutes with the *Mona Lisa.*

"On the third floor, along with the Emperor's personal belongings and other items relating to the decadence and fall of the Empire." She emphasized the word "decadence," eyeing Tom disapprovingly. "It's all on page three."

He quickly read the passage she had indicated and then nodded.

"Thank you."

They took the stairs up to the third floor, Jennifer catching a glimpse of the Great Hall, which housed a fragment of the Declaration of the Rights of Man and a triumphal painting of Napoleon's coronation by Jean Vivert.

"It's amazing that all this stuff ended up here," she mused as they approached the third-floor landing.

"It's even more amazing that it's still here." Tom gave a short laugh. "Napoleon's hardly a Communist poster boy."

The first room was decorated with uniforms and other personal items: his pistols from the Battle of Borodino; a hat and spyglass used on St. Helena. The second room, meanwhile, had been laid out to resemble a bedchamber.

"Look—" Jennifer pointed at the gold N surrounded with laurel leaves embroidered on to the bedspread. "It's the same symbol as was on the key we found in the obelisk."

"It's the bed he died in," said Tom, reading the sign next to it. "Maybe the one where he told Antommarchi his secret. And look here—"

He nodded toward a polished plaster death mask more or less identical to the one that they had recovered in the catacombs.

"So we're in the right place. But I still don't see how we're going to know which is the right one." She glanced despairingly at the paintings lining the walls.

"My question exactly," a voice echoed from behind them as Milo, flanked by four armed men, swept into the room. Jennifer recognized a large man with tribal scarring on his cheeks from a series of mug shots of Milo's known associates that Ferrat had shown her when she was being interrogated.

"How the hell did you find . . . ?"

"Give me some credit," Milo scoffed. "A death mask created by the same person who used to own that book you were so keen to get hold of—I can read between the lines as well as you. Although, I have to say, you did make life a little easier by asking Takeshi to borrow his plane. In case you hadn't realized it by now, he's one of my buyers." He jerked his head at the two men closest to the door. "Go and round up the other guards. Quietly. There's only three or four of them."

"If you think—"

"You need to do the thinking, Tom," Milo said coldly as Djoulou pushed Eva into the room.

"Eva?" Tom called out in concern. "Are you okay?"

Eva looked worn, far worse than Jennifer had expected, her arm in a sling, hair falling over her face, eyes red where she'd been crying. Tom's anguished tone suggested that he had also been shocked by her appearance, and she guessed that the only thing holding his anger in check were the guns being aimed squarely at his chest.

"That rather depends on you," Milo warned him with a thin smile.

"This has nothing to do with her," Tom said angrily. "It never did."

"And as soon as you hand over the painting, it won't have anything to do with you either."

"As soon as I hand over the painting we lose the one thing keeping us all alive. I can read between the lines too."

"Give me the *Mona Lisa* and this ends now," Milo reassured him.

"Don't listen to him, Tom," Jennifer warned him, her eyes fixed on Milo's with a kind of horrified fascination. "You can't trust him."

"This isn't about trust," Tom insisted. "This is about honor, isn't it Milo? About the old ways. You remember the debt between us, don't you? The life you owe me. Well, now's your chance to honor that debt."

"What are you proposing?" Milo eyed him carefully.

"I give you the *Mona Lisa.* You give me Eva and walk away. This time, there doesn't have to be a winner or a loser. We can both get what we want."

Milo paused, gazing intently at Tom as if trying to sniff out the trap that might be lurking behind his offer.

"Fine." He nodded at his men to lower their guns and then pushed Eva toward Tom. She fell into his arms and nestled her head in his collar, sobbing with relief. "I accept your offer. Where is it?"

"Don't Tom," Jennifer grabbed Tom's arm in alarm, certain that Milo would betray them as soon as he had what he wanted.

"I know what I'm doing." Tom shook her off, his eyes locked with Milo's. "Look behind you."

Jennifer followed Milo's gaze to where a small painting of Napoleon was hanging on the wall over a display case. Dressed in black, he was staring straight into the room, a curious smile on his face.

"Why so sure?" Milo approached it skeptically.

"Because there's only one subject Napoleon would have considered worthy of being painted over the *Mona Lisa*," Tom explained. "Himself."

"The size matches," Milo nodded. He unhooked it from the wall and turned it over. "Oil on poplar. Louvre markings on the back. Yes, this must be it. Captain?" He snapped his fingers and a briefcase appeared into which he carefully placed the painting. "Excellent." He flashed them a triumphant smile. "I believe our business here is done and my debt repaid. Enjoy Havana."

Milo backed cautiously out of the room, and then with a final bow, he turned and the door closed behind him. They heard the sound of the key in the lock.

"Are you okay?" Tom pulled Eva away from him and gazed into her eyes. "What did he do to you? What's happened to your arm?"

"You came back for me?" Her voice, although weary and crushed, had a hint of hope in it now.

"I promised I would." He smiled at her.

"I can't believe you just handed them the painting," Jennifer blurted angrily, trying to ignore the sight of Tom gently caressing Eva's tear-stained cheek. "After everything we've been through to get it back. We're left with nothing."

"This was never just about the painting," Tom insisted. "Besides," he grinned, "give me some credit."

"What have you . . . You gave him the wrong one, didn't you?" Jennifer fixed him with an incredulous look.

"There's only one painting here that fits the clues we've seen." He pointed at a small painting over the bed. It showed a group of Egyptian workmen erecting an obelisk in the desert. "The Egyptian dinner service. The *Déscription de L'Egypte*. The Altar of Obelisks. They've all been pointing us to this—"

Eva broke away and gazed up at the painting before turning and considering them each in turn, a mocking smile twisting the corners of her mouth, her posture somehow stiffening and stretching before them as if up until then she had been hunched inside a small shell.

"You can come back in now," she called out confidently. "I've got it."

CHAPTER EIGHTY-SIX

25th April—10:26 A.M.

The color drained from Tom's face, his eyes wide and disbelieving.

"Eva?" He breathed. "What are you doing?"

"Showing you what it feels like to be betrayed." She smiled as the door was unlocked and Milo marched back in. "It's the one over the bed."

"You're together?"

"Don't tell me you're jealous," she shot back.

"The kidnapping in Seville? The telephone calls?" He shook his head as if trying to unjumble the past few days in his mind. "You set me up."

"Did you really think that Rafael came out of retirement for me?" Milo scoffed as he unhooked the painting and swapped it with the one he had previously put inside the case. "He did it for her."

"He was always a poor father to me and he knew it." Her eyes flashed angrily, and Tom now appreciated the scale and artistry of her deception by the speed with which any trace of hurt or distress at Milo's hands had vanished. "I gave him a chance to make amends and he took it."

"Ledoux hired me to steal the *Mona Lisa*. It was Eva's idea to create the copies and sell them on." Milo smiled, kissing her on the forehead. "She's more like her father than he ever suspected."

"And the *Madonna of the Yarnwinder*? What was that for?"

"I never counted on Takeshi killing Rafael." Milo's voice hardened. "I knew that you'd come running as soon as you found out. The idea was to keep you focused somewhere else for a few days until I had the *Mona Lisa*. It didn't quite work out as I'd hoped."

"Didn't it?" Tom gave a resigned shrug. "You've got the painting and, from the looks of it, the girl too. Looks to me like you played your hand pretty well." A pause. "What happens now?"

"Now?" Milo sighed. "Now, I'm going to do us both a favor."

With a sudden flash of steel he drew a knife across Eva's throat. She collapsed, her mouth making a gurgling noise like an emptying bath, the blood streaming down her front as she pressed her hands to her neck. Tom jumped forward but was forced back by the point of Djoulou's gun. Eva looked up, first at Tom, then at Milo, her eyes wide, questioning and scared as she reached helplessly toward them. Gradually they fluttered shut.

"One of us is not going to leave this room alive," Tom hissed through clenched teeth.

"She betrayed you, Felix. She betrayed me. She betrayed her own father, for God's sake!" Milo wiped the blade of his knife across her jeans. "Did you know the FBI had her DNA on file? Our entire operation jeopardized, all because of her lies. Well, this is the price of betrayal. You of all people should know that."

"I know you hide behind your twisted code of honor, when all you really are is a killer."

"My twisted code of honor is the only reason you're still alive," Milo said tersely. "My offer still stands, if you want it. We both walk away from this with the slate wiped clean, my debt repaid." He held out his hand, but Tom ignored him. "Just remember, I owe Agent Browne no such debt," Milo continued slowly, his voice hardening.

Tom glanced at Jennifer, knowing that he had no choice.

She only seemed to be half listening to them, her gaze fixed instead on Eva's staring eyes. His jaw clenched tight, heart pounding, he reluctantly shook Milo's hand. Milo gripped him tightly, pulling him close and whispering in his ear.

"By the way, you were wrong about there not needing to be a winner. Quite wrong. There's always a winner."

He released Tom with a wink, and then led his men out of the room. He paused at the doorway and glanced down at Eva, his tone surprisingly gentle.

"You know, I was actually getting quite attached to her. You of all people know how dangerous that is, don't you, Tom? How it opens you up, makes you vulnerable?"

He paused, and just for a moment Tom thought he detected a slight tremor play across his lips. But it vanished almost as soon as it had appeared and when he next spoke, his voice had recovered its characteristic authority.

"It's not a mistake I'll be making again," he declared firmly, before closing the door behind him.

There was a long silence. Jennifer stepped forward and clutched Tom's arm, searching out his eyes. He glanced at her and then looked back to Eva's body with a sad smile.

"I'm so sorry Tom."

"Whatever she'd done, she didn't deserve that."

"No."

Tom stepped over to the bed. Pulling the bedspread on to the floor, he gently laid it across Eva's body, pausing for a few moments before covering her face. The silk material settled over her like a black shroud, Napoleon's embroidered monogram forming a rich burst of golden flames at its center. The room felt strangely quiet. He realized then that he'd allowed the persistent echo of Eva's voice to creep into his thoughts with growing intensity over the past few days: *There's something you should know. Something Rafael told me about your father. About how he died.* He'd allowed himself to hope. Now, however, she was gone, and with her passing another window on to his father had been bolted shut, never to be opened again.

"You need to call Green," he said, turning suddenly. "Tell him where we are and what's happened. This town must be crawling with Agency people. See if he can organize some sort of extraction via Guantanamo Bay before the police get here."

"It's okay, they've gone." The girl who had been on reception downstairs appeared at the door, her triumphant smile fading away when she saw Eva's body. "He killed her?"

Jennifer frowned in confusion.

"Who are you?"

"You haven't met Dominique before, have you?" Tom asked. "She works with Archie and me."

"What's going on?" Jennifer stepped back and eyed them both suspiciously. "I thought we agreed: no secrets."

"I didn't know she'd be here myself until I turned up just now," Tom protested.

"Archie sent me," Dominique explained. "Dumas found out that Eva was working with Milo and that Takeshi was one of their buyers."

"So you knew they'd be here? You knew she'd betray you?" she said to Tom.

"Once I read this, yes." Tom held up the guide book Dominique had handed him when they had first arrived. He opened it to the third page. A small note had been taped inside. "But I had to play along. I know Milo. I knew he'd never believe that I had given him the real painting unless he thought he'd somehow tricked me into it. Unless he thought he'd somehow won."

"He did win. He took the painting."

"He took the painting I hung there this morning," Dominique corrected her. "But he left you one too." She unhooked the Napoleon portrait Milo had replaced on the wall and turned it over. "Look at the stamp on the back. An N surrounded by laurel leaves. Napoleon's seal. This is the *Mona Lisa*."

Jennifer frowned.

"Then what has Milo got?"

Tom reached into his top pocket and handed her a crumpled business card with a grin.

"You want that journalist off your back once and for all? Why don't you ask him to find out?"

CHAPTER EIGHTY-SEVEN

MOHAMED V AIRPORT, CASABLANCA, MOROCCO

28th April—8:48 A.M.

It was a long narrow room with a single, windowless door and a large rectangular mirror along the right-hand wall. The light was operated from the outside, the table and chairs screwed down to the uncarpeted floor. Milo sat in one of the plastic seats, waiting, his nails tap-tapping impatiently on the desk's laminated surface.

His head snapped up at the sound of a key in the lock and the sight of two men entering the room, one in dirty jeans with a limp and two black eyes, the other a Customs officer whose name badge identified him as Mohammed Kalou.

"What the hell is going on?"

"Mr. . . . Martell, is that right?" Kalou looked up questioningly from his passport.

"You can read, can't you?"

"Yes, it's very clear. Very *fresh*." He gave him a smile.

"What are you insinuating?"

"Nothing."

"Then why are you holding me here?"

Kalou turned over a few pages attached to a clipboard.

"I understand you're importing a painting into Morocco. A

small piece showing a group of workmen erecting an obelisk in the desert. Mid-nineteenth century."

"That's right."

"Is it valuable?"

"I've provided the sales receipt and paid the relevant import duty, as you would know if you had bothered reading the paperwork."

"Mmmm . . ." The officer looked up, his eyes narrowing. "Have you met Mr. Lewis, by the way?"

Milo glanced across to the other man, who had so far said nothing.

"Should I have done?"

"Mr. Lewis works for a U.S. newspaper—*American Lives*."

"*Voice*," Lewis corrected him with a frown.

"*Voice*. Yes. Mr. Lewis believes that there's rather more to your painting than meets the eye."

"Mr. Lewis is wasting your time and mine," Milo said through clenched teeth. "I want to speak to someone in charge."

"Let's begin." Kalou snapped his fingers and the light dimmed. The mirror became suddenly transparent as a light flickered on in the adjacent room.

"What is this?"

"We maintain a small mobile laboratory at the airport," said Kalou proudly. "We thought some basic tests might help clear this up. An X-ray, for example."

"You have no right to . . ."

"Oh, I can assure you, Mr. Martell, we have every right. It will only take a few minutes and then you and your painting will be free to go."

All three men looked on through the rectangular window as the painting was gingerly lifted out of its climate-controlled packing case and placed under the X-ray machine. Satisfied that all the settings were right, the technicians stepped back behind a protective shield and remotely activated the machine.

Milo looked on, a sweat breaking out across his forehead, his mouth suddenly dry.

"Only a few more minutes now," the officer reassured him with a smile. "Ah, here we go."

The technicians approached the inspection window and held up the negatives so that they could see them.

"It looks like there's something else painted under your obelisk." Kalou frowned.

"It's very common for artists to re-use older paintings to save money," Milo blustered.

"It's a woman," Kalou continued as if he hadn't heard. "She seems to have something on her lap. A child—" he exclaimed. "A child holding something."

"It's known as a yarnwinder," Lewis said slowly. "I believe you'll find the painting is the *Madonna of the Yarnwinder.* It's by Leonardo da Vinci."

"Kirk, you bastard!" Milo shrieked, his fists clenching white at his sides.

"Can I quote you on that?" Lewis intoned.

CHAPTER EIGHTY-EIGHT

PALAIS DU LOUVRE, PARIS

28th April—9:05 A.M.

"Please accept this with the best wishes of the government of the United States of America." FBI Director Green gave a small bow as he held out the painting for Maurice Fabius, the French Minister of Culture.

Tom and Jennifer swapped a look but said nothing. Green's small moment of theater was a small price to pay for his assistance in getting them out of Cuba in one piece.

"On behalf of the people of France, thank you." For a moment Fabius seemed quite overcome, his eyes glistening and his thin lips compressing as he reached for the frame.

"As you requested, we haven't touched it beyond conducting some initial infrared reflectography tests." Green pulled the painting back toward him. "It clearly shows the *Mona Lisa* under the top painting, together with several preliminary sketches and re-workings." He held the painting out again and then, as Fabius was about to grasp it, drew it away as another thought occurred to him. "Interestingly, our experts believe that there may be a thin, almost transparent veil around her shoulders. I'm told it was called a *guarnello* and that this was typically worn by expectant mothers at the time. Maybe the *Mona Lisa*'s smile is that of a pregnant woman?"

"Fascinating," said Fabius, finally managing to grip the frame and wrestle it free from Green. "We will certainly see if we can confirm those findings for ourselves." He handed the painting to an aide who lowered it into a container and sealed it shut. Fabius coughed and straightened his tie. "Please, sit."

He gestured toward the four seats that had been arranged around a low table. Tom and Jennifer sat on one side, Fabius and Green on the other. Tea and coffee had been laid out.

"So it's all Napoleon's fault," Fabius smiled as he handed Tom a cup of coffee. "Milk?"

Tom shook his head.

"All we know for sure is that at some stage between 1800 and 1804 when he had the painting up on his bedroom wall, he replaced it with a forgery that was then transferred back to the Louvre. Then he had the original covered up with the self-portrait you have just seen, allowing him to secretly take the *Mona Lisa* with him wherever he went."

"No one would have been surprised that he carried around a painting of himself," Fabius laughed. "Modesty was never his strongest suit."

"The Egyptian dinner service was made between 1810 and 1812, so it's likely that that was when he conceived of his plan to permanently hide the painting," Tom continued.

"Keeping with the Egyptian theme, he constructed the Altar of the Obelisks in the catacombs, placed the painting behind it, and then had it sealed up, obliterating all signs of that section of the catacombs ever having existed," Jennifer added.

"Then he placed a map and a key inside one of the obelisks from the centerpiece and hid the cipher to the code in his copy of the newly published *Déscription de L'Egypte*."

"But why go to such lengths?" Fabius frowned. "He was the Emperor. He could simply have kept the painting for himself if he'd wanted."

"Who knows?" Tom shrugged. "Perhaps he fell in love. You're laughing, but I've seen it happen before. People get obsessed. They get jealous. It's not enough that they own it now. They want it to be theirs forever. Often, they would rather destroy it than contemplate losing it."

"He tried to give the Egyptian dinner service to the Empress Josephine after he divorced her," Jennifer reflected. "So in a way, he was giving her the painting for safekeeping."

"If she'd known, she might have kept it." Green gave the bitter laugh of someone who knew a thing or two about divorce. "That's some alimony."

"But he never got a chance to retrieve it?"

"Again, we're guessing, but at some stage on St. Helena, when he knew he was dying, he must have confided in Antommarchi. He gave him the book and told him about the dinner service."

"The problem was that by then the newly restored King of France had gifted the dinner service to the Duke of Wellington," Jennifer added.

"Napoleon must have been able to give Antommarchi the location from memory and supply him with a duplicate key. When the good doctor returned to Paris he found the painting, replaced it with a death mask as some sort of tribute to his beloved Emperor, and then covered his tracks. When he died in Cuba in 1838, the secret died with him."

"It's an incredible story," Fabius marveled. "Absolutely incredible."

"And one that might never have come to light," Tom commented.

"One that, hopefully, never will," Fabius immediately responded. "While the French Government deeply regrets the actions of Monsieur Ledoux and Mademoiselle Levy, no good will come to anyone from publicizing these individual transgressions."

"I agree," Green said firmly, fixing Tom and then Jennifer with a look. "What's done is done. The important thing is that the *Mona Lisa* is back where she belongs."

"How long will she take to clean up?" Tom asked.

"Six months. Maybe more." Fabius shrugged. "Neither time nor money matter in this case."

"And what will you tell people?" Jennifer inquired.

"The truth. That, thanks to the vigilance of the French police, the *Mona Lisa* has been recovered. That she has unfortunately been damaged. But that she will go back on display as soon as possible."

"So I'm off the hook." Tom breathed a sigh of relief.

"Indeed you are," Fabius said earnestly. "You both are. Again, you have my apologies for the confusion. I'm sure you understand that Commissaire Ferrat was only acting on the evidence available at the time."

"I think we have all been guilty of jumping to conclusions." Green smiled sheepishly at Jennifer.

"In fact, to signal our gratitude for the efforts you have made and the hardships you have endured over the past few weeks, the President has asked me to present you with something."

He snapped his fingers twice and an aide appeared at his shoulder, carrying three small boxes on a velvet cushion. He stood up and motioned that they should do the same.

"This is the insignia of an Officer of the Legion of Honor," he announced grandly, picking up one of the cases and snapping it open to reveal a gilded five-armed Maltese Cross decorated with an enameled laurel and oak wreath and suspended from a crimson ribbon. "It is granted to recognize outstanding achievements in military or civilian life. It is the highest honor that France can bestow."

Tom swapped an amused look with Jennifer. Green looked slightly pale.

"Appropriately enough, it was established by the Emperor Napoleon himself in 1802, the year his Egyptian campaign ended. And it is on behalf of a grateful French nation that I present this insignia to you now."

He stepped forward and with a flourish hung the first ribbon around Green's neck before grasping him firmly by the shoulders and kissing him on both cheeks. Green said nothing, an expression of dazed delight spreading across his face.

Fabius then went through the same routine with Jennifer, before turning to Tom.

"Thank you, but I'm afraid I can't accept this." Tom gave a firm shake of his head. "If you want to give it to anyone, give it to Jean-Pierre Dumas."

"Dumas was suspended from the DST for a series of infractions," Fabius spluttered. "He would be an entirely inappropriate recipient, whatever small assistance he may have provided you."

Tom leaned forward and whispered something in Fabius's ear. The color drained from the minister's face as he listened, his breathing becoming strained. When he spoke, there was a slight tremor in his voice.

"Perhaps your suggestion has some merit after all. I'll see what can be arranged."

CHAPTER EIGHTY-NINE

RUE DE RIVOLI, 1ST ARRONDISSEMENT, PARIS

28th April—9:37 A.M.

"What did you say to him?" Jennifer laughed as they made their way down on to the street.

"I just asked him if he had any idea where Ledoux had got the money to hire Milo."

"You think he was behind that?"

"I think it's pretty unlikely that Ledoux and Levy were acting alone. Someone must have funded them. Someone must have greased the diplomatic wheels to get the Chinese to release Milo only two years into a ten-year sentence. If not Fabius himself, then someone close to him. Close enough to bring him down if it came out."

"Well, either way, Green was happy." She smiled.

"Green looked like he'll be wearing his in bed," Tom agreed with a laugh. "Where's yours?"

"In here." She patted her handbag. "I'll dust it off next time the French ambassador invites me over for drinks." She had a playful tone, but Tom could tell she too was pleased. "Why did you turn yours down?"

"Because it's with such baubles that men are led," Tom quoted.

"Who said that?"

"Believe it or not, Napoleon." He gave a rueful smile. "I figure I'm probably better off without it."

"Any news on Milo?"

"He's being extradited from Morocco to stand trial in the UK for the *Yarnwinder* theft. And I expect the Cubans and the French will want their turn, too, eventually. They're still trying to round up Djoulou and his men."

"And the painting?"

"Didn't you read Lewis's exclusive in the *New York Times*? All the experts are convinced that Rafael's forgery is the real *Madonna of the Yarnwinder*. As soon as they clean it up, it's going back on display in Scotland."

"I heard that Takeshi's auctioning his paintings too."

"Even though they could be forgeries?" Tom asked in surprise.

"He's got the originals and the certificates of authenticity." She shrugged. "As far as anyone else is concerned, the forgeries never existed."

"And Razi?"

"We arranged for him to be sent photos of what Takeshi had done to Hammon. He took the next flight home and has rolled over on everything in return for being put into witness protection."

"No sign of Takeshi himself, I suppose?" he asked.

"Who knows?" She shrugged. "No one's seen him for the last six years. It'll probably be another six before he emerges again."

They paused in the middle of the courtyard.

"You know, this is where I first saw you. This is where this whole thing started."

"I made sure you saw me," Tom reminded her.

She turned to face him, her face suddenly serious.

"Is this where it ends too? For you and me?"

Tom reached for her hand and went to say something, but was cut off by a sudden shout from across the courtyard.

"Felix?" Archie bellowed.

They looked up and saw Archie, Dominique and Dumas heading toward them.

"I should go." Jennifer backed away, her tone suddenly

changing. "Green's flying home today and wants me to go with him."

"Stay," he urged her. "I'll show you the real Paris. Just the two of us. We can start all over again."

"I'd love to think you meant that."

"Of course I mean it," he insisted.

"I know you *think* you mean it." She lowered her head with a sigh. "It's not your fault. It's just the way you've always needed to be to survive. Never getting too close to anyone, never opening yourself up in case it makes you vulnerable. You heard what Milo said about Eva. He was talking about you too."

"People change, Jen."

"Some do, some don't. Some want to and can't, and all that happens is that others get hurt along the way. I don't want that to be me." She hesitated and then leaned forward and pressed her lips to his cheek. "Take care, Tom."

With a sad, almost resigned smile, she turned and headed toward the Rue de Rivoli as Archie and the others reached Tom.

"What did you say?" Archie frowned at her retreating back.

"It's what I didn't say," Tom sighed, her words still echoing in his head as he sat down on the side of the fountain's triangular basin. "Anyway, the good news is I think I may have got J-P his old job back. Provided he stays on the wagon."

"Bugger," Archie sighed. "I was going to suggest a celebratory piss-up, but it sounds like you're off the sauce, J-P. Unlucky, mate. You'll have to watch."

"As long as I don't have to watch you try to Tango, I don't care," Dominique chided him, with a playful slap across the arm. "It's never a pretty sight."

"What do you mean, I'm a brilliant dancer," Archie protested. "In fact the more I drink, the better I get. Watch this." He tried to spin on his heels, but lost his footing and nearly toppled into the fountain.

Their laughter evaporated in the rainbow-flecked spray of

the fountains behind them. Tom glanced up and saw that Jennifer had almost reached the street. She paused and he stood up, thinking for a second that she might look back. But with a small shake of her head, she continued out of the courtyard. Then she was gone.

EPILOGUE

This questionable notoriety, at once comic and tragic, concerns an object that no longer has anything to do with Leonardo da Vinci . . . She is rather caught up in the insatiable production line of the media, whose lies assault celebrities, those figures destined for mass consumption. She is therefore detached from all historical and human reality . . . But the strangest fiction of all is that Mona Lisa does not exist.

André de Chastel

SUB-LEVEL THREE, PALAIS DU LOUVRE,

1ST ARRONDISSEMENT, PARIS

13th November—6:32 A.M.

The corridor stretched before them, the unpainted concrete walls closing in slightly as if they were being gently squeezed, before vanishing into darkness. Every so often, a new section would blink and stutter into life, the lighting triggered by their passing under a sensor. Then the neon tubes would hum lustily, the dull beat of their footsteps and occasional piano play of loose change or keys creating its own strange music, the horizon stretching endlessly in front of them.

The guard stationed outside the vault saw them coming and had time to smooth his hair down and rearrange his uniform.

"Today's the big day then, is it, sir?" the guard called as the two men approached him.

"It certainly is," Fabius nodded with a smile. "The press briefing's at nine and we want to make sure she looks beautiful for all her guests."

The guard placed his key in one of the locks and Fabius did the same in the other. The door opened with a gasp as the airtight seal was released. The two men stepped inside and waited for the door to slam shut behind them before turning the light on.

A single bulb fizzed on, its light trained on the painting fixed to the wall beneath it, the rest of the room swathed in darkness.

"So that's *La Joconde*?" Fabius breathed. "Not bad, given what it's been through."

"She looks beautiful," the other man cooed. "I think the Louvre's work on this is unsurpassed."

"The problem is, they all look beautiful."

Fabius flicked a series of switches. Four lights flickered on, each one bathing another section of the wall in their cool glow. And under each light, was another *Mona Lisa*.

"The problem is that we've no idea which one is the original *Léonard* any more." The man shook his head and gazed at the five identical paintings staring back at him.

"It's whichever one you say it is," Fabius replied tersely. "You're the Museum Director now. That makes you St. Peter at the gates of heaven. You decide who comes upstairs and who stays down here in purgatory. You decide what people believe. Reality is nothing more than perception."

With a resigned shrug, the curator raised his arm, took a deep breath and then began to recite.

"Eeny, meeny, miny, moe . . ."

NOTE FROM THE AUTHOR

The *Mona Lisa* is probably the world's most famous painting. Widely considered to be da Vinci's masterpiece, *La Joconde*, as the French call her, has been on permanent display in the Louvre since the Revolution, apart from 1800–1804 when the Emperor Napoleon Bonaparte insisted on hanging her on his bedroom wall in the Tuileries Palace.

The theft of the *Mona Lisa* in 1911 triggered one of the biggest criminal investigations in French history and was the first truly global news story. The robbery was masterminded by Eduardo de Valfierno, a Brazilian conman famous for selling a gullible businessman the Eiffel Tower for scrap. He teamed up with Yves Chaudron, a master-forger, who painted six copies of the *Mona Lisa*, and Vincenzo Peruggia, an Italian carpenter turned inside man. As soon as news of the theft broke, de Valfierno sold his six copies to unscrupulous American collectors. Peruggia was left holding the original and was arrested two years later when he tried to sell it to the Uffizi, claiming to be trying to rectify the despoiling of Italy by Napoleon by returning the *Mona Lisa* to her homeland. The painting was returned to France amidst great national celebration, although some questioned whether it was indeed the genuine *Mona Lisa* or one of Chaudron's elaborate forgeries.

The theft of the *Madonna of the Yarnwinder* from Drumlanrig Castle in August 2003 remains one of the art world's most notorious crimes. The painting, commissioned in 1501 by Florimund Robertet, the Secretary of State for King Louis XII of France, depicts the infant Christ clutching a cruciform yarnwinder. He is, however, turned away from his mother, to indicate that there is nothing she or anyone can do to save him from his fate. The *Yarnwinder* was one of only a handful of paintings known to be authentic da Vinci works and had been in the family collection of the Dukes of Buccleuch since 1756. Glasgow police recovered the painting in a raid on a solicitor's office in October 2007. Four men were arrested in what some have speculated was an abortive attempt to ransom the painting back to its owners.

The *Description de L'Egypte* was the result of a unique collaboration between 167 civilian scholars and scientists, known popularly as *Les Savants*, who accompanied Napoleon's military expedition to Egypt between 1798 and 1801. Comprising 23 volumes, and taking almost twenty years to publish in its entirety, the *Description de l'Egypte* includes 900 plates bound in eleven volumes, nine volumes of text and three volumes of "grand format," each measuring three and a half feet long and over two feet wide. Only one thousand copies of the original edition were ever published and today most of these are in museum or library collections.

The Sèvres Egyptian dinner service is the grandest example of French porcelain to have survived from the Empire period. Inspired by Napoleon's Egyptian campaign, it consists of a desert service decorated with different Egyptian scenes and a twenty-two-foot long centerpiece comprising temples, obelisks, gateways, seated figures and sacred rams, all engraved with hieroglyphs. Two almost identical services were produced. The first was a gift from Napoleon to Tsar Alexander I of Russia, while the second, originally commissioned by the Empress Josephine, was eventually gifted to the Duke of Wellington by a grateful Louis XVIII. It can still be seen in the Wellington Museum at Apsley House, London.

The Paris Catacombs are a 186-mile-long network of subterranean tunnels and rooms located in what were once mainly Roman-era limestone quarries. With Napoleon's approval, the quarries were converted into a mass tomb near the end of the eighteenth century as Paris's cemeteries were emptied to try and rid the city of disease caused by improper burials and mass graves. Today, only small parts of the catacombs are officially open to the public. However, unofficial (and since 1955 illegal) visits to sites such as the underground bunker established in the catacombs by the Nazis below the Lycée Montaigne, a high school in the 6th arrondissement, can be made through secret entrances reached through sewers, the Metro, and certain manholes. Dedicated catacomb explorers, known as *cataphiles*, regularly meet and even live down in the tunnels. In September 2004, the French police found an underground cinema complete with electricity and running toilets near the Trocadéro. It is not believed to be the only one of its type.

Napoleon's Death Mask, or mold of his face, was made over forty hours after his death on 5th May 1821. The mask was cast by the British surgeon Francis Burton of the 66th Regiment stationed in St. Helena. Burton later gave Dr. Francesco Antommarchi, Napoleon's personal physician and close confidant, a secondary plaster mold from this original cast. It was from this cast that Antommarchi later made the bronze and plaster replicas that have survived until today. In 1834, Antommarchi traveled to the United States, presenting the city of New Orleans with a bronze copy of the mask after a brief stay there. Other examples survive in the collection of the University of North Carolina, and other museums across North America and Europe. Antommarchi eventually settled in Cuba, but died of yellow fever only four months after arriving. Several of his personal belongings survive today in the Napoleonic Museum in Havana, one of the world's most important collection of items associated with the Emperor, including his personal copy of the Death Mask. Engraved on its base are the words *"Tête d'Armée"* (Head of the Army), reportedly Napoleon's last words.